# ROAD-TRIPPED

*A Romantic Comedy*

## Nicole Archer

*To my beloved son, the muse in my life.*

# Road-Tripped Soundtrack

This book comes with its own soundtrack. If you're reading on a device with Internet access, simply click the link at the beginning of each scene. If you don't already have a Spotify account, you'll need to sign up for the free streaming service and download the app.

If you're reading a print version or have a device without Internet access, you can find the Road-Tripped playlist on the author's website: www.nicolearcher.com, or on Spotify.com under the username: nicolearcherauthor.

# Road-Tripped Map

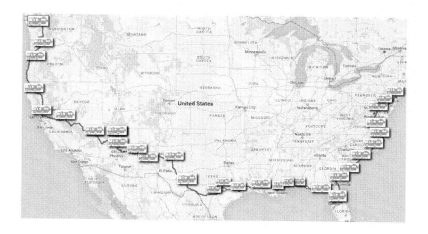

*Calliope, whose name means fine, strong voice, is the muse of epic poetry. She inspired eloquence and beauty in all forms and is often portrayed holding stringed instruments or tablets. Epic poems tell the story of a heroic journey.*

# Chapter 1

## Flippin'

### Manhattan, New York

*"I do not like my state of mind. I'm bitter, querulous, unkind. I hate my legs, I hate my hands, I do not yearn for lovelier lands. I dread the dawn's recurrent light. I hate to go to bed at night."—Dorothy Parker*

**Soundtrack:** Heartless Bastards, "Blue Day"

*1.* String razor wire across the bottom of the slide. 2. Disguise a bomb detonator in the video game controllers. 3. Mix poisonous ricin in with the pool table hand chalk. 4. Spike the liquor bottles with sleeping pills.

Rather than laugh like the evil genius she was, Callie Murphy released a far-reaching sigh. *Her list of Murder Methods for Merrymaking Coworkers* was the most creative thing she'd written in months—and it wasn't even billable.

Across from her desk, more Shimura Ad Agency employees gathered in the break room nicknamed The Hive. It should have called it The Suck since it was a total office productivity vacuum. Staff played in there all day. In fact, she had yet to see a single employee work more than four hours.

It was a mystery how the agency managed to stay in business with all those unbillable hours. On second thought, her boss probably kept it afloat with his enormous inheritance.

Pool balls cracked, video game machine guns rattled, and shrieking laughter erupted. The blender started crunching and whirring. What next? A drum circle? She rewrote the title and added few more methods to her list.

Just then, the office manager burst from the ceiling, screamed down the slide, and landed at the bottom in a crumpled pile.

Every day someone got injured on that thing. Skip should have made every last one of his employees sign a waiver not to drink and ride it. He'd installed the bright yellow liability after he took over his father's business.

"It boosts office morale," he told her.

"Know what boosts morale even better?" she replied. "Money."

But Skip knew dick about workplace morale or legal matters. He was clueless about running a business in general. Not surprising, since up until six months ago, the man had never worked a day in his life.

Hard to believe Skip "Stoner" Shimura, her childhood surfer friend from California, owned an ad agency in New York. Particularly since his biggest talent in life was throwing killer parties.

Now he threw killer parties . . . at work.

Every. Single. Day. He held a booze fest cleverly camouflaged as a mandatory staff-bonding event. Monday was mojito night. Wednesday was Wallbangers. Thursday was Tom Collins night.

As a form of protest, she boycotted every event. Standing up for herself was part of her new personal brand standards. And no one, not even her fake boss, was ever going to tell her what to do again. By God, if she didn't want to have fun, then no one was going to force her to.

She glanced at the clock. *Ugh.* Twenty more minutes. An eternity.

Lately, time ticked by at an evolutionary pace. The last six weeks had felt like sixty years. If time were indeed the cure for pain, then at that rate, she'd never stop feeling like shit.

Speaking of pain, a tap, tap, tapping on the floor grew louder. The sound triggered an almost Pavlovian jaw-clenching response. Sure enough, Account Manager Barbie appeared, wearing blood-red stilettos and painted fingernails to match.

Her real name was Sabrina Driver, but like the doll, she was blonde, big-boobed, and brainless. As if those traits weren't enough to cause a TMJ flare-up, Barbie also littered her speech with the word "like." Even the laws of physics sounded asinine coming from her mouth. "Like, for every action, there's, like, an equal and opposite reaction, like, you know?"

Then there was her escort service attire. To put it another way, plunging, revealing, and skin-tight had to be her keyword search phases when she shopped at hookers.com. Of course if anyone else dressed like that at work, they'd be fired.

What bothered Callie the most though was Barbie's striking resemblance to her friend Hillary. Scratch that. Her *nemesis* Hillary.

Barbie clicked straight toward Eli James. "Oh my Gawd," she cried. "You were so awesome last night."

Was she talking about his bedroom skills or his music skills? Hard to tell with her.

During the day, Eli was a graphic designer at Shimura. At night, he DJed and produced music. Around Manhattan, his popularity was exploding.

Almost as much as Barbie's shirt buttons were.

Eli told Barbie's tits thank you and asked them if they wanted a drink. They replied, "Like sure, why not?" And he strolled off to get them one.

Avery, another senior writer there, flew to the restroom with her cheeks puffed out and a hand over her mouth. *Uh-oh.* Miss Adams must have had a little too much to drink. That or she had the flu.

Callie made a mental note to stay out of her projectile vomit range and focused on something else nauseating.

Walker Rhodes.

Once he stepped inside the room, dumbassaphoria took hold, and every female brain within a six-foot radius shrunk to the size of a Tic-Tac.

With swept-back coffee-colored hair, a big dimpled grin, and a tall muscular body that rivaled Mr. June in the Olympic Men's Swim Team calendar—he often had that effect on women. Perfectly demonstrating this, a crowd of drooling, lash-batting, hair-flipping vultures circled him and giggled like idiots.

From behind a pair of black-framed glasses, he winked an electric blue eye at his fan club members. "Look at all the beautiful women in here. Y'all are the best birthday present ever."

Blushes and smiles galore filled their faces. Amazing how they gobbled up his bullshit.

In essence, Walker was Shimura's sacred white buffalo— women worshipped him. Oh how the office ladies swooned over his slow syrupy Southern charm. They practically fainted when he held out chairs, opened doors, let them sit first, and stood when they did. That reaction was somewhat understandable. After all, perfect gentlemen *were* the last of a dying breed. And let's face it, hot perfect gentleman were damn near extinct.

Handsome, gentlemanly, smart, and talented. Walker seemed like the perfect catch. Except for one thing.

He was a colossal manslut.

That nice-guy act was just part of his get-under-your-panties game. And given all the touching, whispering, flirting, and eventual tears that followed in his wake—he was winning.

In other words, she was the only woman there he hadn't tapped.

And it was going to stay that way.

To fortify that decree, she'd perfected the art of avoiding him—hiding behind her desk, taking the stairs, coming in and leaving before everyone else. Invisibility was the only way. Otherwise she'd weaken and end up in the Walker cult.

She stayed strong though, because womanizers like him deserved an engraved invitation to Hell. And if need be, she'd learn the ancient art of calligraphy to hand-address the envelope.

Don Juan lifted a shot glass and toasted to himself. "Here's to being single, seeing double, sleeping triple, and having a multiple."

More giggling ensued. One woman moaned. For crying in the locker room, the guy could talk about bowel movements and turn women on. Cult leader.

The moaner, Liberty, the social media manager and former mid-western beauty queen, smacked his butt. "Twenty-nine more, birthday boy!"

"Nun-uh, sugar," he drawled. "On my birthday, it's me who does the spanking."

She squealed with delight. "I can't wait!"

"Unbelievable," Callie muttered. The way women Velcroed themselves to him! And for what? A one-night stand? How desperate could you get?

"Happy dirty thirty, Walkie," Barbie said, splaying her hands across his chest. "Sorry about tonight. I'll make it up to you later. Cross my heart." She slowly traced an "X" over her knockers and gave him a kiss on the lips.

From what it looked like, she'd be making it up to him later in bed. If she really wanted to make it up to him, she ought to let Liberty join in.

There's an idea. Shimura should add threesomes to the staff social calendar. Talk about bonding with your coworkers.

Only five minutes had passed since she'd last looked at the clock. Five minutes of torture. Loud music. That's what she needed. Just when she cranked up the tunes, someone tapped her shoulder.

She jerked around and found Skip staring down at her with smug superiority—a look he'd perfected by age twelve. He tossed his intentionally shaggy, black mop out of his eyes and moved his mouth.

"I can't hear you," she said, as if it weren't obvious.

He peeled off her headphones, put them on, and listened for a spell. His upper lip jacked up. "What is this vagina rock you're listening to?" he shouted. "Is this band called *I Hate Men*?"

She stopped the music. "Hey, thanks, Skip."

He tossed her headphones on the desk. "For what?"

"For taking time out of your busy drinking schedule to come over and insult me."

"What? You can't even take a joke anymore?"

She scratched her temple with a middle finger. "Doesn't something have to be funny to be considered a joke?"

He hit her with a down-the-nose stare then shook his head and said, "I ordered the bubbly blonde writer. What happened to her?"

"You mean the doormat? She died back in Chicago."

Was that sympathy on his face? How odd. And mildly unnerving.

*Nah*, he was probably stoned.

"Is that where I return the black-haired bitchsplosion I received by mistake?" he asked.

"Bitchsplosion, huh? Did you come up with that on your own?"

"Overheard it at lunch today. Thought it perfectly described how your crappy attitude is destroying agency morale."

"Yeah, I can see I'm doing some damage." She swept a hand toward the burgeoning celebration where everyone was now wearing sombrero hats and drinking the finance guy's frozen margaritas.

He leaned against her desk and crossed his ankles. "You know, it looks pretty bad when the friend I hired is the only one who doesn't attend the bonding events."

"I can imagine. It must be horrifying to see one of your employees work for a living."

Three, two, one . . .

"I should fire you for insubordination," he said.

Yep, right on cue. Skip threatened to fire her at least forty-seven times a day. The joke had grown so old it had mold on it.

She shifted her attention back to her computer. "Well, hey, I'm kind of in middle of something, so . . ."

He glanced over her shoulder and read the screen. "*Ways to Whack Your Loud Coworkers?*" He read the rest silently with his mouth open. "Dude, you need help."

"I keep begging you to move me to a quieter spot."

"But how would I know when you were about to blast me with poison gas?"

She sighed and folded her hands in her lap. "What do you want, Shimmy?"

"Sorry, your mental health issues sidetracked me for a minute. So tonight, I'm taking the whole agency out to the Boom Club for Rhodes's birthday. And guess what?" A counterfeit smile rolled up his face.

When Skip smiled, something shitty usually followed. She sank down in her chair. "Oh, God."

"Strap on your dancing Chucks, Murph." He slapped her back. "We're going clubbing."

"Can't make it," she said, shutting down her laptop. "I'm busy."

"Ha! Busy. Good one. But I'm afraid your attendance is mandatory."

She let loose a lip-flapping laugh. "Which page in the employee handbook states I have get wasted with my boss after hours?"

His gaze drifted to her chest. "Did you rob a teen-aged boy or something? What are you wearing?"

"There's a t-shirt shop in the hotel lobby. Haven't had time to replace my clothes, yet." Time wasn't the problem. It was the desire she lacked. She could barely muster the will to get dressed in the morning, let alone care about what she wore. There was also the matter of her changing body shape.

"Don't you have something a little less potato sack-y you can wear?" He flicked a finger over her. "What size is that anyway?"

She shrugged. "Medium?"

"Medium in what? Hippo sizes? You can't go out in that. Don't you ever want to get laid again?"

Actually, just talking about sex made her want to make modern art in the toilet. "Aw, sorry my clothes aren't slutty enough. Guess I can't make it tonight." Adding an extra dash of sarcasm, she pouted and blinked sad puppy dog eyes.

"Tell you what." He struggled to dislodge the phone from the back pocket of his skinny jeans. "I'll call my personal shopper and have her buy you something besides"—he shuddered—"that."

Of course he had a personal shopper. Only peasants bought clothes for themselves. "Have you been smoking weed in the stairwell again?" She snatched his phone. "You think I feel like trying on cute outfits right now?"

"Wear that then and get your bag of bloody hearts, Wednesday Addams, we're going clubbing." He pumped his fists in the air. "*Oonce. Oonce. Oonce.*"

She blasted him a Mach-Ten-Level-Murphy-Death-Glare.™

He flipped over his palms like the patron saint of innocence. "What? That's not the look you were aiming for when you dyed your hair and chopped it all off?"

"You know what?" She propped her feet on the desk and placed her hands behind her head. "I think *someone* needs a good Harrasselhoffing."

His eyes slid into angry black slits. "You wouldn't dare . . ."

"Oh, I think it's high time your employees knew their boss sat in David Hasselhoff's lap and got a stiffy."

"I was five! And an extra on Baywatch!"

"You had a tiny boner!"

"It was the tight suit they made me wear!"

She discharged a villainous comic-book laugh—one that had yet to be trademarked—and watched him sweat for a painfully long moment.

He squinted and raised his chin. "You don't even have that picture anymore, do you?"

"You really want to chance it?"

"Meet me up front in five." He spun on his four hundred dollar sneakers.

"Yeah, right." She snorted. "Be right there."

He turned. "I'll move your desk if you go."

"Damn you."

"Oh, and bonus! Tonight's on Double Dick's tab. So drink to your shriveled-up black heart's content, dude."

"Double Dick?"

"New client. Richard Dickson. Total penis. Like I said, order as many expensive froufrou designer cocktails as you can, because that guy is my second asshole right now, and he needs to pay for papa's extra toilet paper." He sauntered to the front, humming the *Addam's Family* theme song.

Speaking of toilet paper, know what sounded better than celebrating a manwhore? An explosive case of diarrhea on an airplane. Add in a drunken crowd and loud club music, and it'd be a close approximation of what her personal version of Hell looked like.

"Chop, chop, Murphy." Skip snapped his fingers. "What's taking you so long? Baggy-ass shirt weighing you down?"

"Your *mom's* weighing me down."

The side of his cheek moved up slightly, intensifying his usual smirk. "Guess you haven't totally lost your sense of humor."

Maybe not, but she'd lost everything else.

**Soundtrack:** Goldfrapp, "Ooh La La"

The Boom Club's lights lowered as the Manhattan summer sky darkened to a starless cobalt blue. Walker nursed his scotch at the bar while heavy bass-driven music pulsed through his brain.

A rail-thin blonde squeezed next to him, followed by a cumulus cloud of perfume. She shouted her name—Alexa Something. After that, ten words per second came out of her mouth with gusts up to fifty. Blah, blah, blah, she was Russian, a model, and obviously coked out of her damn mind. Her phone rang and the yammering stopped.

He made a break for the men's room. Just when he thought he'd escaped, the model walked through the door and rammed her bony pelvis into him. "I vant you, Valker." Her skeletal fingers ran down his zipper.

Despite her drugged-out superhuman state, he managed to peel her claws off his crotch. "No, honey. Not interested. Nyet. Nyet." What the hell was the Russian translation for *I wouldn't touch you with a borrowed dick?*

Locking her giant pupils on him, she ground her jaw and pulled out a rolled up dollar bill. "Want some coke?"

A guy in the next stall screamed, "I do!"

Christ almighty. What a nightmare. He marched to the door and held it open. "All right, honey. You have a nice night."

Oversized lips out in a pout, she pushed past him with her red nose in the air. "I suck you cock good, Valker," she hollered in the doorway. "Find me later, if change mind."

He cringed. Damn models. Just skinny messes beaten down by a twisted industry until nothing was left but an empty vessel filled with drugs and insecurities.

A while ago, he dated a six-foot tall bag of elbows and antlers who destroyed his boyhood swimsuit-model fantasies faster than you could say, "No, honey. I swear you don't look fat." After her he'd developed a severe allergy to models.

God, her stank was all over him. He sniffed his shirt. It'd take bleach and a wire brush to get it off. As he was washing the stink away, the guy in the stall came out shaking his head. "You must be drowning in pussy to turn that down."

A sudden headache blasted him. How much longer was he obligated to stay at that shit show? He walked out and ran into Liberty. She weaved and wobbled and clutched his shirt to stay upright. "Hey, Lib. Feeling all right?"

She gave him a sloppy smile. "I like you, Walker."

He patted her head. "I like you too, Lib."

"No, I *really* like you." She reached between his legs and massaged his balls.

He batted her hand away. "Christ girl, what's wrong with you?"

She mumbled something to the ground.

"What's that?" He cupped his ear.

"For your birthday, I want to give you a blow job." The entire club heard her that time.

A melodramatic laugh burst out behind him. He glanced over his shoulder. The new girl stood in the bathroom line, her nose wrinkled up in disgust. The music was loud, but he had zero trouble reading the words "what a fucking tool" on her lips.

*That thar's what you call an eyeful of the wrong impression.* Liberty's little drunken demonstration was liable to turn into a big pain in his ass if he didn't set that woman straight and pronto. Before he had a chance though, the new girl disappeared inside the restroom.

His wasted goo-goo-eyed coworker tugged his hand. He yanked it free and shepherded her toward the entrance. "Let's get you home, darlin'."

Once he stuck her in a cab, she begged him. "Come home with me, Walker. Please. *Please.*" Saddest thing ever.

"Night, Lib. Drink lots of water before bed."

"Nobody wants me." She burst into tears.

He shut the door and handed the driver more cash. "Better get her home quick, before she loses her lunch in your cab."

Too weighed down with misery to move, Walker stared down the street long after they left, feeling more like sixty than his real age. Thirty-years-old, working at a job he hated, in a city he didn't like, and getting man-handled by women he didn't want.

Not the way he'd imagined his life turning out.

But next week he was going to fix that. Like a kid at Christmas, he'd been counting down the days. Only seven more and he'd be sitting pretty on a fancy motorhome, taking an all-expense-paid trip across the country on the client's dime. An adventure was exactly what he needed to fire up the passion that had burned out many moons ago, back before he started slinging ads for a living.

It was the perfect opportunity to make a change, and the new girl could ruin it with one little conversation with her buddy, Skip. If he didn't explain what happened back there, he'd be kicked off that tour faster than a prom dress.

Back inside, he swam through the sweaty crowd until he found her at the bar hunched over a drink, looking lost at sea. Such a tiny thing she was, sitting there all by her lonesome. He almost felt sorry for her. He pushed a couple of douchebags out of the way and squeezed in next to her. "Haven't had the pleasure to meet you yet." He stuck out a hand. "I'm Walker."

She didn't take it. Didn't even give him a sideways glance. Maybe she hadn't heard him. "Casey is it?" he shouted.

"Callie." She spun her stool and faced him with a steely glare. "And I know who you are." Her look warned him to say one more thing, *just one more thing,* and she'd tear off his nuts and feed them to the wolves.

Kind of disturbing.

Even more disturbing, it turned him on.

He loved a feisty woman, and she was feisty, times three. Her eyes were a dead giveaway. They were the color of ice—transparent almost—and outlined in black. Against her pale, whipped-cream skin they stood out like blue diamonds on snow. Striking. That's how he'd describe them.

Actually, piercing was probably a better word since that's what they were doing—stabbing a hole right through him

He should submit a new Pantone color dedicated to her and call it *Lethal Arctic Blue*.

Why hadn't he noticed her before? She never showed up at the stupid bonding events. He didn't even know where she sat.

A liquid, grinding beat flooded the club. Drowning in a sexual stupor, he pictured those blue orbs half closed while she rode him at the same slow tempo. Somehow he had to make that happen. "Need a drink?" he asked.

She held up a full glass of water.

Strike one.

On her shirt was a donkey piñata with a speech bubble that said *I'd hit that*. He chuckled. "Like that shirt." And the pert little rack under it. Though he could barely see it underneath all that fabric. Was that a man's shirt? Hopefully, it didn't belong to her boyfriend.

Callie swiveled her bar stool and closed him off.

Maybe she was shy? If he hauled her out of Douchebagastan, she'd probably feel better. Hell, he would. He leaned closer and propped an elbow on the bar. "Want to get out of here? Go some place quieter?"

She dropped back her head and groaned. "God, can't you take a hint?" She shooed him with her hand. "Go away. Pick up someone else. I'm not interested in being another one of your whores for the night."

*What the —?* He straightened and scratched his cheek. "Funny, I don't recall asking you to be my 'whore for the night.'"

Rather than challenge him, she pointed a middle finger gun at her temple and fired.

*You can catch more flies with honey than vinegar*, his grandmother always said. Of course you can catch more flies with shit too, but that was neither here nor there.

All in all, he considered himself a pretty nice guy. Ask anyone, and they'd tell you the same. He'd even won 'nicest guy in the class' his senior year of high school. Admittedly, it felt like more of an insult at the time, but still . . . The point was he'd been nothing but kind to her. And the "vinegar" she'd just spat out fermented his already sour mood.

"Thought you might be lonely since you just moved here," he said, backing away with his hands up in surrender. "But I'm guessing with that warm personality of yours, you're probably used to being alone."

Her mouth dropped open, and a gouging, wounded look flew across her features.

"I'm sorry." He touched her shoulder. "I don't know what came over me. It's been a long day . . ."

She jerked away and scraped out a dry laugh. "I bet. Being such an asshole must be exhausting."

The woman was meaner than a skillet full of rattlesnakes. He took off his glasses, grabbed her gaze, and didn't let go. "I'm confused. Did I do something to you? Or are you normally this rude?"

A seductive smile crept up her face. It was the prettiest thing he'd ever seen . . . and the scariest. She beckoned him closer, and like a spellbound fool, he lowered until her mouth brushed against his ear.

"Ready for your birthday blow job?" she purred.

The words wrapped around his cock like velvet fingers and blasted a thousand jolts of lightning to his balls. He choked on nothing and pounded a fist into his chest.

"You seem shocked," she said innocently. "That's the kind of polite conversation you're used to, right? Bet you think I'm warm and friendly now."

All he could do was stare. She'd rendered him completely speechless.

She scoffed. "What's the matter, asshole? Pussy got your tongue?"

Everything around him blurred as a haunting memory from the eighth grade came barreling back. Skinny as willow stick, wearing thrift store clothes and bug-eyed glasses, he'd asked Summer Jenkins to the school dance and she'd run away laughing.

"My dick'd probably wither up if you touched it." The comeback was about a year too late, but he couldn't let her have the last line.

"Good one," she said, socking him in the arm with the force of a linebacker. "You get that off redneck jokes dot com?"

*That's it.* Stick a fork in him—he was done. He gulped down the rest of his drink and said what he came there to say. "Look, what you saw by the restrooms? Keep that on the down low, would you? Liberty had a little too much to drink, and I don't want that to get out."

"I'm surprised you refused." She pressed a finger to her parted lips. "Oh, but I guess you couldn't get it up so soon after the woman before her, right?"

*Ah, hell.* She'd seen that too. He was screwed. But he wasn't giving up yet. "Woman, I'm fixin' to bend you over my knee—"

"Sorry, unlike our social media maven, I don't get off on spanking."

In spite of himself, he chuckled. It was turning out to be the worst birthday ever, laughably so. "You ever take a break from ball-busting?"

Instead of answering, she slid off the stool. "Welp, I'm sure you have a few more mindless babes to bang tonight, so I better skedaddle." She mocked his accent on the last word. "It's been real . . . *Valker.* Hope you enjoyed your birthday more than I did."

Like a spark, she flew out the door and vanished into the night. And damned if he wasn't sorry to see her go. For five long minutes, he thought about running after her. But he couldn't decide what he wanted to do more—fight her, or fuck her, or both?

# Chapter 2

## Trippin'

*"This wasn't just plain terrible, this was fancy terrible.*
*This was terrible with raisins in it."—Dorothy Parker*

n Monday, Skip strolled into work around lunchtime, wearing a pair of yellow jeans. "My office, Murphy, now."

"Are you gonna wear those pants? Because they kind of hurt my eyes." She pretended to block the glare with her hands.

"Now," he said.

Out of nothing more than bored curiosity, she followed him. His office reminded her of a fish bowl. Inside he swam around like an exotic fish all day, doing nothing particularly productive, and everyone on the outside watched. There were no books or anything of a business nature in there, just toy-filled shelves, a glass desk, a laptop, and a white sofa, where she parked herself and closed her eyes.

"Don't sit there. You'll get it dirty!"

"Are you implying my ass is dirty?"

"Dude—"

"Where else should I sit? Your lap?"

"Fine, sit your sparkling clean ass down and listen up." A sham of a smile appeared.

She blocked her eyes with her forearm. "Oh, God, you're smiling."

"Ever heard of RoadStream RV's?" he said.

"The metal campers from the sixties?"

"Fifties, and yes. They're a new client." He shook a bottle of green liquid and popped off the top. "This shit tastes like hay, but it kills hangovers like that."

A ding signaled incoming email and he glanced over at the laptop. "Check this out, some anal twitch downstairs just complained our free coffee isn't earth-friendly." He pounded the delete key with his bottle of hay.

Callie exhaled an asthmatic sigh.

He folded his hands on the desk. "Anyhoo, we sold RoadStream this hip-couple-on-a-road-trip concept." He air-quoted concept. "They travel across the country in an RV and blog about their adventures. Pictures, videos, blah, blah, blah, you get the idea. I'm hoping it'll go viral and make me piles of money. Exciting stuff, right?" It sounded like he was delivering a eulogy.

"And?"

"And . . . since we don't have an enormous budget to hire actors and a camera crew, we're sending two of our hip staff. Doesn't that sound fun?" Only a dead guy could rival the level of enthusiasm in his voice.

She yawned. "Loads."

He blinked a few times and continued. "This weekend, Avery, the female half of the couple, tells me she's pregnant and has hyper-fucking-gravi-something."

"Huh?"

"Morning sickness. Can't stop puking. Now she can't go, and the tour starts in four days. What a cunt, right?"

You know who felt like vomiting? She did. And not because her boss just called a pregnant woman a cunt. Pregnancy simply wasn't a topic she could stomach at the moment.

"Anyhoo," he said again. "You're taking Avery's place. Isn't that wonderful?"

She bolted up. "Say that again?"

He wiggled his fingers in the air like he was translating in sign language. "You are going on the RV tour."

"You sound like a seal."

"I was trying to sound deaf."

"For fuck's sake, Skip, you've violated about twenty employer codes of conduct in about fourteen-seconds. You're gonna get sued one of these days."

He unwrapped something and held it up for inspection. "Bagel Monday, Murphy. Did you get one?" He took a bite and chewed it for an excruciatingly long amount of time.

"If you don't put that bagel down, I'm gonna tell the world about your little high school crush on Céline Dion."

He dropped the bagel and licked his fingers. "Two months in a rockin' camper, all expenses paid . . . Why aren't you jumping for joy?"

"Holyshitfuck! You're serious. No way. I can't even write a check, let alone a campaign right now. Skip, you know I'm homeless and . . ." fucked up, but she omitted that information because let's face it, he already knew. "Send someone else."

"There *is* no one else. Everyone has dogs, cats, monkeys, kids . . . obligations, Murphy, and you've got nada. Like you said, you don't even have a home."

"Lovely. Go ahead and pour a little more acid in the gaping wound," she said. "Why don't you go? You don't have any obligations."

"Duh. Because last time I checked, I wasn't a female writer. Plus, I'm the boss, and I'd rather have my testicles dug out with a plastic spork than travel around in an RV. Have you seen the people who drive those things?" He stuck out his tongue. "Stop manhandling my couch! You're gonna tear the fabric."

"I'm gonna stick this couch up your—"

Once again he smiled. "Pack up those shitty t-shirts, dude. You're leaving Friday. BTW, your better half is Rhodes out there."

Walker passed by the window and waved. She coughed out a gasp. "Walker! Are you joking?"

"Does it look like I'm joking?" He pointed to his expressionless face.

"You want me to live with that . . . *manwhore*? On a motorhome? For two months!"

"Manwhore? Rhodes? Ha! You wish. Actually, every woman in New York wishes—"

"This isn't funny, Skip."

"I'm not laughing."

"Well, I can't do it. No."

He shot up and stabbed a finger at her. "Then you'll be out on your ass along with everyone else when I lose the client and have to shut this place down."

"What are you talking about? Shut it down? Use your inheritance."

He flopped next to her on the couch and gripped his forehead. "It's not mine unless I run the agency profitably for five years."

"What!"

"My father, may he rest in hell, thought he'd teach me a lesson. Said for once in my life I needed to learn the value of hard work." He air-quoted hard work.

"True. But why would you close? You've got other clients."

"Oh, silly me. Did I forget to mention the VP embezzled a shit-ton of money?"

Skip fired the guy before she'd started. The inner workings of his agency weren't something they discussed. "Did your dad know?"

"Unfortunately, he was too busy dying." He tipped back his head and stared at the ceiling. "Until the popo catch the guy, I'm running this joint on nothing but hopes and dreams. And if RoadStream fires us . . ."

"Why didn't you tell me all of this before?"

"Yeah, well, you had other things on your mind."

Guilt squeezed her stomach. It was the first time she noticed how weary he looked.

*Nah*, he was probably just high.

"Bottom line, Murph? I didn't hire you because you needed a job. I hired you because you're a damn good writer, and I need to make a name for this place. But if you don't go on this trip, I *am* going to fire you. For reals."

If he did, she'd be jobless, homeless, penniless, friendless, and more screwed than a gang-bang porn star. She jammed her palms against her eye sockets, damming the flood of emotion threatening to break free.

He laid a hand on her leg. "I'm worried about you, Murph. Sure you don't want to talk about it?"

The sentiment nearly doubled her over. Her friend rarely doled out affection, much less discussed personal problems. If she told him what had happened, she'd break down, and in that fish bowl office, the whole agency would see.

They stared straight ahead saying nothing. After what seemed like hours, he blew out a long breath. "Maybe this trip is exactly what you need. See the country. Get laid by the so-called manwhore. Rhodes is a cool guy. It'll be great."

Riding across the country with a womanizer was his idea of fun? "Are you high? Look Skip, I'll do it, mostly because I owe you a shitload, and I love you like a brother. But don't patronize me. This is not some spring break spa retreat."

"On the bright side, at least you don't have to keep paying for that hotel room." He messed up her hair and rose to his feet. "Remember all those times you snuck in my house? Back when my parents left me alone like a piece of neglected dog shit? You used to say, 'Shimmy, stop being such a pussy. Forget about everything, and go have fun.'"

He strode toward the door and swooped a hand outside. "Stop being such a pussy, Murph." He slapped her back. "Forget about everything and go have fun." He closed the door in her face and waved.

With a pretend handle, she unfurled her middle finger then ran to the bathroom and threw up.

*"The first thing I do in the morning is brush my teeth and sharpen my tongue."*—Dorothy Parker

The new RoadStream creative team met for lunch in the conference room. Chinese takeout littered the red metal table, and the stench of sweet and sour pork permeated the recycled air. Callie stared at the uneaten food on her plate and listened to Barbie drone on.

"Like, Avery came up with the tagline, *Roam Riveted*, but that's as far as she got." She handed out a packet. "This is the budget and the timeline. We need a post four times a week. We're also shooting two commercials on the road—one in Orlando and one in Las Vegas."

She thumbed through the packet. Strange that Hell wasn't on the map. Neither was anything else. "Where are we going?" She waved the map. "I don't see any places on here."

"That's up to you guys," Skip said, not moving his eyes from his laptop. "There's a general route we planned that goes through the states where the biggest sales are, but otherwise, it's a free-for-all. Find someplace interesting, write about it, and make me piles of money."

"Are you serious? There's no plan, no brand, no concept? What am I supposed to write? You just want me to wing it? With your biggest client? That's insane."

Skip sat back and smiled so hard the cords on his neck popped. "No, Murphy, I don't want you to wing it." He air-quoted the last words. "I want you to do your job and come up with a brilliant campaign. Make papa proud."

"Refer to yourself as papa again," she said, mocking his smile, "and I'm afraid I'm gonna have to regurgitate that incident between you and Corey Feldman."

The room went dead silent.

Everyone's jobs were at stake and Skip had just tossed the entire responsibility in her lap. In a normal agency, huge teams of people worked together on a campaign, not just a copywriter and a manslut. She massaged her temples.

"Avery had a few ideas and somewhat of an agenda," Walker said. "We can start there."

She looked over at him and landed on his mouth. A sexy smirk slid up and flashed his dimples. Hot tingles swirled between her thighs. Those things should come with a warning label.

And his eyes were just as dangerous—swirls of blue, green, and gold—like peacock feathers and sex.

Even more frustrated than before, she clenched her teeth and asked, "Who's going to shoot the pictures and video footage?"

"Walker," Barbie cooed. "He's good at everything. Aren't you?"

"Pretty much." He winked.

*Ick.* Could they be any more obvious?

"Meeting adjourned," Skip said. "I've got shit to do."

*Like what? Go shopping?* She buried her head in her hands while everyone filed out of the room.

"You okay?"

Almost everyone.

She looked up and gave Walker the thumbs up. "I'm fucking great. How 'bout you?"

"Want to grab a drink after work and talk about the trip?"

"Can't," she said. "I'm hanging myself tonight."

He rose to his feet and swaggered out the door. "Let me know if you need any help with that."

*"A tear contains an ocean. A photographer is aware of the tiny moments in a person's life that reveal greater truths."—Anonymous*

Walker emailed Skip right after the meeting and quit. Not even a minute later, his boss waltzed in and kneeled on the floor.

"Money, fame, a promotion, whores, anything . . . name the price." His eye twitched as he begged.

"Sorry, Skip. Can't do it."

He threw his hands in the air and flew out the door. "I'm fucked. I'll be at the bar, if you need me."

Later, Avery met him in the coffee shop downstairs. Sick as a dog and she'd come all that way—on the subway no less—just to con him into staying. Too bad it wasn't going to work.

A sickly clone of his friend sat at a table in the back, wearing Audrey Hepburn sunglasses and a maternity dress she didn't need. He sat next to her. "Is that you, Avery?"

"That bad, huh?" She removed her sunglasses and gave him an anemic smile.

He winced. "Argh! What happened?" One eye looked like it'd been shot out.

"I broke a blood vessel heaving my guts out."

"Why are you here? Go back to bed!"

"Stop staring at it!"

"I can't help it." He blocked the view with a napkin. "It's freaky. Seriously, go home."

"Begging's more effective in person."

"Ah, I see." He wadded up the napkin. "Well, your evil eye trick won't work on me."

"Har. Har."

"Besides, Skip already got down on his knees and offered me hookers."

Avery didn't laugh. "I've been on my knees in front of the toilet all day."

He tried not to frown.

Hands in prayer position, she pleaded with him. "Boo, please, I can't get to the kitchen without throwing up, let alone across the country. Please don't quit. Skip's going to close the agency, and I cannot lose my job right now. No one will hire a pregnant writer. And I need the maternity coverage. Please." Her big brown eye and evil red one welled up with tears.

*Bravo.* An award-winning guilt trip. And he wasn't falling for it. Avery was talented as hell. She'd find something else in a heartbeat. So would everyone else. "Sorry, no can do." He threw a pointed look over at the counter where Callie had just taken a seat. "I'm not living with that snake for two months."

A brow arched over her blown-out eye. "Did you just call her a snake?" She tsked. "Shame on you."

Avery waved at their bitchy coworker. Callie smiled and waved back. Then he waved and her hand dropped. So did her smile.

"See that?" he said. "Acted like I gave her the Nazi salute. Bet she'd spit in my face if I went up there and said hi." He crossed his arms and shook his head. "Nope, I'm not living with that ice queen for two-months. Bet her own dog bites her when she gets home. Not a nice lady."

"I don't get it. Maybe she's shy with men. She's super sweet to me."

"Sweet! Yeah, right." He cackled like an old woman.

The laugh caught Callie's attention and their glares locked. *That's right, I'm laughing at you, you tiny terror.* She frowned like she'd kissed the wrong end of a baby and turned away.

"What'd you do to her?"

He straightened. "Not a damn thing."

"Well, she's a great writer, and there's no one else, so suck it up."

"Ha! Great writer? Come on. She got that job through straight-up nepotism and you know it."

"No, really, she's good. Google her. In fact, I don't know how Skip got her to work for him." Her voice lowered. "Something bad happened to her I think."

He didn't lower his voice. "Probably cut off some guy's balls and now he's after her."

Avery's head dropped to her palm. In a matter of minutes, her pallor had gone from grey to a shade above dead.

"You okay?"

"No," she whimpered. "I'm sick . . . and alone. I spent all my money on this baby. Now I'm about to lose my job. I shouldn't have done this—gotten pregnant on my own. This was a bad idea."

Her words cleaved his heart in two. More than anything Avery wanted to be a mom, but she never found the right guy. She finally quit looking for a man and found a sperm donor instead. Spent a year and every penny she had on fertility treatments. The day she found out she was pregnant, she cried in Walker's arms. He'd never seen anyone so happy in his life.

After witnessing her joy, he kept feeling as though he were missing out on something important—something worth fighting for.

Photography and painting were the only things he truly cared about. From the time he was two-years-old, he'd known art was his calling. But he ended up going into graphic design for a steady salary. Ads, logos, websites, endless meetings, and kissing ass—God, he hated it.

A lousy job. His only passion in life and he'd given it up for a bigger paycheck.

But Avery hadn't given up. She'd sacrificed everything to get pregnant. Her finances, her disapproving friends and family, her health—she'd given it all up to be a mom. She'd fought hard and found her missing piece. And now she was questioning her decision because he couldn't handle a tiny blue-eyed road bump on the way to finding himself.

He had to go. Not just for her sake—for his. He had to grab sack and fight for what he loved. Even if it meant riding in a tin can for two months with the smallest biggest bitch in the world. "Okay, Ave."

She sniffled. "Okay what?"

"I'll do it. I'll go."

"Wow, I didn't even have to buy you lunch." Her clammy hand squeezed his. "Thank you, Walker. Seriously, I owe you."

"Darlin', you just worry about yourself and that baby."

"Nothing's changed, you know," she pointed out. "Just stick with the original plan. Get the work done then do your own thing. Just ignore her—" Her hand flew to her mouth, and faster than a bee-stung cheetah, she bolted to the bathroom.

"You all right, Ave?" He tapped on the door. "Need anything?"

She retched and moaned in response.

*Ah, Christ.* Riding with *Rosemary's Baby* couldn't be all that different from riding with the devil. Either way, it'd be hell on wheels.

# Chapter 3

## Slippin'

*"Yet, as only New Yorkers know, if you can get through the twilight, you'll live through the night."—Dorothy Parker*

**Soundtrack:** Lorde, "A World Alone"

The sounds of New York were a constant alarm clock. Callie hadn't slept in months. That night, instead of sleeping, she took stock of the beige in her hotel room. The carpet, bedspread, chair, dresser, lamp, curtains, desk, and door were all a different shade of bland. The color of numbness—the new hue in her life.

Out the window, she glanced at the sidewalks below, searching for something—answers maybe? The only thing she discovered was that from the thirtieth floor, people looked like insects. A million and a half bugs in New York and she was all alone.

She called her sister Effie, thinking it would help, but knowing deep down it wouldn't.

"I'm fucked," Callie said right out of the gate.

"Me, too," Effie said. "But you go first, and we'll see who wins."

Neither laughed.

Callie relayed her disastrous day, and her sister didn't utter a peep. "Eff?"

She came back on the line. "Sorry, I was laughing so hard, I put myself on mute."

"What's so funny?"

"You are," she snorted. "Did you really call to bitch about taking a free road trip with a hottie? After all you've been through? Let's do the twin switcheroo. I'll take your place. You take mine."

A black dog darted into traffic below. "Stop!" she cried then snapped the curtain shut.

"Geeze, I'm kidding," Effie said, thinking the command was meant for her. "Where's your sense of humor?"

It'd been months since she'd laughed. Nothing was funny anymore.

"You need therapy," her sister added.

"Because I don't want to take a trip with a male hooker?"

"No, because you're a mess. You won't talk about what happened. You don't care about anything. And now you're upset over nothing."

"Nothing!"

She sighed. "What are you worried about? It's not like you have to sleep with him. Besides, he must have a few redeeming qualities, otherwise the ladies wouldn't be after him. Be friends with the guy. You need friends—"

"I don't want friends like him."

"So you're gonna avoid people for the rest of your life and be one of those creepy Internet freaks who communicate through an avatar? God, Cal, you need help. There's something wrong with you."

*Impressive.* Her sister had found a way to make her feel even shittier about herself. "So, what's up with you?" she asked Effie, taking the focus off her abysmal situation. "What happened today?"

Effie lit up a cigarette on the other line and puffed. "My ex-drug dealer's son is one of my violin pupils. After the lesson, he shoved a dime bag in my hand."

Her stomach tensed. "Oh, Eff. What did you do?"

"I quit then ran ten miles."

"Ten miles!"

"My addiction was chasing me."

"Now what are you going to do?"

"Wait tables I guess."

"God, you need to get out of California."

"And go where? And with what money?"

*Why don't you use the money you stole from me*, she wanted to say. But that money had been snorted up her nose ages ago. "Finish your concerto and get your scholarship to Juilliard back," Callie said.

"Where would I live?"

"With me."

"Really? You'd do that?"

The uptick of excitement in her voice delivered a swift punch of reality. Rotten idea inviting her druggie sis to live with her. Sleep deprivation must have damaged the rational part of her brain. "Let's talk about it later."

Dead air.

"I'm clean, Cal. I swear."

Unfortunately, her promises were just words in the wind. "I need to get some sleep. We'll talk later."

"Okay, have fun on your trip," Effie said.

"Yeah, right."

After the call, a heavy blanket of anxiety covered her. Grief was a rude bastard, always showing up without invitation. Ah, New York, the city where she'd never sleep.

Not that it mattered. In four days, she'd be not sleeping somewhere else.

# Chapter 4

## Leavin'

*"Trapped like a trap in a trap."*—*Dorothy Parker*

The scorching weather amplified New York's rotting garbage smell—the perfect scent for doomsday, which had arrived, along with the gleaming metal camper, her transport to the underworld.

Walker leaned against the RV, and Barbie, encased in a slit-up-the-back skirt, toddled over in four-inch heels and careened into his side. She'd better be careful. One misstep and she'd expose her asshole to the crowd. Take that back, the asshole was already exposed and standing right next to her.

Skip worked his way through the bystanders, wielding a magnum of champagne. He tore Walker from Barbie's side and placed him next to Callie. "All right," he said. "Let's get the happy couple on the road. All aboard the—" He swept a hand toward her to fill in the blank.

She shrugged. It looked like a giant silver dildo to her.

"All aboard the?" He squeezed his eyes shut. "Meh, I got nothing." Celebrating his lack of creativity, he slugged alcohol right from the bottle.

"Psst," he said from the side of his mouth. "Need any more supplies"—he waved the champagne and winked repeatedly— "put it under groceries." Louder to the other staff he said, "But, don't drink and drive! Right, kids?"

Skip high-fived Walker's shoulder then fist-bumped Callie's face. She ripped the bottle from his grasp. "You need an intervention."

He narrowed his almond-shaped eyes to threads and yanked it back. "Also," he slurred on, "this thing is over a hundred grand. You break it, you buy it."

Barbie filled plastic flutes and handed them to bored Shimura employees. Skip grabbed one off her tray and spilled it on his crotch. He swatted the stain. "Let's have a toast. Here's to—"

"Fuck you, asshole! Move that fucking bus. You're blocking traffic."

Skip raised his glass to the belligerent driver and with a merry old English accent said, "And a big fuck you to you too, sir!"

He turned back to the staff. "Where was I? Oh! Make sure you—" Car horns drowned out the rest of his speech, so he staggered to the bumper and broke the champagne bottle across it, launching glass shards and booze everywhere. "Bon voyage, motherfuckers," he said flatly.

The man was a menace.

Walker snatched the keys from him and stormed up the steps, grumbling about the sorry excuse for management.

"Try not to have fun, Murph," Skip said, daring to pat her behind. She spun around and flung him a Touch-Me-Again-And-You-Die Look™ and waved goodbye with her middle fingers.

She closed the door and gasped internally. That thing wasn't a motorhome. It was a mid-century apartment on wheels. In any other circumstance, she'd dance a little jig. Instead, she dragged her feet through the dildo mobile, her only home at the moment, and checked out her living quarters for the next two months.

She scanned the dashboard and its buttons and knobs galore and resisted the urge to play Commander Murphy because *he* was there.

The rest of the setup was pretty damned sweet. Funky lime green and silver fabric covered windows, seats, and beds. Light blonde wood overlaid the floors. Everything else was white leather, steel, and chrome.

In the miniature kitchen, space-saving stainless steel appliances were tucked under the counter. They'd sure be roughing it out there in the wilderness with a microwave oven and dishwasher.

Across from the kitchen was a table surrounded by benches. Somehow the benches converted to a sofa bed. But she didn't futz with it because she'd sleep out in the open over her dead body.

She flipped open the cabinet doors and found a flat-screen TV in one, and lighting, sound, and climate controls in another.

A folding table popped out of a closet. Camp chairs were stashed behind it, as well as miscellaneous equipment, sleeping bags, backpacks, water bottles, and a portable stove.

The master suite was stationed in the rear. Windows curved around the bed, making the minuscule space feel open and airy

A loft, accessible by a ladder, lay above the master bed. A single bed with a built-in drawer and nightstand packed the space. Thank God for the skylight and window, or it'd be like sleeping in a coffin. Most likely that's where she'd be resting in anything other than peace since Walker would never fit up there.

She slumped down in the passenger's seat and slid Walker a peek. No dimples on him that day, just a tight frown. *Aw,* manwhore was sad. Probably didn't want to leave his harem behind.

He started the engine and edged into traffic. A symphony of horns and a chorus of expletives followed them through Manhattan.

*Off we go,* she thought, *to Hell in an RV.*

**Soundtrack:** The Rolling Stones, "Emotional Rescue"

Resentment grew in Walker like thistles. Callie hadn't said one damn thing to him in two hours. Know that old movie *Weekend at Bernie's*? Driving with her was just like that—like taking a road trip with a dead guy.

It's not like he expected mind-blowing conversation, but they could at least shoot the breeze in a while. How was he going to work with her? Write notes?

There had to be some way to melt that ice queen.

Setting her on fire might work.

At a stoplight, he checked her out. Jaw tight, spine rigid, big frown on her face—she was pricklier than a porcupine in a cactus patch. Not an ounce of glee in that woman.

She had good taste in shoes at least. Like him, she wore Chucks, but hers were pink. They were so cute and sweet and not at all like her.

Might as well break the ice, he reckoned. Too bad he didn't have a sledgehammer. But he *could* kill her with kindness.

Forcing a dental-brochure smile on his face, he made his first attempt. "Why don't you hook us up with some tunes, sweetheart?"

Not a peep from her, not even a nasty look—just kept her eyes bonded to her book. Deaf *and* mute.

*Let's see how deaf.* On the satellite radio, he cranked up a death metal station until the camper shook. She didn't seem bothered by the angry music. To her it was probably a lullaby.

"Is the music too loud?" he shouted.

"What?"

He turned it down and tugged on his earlobe. "I feel like beating the sh—*poo* out of someone now."

"Shampoo?"

"Never mind."

Worn out from blabbing so much, the Queen of Conversation went back to her book.

"What are you reading?" he asked, just as friendly as all get out.

She didn't answer.

He tried another tactic. "Is it hard living with gonorrhea?"

Her head jerked up. "What did you say?"

"I *said* . . . I'm bestowing you the honor of choosing the soundtrack for our trip."

"Just pick something. I don't care."

"Nope. That's your job, woman."

Her back slapped against the seat, and she glared at the ceiling. "Will it shut you up?"

"No, but it might fill the void in the seat next to me."

She reached for the dial.

"Wait. There's something you need to know first. I'm allergic to female pop singers."

"What, pray tell, does that mean?"

"Britney Spears, No Doubt, Pink, Lady Gaga, Taylor Swift"—he went up an octave—"Christina Aguilera, Mariah Carey, Adele . . . anyone with a shrieking voice like that. I can't handle it."

"What happens?"

"My boys shrivel up." He motioned over his crotchal region.

A second later, Katie Perry blasted out of the speakers.

He covered his nuts. "Nooo! Help! Turn it off."

Ever so slowly, the passenger's first signs of life appeared— the teensiest smile in the world sprouted on her face. A second later, she turned on the Stones.

"Whew." He wiped his brow and sang "Emotional Rescue" in a falsetto voice.

The smile grew a millimeter.

*Baby steps,* he thought, and continued his awful singing.

# Chapter 5

## Ringin'

### Liberty Bell Park, Philadelphia, Pennsylvania

**Soundtrack:** Iggy Pop, "The Passenger"

Walker circled the Liberty Bell parking lot three times in search of a space. "Guess we're not gonna hear freedom ring today," he said.

Callie pointed out a spot along the street. "Park between those buses."

"I'm a man of many talents, but parallel parking a giant motorhome isn't one of them."

"Get up. I'll park it."

He didn't budge.

Mumbling what a fucking moron he was, she jumped over the console and sat in his lap. While his dick appreciated the move, he didn't. A whiff of her scent changed his mind. It was like caramel and sunshine. He buried his nose in her hair. "Mmm, you smell good."

"Get out!" She kicked him in the shin.

"Ow! Damn, you're mean. Okay, okay." He stepped out of the vehicle with his hands in the air. She punched the gas and nearly ran over his foot. "Crazier than a bullbat," he muttered.

In an act that could only be described as badass, she whipped the motorhome between the two buses and parked. *I'll be damned,* he thought, *she pulled it off.*

The driver's side door swung open and she got out with her nose in the air.

"Pretty proud of yourself, huh?" he said.

"Ever feel like less of a man because you can't park?"

"My bedroom skills make up for it." He winked.

She shut her mouth and scampered toward the security line wrapped around the entrance. "Let's get out of here," he said. He'd rather stand in Hell, wearing gasoline underwear, than stand in line. There wasn't an attraction on planet earth worth wasting his life like that. But Callie stood steadfast and forced him to stay.

It was free to get in, but once he finally laid eyes on the landmark, he felt like the state of Pennsylvania should have paid him to see it.

The bell, in dire need of a polish, hung between two metal poles cemented in an outdoor amphitheater. Behind the velvet ropes surrounding it, a colorful bunch of tourists gathered around, with cameras glued to their faces.

Towering over everyone's heads, Walker stood in back and watched his coworker. Looking as bored as he was, she yawned as the guide blabbed on. A hugely pregnant woman squeezed next to her. Callie glanced down at the woman's belly and wilted. Eyes, mouth, and shoulders sagging, she clutched her throat and sidestepped away from the lady.

Now that was just plumb strange. He slipped the zoom lens on his camera and dialed in until he had her in sight. She wrapped her arms around herself like straitjacket and stared at the bell's crack like something horrible was crawling out of it. He pressed the shutter. *Beep!*

As he stared at the picture, melancholia washed over him. It was the first decent photo he'd taken in years, but the moment he'd captured wasn't a happy one.

Maybe he could cheer her up. It wouldn't be an easy task, but he was always up for a challenge. In short order, he sidled up to her. "Freedom not all it's cracked up to be, huh?"

"Very punny," she replied, not moving her gaze from the landmark.

The woman had no sense of humor. Zero. Zilch. "How come you never smile?" he asked. "I'm dying to see what it looks like. Do it for me. Show me a smile."

An upside-down smile hit him instead. "I hate when men tell me that. It's so patronizing."

"Maybe you should smile then."

"And maybe you should wipe that stupid grin off your face."

He didn't quit the alleged stupid grinning. "Maybe you need *your* bell rung. Bet you'd smile more."

"Let me guess, you think you're the man for the job?"

If banging his coworker made her easier to be around, then sign him up. "I'd definitely put a stupid grin on your face."

She blasted out a chilly laugh. "The only way you'll get a stupid grin out of me is if you gave me a lobotomy."

Boy, did he want to prove her wrong—just take her up against the bell and fuck that smug look off her face. No doubt they'd add a few more cracks in the thing.

He unbuckled his belt and bellowed, "Get back to the trailer, woman. I'm gonna teach you a lesson."

Everyone in the crowd stared. Callie stabbed him with a brutal glare.

"Go on," he said. "And take your panties off before I get there."

She jammed a hand on her hip. "Billy Bob, did you get into the moonshine again?"

"I don't sound like that," he said, remarking on her terrible Southern twang.

"Guess I better practice up on my hick accent."

That woman would make a preacher cuss. "Meet you out front. Make sure you take off those panties first." He winked and rushed out before she noticed his hard dick.

Back inside the camper, he counted backwards from a hundred until he got ahold of himself. Five minutes later, she showed up, raising his hackles again. He plastered on a plastic smile. "Where to next, Bluebell?"

She plopped in the passenger seat. "I thought you had a list?"

"Avery did, but evidently she didn't know about my line allergy."

"Oh my God." She rolled her head side-to-side. "We were only there for fifteen minutes, and you acted like it was hours! A freaking toddler has more patience than you. Are we there yet? Are we there yet? I never want to stand in line with you again."

When he wanted her to shut up, she wouldn't.

"I have to write about this shit, you know. All you have to do is snap pretty pictures."

"What's your point?"

"We can't just run in and out of random places. We need an idea that ties everything together. And I need time to absorb and learn."

"Where do you want to go then? Some place with lines?"

"We need an agenda."

"I'm more of a go-with-the-flow kinda guy. Let's just wing it and see what happens." He sat back and waited for her to explode.

But instead, she stared straight ahead, popping her jaw muscle back and forth. "Screw it. I don't care."

"So that's it? You're not gonna participate? You can't even come up with one place you want to go?"

"Who cares? I'll just"—she flapped her arms—"wing it. What does it matter if the whole agency shuts down? As long as you're free to wander the country."

No telling what else she was rambling on about, he was already focusing on something else—the perspiration beading in the dip of her neck. He wanted to lick it out.

"*Yoo-hoo!*" She waved a hand in front of his eyes. "Are we going to sit here all fucking day?"

Honestly, he should have quit while he was behind, but pissing her off was becoming his new favorite sport. "How does all that filthy language fit in that tiny body?" He started the engine. "You're as much fun as poison ivy, you know that?

Why don't you ride in back, and I'll pick up a hitchhiker. I'd have someone to talk to at least."

"Great idea, hoss," she said, imitating his accent once again. "Not at all dangerous."

"Tell you what, driving with a serial killer would be a helluva lot better than riding with you."

Sharp breaths fired out her flared nostrils. "God, you're like the Asshole Club president." Then like a wild hair, she leapt out of the seat and sprang up to the loft.

He pinched the bridge of his nose. They weren't going to make it out of Pennsylvania without killing each other, much less across the country. But what else could he do? He had no other choice but to keep moving. Dialing the punk station up to fifty, he threw the camper in drive and took the next exit to wherever it led.

# Chapter 6

## Dinin'

### Intercourse, Pennsylvania

**Soundtrack:** Cage The Elephant, "Ain't No Rest for the Wicked"

*T*he exit led to Lancaster County. More precisely, Intercourse, home of the Pennsylvania Dutch, and where every business sounded like a dirty joke. *Intercourse cleaners. Intercourse liquors. Intercourse gas.* His inner adolescent giggled endlessly.

In the last hour, his mood had improved substantially. Wandering felt liberating. A little too liberating, as in he had no clue where to park the RV for the night. Maybe they needed a plan after all.

But he'd never admit that to *her*.

When he passed a sign for Intercourse Grill, he stopped for supper. Once he parked, he glanced back and blew out a lip-trilling sigh. It'd been four hours since he'd last seen his mean coworker. He loped to the back, figuring he ought to at least check on her.

At the top of the ladder, he stopped breathing. The summer evening sun showered down from the skylight and bathed her sleeping body in white light. Curled delicately on her side, she looked like a pixie—delicate, feminine, serene—completely unlike alert Callie.

All she had on were panties and a tank top, the strap of which had slipped down, exposing a glorious plum—one beautiful, hot, glowing tit.

He climbed another rung, and caught sight of her ass cheek, peeking out from her undies to say hello. His cock, traitor that it was, shot up and said *nice to meet you*.

Why didn't she show that body off? If she did, maybe he'd be able to tolerate her.

A compulsion took over—he wanted—*needed*—a picture of her, all sweet and succulent and bare-breasted. He'd take it and refer back to it in desperate times. Like when he wanted to strangle her.

Which was often.

He should probably take two.

Camera in hand, he shimmied back up the ladder and inched beside her. He pushed the button.

*Beep*!

She stretched, opened her eyes, and blinked. "What are you doing?"

He cleared his throat. "I...um..." *Can't think of a goddamned thing.*

Her gaze dropped to his lap, traveled over to the camera in his hand, then moved to her chest. She yanked up her strap and sat up. "What. Are. You. Doing?" Her teeth were clenched tight, probably hiding the fangs that had just popped out.

Honesty was probably not the best policy in that situation. "Nothing," he said, trying not to wince at his own stupidity.

"Get out." She tossed a pink Chuck at his head.

The surprise attack upset his balance, and he tumbled out of the loft onto his back. The air whooshed out of him. "Further mucking bun of a sich—"

She peered over the railing, muffling a sadistic laugh with her hand. "You all right?"

"No, goddamn it! What do you think this floor's made out of? Pillows and clouds?" He grimaced and rubbed his butt. "Thought you might want dinner, but the hell with it." Nice excuse. Had his dick not sucked away all his brainpower, he'd have come up with that *before* she tried to kill him.

"Okay," she said. "Let me just get some clothes on."

*Yes, please, for the love of Christ, get your clothes on.*

He needed a stiff drink. When he opened the pantry door, angels sang from above. Behind those shiny metal doors were shelves upon shelves overflowing with liquor. The bar was completely stocked. Beer, mixers, four kinds of olives — there were even maraschino cherries in there! Skip bought them more booze than food—that beautiful son-of-a-bitch. If he were there, he'd give that man a sloppy kiss right on the lips.

He made a nice tall scotch on the rocks and drank down the burn. Callie descended, wearing shorty shorts and the illustrious tank top. Her evening attire was a helluva lot better than that pillowcase she had on earlier. Other than the boob show upstairs, it was the first time he'd seen her in clothes that fit.

The pain in his back reminded him not to think of her as anything other than his surly coworker.

"Are you staring at my tits?"

"Sure am. What you got on there?" Lifting his glasses, he examined her shirt. A black kitten sat on each boob. Something was scrawled underneath. "Nice kitties?" He clucked his tongue. "Can't believe you'd wear such a suggestive thing."

Ignoring his remark as usual, she strode toward the open cabinet. "Holyshitballs! We've hit the mother lode."

"Skip outdid himself."

"He certainly did! What's this?" She shook out a plastic disk. "Collapsible martini glasses! What will they think of next?"

In one drawer, she found a stack of blue bar towels embroidered with the words *Screw It*. "Well, aren't these cute?" She grabbed the ice shaker from another shelf and made herself a martini. "Guess Skip's off the shit list for the day."

Walker chuckled and held up his drink. "Amen! This might make up for that staff bonding bullsh—*poop* he makes us do."

She groaned. "God, I know. What next? Trust fall exercises and motivational posters?"

"I've never seen you at one."

"And you never will."

"How'd you get away with that?"

"I've got dirt on him."

"Bribery, huh? I like your style." He raised his cup, and she met it with her martini glass.

"How's your back?" A naughty twinkle sparkled in her eyes.

"There's an appalling lack of sympathy in your tone, Bluebell." He waited for an apology and received none. "You didn't happen to step on my kidney back there, did you? Think it fell out."

"What were you doing up there with your camera, anyway?"

He answered her question with another. "Ready for intercourse?"

She damn near spit out her drink.

Sidestepped the hell out of that, didn't he? "Look out the window."

"Intercourse Bar and Grill. All-You-Can-Eat Buffet," she read. "Wow. Wonder what they serve?"

"Sausages," he said.

"Banana cream pie," she said.

"Ham sandwiches."

"Beef jerky."

"Tea bags."

He gave her a sideways grin. "What a cunning linguist you are."

In one move, her smile slid into a frown. What a little hater—couldn't even manage a single second of fun.

**Soundtrack:** Electric Light Orchestra, "Evil Woman"
**Soundtrack:** Foreigner, "Cold as Ice"

*Meatloaf.* That's who was playing on the jukebox, and that's what the Intercourse Bar & Grill smelled like: meatloaf.

A freckled redhead greeted them at the door, wearing a T-shirt knotted up to her boobs. She led them past a table of crusty men in baseball caps.

"Thanks, sweet thing," Walker said, sliding in a red vinyl booth.

She beamed. "Anytime. My name's Poppy if you need anything else." Twice she looked back.

He winked and waved then pored his focus into finding more sexual innuendo items on the menu to make Callie laugh. Coming up short, he folded the menu and lifted his gaze. A dissecting blue glare hit him. "Now what?"

"Out of curiosity? Do you come on to every woman you meet?"

He draped an arm over the back of the booth. "Aw, Bluebell, are you jealous of that sweet waitress?"

She examined her fingernails. "Horribly."

"Just being friendly is all. Not that you'd know what that means."

She rubbed her chin. "Friendly? Is that the hillbilly translation for acting like a dick?"

Getting all bent out of shape wouldn't do him any good—that'd just give her more ammunition. He needed to stay calm or at least *appear* to be calm. He stretched his legs in the aisle and put his hands behind his head. "I know it's difficult, but try to focus on something besides my dick."

"It's hard when it's over six feet and spewing bullshit."

"It's hard and spewing all right."

With a loud exaggerated sigh, she stuck the menu in front of her face, cutting off eye contact, as well as his awesome retort.

After a peaceful few minutes of Callie shutting her pie hole, the waitress returned for their order. "Tell me about the Intercourse special, pretty girl." He dialed up the Cheese-a-Tron 3000 for his coworker's benefit.

Poppy chattered on about the amazing steak until his ears bled.

"Perfect, darlin'. We'll have two of those. Medium-rare." He handed the menu back. "Can't wait to see what you have for dessert." Leading the waitress on wasn't very nice, but riling Callie up gave him such a perverse thrill.

An ice cube hit him in the head. "Ow!" He rubbed his head. "Are you insane? Do I need to hide sharp objects from you now?"

"Did you just fucking order for me?"

"Thought you could use a nice big piece of meat. Not sure how you're gonna eat it though with that filthy mouth of yours."

She gripped the table. "Ever consider I was a vegetarian."

Of course she was. "No wonder you're so violent."

Bogus laughter roared out. Eventually, she stopped and wiped fake tears from her eyes with both middle fingers. "God, you're so funny."

Heat surged through his balls. She had to be a hellcat in bed. But that was dick logic talking. It'd be a cold day in hell before they ever hooked up. And if they did, she'd probably kill him in his sleep.

That being the case, he gathered his scattered wits and headed for the jukebox. After carefully making his selections, "Evil Woman" blared from blown-out speakers by the bar.

Chuckling, he hurried back to the table to see if the devil had heard her theme song. Unfortunately, Poppy showed up right then, bearing juicy steaks and a flirty smile.

"Thanks, beautiful," he said. "Bet they're as delicious as you are."

Callie snorted. "Un-fucking-believable."

Poppy frowned and dragged her feet back to the bar.

"Something funny, Bluebell?"

"Stop calling me that!"

"But it fits you so well. You're so dainty and sweet. And with those great big blue eyes of yours, you look just like a bluebell blossom." The truth? He'd come up with the nickname at the Liberty Bell because her ball-busting had given him the blues.

"Cute," she said. "I have a pet name for you too, but since you don't like potty language. . ." She sliced off a piece of steak and stuck it in her mouth.

"Hold on. I thought you were a vegetarian?"

She swallowed. "No, I'm a don't-tell-me-what-to-do-atarian." She licked her saucy lips and took another bite. A soft "mmm" slipped out while she chewed.

"Still thinking about servicing me, Bluebell? Don't worry, darlin', there's plenty of time to do it while I drive."

"I wish," she said, dripping with sarcasm. "But I'm not a fan of STDs."

"I'm squeaky clean, honey. But I'll wear a rubber anyway. Maybe it'll protect me from your fangs."

Her fork dropped with a loud clang. "Are you done acting like a pig?"

"Are you done acting like a brat?"

"Think I can eat my dinner without being sexually harassed?"

Since sexual harassment wasn't funny, he shut his trap. But Foreigner's "Cold as Ice" came on and summed up his feelings perfectly. He sang along.

Unaffected by his spiteful serenade, she buttered her roll and popped a piece in her mouth, softly moaning as she chewed.

Boy, he'd like to butter *her* roll. "Taste good, Bluebell?"

She ignored his question and reached for another. Her appetite surprised him. It didn't look like she ate much at all. In fact, she looked downright frail. Her personality made her seem a lot bigger though—kind of like a tiny Chihuahua with a St. Bernard bark.

After the Liberty Bell incident, he was starting to think maybe Avery's story was true—something bad must have happened to her. Maybe he'd be able to stomach her biting personality if he knew what he was dealing with. Since he had to live with her for two-months, he'd better find out. "Why'd you leave Chicago?" he asked.

The color drained from her face and sweat beaded on her forehead.

He stood. "You all right?"

She shook her head and bolted to the bathroom, clutching her throat.

Maybe it was something she ate. But he'd had the same thing and felt fine. Another woman entered the restroom, taking a load off his mind. Surely, if she were dying, the other woman would come out and call for help.

Callie shuffled out five minutes later, still pale and damp. She didn't offer an explanation, and figuring it wasn't polite dinner conversation, he didn't ask for one.

Poppy came by with more water.

"How 'bout some of your cherry pie, darlin'?" He didn't even like cherry pie, but Callie's reaction had to be vastly entertaining.

"Sure thing, sweets," Poppy said. She set the check on the table and walked off, swaying her hips in a way that couldn't be natural.

Callie picked up the check and sneered. "She wrote her phone number on here."

"Gimme that." He smiled down at it.

"Are you planning on bringing home stray hoes everywhere we go?"

Had he heard that right? He needed clarification. "Stray hoes?"

"Yeah, do me a favor? Get a motel room when you do. I'm not keen on listening to you and your groupies go at it all night."

He took off his glasses and scrubbed a hand down his face. "That cold-bitter-bitch routine of yours is getting mighty old."

He put his glasses back on. "I keep thinking there's gotta be more to you—that you couldn't possibly be so nasty all the time." He shook his head and took out his wallet. "But you just keep proving me wrong."

The hardness on her face cracked and fell off. He'd expected a fight. Instead she fled . . . right out the door.

Rage and remorse wrestled inside him as he watched her jog across the street. She was a pint-sized pain-in-the ass for sure, but he was ninety-nine percent certain someone had made her that way.

*"I'm quite all right. I'm not even scared. You see, I've learned from looking around, there is something worse than loneliness—and that's the fear of it."—Dorothy Parker*

**Soundtrack:** Joss Stone, "Let Me Breathe"

Callie rested her forehead on the camper's cool chrome table while anxiety crawled over her like Black Death.

The panic attacks had started after she left Chicago. Most of the time she had them under control, but back in the restaurant, she'd almost passed out.

Walker would've loved that—more proof of how fucked up she was. Fucked up, cold, bitter, and nasty. At least she wasn't weak.

Why wouldn't his words stop echoing in her brain? After all she'd been through, her skin should have been thicker by now. But evidently it hadn't grown back yet, after years of having it shredded to the bone.

Once upon a time, people thought she was too nice. The hostile fallout of her parents' divorce, her mother's dictatorship, her sister's drug addiction—none of it had broken her spirit. Back then she was so optimistic others proclaimed it as weakness.

But Walker had never met the free-spirited-surfer-yoga-teacher-high-on-life version of her. He'd met the war-torn veteran, who flinched at intimacy of any kind, and who thought happiness was the mark of the apocalypse, signaling the world was about to end.

Now she was just an empty shell. Thanks to Daniel. He'd turned her against the world and made her wage war with herself. He'd stolen her soul and replaced it with a cold, bitter bitch.

Breathing, sleeping . . . *living*—she couldn't do anything right in his eyes. According to him, her list of faults was a mile long. *You dress like shit. Your hair is stringy. You're stupid. Your tits are too small. Don't open your mouth—*

When he wasn't beating her down, her best friend took his place. "You're lucky to have him," Hillary told her. "Most men don't go out with women like you. We'd all be better off though, if you just left him and found someone who can deal with you."

Had she known her friend's advice was really a warning, maybe things would have turned out differently.

And now there was a new antagonist in her life—Walker. But hey, two months of misery was nothing compared to three years, right?

Two more months of doing what she vowed never to do again—act like a good little girl and keep her mouth shut. Two more months of pretending to be someone she wasn't.

She wadded up the bar towel and threw it against the wall as hard as she could. "God fucking dammit!"

In the middle of her rage fest, the driver's side door opened and Walker jumped in. Without a word or even a glance back to see if she was there, he started the engine and drove down the street.

Several deep breaths later, she glanced out the window. They passed a family of smiling Intercoursians (Intercoursers?) in a horse-drawn carriage.

How lucky were they, not to have to deal with modern life? They didn't have to deal with advertising campaigns, or constant bad news, or mobile phones that never rang, or status updates from ex-boyfriends.

Their lives were simple. They worked hard in their fields and dined at long communal tables with their Amish friends and family surrounding them. They didn't have to sit on their ass all day in front of a computer. They didn't buy frozen meals or fast food—they grew their own.

Maybe that's what she needed—a strict-ass religion.

Just as she was getting all esoteric and shit, they drove past a horse and carriage in front of a McDonald's. A bunch of bearded men sat in the back cart, stuffing Big Macs in their faces.

*Jesus.* The world was full of actors—everyone pretending to be someone they weren't.

Including her.

Half a mile down the road, Walker stopped at a gas station. After he filled up the tank, he wandered into the store and came out ten-minutes later holding a piece of paper that turned out to be a hand-drawn map. It led several miles outside of Intercourse, to an unmarked dirt road between two cornfields.

Hot dust clouds followed them until they dead-ended next to a crooked red barn with a droopy roof.

"That old man back at the gas station said we could stay on his land for the night," Walker said, finally gracing her with an explanation. He jumped off the camper and left her there in shock.

They were spending the night in a cornfield?! Hadn't he ever seen *Children of the Corn*? At that very moment, scary Amish teenagers were probably sharpening their scythes, just waiting for it to get dark.

At least she'd die in a pretty setting. Outside, she stretched and let the green fragrance wash the city from her mind. A wildflower-filled valley—tinted pink by the summer evening sun—spread out between them and another barn in the distance. A cluster of maples surrounded a kidney-shaped pond, and two rainbow-colored hammocks dangled between the trees. She wandered over and settled in one.

The breeze rocked her gently as purple clouds drifted overhead. It'd been a long time since she'd been outside. Too long. For a brief second, she let go. Then Walker moseyed over and ruined the whole moment.

Still refusing to acknowledge her presence, he eased himself into the other hammock and folded his tattooed arms behind his head. His breathing deepened, and in less than a minute, he fell asleep.

God, she wished she could fall asleep that easily.

Taking full advantage of his unconscious state, she studied the sleeping manwhore. Other than his girly long eyelashes and plump kissy lips, the man screamed testosterone from head to toe—even while he snoozed. His eyeballs danced under his lids, and a smile ticked up one side of his cheek.

*Probably dreaming about pussy,* she thought and crashed a few minutes later.

# Chapter 7

## Darin'

### Random Cornfield, Intercourse, Pennsylvania

*"There's a hell of a distance between wise-cracking and wit. Wit has truth in it; wise-cracking is simply calisthenics with words."—Dorothy Parker*

*W*rapped up tight in a hammock burrito, Callie awakened in smoky darkness. A campfire blazed next to the Silver Dildo, and Walker sat beside it, staring into the flames.

She stumbled over, stopped midway, and gasped. Flickering lights floated over the valley like fairies dancing in the field. "What are they?"

"Lightning bugs," he said. "Guess Pennsylvania's known for them."

The splendid scene reminded her of a poem, and so she recited one. "'It's time to make love, douse the glim; the fireflies twinkle and dim; the stars lean together like birds of a feather, and the loin lies down with the limb.'"

"You make that up, just now?"

She unfolded another chair and placed it front of the fire. "I wish. An obscure poet from Savannah, Georgia, wrote it."

"Aiken?" Walker asked.

"Wow, I'm impressed." Seriously, no one knew Aiken's work, let alone backwoods manwhores.

"I was born and bred in Savannah."

"Hence the accent."

"Hence the accent," he confirmed.

"I saw cookies in the pantry. Want some?"

"Does a fat baby fart?"

She wrinkled her nose. "Does that mean yes?"

"Yes, ma'am, cookies please."

A short while later, she returned with the cookies and two sloshing martini glasses full of milk. He watched her eat with narrowed eyes.

She wiped her mouth. "Something on my face?"

"How come you're being so nice all of a sudden?"

"Guess I'm too tired to be a cold, bitter bitch."

He placed his forearms on his knees and hung his head. "Sorry about dinner earlier, Bluebell. Wasn't my finest hour."

A chorus of crickets sang while she gathered her mouth off the ground. *Wow*, an apology. That was something she'd never heard before. From anyone.

"I'm sorry, too," she said, finally managing to speak. "What you do in your free time's none of my business."

He sighed and sat up. "Why are you so tired? You slept all day."

"I have insomnia."

"Why's that?"

Because every time she closed her eyes, an endless loop of the same scene played over and over.

After a long crackling silence he said, "Ever play the question game?"

"Is that a drinking game?"

"If that's what you want."

The last time she'd played a drinking game was in college, and she'd woken up with a mustache and the words *I'm wasted* written in permanent black marker on her forehead.

"No thanks, I'm not up for passing out in my own vomit tonight."

"We don't have to drink. What's that other game like it? Truth or Dare? That's it. Let's play that."

"What are you, a junior high girl?"

He raised his hands. "Just trying to get to know you. Have a conversation. Maybe have a little fun. But if you'd rather just sit there like a statue."

Truth or Dare sounded about as much fun as frolicking through the Children of the Corn-laden fields with her pants down. But for the sake of harmony, she went along with it.

"All right," she grumbled.

"You sound thrilled."

"Just ask the question."

"Truth or Dare?"

"Truth."

"Why'd you leave Chicago?"

Her pulse kicked up. "You asked me that earlier."

"And you didn't answer. You get fired?"

"That's two questions. And the answer to the last one is no. I didn't get fired. But thanks for assuming I'm incompetent."

"Boyfriend dump you, then?"

"It's my turn," she blustered. "What do you want? Truth or dare?"

"Truth." He crossed his arms across his chest. "Unlike you, I've got nothing to hide."

Since he opened the door, she went inside. "Great. Then you'll have no trouble telling me how many women in the office you've slept with."

"Why are you so concerned with my love life?"

"Why are you so concerned with mine?"

"A gentleman never kisses and tells."

She snorted. "Oh, puh-lease. It's obvious you've made the rounds."

"Is that right?" He barked out a laugh. "Obvious is it? Well, since you already know the answer, I guess it's my turn then. You have a boyfriend?"

Was this the Inquisition or a party game? "Why the hell am I doing this?" she asked the sky. "You didn't ask if I wanted a truth or a dare. And the answer is a dare."

He heaved another log on the fire and reclined in his chair. "Dare it is then."

She put her hands in a T. "Time out. We need to set some ground rules first."

"All right, go for it."

She held up a finger. "One, no dares in corn fields."

"M'kay."

"Two, no naked dares."

He snapped his fingers. "Darn."

"Three, no objects in any of my orifices."

He drew back in horror. "What the hell kind of Truth or Dare have you been playing?" He shook his head. "No stuff in body cavities, check."

"Go on. You may proceed with your dare."

He rubbed his hands together. "I dare you to . . ." He scanned the area. "Go sit in that barn." He pointed to the leaning tower of shitza behind them.

"Are you serious? You really need to up your dare game, dude."

"I'm not finished! Ten minutes inside. Door closed. No flashlight."

"Oh, scawy." For extra special sarcasm, she added jazz hands.

"Hop to it then, tough girl."

She trudged toward the barn. Behind her, he wailed and moaned like a movie ghost. Her middle finger twitched, but she stayed on task.

A slight wave of the hand could have toppled the barn. If anything, she was more scared it would collapse on her. The door creaked open like the entrance to a tomb and darkness swallowed her up.

"Shut the door," Walker shouted.

She slammed it closed and flipped him off behind it.

*Ugh*, it smelled like something died in there. That couldn't be good. As her eyes adjusted to the dark, she stumbled around looking for somewhere to sit. A scratching sound stopped her in her tracks.

Metal cans crashed to the ground and something screeched.

Every hair on her body shot up. She held her breath. Just then, something horrible ran across her foot. She let loose a barn-toppling scream.

Whatever it was screamed too.

Blindly, she tore ass toward the door and smacked into something. A scythe! *Children of the Corn*! Another blood-curdling shriek ripped out of her.

The door flew open, and a shadowy shape stepped inside. "Callie?"

She leapt into Walker's arms. "Don't go in there! There's something awful inside."

He frowned. "What happened to your head?"

Hot liquid trickled into her eye. She wiped it away and tugged his arm. "We need to leave. Right now. Let's go."

He stepped inside the barn.

"Don't!" She grabbed his hand.

"I'm gonna get a flashlight." He ran off and left her there.

"Asshole," she yelled and sprinted after him.

A second later, he bounced off the camper, shining the light in her face. "Good grief, woman." He threw an arm around her. "You're shaking like a North Pole stripper. Shh, calm down."

Despite the monster in the barn, she felt surprisingly safe in his warm campfire and cookie-scented arms. If only she could unzip him, climb inside, and never come out.

"You okay?" He pulled back a fraction of an inch.

"Oh, no! I got blood on your shirt." She rubbed the stain.

"Don't worry about it. Let's go see what the fuss is. It's probably nothing."

She slapped her hands on her hips. "That *nothing* screamed its ass off!"

"No, you screamed *your* ass off."

"So you're gonna be like the stupid dude in every horror film? The moron who checks out the scary sound in the basement?" She sliced a finger across her neck. "Bad idea. Let's just get out of here."

He widened his chest and made his voice sound like a cartoon superhero. "Don't worry, ma'am, I'll protect you."

"With what? You have a gun?"

"Just these babies." He flexed his biceps and kissed each one.

"For fuck's sake. Give me the keys."

"Nope, you're coming with me."

Legs wide and arms crossed—she planted her feet and refused to move. "I am *not* going back in there."

"Stay here by yourself then." Whistling a little tune, he ambled toward the barn, perfectly at ease.

She grabbed the back of his shirt and trailed after him. "If we aren't murdered, I'm going to kill you."

At the door, he flipped on the flashlight and stepped inside. Five-seconds later, he backed out, roaring with laughter. It took three tries for him to spit out the words.

She shot him a Murphy-I'm-Gonna-Serve-Your-Balls-On-Toothpicks-At-My-Next-Party glare.™

He cleared his throat. "It's just an old 'coon."

"'Coon?"

"Raccoon. Little thing. Yay big." He moved his hands a foot apart. "Come see."

That couldn't have been the same beast she'd encountered. She peeked inside. Cowering in the corner, the terrifying creature, no bigger than a large house cat, clutched a corncob in its tiny hands.

Walker bent over and laughed.

"Hilarious. What if it's rabid?"

His expression grew serious. "Did it bite you?"

"No, but . . ."

"Haven't you ever been outside before?"

"I've always lived in cities."

"What about nature shows?"

She drew a circle in the dirt with a foot.

"Weren't you ever a scout?"

"I didn't want to be another pawn in their cookie pyramid scheme."

He laughed. "Woman, you're weirder than a wagon full of one-eyed monkeys. I thought you'd impaled yourself on something."

She narrowed her eyes until he was barely visible.

"Come on." He snagged her elbow. "I'll get the first-aid kit. Shoulda just answered my questions."

She shoved his arm. He hip-bumped her back.

Bandage in hand, he knelt in front of her and placed it on her cut. "There you go. Want me to kiss it and make it better?"

In a hormonal trance, she stared at his wet lips and nodded. "I mean, no. No!"

"Sure? I've been known to heal people with my kisses."

She crossed her fingers. "Get those things away from me! I don't know where they've been."

A starchy grin replaced his warm smile. Stiffly, he strode toward the fire and sat in his chair. He poked the coals with a stick, and the flames kicked back up. "Man, I haven't laughed that hard in ages."

"Glad I could entertain you," she said dryly.

Blatant contempt seeping out of his pores, he studied her as if she were a creature in a zoo. *And over here we have the frozen bitch from Chicago.*

"Why can't you just let go and have a little fun? Loosen up for Christ's sake. You're wound up so tight I can see your religion."

Her ribs squeezed her lungs. *Fuck it*, she'd had enough. Only one day in, he was already listing her faults and telling her what to do. She jumped up and ran to the camper.

He followed her. "You okay?"

The door wouldn't open. She yanked and yanked then kicked the door. "I can't get in."

He reached around and flipped up the handle. "Stop for a sec. What's wrong?"

"I'm just tired." Her shaky voice wasn't backing up the lie.

He tipped her chin and gave her a peacock examination. "Doesn't look like you have a concussion. How hard did you hit your head?"

"I'm fine." She ducked out of his way.

"All right. Get some sleep, Bluebell."

Absolutely, she'd get right on that—just as soon as she finished having a panic attack.

**Soundtrack:** Too $hort, "Just Another Day"

The loud thunder of heavy bass woke Callie from a nightmare starring Daniel and Hillary. She threw off the covers and jerked the curtain open.

"*Psst*, you asleep?" Walker's head poked over the railing.

"What's that noise?" She turned on the light.

He crawled beside her, wearing pinstriped pajama bottoms and nothing else. She tried like hell to keep her eyes off his chest—smooth cut ridges of muscle, narrowing down to his hips—and focused instead on his ink.

On one arm, a multi-colored camera and a roll of film curled around his bicep. An oak tree with a tree house branched over the other.

His stupid take-off-your-clothes-darlin' grin slid up. "Like what you see?"

She clamped her thighs shut and peered out the window. A bonfire raged by the barn in the distance and dozens of cars and people were scattered around it.

"Looks like a kegger," he whispered.

"Why are you whispering?" she whispered.

His skin brushed against hers and triggered a tight tingle in both nipples. It was torture being trapped up in that tiny space with him. "Quit touching me," she snapped.

Like a bratty little brother, he smeared his arm all over her.

Like a bratty little sister, she cried, "I'm gonna tell Mom!"

He kept doing it.

"Careful," she warned. "Don't want you tumbling off the ladder again."

They resumed their covert party-spying operation from their overt Silver Dildo lookout. Seriously, parked in an open field like that? They were totally conspicuous. They stood out like a sore middle finger.

"Let's go check it out," he whispered.

"It's almost two a.m."

"Oh, sorry, Grandma. Didn't realize you had bingo in the morning."

"Cute. I'm still not going."

"Fine, I'll go by myself."

The chances of falling back asleep were anorexically slim. "The minute rabid raccoons or corn children show up, I'm outtie."

His eyes widened. "Is that a see-through nighty you're wearing?"

She looked down at a pair of serious titty hard-ons and yanked up the covers. "Out!"

He bounced his brows obscenely. "Did I do that?"

Even the thought of him touching her boobs made her moist. She chucked a pillow at him.

He ducked and dashed down the ladder. "Hurry up. I'm leaving in five minutes."

*Ten* minutes later, she met him outside.

"Let's march," he said, slinging his camera over a shoulder.

"What's that for?" she shouted, intentionally blowing their cover wide open. "Are you gonna film them murdering us?"

"You mean am I gonna film myself murdering you? Yes."

Frogs croaked in the thick cotton night, and off they went, thrashing through waist-high weeds. Halfway there, Walker stopped. "Think there's corn stalk camouflage?"

She pulled a sticker out of her shoe. "Think this is a good time for your random musings? On the way to our deaths?"

A rap song thumped in the smoke-filled breeze. She rapped along, singing about pussy, big assess, and n-words.

He arched a strongly disapproving brow.

"What? I like this song."

They marched on. As they drew nearer, he crouched by pickup truck. "What are we doing?" she asked.

He yanked her down next to him and struck a stern shut-the-fuck-up finger against his lips.

She whispered, "What are we doing?"

"Stay here."

*Pfft.* As if she were going anywhere else.

He belly crawled under the pickup as if he were leading an ambush in the Viet Cong. The sheer absurdity of it made her giggle. She clamped a hand over her mouth, but it didn't work. The more she tried to stifle her laughter, the harder it was to contain. It wasn't long before she was convulsing and snorting like an elephant.

"What are you doing over by my truck?"

She flinched and whipped around. Three teenaged boys—Drunk, Zitty, and Leery—eyed her with hostile suspicion. Since she had no idea what they were doing, she fabricated an answer. "Um . . . nothing?"

The sound of loose gravel scraping stole their attention. Walker shimmied out from under the truck, straightened, and gave the boys a gangsta nod. "Gentlemen."

Zitty and Drunk, lowered their heads. Leery, however, lifted his chin in defiance. Walker stepped forward. Leery stepped back and jammed his hands in his pockets.

"Dropped this under the truck." Walker held out his lens cap for proof.

Callie gawked at her coworker, amazed at how easily he'd alpha-dogged the three pups. His towering height alone spoke strength. But the way he'd handled them with such cool confidence? She was almost impressed.

Following his example, she straightened to her full five-foot-two height and tossed them an un-trademarked Bugged-Out-Steve-Buscemi-In-*Fargo* glare. He was small but ferocious. And so was she.

"Any beer left?" Walker asked the kids

Zitty nodded and pointed to the bonfire.

*Beer!* Why not ask them where the nearest Chinese restaurant was? Un-fucking-believable. *Beer.*

A wave and another gangsta nod later, they sallied forth to the keg. "What's that crazy look on your face?" Walker whispered.

"I'm trying to be scary."

"I'll say. Looks like you just crapped your pants."

"I almost did."

"Act casual," he said through the side of his mouth.

"As opposed to what? Acting professional?"

"God bless, woman. First, I couldn't get you to talk, now you won't shut up."

She pulled down an eyelid with a middle finger. "Do I have something in my eye?"

He shook his head and surveyed the scene. They must have crashed a private high school party. Everyone was wearing the same drab uniform—boys in blue short-sleeved shirts and black pants, and girls in some sort of . . .

*Wait a minute.* Those losers weren't in private school— they were Amish. "Notice anything unusual?" She tugged his sleeve.

"Are they smoking crack over there?" He gestured to a group by the barn. A barely functioning human lit up a bubble pipe, similar to the one she'd found in her sister's room.

"Whoa," she said. "Wonder what Amish communion's like?"

"Damn, you're right! They *are* Amish." He focused the camera on the crack crew.

She smacked his arm. "Stop that. They'll see."

The bulb flashed. "What are they gonna do? Smoke me out? Those kids are useless."

"We should go. I don't want the law busting us with all these Pennsylvania Dutch druggies."

"Are you nuts? Leave Amish Bizarro world? No way. This is the photo op of a lifetime." With that, he ambled off with the camera sewn to his face.

As a writer, she considered herself an amateur social anthropologist. Given that, she parked herself in her laboratory—i.e. a rusty flatbed trailer—and observed the subjects—i.e. the repressed religious crackheads who were currently jamming out to Tupac's greatest hits.

Her objective findings? Those peeps were all sorts of fucked up.

Meanwhile, Walker made the rounds like the Southern politician he was, taking pictures, shaking hands, patting backs, and making the girls swoon. Later, he joined her on the flatbed.

"This should be a reality show," she said, squaring her fingers. "I'll call it Divine Intervention. Think I'll win an EMMY?"

"Sounds like an award-winning hunk of sh—poo."

"Shampoo?"

"Never mind. What are you looking at?" he asked.

"See how sad that one is." A lone mousy girl sat crisscross applesauce and stared at nothing. "Wonder if she's being shunned because her dad has a computer."

"She's probably just higher than a giraffe's puss . . ." he trailed off.

"A giraffe's what?" She knew exactly what he'd said. But his ridiculous censorship amused her so. It was sort of knight-in-shining-armorish—super sweet—but completely un-fucking-necessary.

He stood and brushed himself off. "Let's get some beer."

She pumped the keg while Walker poured. Sleep-deprived delirium took over, and she made a wild bet she could chug beer faster than him.

"What are the stakes?" he asked.

"Loser has to empty the shitter for a week?"

"You're on." He tapped his cup against hers.

Technically, the bet was dirty. Then again, so was pumping poo. On the count of three, she downed the beer in four gulps, raised her fists in the air, and belched so loudly it echoed for miles.

Walker curled his lip. "Jesus, were you a frat boy in another life?"

She shrugged. "Grew up with a bunch of surfer dudes."

He looked shocked. "You surf?"

"Why does that surprise you?"

"Can't really picture you hanging ten."

"Why?"

"Croquet seems more like your sport. Or maybe badminton. Something prissy like that."

"I've never played badminton before. Does it use these?" She flipped him the double bird.

"So ladylike."

"Your dad's so ladylike."

"Boy, you're on a roll, aren't you?" He chucked his cup in the trash. "Ready to go?"

She followed him down the hill. Midway back to the camper, he paused. "I almost forgot about the miraculous event earlier."

Expecting another fascinating anthropological discovery, she cried, "What?"

"You laughed! Over by the pickup, you laughed!"

"Oh, when you went all G.I. Joe back there?" She snickered. "Yeah, that was hilarious."

Another minute later, he stopped again. "That would have been the perfect opportunity for corn camo. We would have been virtually undetectable."

"You were under a red pickup truck."

"Still . . ."

Thinking about his *Soldier of Fortune* stunt made her giggle again.

"Uh-oh," he said, "you're doing it again. Oh, no! You're smiling too! Oops, there it goes. It's fleeting. Kinda like a firefly. Turns off and on"—he snapped his fingers—"just like that."

**Soundtrack:** The White Stripes, "Ball And Biscuit"

Sun blasted through the skylight, stirring Callie from another dark saga with the usual actors. She yawned and looked down at her phone with disbelief—she'd slept a whole eight hours. It was as if she'd just come out of a coma. She felt revived—even, dare she say—peppy?

The prospect of creating a campaign didn't seem as daunting after a few hours of shut-eye. With a shower, a decent meal, and some coffee, she might actually feel like a human being.

Bathing was the first priority. She smelled like a smokestack. She threw on some clothes and climbed down the ladder. The partition to Walker's bedroom was shut. She tiptoed to the bathroom and slid open the door just as a wet naked man stepped out of the shower.

"Oh, I didn't know you were . . ." she glanced between his legs, and her brain shut down. From the billowing steam, his erection jutted out like a flesh-colored obelisk rising above the clouds. It was magnificent. She wanted to worship it, put a shrine around it . . . take a field trip to it. Heat spasmed through the neglected area between her thighs. "Oh," she said again.

He made no move to cover himself—he displayed his dick proudly with his hands on his hips. As well he should have.

A rumbling sound came from somewhere above The Most Beautiful Cock In The World (trademark pending). Did it say something?

"Callie?"

"Hmm?" *God*, he wasn't wearing glasses.

"I *said*, hand me a towel."

She reached for the towel, dropped it, picked it back up, and dropped it again. Making herself look like even more of an ass, she exploded into a maniacal fit of giggles.

Another sound cut through the haze. Was it a sigh?

"Get out," someone said.

The gruff tone slapped her out of her daze. "Oh," she said for the third time and backed out. He slid the door shut in her face, grumbling something about the piece-of-crap lock.

On the way to the kitchen, a drop slipped down her chin. *Jesus*, was she drooling?

The bathroom door slid back open, and he padded over with a towel clinging to his hips for dear life. A waft of freshly applied citrus aftershave drifted under her nose. She clenched her jaw and snatched the coffee pot. Who knew making coffee could be so sexually frustrating?

"Something wrong?" he asked.

"Would you put your clothes on!"

A scandalous grin slid up one side of his mouth. "Why? You've already seen everything."

Huffing out her frustration, she shielded her eyes and scrambled for the laptop. Gaze glued to the screen, she booted it up. The half-naked rat bastard sat down next to her. She glared at him while he hooked up his camera to his computer.

"Problem?" he asked innocently.

"Gosh, it's hot in here." She tugged at the hem of her shirt. "I think I'll work topless."

His eyes flicked to her boobs and a grin formed.

"Dammit, I'm not working with you in a towel!"

"Just give me a cotton pickin' minute, would you." Once the images started flashing on the screen, he strutted back to his room with the tops of his muscled ass cheeks peeking out from the towel.

More ground rules were in order. No prancing about in towels for one, and for two, no giant hard-ons.

Without his nude body next to her, the dumbassaphoria faded away, and her brain switched back on. For the hell of it, she googled "Amish drugs." Remarkably, a page of results came up. She opened the first link and read.

*"The Pennsylvania Dutch rite of passage Rumspringa encourages young Amish men and women to leave behind the confines of their strict religion before they take their lifetime vows. At sixteen, teenagers are encouraged to try movies, dating, or team sports. In other communities, more extreme vices are explored, such as drugs, alcohol, sex, cars, and music."*

They'd crashed a Rumspringa. What a story! But how was she going to make that work with an RV ad campaign? Wondering what images she had to work with, she glanced over at Walker's screen.

A gallery of thumbnails popped up. The first one was a gloomy portrait of a woman staring at a crack in the wall. Pain and bleakness carved the subject's dreary expression. She squinted. No, it wasn't a wall. It was the Liberty Bell. She clicked on the image and zoomed in. Walker jogged over and slammed the lid shut.

"Open it."

"No."

"Open that fucking laptop."

Two inches from her face, he said it again. "No."

She grabbed ahold of his bare nipple and twisted. "Open it!"

"Ow, Jesus. All right! Uncle. Let go! I'll open it." Rubbing his chest, he logged in again then pushed the laptop over.

After one quick look, she darted outside.

*"In photography there are no shadows that cannot be illuminated."—August Sander*

Walker studied the portrait of Callie. The color, composition, and lighting were all perfect. The most captivating part was her eyes—blue-glazed and painted with anguish.

The only decent picture he'd taken in ages, and of course, she'd have to ruin it. What a walking buzzkill, that woman.

Mad as spit on the griddle, he blasted out of the door. The trees screamed and squawked as he stalked toward her. Two crows flapped off and left an empty silence.

"Why'd you run off?" he asked

She flinched and glanced away. "I needed some air."

"Uh-huh, bull. Let's hear it. What's wrong with the picture? You worried about social media? If so, I'm not on it."

Fury flashed in her eyes.

Go ahead and take out the tigress, lady—I'm ripe for a fight.

"I don't give a fuck about Facebook. You're not doing your job. Instead of taking pictures for the blog, you're taking shitty pictures of me. And why were you in the loft yesterday?"

For his own safety, he left the last question alone. "It's *not* a shitty picture."

"You have no right to invade my privacy. Delete it."

"No way. Not unless you have a damn good reason. And so far, you haven't given me one."

Her body shook with anger. Instead of exploding like he thought she'd do, she imploded and rolled in a ball, hugging her knees tight and burying her face.

Anger he could deal with but not emotional withdrawal. That's what his mother used to do.

He softened his tone. "It's a beautiful picture, Callie. Tell me why you're so upset."

"It's awful." Her head lifted. "It's depressing. I look sick. If you post that on the blog, I'll . . ." She stopped herself from saying what he suspected was the granddaddy of all curses. "Get rid of it."

Her words beat inside him like a funeral drum. The crows flew back and cawed. "How about I Photoshop a smile on your face, then? Hell, I'm curious to know what that'd look like myself."

She curled up again. Face still buried, she murmured, "Is that what I . . . Do I look like that all the time? Sad like that?"

"Are you?"

She looked up. "Am I what?"

"Sad?"

Once again, she rolled in a ball like a giant roly-poly bug.

"Something tells me you've got a good reason to feel that way or you wouldn't be trying to hide it." He kept quiet for a minute. "Be sad if you need to be sad. There's nothing wrong with feeling blue. There's a lot of beauty borne from sorrow—music, art . . . poetry. Put your feelings in your writing. Make something great out of something sad."

She picked up a stick and dug in the ground.

"Truth be told," he said. "I'm not all that happy myself. I'm not doing what I want, and my job's sucking the life out of me. Went to school for photography, but I haven't taken a decent picture in years. Been too tired and uninspired. When I saw you yesterday, you looked so . . ." He took a breath to gather his thoughts. "Raw emotion—that's what I see in that image. It's real, and that's what makes it so beautiful."

"I didn't realize you were so disgruntled," she said, completely ignoring his heartfelt confession. "At work, you seem so . . . cheerful." She made cheerful sound like a case of the clap. "Are you gonna quit?"

"Already did. Promised Avery I wouldn't leave until after the tour finished."

"Why are you here, if you're so miserable?"

"I was hoping to stimulate my creativity. But then—"

"But then I showed up. I'm not exactly thrilled to be here either, you know. But Skip can't afford to lose the client and . . ." She chewed her lips like she was contemplating whether to admit the next statement. "And I can't really handle finding another job right now. The last few months have been pretty stressful."

That revealed absolutely nothing about why she was so distraught.

She stared out at the pond. "Sorry I ruined your trip."

"You didn't." He wasn't sure what shocked him most—his statement? Or that it was true? "I've never laughed harder or been more inspired than in the last day and a half with you. If that's what the first thirty-six hours was like, I can't wait to see what happens next. Hell, we might even start liking each other."

A soft smile curled up. When she wasn't sad, she was lovely, and the world looked warmer. A sudden craving took over his thoughts. He wanted to be responsible for that, for making her smile, for making her happy.

"I haven't written anything creative in years," she said. "God, it's been so long, I don't even know if I can write anymore. Maybe you're right. At least I'd have something to focus on besides . . ."

He waited for her to finish but she didn't. "Darlin', I'm always right."

"How do you get that enormous head of yours through the door?"

He wiggled his brows. "That's what she said."

She rolled her eyes. "Can we set some ground rules on the photography?"

He slumped over. "Here comes the disclaimer."

"Don't be such a drama queen. If you must take pictures of me outside of the campaign, fine. But I don't want to see any more of my 'raw emotion.' Keep your personal work to yourself."

That didn't sit well with him. He'd rather share his work with her. But if that's the way it had to be, then so be it. On that disappointing note, he stood and held out a hand. "Come on, Bluebell, let's go figure out where we're going."

"Thought you didn't want to plan anything?"

"We need a daily destination, not a plan. I still want the freedom to wander." He stopped. "What if we take turns picking places?"

"You don't want to plan the trip together?"

"I doubt we'd agree. I need to visit my grandma in Georgia and my friends in South Carolina. Other than that, I'm game for anything."

"Anything?"

Knowing her, he'd probably end up riding a unicycle naked with a monkey on his shoulder. "Within reason," he added.

"What do you consider reasonable?"

"Don't really know, but there's no doubt in my mind you'd do the exact opposite if I told you."

# Chapter 8

## Freakin'

### Baltimore, Maryland

*"I'd rather have a bottle in front of me than a frontal lobotomy."—Dorothy Parker*

**Soundtrack:** Ghostland Observatory, "How Does It Drive"

"amn, woman, have you lost your vertical hold? You can't pass that semi in this thing. Stop! Christ! That's a double yellow line."

She punched the accelerator up to ninety. "Come on!" she coaxed. "Faster, baby, faster. You can do it." Thirty seconds before a head-on collision, she yanked the camper back into the right lane, cutting off the honking semi.

"Good job, Greased Lightning." She patted the dashboard affectionately and glanced at him. "What?"

"Pull over! I need my heart palpated."

"Don't be so dramatic."

"Where's your driver's license? There's no way you passed the test."

"A dead person could pass the test. I grew up in Los Angeles, for fuck's sake."

"A terrible driver from L.A.—I never would have guessed."

"Just because you drive like a grandpa, doesn't mean I'm a bad driver."

She focused on the road and he focused on her. He liked that she didn't wear makeup. Except for the faint grey circles under her eyes and the delicate spray of freckles across her nose, her vanilla ice cream skin was flawless. Smooth as a pearl.

"Why are you staring at me like that?"

"Just wondering if I should prepare my will."

"Who knew you were such a little girl?" She turned up the stereo.

He turned it down. "Surprised to hear you say that after your little bathroom break-in this morning."

Pink bloomed on her cheeks and she cranked up the volume again.

He let her squirm for a bit. "Where are you taking me, anyway?"

"It's a surprise."

"I don't like the sound of that."

"Don't worry your pretty little face. We're almost there."

Not long after, she slammed on the brakes in front of a ramshackle pile of bricks, overgrown with weeds.

"We're here." She swept her hand over the scene as if she were Glinda the Good Witch showcasing OZ.

"An abandoned building?"

"Not just any abandoned building. A haunted one!"

"And from the looks of that thing, we won't be making it out alive either. Is it condemned?"

"Probably."

"Great place to hide dead bodies. Is this where you're gonna do me in?"

"Good idea."

The phrase *we are all lost souls* was tagged across the building in red paint. He read the sign over the entrance. "Forrest Hills Asylum! What the—? You brought us to a funny farm?"

She stuck a finger in the air. "A *haunted* funny farm."

Her melodious tone disturbed him more than he was willing to admit. *The hell with it.* He went ahead and flat out told her what he thought. "You scare me."

"Don't be silly. Think of it like a movie location. We can do all sorts of cool things here. Make a modern *One Flew Over the Cuckoo's Nest* or do something fun like that."

"*If* we get in."

"We will."

He sincerely hoped not.

After he gathered the camera equipment, he tried the front entrance. The door's rusty hinges scraped like a saw on metal as it opened. He motioned her inside. "Welcome home, crazy."

Hospital-green paint peeled off walls like shedding skin, and rows of rusty overturned wheelchairs bracketed the corridor. Rat turds, urine, mildew, and hot decay—it smelled like insanity in there.

The door slammed shut and her eyes widened with mock fear. He shook his head and wandered down the hallway, crunching through broken glass.

While he set up a few shots, she lounged in a battered wheelchair and waited. When she wasn't looking, he took a candid. Another perfect shot. Photogenic little so-and-so. Pity she'd never see it.

They wandered through a steel door and stepped into what was once a surgical room. She pointed out dangling wires in the ceiling. "Bet this is where they did shock therapy."

He unfolded the tripod. "Hook 'em up. Maybe it'll work on you."

"Did it work on your mom?"

He gritted his teeth and set up his camera. Once he started filming, he didn't notice she was gone until something crashed down the hall.

He crept down the dark corridor until he found her in a room, sitting cross-legged on the floor. Light beamed down on her from a barred window

Beep!

She flipped around and screamed.

"Jesus Christ." He clutched his heart.

"You scared the fuck out of me."

He sat beside her. "Sorry, filthy, thought you heard me coming."

"Not cool to sneak up on someone in this joint. I almost shit my pants."

"TMI."

"Yeah, well scare me again, and it'll be TMS."

"TMS?"

"Too much shit."

"Your mind is a dangerous place, Bluebell."

He took in the room. Decayed vinyl covered the walls and rock-hard foam poured out the cracks like puss from a wound. In the corner, a crumpled, brown-stained straitjacket lay in a dead heap. "Is that blood?"

"Probably," she breezed.

"You don't find that unusual?"

"Pardon the pun, but things were crazy back then. They institutionalized women for PMS and postpartum depression. God knows what they did in these rooms."

"Did you learn that playing trivia down at the local cemetery?"

"I wrote a paper on it in college." She leaned back on her hands. "Rather than deal with the social ramifications of divorce, husbands locked up their wives all the time."

"I don't see anything wrong with that," he said with a straight face. "Things have definitely changed. My mama was in a mental health facility, and it was more like a nursing home, not like this hell hole." Why he shared that information with her was as mysterious as the blood-splattered straitjacket.

She gripped her forehead. "The mom joke. Oh, shit. I'm so sorry."

"You didn't know."

"Why was she in there?" she asked after a long silence.

"My dad cheated on her all the time. She went to a dark place." He paused. "I blame him, but her brain probably wasn't wired right to begin with."

"Where is she now?"

"She died. Grandma's convinced she killed herself. But the doctors told us her drug cocktail caused it."

"How old were you?"

"Eight. My grandma raised me after that."

"What about your father?" she asked.

"Never heard from him again."

She placed her hand on his. "That must have been so hard for you." The tenderness surprised him. It must have surprised her too because she quickly yanked it back.

Despite the furnace-like temperature, he shivered. His childhood had been a horrid, and rehashing it left him chilled. He jumped up and bounced on his feet. Discussing his past, in a loony bin of all places, made his skin crawl. "Let's go," he said. "This place is giving me the creeps."

They loaded up the equipment, and she sat in the driver's seat. "That was fun," he said, hoping she'd picked up on the sarcasm.

She flashed a sinister smile. "Wait until you see what's next."

"Did I mention you scare me?"

## Enchanted Forrest, Ellicot, Maryland

*"A picture is a secret about a secret, the more it tells you the less you know."—Diane Arbus*

**Soundtrack:** Antonio Vivaldi, Janine Jensen, "Concerto No. 2 in G minor: The Four Seasons

For their next nutty adventure, Callie drove them to an abandoned amusement park outside of Baltimore. In its heyday forty years prior, the park was probably a fun family adventure.

Now it was just creepy.

"Did you find this by googling freaky stuff in Maryland?"

"At least there aren't any lines. Besides, this place is a photography goldmine."

Indeed it was. In any other circumstance, he'd have told her to go on without him while he got a beer. But moving outside his comfort-zone was so far proving to be a good thing. Freaky or not, in fifteen minutes, he'd already taken some stellar pictures.

After taking pictures of a Giant Mother Goose, an evil Humpty Dumpty tumbling off a collapsing brick wall, and Callie running through a field of weeds and beat-up gingerbread men, he set the timer and took a selfie of them in front of Hansel and Gretel's graffiti-covered candy house. He'd have to edit out the *Fuk Yur Black Dick* graffiti over the door and her *Let's Get Sith-Faced* Star Wars shirt, but otherwise, the picture rocked.

"Look! A rainbow bridge!" She skipped over to a mangled pile of colored wood by the fetid pond. "Think this is where childhood dreams come to die?"

"Probably." Not that I'm complaining, but any idea how to spin your freaky field trips for the campaign?"

"Why, I'm glad you asked. I think we should weave a vintage-retro thread through everything. Use the look and feel of old movies, postcards, and posters, and tie it into their long-lasting design. *Some things weren't meant to last as long as RoadStream RV's*—that's what we can say about today's venues."

"Not bad," he said. Maybe she really was talented. He made a mental note to check out her work later.

They wandered over to a pint-sized roller coaster. Half its tracks were buried in the ground like dinosaur bones. Callie nodded to a monstrous witch's head tunnel above it. "It looks like she ate the train."

"Must have scared the bejeezus out of the kids."

"Roller coasters are the best. The last time I rode one was before my parents' divorce."

He glanced up from his camera. "Never been on one."

"Shut up!" She stared at him like he was a circus freak. "We're going to have to fix that."

"No, ma'am—" Before he had a chance to erase that thought from her mind, her phone rang. Lord, he hoped she'd forget all about fixing that.

While she talked, she straddled the back of a fiberglass dragon. He attached the zoom lens and caught a solitary tear rolling down her cheek. She batted it away like a bug and continued her conversation.

He rubbed a knot out of his shoulder and paced in a circle. Whoever was on the phone was messing with her mood, and after a gloomy morning, the last thing they needed was a dismal afternoon.

The call ended, and she plodded over with her head hanging a touch lower. "Ready?" she asked.

If he hadn't witnessed it himself, he'd never have known she'd been crying. It didn't seem like she wanted to talk about it, and frankly, neither did he. Her sad business wasn't his, and drama was for actors, not defeated photographers.

## Maryland East Coast

The insanely popular Seafood Shack was, in fact, a shack. In the tiny restaurant, Jimmy Buffet music played in the background, and the smell of fried seafood clung to the air.

The server delivered a plastic basket with a fried soft-shell crab sandwich for Callie and a plate of oysters on the half shell for Walker.

She frowned at the sandwich. Splayed across the bun like a fried spider was a whole crab—shell, legs, and yuck. After one bite, she pushed the basket away.

"You look like you just stepped in dog sh—poo," Walker said.

"Dog shampoo?" As long as he kept up the gentleman charade, the joke never grew old.

"Never mind," he said.

"The crunchy texture kinda grossed me out." She added an overdramatic shudder. "It was like eating a cockroach."

"Want one of these?" He squeezed lemon on the slime and held it out.

She turned away, trying not to gag. "No, thank you."

"What? You don't like sea vagina?" He fingered the oyster's folds and tongued it like an oral sex superstar.

Heat pulsed between her legs.

Over his frames, he arched a devious brow. "Are you blushing, Bluebell?"

"I'm hot. Are you hot?" She fanned herself with the menu. "God, I'm roasting. What do they have against AC in Maryland? Holyshitnipples! I'm melting."

"No oysters in California?" he asked, still smirking.

If he didn't clam up about those oysters, she was going to . . . "I don't know. Obviously, I don't eat sea vagina."

"You grew up there, right?"

She nodded. "Skip did, too."

"No kidding?"

"I met him surfing."

"Still can't picture either of you as the laid-back surfer-type."

Back then, it was non-stop fun in the sun, and yes, despite their terrible family lives, she and Skip were definitely laid-back. Though his chillness mostly originated from pot.

"I won a silver medal surfing in the Nationals in high school. Thought about going pro for a while."

"How come you didn't?"

She shrugged. Her surfing career ended when her tyrannical mother found out she wasn't practicing music all hours of the day.

"How'd you end up in advertising?" he asked.

"I sort of fell into it." More like fell in love with an asshole. In college, she'd majored in creative writing. But high-paying jobs for writers were scarce. She thought she'd end up bartending for the rest of her life until one day, a gorgeous ad executive showed up at the bar, promising the world and a job writing at his ad agency. Swept up in a cloud of lust and dreams, she moved to Chicago a month later.

"I got sucked into it for the money," Walker said.

"It *does* pay the bills," she agreed soberly.

"Family still in L.A.?"

"My dad is. My mom lives in Europe. My sister lives in San Diego." Her limbs grew heavy. Family was an exhausting subject.

"How old's your sister?"

"Same age. We're identical twins."

"No kidding?"

"She called earlier. She's a recovering drug addict." Callie poked a fork in the crab. "Effie's a phenomenal violinist. She's composing a concerto."

"No kidding? That's cool." He defiled the final oyster.

"She played part of it on the phone for me earlier. It makes me crazy. She should be performing at the Met, not playing out of her car while she's on break at her shitty restaurant job." The back of her throat tightened. "I'm scared she's going to relapse and I'll be the only one who hears it." With all her drama, he probably thought she belonged on a shrink's couch instead of an RV tour.

"Bet it's beautiful. I'd love to hear it. Think she'd let me listen?"

The sincerity of his statement bubbled up gushy feelings she didn't care to let out.

"What's your middle name?" he asked.

"That was random."

"You seem upset. I'm trying to take your mind off your sister. So what is it?"

"I don't have a middle name."

He reared back dramatically. "What! No middle name! That's a sacrilege in the South!"

"Nope. Just Calliope Rhodes."

"You planning on marrying me, Bluebell?" he asked in a bedroom voice.

She hiked up a smug cheek. "Uh-*no*."

"You said your name was Calliope Rhodes."

"I did not!"

He grinned and nodded. "Yes, you did."

Broiling heat crawled up her face. Good God. Did she? How mortifying!

"Yep, took a nice long run down the ole Freudian Slip-N-Slide, didn't you? Have you been writing our name in hearts all over your notebook, too?"

"Yeah, right." She fake laughed and raised her hand for the check. Time slowed to a sloth-like pace as Walker taunted her with a suggestive brow wiggle. He was still chuckling and smirking by the time the bill arrived.

After they paid, he helped her out of the chair and motioned toward the door. "After you, Mrs. Calliope Rhodes."

She groaned. "You're never gonna let me live that down, are you?"

"Never."

# Chapter 9

## Rollin'

### Coaster City Amusement Park, Williamsburg, Virginia

*"There are no bad pictures. That's just how your face looks sometimes."—Abraham Lincoln*

**Soundtrack:** Wolfmother, "Woman"

In Williamsburg, Virginia, Callie pulled over and fetched something from the kitchen then came back dangling a bar towel. "Blindfold yourself."

Walker narrowed his eyes. "What are you up to, woman?"

"It's a surprise."

"I don't like the way you said that. What kind of surprise?"

"You'll see." A demonic grin slid up.

"You scare me." He sniffed the towel. "Is there chloroform on here?"

"For fuck's sake, I'll do it." She tied the rag around his head.

"Jesus, you're cutting off the circulation to my brain."

"It's not like you use it."

"Funny lady."

As she started up the engine, a billion crazy scenarios ran through his mind. "Insane asylum. Beat-up kiddie park. What next? A torture chamber?"

"Quiet, big man, or I'll gag you too."

A few minutes later, she parked and opened his door. "We're here," she sang.

"Where? I can't see a thing." He stepped out and felt her face like he was blind.

She grabbed his hand. "Let's go, Helen Keller."

The humid night made everything sticky. Judging by the sound, she was leading him to a crowd somewhere.

"Surprise!" She whipped off the blindfold.

*Shit fire and save the matches!* She'd hauled him to Coaster City. His heart rate shot up, and his mouth dried out. Everywhere weapons of mass destruction rose skyward like ladders to the afterworld.

A rare smile beamed out from the tiny terrorist. "Yay! Now you can ride your first rollercoaster. Aren't you excited? I'll just go get tickets." The devil skipped off, leaving him there in a cold sweat.

Just as he was about to have a stroke, he spotted a carousel. And bumper cars! He let out a breath. Okay, all right, he could do this. He'd just use the line allergy excuse for the coasters, and they'd go on rides more his speed. Like the teacup ride, for instance.

Callie bounced over a minute later, swinging two passes on strings. "Let's hurry the fuck up. It closes in an hour."

"Where to, sailor mouth?"

"There!" She pointed out a treacherous beast of a ride. "Thunder Rocket. The tallest roller-coaster in the U.S."

And also the most terrifying goddamn thing he'd ever seen. "Look's awesome," he lied. "Lead the way."

*Thank Christ in heaven*, a crowd circled the ride twice. "Darn." He snapped his fingers. "Too bad about my line allergy. I really wanted to ride that sucker, too."

"We have VIP passes. We can skip to the front." She held up the laminated tag.

"Well, isn't that just peachy." *You sick evil woman.*

"Come on. They're waiting." She pranced up the platform.

All cylinders ceased firing—he couldn't process a single thought. In a robotic trance, he put one foot in front of the other and marched to his death.

Callie waited for him in the front car. The most dangerous car. The first car to run off the tracks and explode. She *would* pick the front car.

Without his permission, his body sat next to her. A bunch of mumbo jumbo blared over a distorted loudspeaker.

"Walker—"

"Shh!" he hissed, blocking her with his hand. He didn't understand a goddamn thing. They were probably listing all the critical things he needed to survive. Where were the goddamned parachutes and flotation devices?

Her hand stroked his arm. "Are you feeling okay?"

In a word, no. He was far, far, far, far, far away from being okay. Light years. In fact, he was seconds away from barfing up his dinner.

"You're pale and sweaty," she said. "Were the oysters bad?"

She had to mention the oysters. A wave of nausea rolled through him. He searched the tracks for faulty construction.

"You're not scared, are you?"

"I'm not fu—" *For Christ's sake*, he sounded like a little girl. He cleared his throat. "I'm. Not. Scared."

The safety bar crashed down, nearly castrating him. "Son-of-a—help! Get this thing off me!"

She stared at him.

"What?" he barked.

She patted his leg. "I get scared sometimes, too. There's a line from a poem about fear. It goes, 'What if I fall? Oh, but my darling, what if you fly?'"

*What the hell was she talking about?* "What the hell are you talking about?"

"Let me give you the male translation: stop being such a pussy, and man up!"

Red dots of anger clouded his vision. "Never, ever, call a man a pussy."

She fluttered her eyelashes and flashed a fake smile. "Want to hold my hand?"

"No, I don't want to hold your hand."

The train lurched forward. He slammed his lids shut and grabbed her hand. As they climbed the tracks, she traced circles on his wrist. The tickly distraction slowed his pulse.

"Open your eyes," she said.

Right when he did, they dropped. "Shiiiiiiiiiiiiiiiiiiiiiiiiiiiiit!"

His bones shook like a rattle, and his cheeks flapped like wings. They circled the loop, and his intestines flew down to his ass. Upside down, right side up, tipped over, unzipped— one minute he was laughing like a crazy man, and the next he was whimpering in pain. More jiggling, and jarring, and freaking the hell out, then the train sped back to the station.

Callie's cheeks were pink as cherry blossoms, and her bangs stood straight up. "Well? Were you scared shitless?"

He jacked a fist in the air. "What a friggin' rush! Let's ride it again."

"Really? There are five more."

"Come on then, move that tiny butt!"

They rode all five coasters, the bumper cars, the Ferris wheel, the carousel, and even ate the last batch of cotton candy. Ten minutes before closing, he stopped in front of a knock-over-the-milk-bottle game.

"Those things are rigged," she said. "You might as well throw your cash in the trash."

He slapped said cash on the counter, and a greasy man handed over three baseballs. "Start picking your prize, Bluebell."

On the first try, he knocked down every one of them.

Raising her cheek slightly, she gave him a facial shrug. "Eh, lucky shot."

As if he were in the World Series', he cocked back his arm and threw the next ball. Damned if he didn't do it again. He buried his shock behind a wink. "Figure out what you want, yet?"

"Sorry, I was too busy mopping my mouth off the floor."

Muttering a silent prayer to the carnival gods, he let the last ball fly. The bottles fell clanging to the ground.

Her eyes bugged out. "Ho-lee-shit, you actually won."

"What's it gonna be, Bluebell? The big teddy bear? The purple elephant?"

She pointed to a dusty green atrocity hanging in the back. "I'll take the stuffed beer can, please."

The guy handed it over.

"My very first carnival prize." She nuzzled and kissed it. "Thank you."

He laughed. "You're welcome, nutter."

On the way out, she stopped and picked up the roller coaster pictures. Afterwards, they drove to a campground outside of Williamsburg.

Before bed, he brushed his teeth and admired his reflection in the mirror. Damn, he looked stronger, didn't he? Kicked his fear's ass to the curb.

Thanks to Callie. If she hadn't called him a pussy, he wouldn't have been standing there with a brand new pair of bigger balls.

And what a rollercoaster of a day they'd had too—down, up, back down, all the way the hell up. One thing was for sure—she wasn't boring.

On cue, she burst out laughing. The sound was full and fruity and completely contagious. He cracked a foamy smile and slid open the bathroom door.

Clutching the amusement park pictures to her chest, she rolled on the floor, giggling her butt off.

"Let me see those." He ripped the photos from her grasp.

In every shot, she wore a mile-wide smile. He, on the other hand, looked exactly like *The Scream* painting by Munch. Not one shot, *not one damn shot*, where his face wasn't riddled with terror. "I don't see what's so funny." He tossed the pictures on the table.

She went through them again, crying and shaking like she had palsy. For ten solid minutes, she roared. In the midst of her full-blown hysteria, she made a snack, brushed her teeth, and climbed the ladder, hugging the beer can under an arm.

When he crawled in bed and shut off the light, the snorts and giggles were still going strong. Finally, FINALLY, she shut up. Just as he was about to drift off, her laughter jolted him awake.

"Put the pictures away, Blue."

"I'm not even looking at them," she cried.

He smiled at the ceiling. If she kept laughing like that, he'd gladly take a thousand more humiliating pictures of himself.

"Blue?"

"Yeah?"

"I had a good time today."

"Me, too," she said with a contented sigh. "Goodnight, John Boy."

"'Night, nutter."

# Chapter 10

## Ridin'

### Corolla Island, North Carolina

*"The cure for boredom is curiosity. There is no cure for curiosity."*—Dorothy Parker

**Soundtrack:** Tom Petty & the Heartbreakers, "Rocking' Around (With You)

*O*n Corolla Island, she threaded her toes through the sand and watched the sunrise paint ribbons of grapefruit, blueberry, and cherry colors across the sky.

Hundreds of wild mustangs woke with the sun. They dipped in the ocean for morning showers, rearing and splashing in the waves.

Walker, barefoot and bare-chested, set up his tripod. As he snapped pictures, he beamed.

*Yeah, yeah,* the animals were enchanting and all, but watching a half-naked man in his element was a far more beautiful sight to behold.

A colt danced over and whinnied.

"Come on, boy," Walker coaxed. "Let's get a picture of you, handsome."

The pony stepped forward and pawed the sand. Wind kicked up his forelock, revealing a white star on his chocolate face. He cantered in a circle and stopped short five feet from the photographer.

"That's it," he said. "Little bit more."

He pranced closer and smelled the air as if he were whistling *doot-deet-doot-deet-doo*. From the corner of his soft brown eye, he studied her then curled his muzzle over his teeth.

"He's smiling," she whispered.

The shutter beeped.

The colt's mother jerked up her head, sea grass spilling from her mouth, and cried out to her child. He trotted toward her, and together, they galloped down the beach. Soon after, the rest of the herd thundered away.

Her body hummed. She couldn't wait to write it all down. Lately, writing wasn't just a job—it was a compulsion. Ideas swelled inside her, developing like fetuses. And every day she jumped out of bed, dying to create.

Travel provided an endless supply of inspiration, and Walker motivated her even more. He encouraged her to fine-tune everything, cut out the clutter, and simplify her work. In return, she pushed him to tell more of a story with his photography.

All day long they bounced ideas off each other. She'd been numb for so long, she'd almost forgotten what excitement was like. It was as if he heated up her atoms and made her electrons fire faster.

The articles she wrote, coupled with the pictures he shot, were so much more than advertising—they were poetry and art. And as a result, the RoadStream campaign took off. Receiving a compliment from Skip was a rare and beautiful thing, and he was issuing them daily.

Nothing was boring with him around. Eating, cleaning, driving, sleeping, breathing—it didn't matter, he turned everything into a game. Who could fold laundry the fastest, or have the most awkward conversation. He'd won that bet by asking a homely drugstore clerk if he could use over-the-counter wart medicine on his cock rocket. She'd laughed for an hour straight afterwards.

The morning before, she'd accidentally shaved her legs with his razor.

"You ruined it!"

She handed him her pink one. "Do your worst."

"Are you kidding? I'm not touching my manly face with that girly thing!"

To prove his razor was better, he'd insisted on a bar rag-blindfold test shave. Instead, she shot him in the face with shaving cream, and he chased her around the campground, snapping a towel at her ass.

When they weren't clowning around, or busy with the campaign, they focused on personal projects, working quietly next to each other until bedtime.

Life aboard the Silver Dildo didn't suck a bag of dicks like she'd thought it would. On the contrary, cohabiting with Walker was easy. In fact, she found his constant presence comforting. And their tiny living quarters felt more cozy than cramped.

Shacking up and working with Daniel, on the other hand, was like living in a war-zone. Ten hours a day he'd berate her at work then come home and criticize her all night. He'd drained her—sucked the creativity right out of her bones.

In all fairness though, living and working with someone was one thing, but living, working, *and* having a relationship was an entirely different matter.

Not like she had anything to worry about—that would never happen with Walker.

Ever.

# Chapter 11

## Drinkin'

*"I'm not a writer with a drinking problem, I'm a drinker with a writing problem."—Dorothy Parker*

When she opened her eyes, the evening sky looked like orange sherbet. She yawned and watched tacky tourist stores whiz past the window. "Where are we?" she asked.

"Still in North Carolina," Walker said. "Campground's up ahead."

A short while later, they arrived at a gated entrance, where a round, bald man greeted them.

"Is that guy wearing a Hugh Hefner robe?" she whispered.

The guy in question, who was definitely wearing a Hugh Hefner robe, introduced himself as Cliff. He handed over some brochures. "Here's a map and the dress code policies. Free time is after seven. You're in spot twenty-three, to the left."

"Dress code?" Callie asked after they pulled out.

"No clue." His lips twitched.

She had a funny feeling, but when they pulled into their spot, she forgot all about it. The site had a secluded ocean view—a rarity as far as RV parks went. "Well, well," she said. "Right by the beach. Nice job, dude."

Once they'd set up the Silver Dildo, Walker bounced out, wearing board shorts and a pair of goggles. The dips of his hips pointed like an arrow to the monolith below. He strutted down to the beach—oozing masculinity and confidence—and dove in the ocean.

Past the break, he came up and sliced his arms through the pounding surf as if it were a backyard swimming pool.

Sporty peacock.

She breathed in the warm salty air and smiled. This was where she belonged, by the ocean, not stuck in a dirty city.

"Hey there, cutie!" someone said.

She whipped around and screamed. A furry, pot-bellied naked creature stood before her.

Sasquatch spoke. "Sorry, didn't mean to sneak up on you. I'm Bob. We're camped in the spot next to yours. We ran out of toilet paper. Thought you might have an extra roll."

Could she outrun him? Obviously, he wasn't carrying a gun. She grabbed a stick off the ground and jabbed it in the air.

"Whoa! Whoa!" He covered his nuts. "Don't whack my willy with that thing!" He laughed. And it was the shrillest sound she'd ever heard—like a cheese grater on her eardrum.

"Where are your clothes?" she cried.

He scrunched his mouth to his cheek, looking strangely perplexed. "After seven's free time, hon, clothing optional."

The puzzle pieces gradually came together—the man in the bathrobe, the dress code . . .

WALKER!

"Wait here. I'll get you a roll."

A moment later, she handed off the TP, carefully averting her eyes from the empty balloon between Bob's legs.

Instead of shoving the hell off like she wanted him to, Bob sexually violated her with his eyes for a moment. "Ever been to a nudist resort?" he asked.

"Uh-*no*."

"It's liberating." He stretched his arms out wide and jiggled his penis.

*Ew. Ack. Ugh. Yuck.* Slightly sick to her stomach, she covered her mouth and wrenched her gaze from his crotch.

"Until you live naked, you don't realize how imprisoning our clothing is."

She'd like to put him back in clothing prison.

"It's just you and nature and nothing else."

And the burning sun on her skin and the sand fleas in her vagina.

"I'll think about it, Bob," she lied.

"It'll change your life."

"I'm not really big on change."

"Suit yourself. Or better yet, don't." Another shrill sound blasted her ears, and his belly shook like a bowl-full of fur-covered jelly.

At last, bare-assed Bob waved goodbye and flopped down the trail with the toilet paper streaming behind him.

Immediately after he left, Callie plotted her revenge.

*"A hangover is the wrath of grapes."*—Dorothy Parker

**Soundtrack:** Led Zeppelin, "You Shook Me"

On the beach, a naked woman waved at him. Before you get excited, she had bright red clown hair and skin with more cracks than a desert road.

*That thar's what you call rode hard and put away wet.*

Definitely not what he'd pictured when he'd booked that place.

"Have a nice run, handsome?" the woman asked, chomping on her gum like death eating a cracker.

"Yes, ma'am." He kept moving.

The woman caught up to him, running with remarkable endurance. "I'm Bev," she said. "You by yourself?"

"No, ma'am. Got the little woman back at the camper." Not entirely a lie—there was a small woman waiting for him. He started to run. She did too.

"What a shame. I'm making my special pink potion cocktails later," she panted. "Stop by spot twenty-four later, cutie, and have a drink with me."

"I've gotta get back to my wife, ma'am," he said then ran like hell until he lost her.

Back at the campsite, Callie greeted him with a hot smile and a cold glare. "Welcome back, ass face. Have a nice swim?"

Was the answer to that yes or no? He'd better just keep quiet.

"While you were out frolicking in the ocean, our neighbor came by brandishing a pork sword."

It took an epic amount of restraint not to laugh. "Sorry I missed that."

"Yeah, I bet." She increased the wattage of her smile. "Speaking of schlongs . . . I presume you'll be pulling out your skin flute momentarily?"

He coughed a laugh into his fist. "Mine's more like a skin tuba, darlin'."

"Whatever. Are you disrobing your dong or what?"

"I'll show you mine, if you show me yours."

"Ready when you are," she chimed.

"You serious?" He took off his glasses and studied her. Truthfully, he didn't expect her to get naked. Of course, he wouldn't look away if she did. When he'd picked that place, he was thinking of the story. A nudist RV park? Come on! With her writing and his (cleverly censored) photos? They were bound to win an award.

"Absolutely." She flashed a flirty smile.

Even the remote possibility he'd get to lay his eyes on her sweet naked tits made his logic shut down. Meaning, he actually believed her cockamamie bullshit. All he needed was a quick shower and he'd be ready for a little pre-dinner show.

"Hurry back," she called after him.

Oh, he'd hurry all right.

In the shower, he gripped his skin tuba and rubbed one out in five-seconds flat. Sort of sad how fast he came. But lately, even the crack of dawn turned him on.

Afterwards, he dressed in shorts and nothing else. Why bother with the extra layers, if he was taking everything off?

He put on the stereo, grabbed a bottle of tequila, and rushed out the door. It was a gorgeous night and bound to get even more gorgeous once Callie stripped.

Not even a second passed before she asked, "Why aren't you naked?"

He smirked. "Why aren't you?"

"You first."

"I'm not building a fire with my pants off. I'll singe my goodies."

"I'd like to singe your goodies," she grumbled.

He whipped around. "You say something?"

"Must be the wind."

At that precise moment, he began to suspect she was up to something. But he carried on as if it were nudist business as usual and started the fire.

Once the sky turned black and the flames were roaring, he sat beside her at the picnic table and drank a nice healthy dose of tequila. "Want some?"

She yanked the bottle from his hand and gulped down the mescal like it was water. Between coughs and sputters, she cried, "Gah! Tastes like ass!"

"Take it you know what ass tastes like?"

"Sooo," she said, ignoring his question. "When are you getting out the giggle stick?"

He chuckled. "Boy, you want it bad, don't you?"

"Oh, yeah." She yawned." I can barely contain myself." Though she may have sounded bored, the hungry look she gave him said otherwise.

Then again, he'd just had two shots and was probably imagining things. "Be my guest."

"Let me just go freshen up."

Oh, boy! What did that entail? Maybe a trim job around the lady parts? He smiled. *That'd be nice.*

A short while later, she returned looking exactly the same. Did she shave her legs? Do her hair? Damn, what'd she do? He slugged down the Mexican gasoline and passed it over to her. "Well? We doing this or what?"

"How about a game of Truth or Dare first? That'll make things more fun."

That sweet smile on her face didn't fool him. *Fun, my ass*, he thought. If it were up to her, she'd have him running around, dangling seaweed from his dick. He'd better beat her to the punch. "Truth or dare?"

"Truth," she said.

A nudie beach and a bottle of booze, and he had her right where he wanted her. "So, Bluebell . . ." He folded his hands across his belly. "Why'd you leave Chicago?"

Her expression turned blank, like he'd somehow extinguished her emotions with a simple question.

"Nun-uh!" He poked her rib. "I'm not falling for that lost puppy look. Out with it."

She blew out a long breath. "For a lot of reasons."

"Name one."

"My fiancée cheated on me."

A prickly ache grew in his shoulder. He rubbed it for a moment. "How long were you together?"

"Three years."

"That's a long time." He shook his head. "I don't get why women go out with creeps like that."

Her posture stiffened. "I didn't know he was going to cheat on me—"

"Not you, the other woman. She went after your man when he was with you. That's just asking for trouble."

"You've never cheated on anyone?"

"Hell, no. If I feel like cheating, it's time to break up."

She dipped her chin and squinted. Either she was drunk or didn't believe him. Not caring either way, he drank another shot.

"Pass me that," she said and drank twice as much. Pounding her chest and coughing, she asked him if he wanted a truth or a dare.

He sighed. "How 'bout we make this easy and just take off our clothes."

"All right, take them off."

"Nun-uh, not without you."

"Let's do it at the same time." She twirled a finger. "Turn around. This isn't a striptease."

*Too bad. A crying shame, really.* "For Christ's sake, I've seen a naked woman before."

"Oh, I'm aware of the vast amount of booty you've seen."

What'd she mean by that? Furthermore, what did she consider vast?

"Turn around and we'll both take off our clothes." Her voice sounded unbelievably innocent. "On the count of three, we'll turn back around."

"This isn't a Wild West show down."

"Humor me."

He pretended to be exasperated. "Fine. Let's get this over with."

On the count of one, he dropped trou and flung his shorts on the table.

She kept counting. "Two . . ."

He rocked on his heels.

"Two and a half. Two and three quarters . . . three!"

He jumped around, ready to feast his eyes on her fleshy delights. "What the—? Why are your clothes still on?"

Grinning like a jack-o'-lantern, she twirled his shorts around her middle finger then dashed over to the fire and threw them in. "Oops! They slipped. Walker, Walker, pants on fire."

"Why you little—" He chased her like a mad bull charging a matador and caught her by the collar. But she kept running, and he tore her shirt.

"Ow! That hurt." She stopped and rubbed her neck.

They glared at each other, nostrils flaring like racehorses.

*Enough of that bullshit.* He ran to the camper, but the little brat had locked the door. "Where are the keys, Blue?"

"Keys? What keys? I thought you had them."

"I'm gonna spank your ass 'til it blisters."

She wasn't paying a lick of attention to his threat. Why? Because she was too busy staring at his dick.

He slammed his hands on his hips and pushed out his pelvis. "Want some popcorn for the show?"

She turned away, cheeks as red as the fire.

Payback time. He was going to make her squirm like a worm in hot ashes. "Man, it feels great out here." He stretched his limbs wide and flexed his muscles.

Not a single word came out of her mouth. Not one biting remark. Couldn't even manage an insult, she was so flustered. He'd have given himself a high-five, but he already looked like a complete jackass.

He paraded around the camp as if he'd been a lifetime nudist then sat across from her and spread his legs as wide as his hips would allow.

She slammed her eyes shut and snatched the bottle off the table.

"Something wrong, Bluebell?" he crossed his ankle over his knee.

The tequila glugged as she sucked it down.

It was balls to the wall after that. Or rather, balls to the face. He grilled steaks bent over in front of her face. For some reason, she didn't touch a bite of her dinner. She did, however, plow through the tequila.

Later, he climbed up on the picnic table and aligned his dick with her view. "Crazy mosquitoes." He swatted at nothing. "We need some damn spray."

She shielded her eyes and chucked the keys at him. "Okay! Okay! You win! Please, for the love of fuck, put your clothes on."

He made her beg a few more times then went inside and put on clothes. On his way out, he glanced through the window and caught her making snow angels in the sand. Good lord, time to cut her off.

"Girl, you are dee-runk. No more tequila for you!" He laughed.

Behind him, a hyena laughed too.

He turned around and met a pair of leathery tits head-on. Mercy! What an ugly sight. It was Bev from the beach, and she was with a guy who looked like he'd just escaped from The Island of Dr. Moreau.

"Here's the welcome wagon," Bev said, setting down a pitcher of what looked like Pepto-Bismol.

"Bob Gentry," the nude dude said, holding out his hand.

Walker nodded. Like hell he'd shake hands with a naked man.

Bob sat at their picnic table, where incidentally, Walker would never sit again. "Met the wifey earlier over a roll of TP," he said. "Guess you met Beverly at the beach?"

Bev blew him a kiss. He cringed and backed away.

"Well, aren't you the cutest thing?" Bev poured his obviously wasted coworker a drink. "You're gonna love this, sweetie."

Callie slugged it and smiled at everyone with a pink mustache.

He snatched the cup away. "I'm afraid she's had a little too much to drink already, haven't you baby cakes?"

Blue diamond daggers shot from her eyes. "Baby cakes?"

"Thought you'd be naked by now, hon," Bob said to Callie.

"Know what? Fuck it!" she declared. "I'm getting naked." Making good on her promise, she tore off her shirt—just grabbed ahold of the tear in the collar and ripped it right off.

Bob whooped. "That's the spirit! Doesn't the wind feel nice on your titties? Oh yeah, look at those hard nips."

Walker vaulted in front of her. "Dammit, put your shirt on," he whispered through clenched teeth. The leering couple craned their necks around him. "They're eye-raping you."

Blatantly ignoring his warning, she circled her arms overhead and twirled. "I feel so light!"

Desperately trying to hide his topless coworker, he dragged her into a tight hug. She fought him like a pissed off bobcat caught in a trap. Ultimately, she gave up and laid her cheek against his chest.

Bev jiggled over and handed him a drink. Maybe it'd make him go blind. He sucked it down like a man dying of thirst.

Surprisingly, it tasted like donuts. "You got another one of those, Bev?" He held out his cup.

"Watch out!" her husband howled. "That'll put hair on yer chest. Looks like you could use some though."

"Guess you've been drinking them daily, huh, Bob?" he replied with a tight smile.

The hairy man bugled and bleated.

Jesus, his laugh was more irritating than licking sandpaper. While Walker endeavored to mop the sound from his memory, Callie caressed him.

"I love your hairless chest." She nuzzled his pecs. "So smooth and sculpted. Like a marble manslut statue."

He covered her mouth. "Shh! Stop talking."

A painfully awkward minute later, Bob cupped his balls and raised his glass. "Here's to rocking out with our cocks out." He followed the gruesome toast by ramming his tongue down his wife's throat.

Walker tipped back the liquid donut and tapped the bottom of the cup until the last drop trickled into his mouth.

"What do y'all do for a living?" Bob asked after eating his wife's face.

"Well, I'm a writer," Callie slurred. "And Walker's a professional drag queen."

"She's kidding." He wrapped his arms around her face. "I'm in advertising."

"Shran't breash."

Like a dumbass, he loosened his grip, and she bent over his arm as if he were dipping her in a tango lesson. Her hard nipples pointed in the air like sexual beacons. He yanked her back up. "Dammit, control yourself."

"You smell so good." She sighed and slid her wiggly plums all over his skin. "Your aftershave makes me wet. Seriously, I have to change my underwear when you put it on in the morning."

His dick shot up, harder than a choirboy's in a porn shop. *Hellfire and damnation.*

"Want another one, sweetie?" Bev headed toward them with the pitcher.

"God, yes." He sounded a little desperate.

She poured him one, and as he lifted the overflowing cup to his mouth, he swore something crawled out of it. Was he hallucinating?

Led Zeppelin came on the stereo, and his topless friend cheered. "Let's have a naked dance party." Rather than wait for the guests to arrive, she had a dance party for one. On his dick. To the beat of the song, she ground against him in a slow-cock-hardening circle.

He didn't dance. He didn't move. He couldn't. He'd lose it if he did. It was so goddamned painful not being able to touch those bouncy boobies—not to mention her unmentionables.

"That's not dancing," he grunted, "that's foreplay."

Her half-lidded eyes traveled down to his hard-on, and a seductive smile pushed up one blushing cheek.

"Go on! Dance with your lady!" Bev said.

"Yeah, show your wife some affection, buddy," Bob added.

Callie slapped his chest and puckered her lips. "Yeah, show me some affection, buddy."

"We're not big into PDA, Bob," he said, smashing her face back against his chest.

"Aw, we don't mind," Bev said. "Go on, give your sweetie a kiss."

Just when he opened his mouth to tell Bev to crawl up a hog's ass and have a ham sandwich, Callie stood on her tippy toes and kissed him.

His heart drummed so loud it felt like he was in a womb. She plucked off his glasses and went at him like a hooker in heat. All his self-control floated away on a pink fluffy cloud.

They attacked each other, swirling, sucking, biting, and grabbing. It was the best kiss he'd ever had. Damn shame he probably wouldn't remember it.

Someone groaned, and he was pretty sure it wasn't him. He peeled his lips off his sexpot coworker and squinted at the blur by the picnic table. "Hold on a sec." He set Callie down and felt for his glasses in the sand. Once they were on, he nearly screamed, for all the sudden, he had a horrifically clear view of Bev blowing Bob.

"You swing?" Bob said with a shit-eating grin. "Let's swap."

His wife okayed the idea with a wink. "Mm-hmm," she mumbled, mouth stuffed full of cock.

"That's it!" Walker clapped. "Time to go! Y'all need to leave."

"Give me a minute," Bob said, still pumping into her mouth. "I'm about to come on my wife's tits."

"Nope. Nope. Come on your wife's tits somewhere else."

Bev scrambled to her feet wearing a look so ugly it'd scare the maggots off road kill. "That was rude!"

"Oh, I'm sorry. Let me rephrase that, please come on your wife's tits somewhere else."

Bob fisted his dick. "I don't like your tone, buddy."

In his addled state, he could barely sort out which of their offenses bothered him more. But one stood out in particular: those swinging sons-of-bitches were cock-blocking him. And that was reason enough to strike an even more unlikeable tone. "Leave, or I'm gonna unleash hell on your asses."

Had he heard that line in a movie? Or was it an original? Either way, he didn't have a clue what sort of hell he'd unleash, nor if he'd be able to do it on their asses. But it sounded tough, and furthermore it worked, because right after the threat, they hightailed it out of there.

Halfway down the trail, Leather Tits shouted, "Maybe if your wife gave you more head, you wouldn't be such an asshole."

She was absolutely right—he needed more head and stat. Where was his wife anyway?

Back in the camper, he locked the door, checked it twice, then staggered to the rear. Sweet Mother of Mercy! Much to his wonderful surprise, he found Callie in his bed, spread out on her tummy, fast asleep.

He knelt beside her and caressed her milky back. Near her right shoulder blade, four freckles formed a smile. He connected the dots with a finger then kissed the spot. Goosebumps pebbled up on her skin.

After that, everything turned pink.

*"Her big heart did not, as is so sadly often the case, inhabit a big bosom."—Dorothy Parker*

Her decapitated head rolled under the Silver Dildo and Walker stepped on the gas. Callie jolted awake. There was an axe in her head and a hand clutching her breast. She blinked. Where was she? She reached around and found Walker attached to the hand.

The last thing she remembered was his dick swinging in front of her face. Everything after that was a painful blur. She tried to crawl out from under him, but he groaned and tightened his hold.

"Walker," she whispered.

Against the back of her neck he mumbled, "Hmm?"

"Your hand."

He plucked her nipple in his sleep.

Heart pounding in her aching head, she sat up and winced. "Walker!"

"Shh. Jesus, stop shouting."

"Why is my shirt off?"

One eye opened and quickly shut. He scrunched up his face and groaned. "Mouth. So dry. Need water. Help. Pain."

She shoved him. "Get up."

Gradually, he rose, grimacing in the sunlight. "I think those freaks roofied me."

"What freaks?"

Both his eyes opened wide and immediately zeroed in on her boobs. A lopsided grin tilted his mouth. "Good morning."

Scorching heat climbed her neck and shot down to groin at the same time. She yanked the sheet up to her chin. "Walker!"

He jerked his gaze to hers. "Sorry, what did you ask me?"

"What freaks?"

"Bob and Bev. The swingers? Don't you remember?" He shuddered. "Ugly situation. Be glad for the memory loss."

"Where's my shirt?"

"You took it off. In fact, you ripped it off." He rubbed his temples. "It feels like a mule kicked my head."

"Walker!"

"What! You were wasted. I tried to stop you."

Nothing made sense. "Did I . . . did *we* sleep together?"

"Jesus, stop yelling. Yes, we slept together. Isn't it obvious?"

A needle on a record scratched.

Several things popped in her mind at once. Number one, they must not have gone at it very hard because her vagina felt surprisingly unscathed. And number two, how fast could she swim across the ocean and get out of there?

A long droning groan leaked out of her.

"Wait a minute," he said. "We slept in the same bed, but we didn't . . . Jesus, I wouldn't do that, not when you were trashed."

She collapsed on the pillow. "Thank fucking God."

He frowned. "You don't have to sound so happy about it."

"I'm wigging out. I don't remember a thing."

His eyes drifted to her breasts again.

"Stop staring at them! I know they're microscopic."

He cocked his head and bunched his brows. "You don't have a clue how beautiful you are, do you?"

She wanted to talk about her tiny tits about as much as she wanted to take a joyride in the back of a hot garbage truck.

"Blue, look at me." He tore the sheet away. "Is that why you hide under all those big clothes? Because you think there's something wrong with your body? Was it that guy? Did he tell you they were too small?"

At least a hundred times, Daniel had offered to pay for a boob job. He wouldn't help her pay off her student loan, but he'd happily pay double the amount for double-D's.

The very idea had repulsed her. It was such a blatantly sexist thing to request. "Get your back hair lasered off and your penis enlarged," she'd told him. "Then we'll talk bigger tits." After that, he'd never mentioned it again.

But when he cheated on her with that whore whose breasts were four times larger, a lingering thought paced the back of her mind—if her tits were bigger, would he have strayed?

"Don't believe a word that jerk told you. They're perfect," he said. "Just right for your frame. Trust me, sweetheart, there's nothing wrong with you. You've got a beautiful body and your skin . . . You ought to be in a lotion ad. Or a dermatologist poster. Christ, I don't even know what the hell I'm saying. My brain's melted, and my body hurts. Shoot me." He rubbed his temples again.

She snorted. "That's ridiculous. I'm so pale, I'm almost transparent."

He took her hand. "Don't cut yourself down like that. You're gorgeous, Bluebell. And I'm not just saying that cause your tits are on display."

The tight harness with which she'd restrained her emotions jerked free and a backlog of tears swamped her throat. With zero saliva and a shoe leather tongue, she swallowed them back down.

He rubbed her back. "Hey . . ."

A tear escaped. *Oh, shit.*

He brushed her cheek. "You okay?"

She jammed her palms in her eye sockets. "I don't know what's wrong with me. I guess I'm still drunk."

He folded her in his arms. "Let it out, Blue."

No way. If she let go, a geyser of grief would shoot out. His heartbeat ticked like a metronome—slow, steady, soothing. The smell of his skin, his hands lightly caressing her back, the strength of his hold—she concentrated on those feelings and shoved her messy emotions back in the closet. "I'm sorry." She pulled away.

"For what?"

*For being a small-boobed-hung-over-emotionally-unstable mess?* she thought, but said, "For passing out in your bed."

"Anytime, as long as you take off your shirt first."

She jerked the sheet over her head. "Whatever happened last night, you better take it to the grave."

"You mean when we made out like teenagers?"

"What!"

"Wish I could tell you about it, but my lips are sealed."

A faint memory desperately tried to crawl out from under the fog of her hangover. *Holy shit,* they *did* kiss. Nineties' jungle music had a slower beat than her heart right then.

"All right," he sighed. "I've gotta get up, throw up, chug a gallon of water, and check my body for signs of rape. My buddy's expecting us in Myrtle Beach by five."

"Walker?"

"Yes, Blue?"

She peeked out from the sheet. "Would you find my shirt?"

The dimples on his cheeks deepened. "No can do." Clutching his head, he crawled over her and weaved toward the bathroom.

The door slid shut and opened back up a second later. "When we get to Myrtle, I'm buying you the skimpiest bikini I can find. Time to show off that body."

# Chapter 12

## Bangin'

### Pawley's Island, South Carolina

*"The lady doth protest too much . . ."—Shakespeare*

**Soundtrack:** The Stray Birds, "Dream in Blue"

*W*alker's friends lived just outside Myrtle Beach on a quaint island called Pawley's. Egrets and blue herons dotted the green, reedy marshes on the western side, and white gulls and pelicans spread out over the waves on the eastern side.

Matt and Patty lived with their two children on the beach side, in a pale pink house perched on stilts.

On the beach earlier, they'd feasted on a low-country boil Matt had spent the whole day cooking. After dinner, as the evening sun sank behind the dunes, Callie sat next to the fire pit and watched a scene torn from the pages of the American Family Dream catalogue.

Walker and his big bear of a friend Matt were building a sand leviathan with the help of Matt's son and the family dog. A few feet away, Patty dipped her baby's toes in the surf.

A sharp pang of longing consumed her. It'd probably always be like that—her alone, admiring someone else's family from afar.

Patty came over with the baby. "You mind watching him? Need to fetch something inside the house."

"No, no! I'm not good with kids."

"It's just for a few minutes. I'll be right back." Patty plopped the baby on her lap and waltzed off.

Panic-stricken, Callie went rigid and held the baby in front of her like he was diseased. He shot her a gummy grin. She smiled back, and he grinned wider. Relaxing her death grip a bit, she bounced him on her knee and sang.

> *Would you like to swing on a star?*
> *Carry Moonbeams home in a jar?*
> *And be better off than you are?*
> *Or would you rather be a pig?*

She snorted like a pig and bounced him higher. Giggling and squealing, he wrapped his tiny hands around her fingers and squeezed her heart hard. Fat tears tumbled from her eyes and dropped on his fuzzy head.

Patty strode toward her. Callie wiped her face and handed the baby back.

"You okay?" she asked.

"Sand in my eye."

A quiet moment of understanding passed between them. Patty nodded and sat beside her. While she nursed the baby, she asked about Walker. "How long have y'all worked together?"

She let out her breath. "A few months."

"Y'all are dating, right?"

"Are you kidding me? Hell, no!" Mentally, she cringed at how offensive that must have sounded to his good friend.

Patty probed her with a hard stare then shook her head. "Girl, I don't know how you do it, living in that box. I wouldn't be able to keep my hands off him."

"Trust me, it's not hard when he's slept with every woman in the office."

Patty cocked her head. "Walker? But he's so picky. I've known him for ten years, and you're the only woman we've ever met. I always thought he was celibate."

Clearly, she hadn't seen her friend in a while.

"Matt said Walker couldn't pick up a girl to save his life back in high school. Said he was skinny as a bird and wore huge glasses. You believe that?"

They shifted their gazes to shirtless Walker, running down the beach as graceful as a gazelle, his chiseled body flexing and glowing in the sunset. Effortlessly, he placed Patty's kid on his broad swimmer's shoulders then swaggered over, flashing a panty-dampening dimpled smile.

"Not a damn bit awkward now," Patty said.

"Not at all."

*"Photography is truth."*—Jean-Luc Godard

On the morning of the Fourth of July, Matt and Walker sat in their golf cart on the eighteenth hole, drinking Bloody Marys. It was so humid you could swing a sponge in the air and mop the floors with it.

Walker wiped the sweat off the back of his neck and watched a sandhill crane tiptoe around the green. "Man, I've missed this."

"No golf in Manhattan?" Matt asked.

"I'm talking about the South. I miss the heat and the beach. The salty air. I've gotta move back here."

"I'd be happy as hell if you did." His buddy took a long drink. "Callie's sure a pretty little thing. Sweet too."

He laughed. "Sweet's not quite the word I'd use to describe her."

"What? You don't like her?"

"She's all right."

"All right? She's finer than frog hair." Matt narrowed his eyes. "You want her, don't you?" He pinched Walker's cheek. "Aw, you do! Look at you! You're blushing. Bet you're just dying to see those sexy blue eyes glaze over when she comes. Oh, Walker! Deeper! Harder!" He bucked his hips in the air.

"Jesus man, don't talk about her like that. She's my friend."

Matt quit the air-fucking and laughed. "So I take it you haven't hit that yet?"

No, he hadn't hit that yet, but he wasn't about to tell Matt that. Instead, he told his buddy the swinger story.

"So, had you not been drugged by the swingers' pink donut poison," Matt said, repeating the events, "You wouldn't have kissed your hot coworker? Am I getting that right? Because she's your buddy, correct?"

Yeah, he didn't believe it either.

"Well, when it happens—because there's no way it won't when you're all snuggled up like a bug in a rug in that camper," Matt said. "Just make sure you're careful. You don't want to end up married with kids, never having sex because you're too tired to do anything but lie in bed and watch TV."

Walker swigged down the rest of his drink, hoping his shock was hidden behind the cup. He couldn't decide which was worse—spending every night watching TV in bed? Or spending every night watching TV in bed *and* not having sex?

"Don't get me wrong," his friend clarified. "I love my wife and kids, but sometimes I miss being single. Marriage is hard work and children are exhausting."

The confession stirred up a heap of disappointment in Walker's gut. Patty and Matt were his role models—the perfect example of a happy marriage. One day he hoped he'd have a relationship like theirs. And hearing his friend wasn't happy, destroyed that hope in one punch.

Not that it mattered. He hadn't even come close to meeting the right woman. After all, where would he find someone creative, funny, passionate, AND sexy? Someone easy to live with? Someone like Callie, but who actually liked him?

Maybe he needed to lower his expectations. Or maybe marriage just wasn't for him.

He pushed aside his moody thoughts and gripped his friend's shoulder. "I'm sure it'll get better, man. It's probably just a rough patch. Maybe when the kids get older . . ."

Matt tugged his ear and gave him a short nod. "Yeah, probably." He sounded doubtful.

Walker didn't blame him. He wasn't really convinced either.

Quiet as a one-handed golf clap, the friends stared out at the green until the sun's blistering heat became unbearable.

His buddy perked up. "Ready to lose this game?"

"S'pose so," he replied. Even if he was losing at golf, he was still winning the game just by staying single.

## Boat parade, Pawley's Island, SC

**Soundtrack:** Elvis Presley, "Island of Love"

That drowsy afternoon, heat waves spiraled off the asphalt. Islanders, decked out in red, white, and blue regalia, waited impatiently for the Fourth of July parade to begin.

The largest water fight in the Carolina's also took place along the parade route, and every grandpa, baby, aunt, and uncle had at least one bucket of ammo—i.e. a bucket of water—beside them.

Locals spent months preparing for the parade—making homemade water guns, creating costumes, and decorating boat floats. Pretty much overkill, considering all that hard work would be destroyed in approximately thirty-five minutes.

Guilty of first-degree overkill, Matt and Patty had won the best float three-years in the running. The year before though, they'd lost to a group of seventy-something women dressed up like pageant contestants, donning bikinis, sashes, and crowns.

"They didn't even decorate their doggone boat," Matt said, still licking his wounds. "It was just old women in swimsuits, sitting on stupid chairs."

Patty chimed in. "Last year, I found out one lady's husband was a judge. Boy, I was fit to be tied. Wanda Jenkins, bless her heart, she looked like one big varicose vein in that white bikini."

Matt nodded. "After that, we blackballed Ernie Jenkins and added a new parade committee bylaw that states judges can't cast a vote on relatives' floats. Of course it's awful hard to find folks around here who aren't related."

Ah, the simplicity of small-town life—no gangs or shootings—only crooked parade judges and incest.

In view of last year's trophy robbery, Matt and Patty went all out with their Elvis *Blue Hawaii* theme. They built a giant paper maché Elvis bust and attached it to the bow like a mermaid on a Viking ship.

They filled the boat trailer with real, not fake, *real* palm trees and sand, to make it look like they were shipwrecked on an island. Matt even built a grass-covered tiki bar in the back of the boat, with totems that breathed fire out of their mouths.

Before the parade, their team finalized last-minute details. Patty dressed her little boy in Hawaiian shorts. Walker draped inflatable pineapples over the sides of the boat. Matt filled water buckets and mixed blue cocktails.

As for her, she slathered on thousand-proof sunblock so she wouldn't turn as pink as the string bikini Walker forced her to buy. After that, she dressed in a lei and a grass skirt then taped a plastic parrot to her shoulder. Though the bird definitely added an extra dash of silly, the comedic value of her costume paled in comparison to Walker's and Matt's.

Walker wore a coconut bra, baby-blue tight retro swim trunks, and a captain's hat like the one Elvis wore. Minus the bra, he looked exactly like a fifties' movie star.

His enormous friend stuffed himself into a tiny, white polyester short jumpsuit, unzipped down to his navel. The outfit cut his junk in half and gave him a frontal wedgie. Walker teased him about it relentlessly.

"Sorry, Vagina Dick, didn't see you there."

"Hand me that bag of ice, Moose Knuckles."

"Ew, get your beef curtains away from me."

"Your dick looks like a ninja boot."

"Is it easier sitting down when you have two assess?"

All afternoon, he made his friend's smashed schlong the butt-dick of all his jokes.

Five minutes before go-time, Matt outlined the parade rules. "Fire your weapons at everyone—kids, grandmas, the handicapped. I don't care who it is—show no mercy! And I want to see some enthusiasm. Holler, yell, scream, go cray-cray. Ladies, flash the judges if you have to. Do whatever it takes to win that trophy."

A foghorn sounded. Matt clapped and cranked up the Elvis soundtrack to a deafening volume. "Showtime, everyone!"

Patty's parents, in charge of towing the boat through town, jumped in the truck with the baby, and the float rolled forward.

"Take no prisoners," Matt yelled then sprayed the crowd with a contraption strapped to his back. While he was going *Full Metal Jacket* on everyone, a kid pegged him in the nuts with a water balloon.

Callie roared and Walker shot a stream of water into her open mouth. She coughed and sputtered and tossed a balloon grenade at his face. He ducked, and it splattered across Patty's face instead. Patty retaliated by nailing her in the back with a wet sponge ball.

The island turned into a water war-zone.

A toothless old man shot her boob with a pump gun. She screeched and Walker sprayed the other. In return, she squirted his crotch. For half the parade they fought each other.

Then a hostile gang of pre-teen boys fired upon Walker. He blasted Matt's water cannon in their faces. "I'm gonna take you out, you *Lord of the Flies* son's-of-bitches!"

"Give me that thing," she said and hit them again.

At the end of the parade, the float passed the judges' table. Matt set off a water bomb and gyrated his junk to "Rock-A Hula Baby." A judge, dressed like Uncle Sam, turned on the fire hose and gunned Matt flat on his back.

With the exception of the rollercoaster picture night, she'd never laughed so hard in her life. Her cheeks hurt. Her ribs ached. And her voice had gone hoarse.

But beyond the big smile on her face, in the space between her heart and throat, a wistful sort of ache grew. So many things she'd missed out on over the years—beach parties, parades, cookouts, and boating. She'd had more fun with Walker in the last few weeks, than she'd had in the last twenty-seven years of her life.

Her sabbatical from the real world wouldn't last forever though. But in the meantime, she'd savor every last second.

All the boats launched after the parade, and as the flotilla made its way down the narrow channel, swarms of people cheered from restaurant patios along the inlet.

Once they arrived in the bay, everyone anchored, and the real party began. Islanders tied together rafts, tubes, blown-up bars, and baby pools, and swam back and forth, sharing food, drinks, and laughs like a big happy family.

Walker crossed his arms, showcasing his beautiful inked biceps, and leaned against the captain's chair, looking like a male swimsuit model. A drop of sweat trickled down his treasure trail. He slid his mirrored aviators down his nose. "Whatcha staring at, Bluebell?"

She jerked her gaze away. "Nothing."

"Didn't look that way to me," he said, his voice a tad deeper.

*God,* she was burning up. And it wasn't from the sun. What she really needed was a cold shower, but a lukewarm ocean would have to suffice. She dove off the back of the boat and scampered on a raft the size of a queen mattress.

As she floated and watched the surviving orange sliver of light fade beyond the horizon, it felt as though her soul were smiling. Days like that inspired poetry—odes to the last twenty-four hours.

Someone cannonballed off the back of the boat, causing a giant wave. Walker surfaced next to her.

"You almost capsized me," she cried, clinging to the rocking vessel.

"Definitely one of my finest cannonballs ever." He tossed his leg over the raft and slid off. "Christ, this sunscreen's making me slipperier than a greased eel."

Throughout his multiple attempts, she laughed hysterically. Finally, he made it on and flopped beside her.

Their gazes fused as they caught their breath. His spiky lashes slowly fanned his sun-bronzed cheek. A piece of seaweed stuck to his shoulder. Using it as an excuse to touch him, she brushed off the kelp and let her fingers linger on his cool skin.

The move struck a match, and his stare turned heated. "You got some sun." He stroked her cheek with back of his knuckles. The tingles remained long after his hand lowered.

A boom thundered in the distance, and brilliant sparks rained over the ocean. Walker snaked an arm under her and folded her into his wet warmth. She opened her mouth to protest, but he shut her up with a kiss.

Another firework went off and he glided his tongue around her lips. "Mmm." He pulled her bottom lip between his teeth. "You taste like peach pie."

And *he* tasted like salted coconut. She wanted to consume him.

He slid aside the top of her suit. "I've been wanting to do this all day."

She panted. "What?"

He answered her question by tonguing her swollen nipple. "Oh, God."

"Feel good?"

"Yesss." She raked her fingers down his back. *Swoosh, bang, crackle*—her body lit up with the fireworks and sang "God Bless America."

His fingers swept shocks across the waistband of her suit. Inviting him to go lower, she dropped one leg off the raft. The ocean licked her foot while he bit her neck. She held her breath and rolled her hips, rocking the raft dangerously.

"That your secret spot?" he asked.

His erection poked her leg. Just the memory of it made her melt. She ground into his hardness. "Is that yours?"

"Careful," he said, his accent thick and buttery. "Keep doing that, and it's gonna go off like a bottle rocket."

Only Walker could make a bad simile and cream her panties at the same time.

Soon the *oohs* and *ahhs* and bangs ceased, and the only sounds left were the waves lapping and their lips smacking.

He circled the fabric over her clit, disintegrating her willpower. Deep in her reserves, she found a smidgen of strength and grabbed his hand. "Not there."

Given the way he jerked back, you'd have thought she'd slapped him.

"Time to go, lovebirds!" Matt called from the stern. She wanted to drown his friend and hug him at the same time.

Walker rubbed two fingers across his mouth, gave her one last longing look, and slipped off the raft with a giant splash—leaving her on fire and drowning in a sea of regret.

# Chapter 13

## Smokin'

### Savannah, Georgia

*"That would be a good thing for them to cut on my tombstone: Wherever she went, including here, it was against her better judgment."*—Dorothy Parker

**Soundtrack:** Rick James, "Mary Jane"

Callie imagined Walker's grandmother would be like the stereotypical Southern lady—charming, polite, refined. She'd wear a big floppy hat, white gloves, pearls, and a smart dress suit. She'd have finishing school manners, and like him, she'd never say anything crass.

The real Josephine Rhodes sported bright purple glasses, purple flowered leggings, and a shirt that said *I'm a virgin, but this is an old shirt.* Her white hair stuck out like Einstein's, and she drank like a fish.

Although judging by the horrified look on Walker's face, that wasn't his grandmother's normal behavior.

"Let's all sit on the porch and chat," Josephine had said when they arrived. Evidently, that was the southern translation for "Let's sit in the oppressive heat and watch grandma get soused on sweet tea and bourbon."

Of course neither Walker nor his grandmother broke a sweat in the Georgia kiln-like weather. She, however, felt like someone had lit her on fire. Sweat dripped down her neck and pooled in her bra. Walker tried to help by turning on the ceiling fan, but all that did was blast hot air in her face like a heater.

An hour later, her brain—deep fried by the scorching weather—stopped working altogether.

"Got a good joke for y'all," Josephine drawled.

Her grandson winced.

"What's the difference between a job and a dead prostitute?"

"Jo—"

"A job still sucks." She whooped out a laugh.

Walker rubbed the back of his neck.

"What do you call cheap circumcision?" She paused for a beat. "A rip-off. Get it?" She scissored her fingers. "Snip, snip."

He cleared his throat and grabbed the glass from his grandma's hand. "Think you've had about enough of those, Grandma—"

"Don't get your panties in a wad, Sugar Bear. Your friend likes my jokes, don't you?" She patted Callie's wet thigh. It sounded like she was slapping a raw chicken breast. "If you don't have a sense of humor, then don't sit next to me. Right, Callie? I bet you've got some good jokes."

*What did she say?* It was too hot to hear. Perhaps if she rocked her chair at light speed, she'd manufacture a slight breeze. The Rhodes family stared at her. "Jokes? Hmm. How about this one? A dyslexic walks into a bra."

Instead of crickets, cicadas rattled. Maybe it was her delivery? She started rocking again.

Josephine turned to Walker. "How 'bout you go to Pie Palace and pick us up a peach pie?"

"I can't drive that camper downtown, Grandma."

"Take Sheila." She tossed a set of keys to him. "Callie and I'll get to know each other while you're gone."

He mouthed an apology to her behind his grandmother's back.

"Later, tater!" She shooed him away with a finger-wiggling wave.

Soon after, he sped past the house in a cherry-red Cadillac convertible, with the top down and his aviators on.

"Sexy," Callie said, not at all talking about the car.

"Real fuel-efficient too," Jo said. "Gets eight miles to the gallon."

"Really? That's as bad as the Silver Dildo." She slammed her eyes shut. "Did I just say—"

"Silver Dildo? Sure did. Better than the big toaster though. That's what I was calling it." She gave Callie the same dimpled grin as her grandson's then rocked her chair back as far as it would go and slingshotted her spindly body to standing. "Let's see if we can't find some trouble."

Walker told Callie he didn't have a lot of money growing up, but their home was enormous. Maybe he was like one of those faux hippie deadlock kids in L.A., who bummed money and cigarettes off people, then drove their Hummers back to their mommy and daddy's house in Malibu.

*Nah*, that didn't seem likely.

Inside the house, the décor was a cross between *Gone with the Wind* and *Willy Wonka's Chocolate Factory*.

A massive crystal chandelier floated from the lofty ceiling in the foy-yay (or foyer as most commoners call it), and an oak butt-sliding staircase winded down from the top floor.

Everything else was an explosion of colorful oddities. Purple velvet chairs, a zebra-skin rug, and a dress dummy with a pirate hat were just a few of the items festooning the living room. Above the fireplace hung a stained-glass portrait of Dolly Parton. "I love what you've done with the place," Callie said. "It's so eccentric."

"Is that a compliment?" Jo asked.

"Definitely." She wandered over to the fireplace. A picture of a handsome man in a William Faulkner suit sat on the mantle.

"My late husband," his grandmother said. "Died before Walker was born. Not great in the sack, but his money made up for it." She pointed to a wall of framed pictures. "These are all Walker's. Boy's got more talent . . ."

Everything from his elementary school crayon drawings to his mesmerizing black-and-white photos covered the wall. She stopped in front of a picture of a weird little kid with braces and pop-bottle glasses. "Who's that?"

"That's Walker when he was thirteen."

She covered her mouth, muffling the "holy shit" she was dying to scream out. His perfect white teeth and dimples were hidden behind atrocious headgear, and his blue-green eyes were three times larger than normal in a pair of glasses that even the worse geek in the world wouldn't wear. "Oh my God. Can I borrow this? I need it for occasional bribery."

Not even batting an eye, his grandmother said, "Take that one. He keeps stealing it, so I made several copies."

Callie slid the photo out of the frame and snorted all the way to her suitcase. Once it was safely hidden, she met up with his grandma, and they went out back to the garden.

An oak sprawled over the yard with a tree house perched on top. It was the same tree house tattooed on Walker's arm. She could just see him up there as a boy, all gangly and covered in paint, wearing those ghastly glasses.

They meandered around a stone path, bordered by blossoms and fountains. "Wow, Mrs. Rhodes, your yard is TV-landscaping-show beautiful!"

"Spent my life making it that way," she said on the way to the greenhouse.

It was air conditioned inside, thank God. His grandma sat in a corduroy recliner and motioned for her to take a seat. From behind a shelf, Jo pulled out a didgeridoo.

*Oh, crap.* Was she seriously going to bust out and start playing that thing? The bad jokes were awkward enough. She sunk a little lower in the chair. This was beyond her acting capabilities.

*Wait a minute . . .* It wasn't a didgeridoo. She was holding a bong the size of a schoolboy!

Mouth gaping wide and eyes probably popping out, she watched Walker's grandma hum a little ditty and pack a bowl. The woman didn't seem the least bit concerned about blazing up in front of her grandson's coworker. Au contraire! She fired it right up, inhaled for nine or ten minutes, then puffed it out in Callie's face with a guffaw.

Still coughing out smoke, she handed over the bong. "Your turn."

Callie waved her hands frantically. "No, thanks, I'm good."

"Go on. It's organic. Grow it myself in the greenhouse. Try it. It'll help you relax. You're more uptight than last year's swimsuit."

"No, really. I can't."

"I won't tell. Go on, take a hit." She pushed the bong over another inch.

Talk about your non-peer pressure. Admittedly though, she was a wee bit tense—mostly because of her grandson. But she'd only smoked pot a handful of times with Skip in college. That wasn't quite like smoking with someone's grandparent.

Exactly what *were* the consequences of getting high with his whacked-out grandmother? On the lighter end of the spectrum, she'd chill out and share a few laughs. On the darker end, she'd pass out in her own vomit and make an ass of herself. That said, it was also highly unlikely she'd ever see the woman again.

*Fuck it.* "Puff, puff, pass, grandma."

Josephine chuckled. "Atta girl."

She lit the weed, pulled in a mass of stinky smoke, and slowly exhaled. Two more hits and she was higher than . . . eh, who knows. Let's just say, she was far too high to think. "That's some good shit."

Josephine winked. "Grandma's special blend."

She burst out laughing. So did his grandmother. They cackled and snickered and grinned at each other for what seemed like hours. Still chortling, Jo said, "So how long have you been sleeping with my grandson?"

Callie choked and pounded a fist against her chest. "I'm not . . . I never . . . Walker and I are just . . . friends."

"No need to pretend, sweetie. I'm not like most grandmas. I'm much more open-minded." She threw a pointed glance at the bong.

"We work together. That's it." It's not like they ever made out on a raft or anything.

"That's it, huh?" She snorted. "Watch out! Your pants are on fire."

Callie gripped her forehead. "Dude, you're harshing my mellow!"

Josephine hooted. She laughed with her—mostly because she was ripped.

"Can I give you a piece of advice about my grandson, sweetie?"

"Please don't."

She kept talking. "Walker doesn't take relationships lightly. He's extremely sensitive and doesn't do the casual sex thing."

Was she joking? All he did was the casual sex thing. Peals of laughter rolled out of her. "You don't have to worry about that." She giggled. "He's not the slightest bit sensitive."

A frown deepened the creases around the old woman's mouth.

Callie groaned. "That didn't come out right." Mostly because she was stoned off her ass. "What I meant to say was you don't have to worry about us. We're not having casual sex. Or serious sex. Or any sex at all."

"Not yet maybe, but you'll be riding on more than that Silver Dildo soon, mark my word. He looks at you like he'd fight tigers in the dark to get to your tent. And you're so hot and bothered, your ears smoke."

*Newsflash!* Walker looked at every woman like that. He was a professional sexy-look giver.

"All I'm saying, honey, is don't lead him on. If you're not serious, let him know upfront. Don't hurt him. That boy's the only family I've got left."

Was she in the freaking *Twilight Zone*? Lead him on? Hurt him? She snickered. "We. Are. Not. Having. Sex. I'm not even sure he likes me."

Josephine's cataract-fogged eyes bore holes through her.

Callie sat up straight and looked around the room for a diversion. Considering how high granny was, anything would work. She pointed out the window. "Is that Ted Turner?"

The old woman's eyebrow raised exactly like her grandson's. "I like you, Callie. You're the kind of woman Walker needs. You're spunky. And you seem like a smart girl. But you haven't got the sense God gave an animal cracker when it comes to my grandson. Pay a little attention, sweetie, that boy likes you, and if you'd stop fighting your feelings"—she coughed—"you'd realize you like him too." She coughed again. Before long, she was in the midst of full-fledged tuberculosis-style coughing fit.

Callie jumped up and smacked Jo's back. "You okay? Need some water?"

"I'm fine." She wheezed and doubled over, her lungs crackling with every breath.

"Maybe you should lay off the pot? That cough doesn't sound good."

"Go see"—she coughed—"if Walker's back with the pie."

Oh yeah. Pie sounded great. Hopefully, he'd bought four or five. But like hell was she going to leave his hacking grandmother alone.

Getting her out of there was going to be a serious chore. While she may be the president of Stubborn, Inc., his grandmother was the CEO.

With the few brain cells she had left, she hatched a plan. Well, not really. In fact, she had no idea what she was doing.

Someone spoke. "I'm not entirely sure I can walk." Weird, that sounded like her voice. *Hmm, not bad.* She should have come up with that idea. *Oh, wait,* she did. "Also, I have no clue where I am." She laughed her ass off. Probably because she was as baked as a loaf of pot bread. *Heh, that was funny.* She snorted.

Josephine chuckled and grimaced as she stood. Callie took her arm and pretended she couldn't walk. Grandma didn't suspect a thing—mostly because she really couldn't walk.

On the back porch, she jabbed a finger at the old lady. "Say one word about any of this—the pot, the sex talk, anything—and you'll be the one shouting I've fallen and can't get up."

She cracked up. "So you don't want me to tell him you're in love with him?"

"You should really cut down on the weed, grandma."

*"Whenever I'm asked why Southern writers particularly have a penchant for writing about freaks, I say it is because we are still able to recognize one."—Flannery O'Connor*

**Soundtrack:** Michael Franti, "Ganja Baby"

Loopier than a lasso in a hula-hoop contest. That's how Callie was acting. He'd caught her staring at him with I-want-to-eat-you eyes about twenty-seven different times that night.

That he could relate to. The way she'd tasted the night before—like hot candied sex—made him just as hungry. He bet the rest of her candy shop tasted just as sweet.

But the go-away-come-closer signals had him as confused as all get out. Since the boat parade, she'd been doing an outstanding job of brushing him off and pretending like nothing had happened. After they'd kissed, he thought their relationship would deepen. Deepen, as in him sinking between her thighs. But she'd kept him at arms-length since then.

Maybe she'd had too much to drink during the parade. One thing was for sure, if he ever kissed her again, she was going to be sober as a judge.

Speaking of sober, he'd never seen his grandmother get drunk like that. That had him shaking his head all afternoon. And with Callie acting nutty too? Something was a half bubble off plumb.

He'd lost count of the times she'd commented on the scenery. On and on she went about how amazing the Spanish moss was, and how it dripped from the trees like "green guts."

Earlier they'd gone to Forsyth Park, and she jumped in the fountain. Right in front of the cops, she climbed over the fence and stuck her feet in the water. He'd had to tell the police she didn't know any better.

When they visited SCAD, where his work was still on display, she'd acted like he'd taken her to the Louvre.

They'd had a drink with his buddy Jim, and she wouldn't stop laughing. Jim wasn't a funny man.

There was also the non-stop yapping. Normally, she lived in her head, and he had to pry the thoughts from her brain. But that night, every bit of minutia that crossed her mind poured out of her mouth like a fountain of crap.

The woman who'd barely cracked a smile at the beginning of the trip? Nowhere to be found. Her smile was so big it'd stop traffic.

Whatever was going on, the woman was adorable. If she acted like that the rest of the trip though, they'd have to have a serious come-to-Jesus.

Callie stumbled on the sidewalk and crouched. "Are these shells?"

"That's tabby concrete. Limestone's scarce around here, so they mix oyster shells in. Some of the houses have it in the walls."

"It's amazing!" She caressed the sidewalk.

He pulled off his glasses. "How much did you have to drink today, young lady?"

"Gee, Dad," she said with teen-aged sarcasm. "When'd you get so tall?"

Her skin wasn't flushed or sweaty, just dewy. Heatstroke couldn't have been the cause of her strange behavior. He hooked her elbow with his. "Come on, nutter."

Farther down the street, she spread her arms wide and danced in a circle as if she were on the set of *The Sound of Music*. "I love it here."

Despite the fact she was losing her mind, he chuckled. "Is that right?"

"It's so eccentric and charming and old and mossy and hot. Really hot." She fanned herself with a pretend fan.

They strolled past the first Girl Scout headquarters, and she rambled on endlessly about how the girls should earn patches for things like flipping off cat-callers and not dressing like whores.

A few times he just stopped and stared.

"I wish I lived here."

"You do, huh?"

"It's like a writer's wet dream."

"I miss it here," he confessed.

"Are you ever going to move back?"

"Someday. Soon, probably. Josephine's not getting any younger. Plus, I can't stand New York City."

Her smile withered.

He stopped. "What's wrong?"

"It's just"—she picked a speck of nothing off her shirt— "I'll . . . miss you. You're the only friend I have, besides Skip."

A twinge of sadness hit him in the chest. He'd really grown to like her. If he were honest with himself, he more than liked her. But when it came to her, he lied to himself on a regular basis. An hourly basis more like it.

"I'll miss you too, Bluebell." He reached for her hand and she took it. He liked holding hands. He liked holding *her* hand.

A little ways down the street, he paused in front of a two-story brick storefront. "See this place? It's Walt Trainor's gallery. He's a famous photographer. Inspired me as a kid."

"You know him?"

"I was always too scared to meet him. Might have burst my boyhood bubble if he turned out to be a crappy human being. Safer to admire him from afar—pretend he was a great man." He peered in the dark windows. "Think he lives in Sweden or somewhere. Once in a blue moon, he has a show here." He whispered in her ear. "Want to know a secret?"

"Do I have to do a dare?"

"Nope. It's a freebie."

She bowed. "Then, by all means."

"When I was a kid, I told everyone Walt was my dad. My father was such a sh—poo head—"

"Shampoo head?" She erupted into a fit of giggles.

He stared at her then finished his thought. "*Anyway* . . . I used to imagine Walt picking me up from school and throwing a football with me. He'd teach me everything he knew about photography. And one day, my work would hang on these walls. Since he didn't live here, and my dad wasn't around, it was an easy lie to pull off. Think that's demented?"

She smiled sweetly. He'd expected her to laugh. "Not at all. I used to imagine my mother was dead." She covered her mouth. "Did I say that out loud? Motherfuck. Don't lock me in the loony bin for saying that." She winced. "Ugh. Do you have a ball gag? My mental filter isn't working."

He leaned in and sniffed. No alcohol. Just smelled like her caramel shampoo. They kept wandering.

"Does you look like Walt?" she asked. "Is that why you picked him as a faux dad?"

"Don't know. Never seen a picture of him. Most photographers are behind the lens most of the time."

On the corner, she stopped in front of another storefront. Windows and glass brick surrounded the entrance, giving the old building a modern feel. The second-floor had a small wrought-iron balcony that wrapped around the building.

"Hey, this place is for sale." She peered in the windows. "Buy it and make your own gallery. Then you can be another little boy's dream father."

"Bet the light's incredible." He pulled out a brochure from a pocket on the door. "Just one point five million."

"Whore yourself out."

"I do that every day in my job."

"True that." She gazed up. "I love the balcony. It's so *Cat on a Hot Tin Roof.*"

With her head tilted back, the sweet spot on her neck was exposed. The spot right above her throbbing pulse. The spot that made her grind against him the night before.

"If I won the lottery," she said, "which would be a fucking miracle since I've never bought a ticket in my life. The odds of winning are ridiculously low. I once saw postal employee spend seventy-five bucks on scratch-offs. If he put that money in his government retirement fund, he'd really make a million someday—"

"Back to what you were saying."

"Hmm? Oh! I'd buy this building and make it a gathering place slash coffee shop for creative people to hang out and brainstorm. Like the old Algonquin Round Table days with Dorothy Parker and all the other writers."

"Dorothy Parker, huh?"

"She's my favorite writer." Hand on heart, she recited. "'Into love and out again, thus I went, and thus I go. Spare your voice and hold your pen—well and bitterly I know. All the songs were ever sung, all the words were ever said, could it be, when I was young, someone dropped me on my head?'"

"Sounds like you wrote that."

"I wish. Then I'd be famous but still broke. Dot never made any money being a snark." She nodded to the top floor. "I'd put a yoga studio up there."

"I've never seen you do yoga."

"I'm . . . taking a hiatus."

"Too much exertion?"

She pointed to the roof. "Looks like the ceilings are super high up there."

Interesting how she skipped right over that question.

"One can dream, right?" She exhaled a wistful sigh.

"That's your dream? A yoga studio, slash coffee shop, slash creative gathering place?"

Her starry-eyed look turned cloudy and the giddiness fled from her face.

"What'd I say?" He squeezed her hand.

"My ex used to make fun of me when I told him that. I was waiting for an insult."

Every detail she revealed about that jerk made him wonder why she stayed with that guy for so long. Especially since he himself couldn't get past a drunken kiss. He hooked a finger under her chin. "I love your idea. But you can't have this building. It's mine."

A sweet smile crept up her cheeks.

Heart beating ten times faster, he moved in for a kiss. She closed her eyes, and just as he was about to lay one on her, someone started up a Harley and revved it obnoxiously. Her eyes popped open and she backed away, looking horrified.

Around her, he didn't know whether to shit or go blind. He shoved his fists in his pockets and filled the awkwardness with more building banter. "I'd love to own this place."

"I'm telling you, sell your body."

"It's worth more than that."

"You're probably right."

They turned and headed back to his grandma's. In front of a streetlamp, he stopped her. "You sure are pretty, you know that?" Then he noticed something: her black pupils completely swallowed up her blue irises. He squinted. "What exactly did you do with my grandmother when I left?"

She rubbed her nose. "Um . . . nothing."

"She didn't take you out back, did she?"

Her eyes widened like a camera flash went off.

"Uh-huh." He whistled for a pedicab. Time to have a chat with his grandma.

At breakfast the next morning, everyone sat around Josephine's scuffed oak table—piled high with food—and feasted on home cooking. Except Josephine, that is—she barely touched a bite.

She was thin as a gnat's whisker and looked like she'd just gotten over a prolonged case of the flu. Women were crazy that way—dieting for no damn reason. "You're not on that low-carb diet again, are you, Grandma?"

She ignored him and pointed to a cardboard box. "I made you kids some snacks for the road."

He stood and peeked inside. Strawberry preserves, honey, fresh-baked bread, garden veggies, roast beef sandwiches, homemade cookies . . . Jesus, a ham! She'd packed her whole damn fridge. "Snacks? This'll last for a week."

"You'll need it to keep up your stamina."

"Stamina?"

"You know, so you can go all night in the Silver Dildo." She winked.

"Tell me my grandmother did not just use the word dildo."

"That's what your girlfriend calls it."

Callie's eyes darted around the room. "Is that a cuckoo clock?"

His grandma smirked. "This here's clover honey. It's an afro-dee-zee-ack." She pulled out a jar. "Not like y'all need help heating things up—you're already boiling over. But it might make things more interesting." She winked.

Someone should invent a mute button for grandmothers. "That's enough, Grandma."

"Oh, hush! It's not like I'm having breakfast with a couple of virgins. Besides, it's my house. I can talk about sliding the bone home if I want to."

He took off his glasses and rubbed his eyes.

"Is that a mood lamp?" Callie asked. Clearly, the subtle art of distraction wasn't a skill she'd yet mastered.

Grandma plucked the lamp off the shelf. "Take it with you. Mood lighting for when you're churning butter."

His coworker narrowed her eyes at the old woman. "Churning butter?"

"You know"—Jo poked a finger through a hole in her fist—"Shaking the sheets? Serving horizontal refreshments? Taking a midnight jockey ride." In case they'd misunderstood her finger-fucking-fist gesture, she added, "You know? Sex."

Was it just him? Or did the last statement seem a bit redundant? He blew out a long, loud breath. On a normal day his grandmother lived on the top floor of silly and weird, but she wasn't tactless.

He inspected her eyes. *Yep*, she was higher than a damn kite. Twelve years before, she'd had breast cancer and started growing her own pot. She beat it, thank God, and since then, he'd only seen her share a joint with friends a handful of times. Baking before noon though? That was out of control.

But it was neither the time nor the place to discuss her drug abuse. Maybe after he'd changed his identity.

"That's enough Sex Ed for the day, Grandma."

She huffed. "Boy, you two are a bunch of prudes. Not for long though! Get me my billfold. I'll bet you forty dollars, you'll be more than coworkers by the time you hit the state line."

"One more word, old woman"—he poked a finger at her—"and I'll drop you off at a nursing home on the way out of town."

Callie burst out laughing. The sound instantly soothed the sting of embarrassment.

"Excuse my grandmother," he said. "She's one fry short of a Happy Meal."

A big cap-toothed smile lit up Jo's face. "That's the nicest thing anyone's ever said."

After breakfast, Josephine gave his travel buddy a tight hug. "Remember what I said—" She whispered the rest in her ear.

"I told you," Callie grumbled, "nothing's going on."

"Uh-huh. Well, have fun doing nothing." Josephine waved.

On the way down the steps, his friend tossed him a look that implied his grandmother was insane. He'd have to agree.

"Wanna tell me what that was about?" he asked the old woman.

"She's pretending not to be in love with you. Not doing a very good job, is she?"

*Stoned meddling fool.* "Don't think she's pretending, Grandma."

"Pshaw. You're just as blind as she is." She patted his arm. "You'll figure it out soon. You better." She took his hands in hers. As a kid, holding her hand magically made him feel better—made him feel loved. "You look so happy, Sugar Bear. I love seeing you like this. I'm so glad you finally met the right woman. And you're following your dreams, too. I couldn't be prouder." Tears rolled down her wrinkled cheeks. Not once had she ever cried in front of him.

A twitchy, nervous feeling consumed him. "Jo? What's going on?"

"Just wish you could stay a little longer, is all." She pulled a tissue from her pocket and dabbed it under her eyes.

"I can stay another night. I'm sure Callie won't mind." Although after his grandma's behavior at breakfast, there was no telling.

"No. No. Don't mind me." She waved the tissue. "Go get your girl. I'm fine."

"She's not my—"

"Oh shush. Go make me some blue-eyed great-grand babies before it's too late."

No point in arguing. The only way to change that hardheaded woman's mind was not to try in the first place. She gave him a kiss on the cheek and squeezed the air out of him with a hug.

He laid a kiss atop her cottony head. "I love you, you crazy old bat."

"Love you too, Sugar Bear. Now go on, have fun."

On the way to the RV, he paused every few steps, torn between staying and going. One more night wouldn't matter. They could make up the time.

Just when he'd made up his mind to stay, Jo hollered, "Remember, Sugar Bear, ladies come first! Especially in the bedroom."

In an instant, his worries dissolved. She was fine. Certifiable. But fine.

# Chapter 14

## Runnin'

### Okefenokee Swamp, Waycross, Georgia

**Soundtrack:** Charlie Daniels Band, "The Devil Went Down to Georgia"

On her list of things never to do again, Callie mentally checked off canoeing in the Okefenokee Swamp. The rain had started fifteen minutes into their three-hour journey and hadn't let up. A dense fog formed and made the swamp seem like it was steaming.

More like steaming hot.

Her skin felt like a winter parka. If only she could have peeled it off. At the very least, maybe she'd get some relief from the goddamned mosquitoes.

As a kid, she'd thought lily pads were somehow magical. Don't ask. It's a long story. Let's just say when she found out the swamp was teeming with magic pads, she'd practically done a cheerleader routine.

That was three hours ago.

You know what? Fuck lily pads. Seriously, if she never saw another lily pad in her life, she would have been ecstatic.

Worst idea in the world to go there, and unfortunately, it was hers. "Let's create swamp stories like *Creature from the Black Lagoon*. It'll be fun."

So far though, she'd been a trooper. Hadn't complained once. But after three hours, her fortitude was shot to hell. "We're so lost," she whined.

Walker wiped his foggy glasses on his shirt. "We're not lost. I know exactly where we are."

She chuffed out an artificial laugh. "Of course not, Captain Cliché. Men don't get lost, right? Seriously, Walker, I need to pee. I'm tired, hungry, wet . . . I've got bites everywhere."

"Got swamp ass, do you?" He waggled his brows.

Her frustration multiplied like a virus. "I'm about two-seconds away from pissing in this boat. Please call for help." She clasped her hands. "Please. Please. *Please.*"

"Since I've got zero bars of reception, I'll get right on that."

She dropped her head in her hand.

He rolled his shoulders. "Another fifteen, twenty minutes max."

That's what he'd said an hour ago. "No, I've had it. I need to go now."

"How 'bout that island over there?"

"You mean that mud pile?"

"Want to jump overboard and go in the water?"

She looked down at the smelly, black soup. "Fine. Take me there."

They rowed over and pushed the canoe ashore. She stepped out of the boat straight into knee-deep ooze. A string of creative curse words flew out of her mouth.

A cross between amusement and disgust crawled up Walker's face. "You're gonna scare off all the critters with that language."

She scratched her nose with a middle finger and searched for a private place to pee. A rock outcropping lay ahead. She slogged through the slime to get to it.

A felled tree blocked her path. She hurdled it and scratched the hell out of her leg. Fire flew up her shin, but the pain in her bladder was far worse.

Onward she trekked.

*Suck. Squish. Suck. Squish.* Fifty feet felt like thirty miles in that crap. Swamps had to be the most miserable places on earth to take a piss. Maybe even worse than a portable toilet during a summer frat party.

Behind the rocks, she pushed down her soaking wet shorts and squatted. Once she let go, she was so thoroughly relieved the hissing didn't even faze her. What the hell was it, anyway? A snake? The wind? The leaves? She scoured the area in search of the culprit.

A growl replaced the hiss. She craned her neck around the rocks and found a pair of black beady eyes staring back. An alligator opened its mouth full of pointy teeth and chomped down.

Her brain clicked off, and her fight-or-flight response kicked in. Without exhaling a single breath, she eased up. The gator growled again.

Ever so slowly, she waddled backwards with her shorts and panties shackled around her ankles. The beast followed her.

"Shoo," she whispered, kicking off one leg of her shorts.

It stopped.

"Go away." She freed her other leg.

It stepped a foot closer.

She stepped a foot back.

It charged.

High-stepping, flapping, and repeatedly screaming fuck, she jumped over the tree and bolted. Well, not bolted, more like slopped quickly. The mud sucked off a shoe. "Fuck!"

Walker chuckled. "You've just won the award for the all-time highest use of f-bombs in a thirty-second period."

The lizard cleared the tree. "Gator!" she shouted. "Fucking go! Fucking go! Get in the fucking boat."

"Holy fuck!" he yelled, finally getting the hint she wasn't screaming obscenities for the fuck of it.

He grabbed the oars and pushed the canoe off the embankment. Two feet from the boat, the mud chained her leg. She yanked out her foot, lost the other shoe, and nearly dislocated her hip.

"Hurry," he cried.

"What the hell do you think I'm doing? Painting a damn princess mural?" She dove in the boat face first.

"Get your legs in!"

"I can't!"

He grabbed both her ass cheeks and hauled her in. The boat flew across the swamp as Walker ground the oars through the brackish water, grunting through gritted teeth from the effort.

"It's not following us." He stopped rowing and tossed her his shirt.

"Don't stop!"

Sweat poured down his heaving bare chest. "You're bleeding. Did it attack you? What happened? Are you hurt? Jesus, look at your leg."

The adrenaline fog lifted and reality hit her like a hard slap to the cheek. Her underwear was gone. And her shorts. And her shoes. And her dignity. And he'd grabbed her naked ass.

Inexplicably, the most humiliating moments in her life played through her mind like an old home movie. In one scene, she walked around campus all day with her skirt tucked in her panties.

Fast-forward to the night her boyfriend freaked out, thinking he'd been stabbed because she'd had her period all over his white sheets.

Another scene featured a pair of balled-up underwear falling out of her pants on the way up to the podium to give a client presentation. Daniel had harangued her about that for months.

Speaking of Daniel, it hadn't been at all humiliating when she'd caught him fucking her best friend. *Not at all.*

But this? This was an all-time, record-beating embarrassing moment. Crying would have been perfectly acceptable. But since she rarely did anything right, she dissolved into a hysterical fit of laughter instead.

Lines of worry etched Walker's forehead. "Did you hit your head back there?"

She kept cracking up. Her laughter echoed through the swamp, rocked the boat, and scared the birds out of the trees. Between giggles, she managed to choke out, "Did you get footage of that? Me? Naked? Being chased by an alligator? Classic B horror movie material." She cackled so hard she nearly blew off her limbs.

His expression turned grave. "Shh, Blue, calm down. I think you're in shock."

The tenderness in his voice uprooted a tangled mess of emotion. She wiped the blood off her shin. "I lost my shoes. I loved those shoes."

"I know, darlin'. I'm so sorry." He brought her legs to his lap and thumbed circles over the arches of her feet. "Just close your eyes for a minute and catch your breath."

Warmth from his touch traveled up her body and expanded her heart. Daniel never touched her unless she'd showered, waxed, and shaved every last hair off her body. And Walker rubbed her gross feet and acted like the mud and blood didn't exist.

He cared about her. No one cared about her. Even Effie cared more about her addiction than her own sister.

Right then, in that rainy, dreary, black swamp, her affection for him bloomed like a rose.

"Feel better now?"

She bit her lip and nodded.

"I really do know where we are. Fifteen-minutes away. I promise. Think you can make it?"

As long as she was with him, she could last another day. Okay, that was a bald-faced lie. She picked up her oars and stuck them in the swamp. "Let's get the fuck out of this shithole."

After paddling for a while she said, "Walker?"

"Yeah?"

"Thanks."

"For what?"

"For caring."

"Of course I care. You don't have to thank me for that." He rowed for another minute then stopped. "Blue?"

"Yeah?"

"Painting a princess mural?"

"Yeah, not sure why I said that."

A deep belly laugh bellowed out of him. She cracked up too. And together, they laughed all the way to the ranger station, which like he said, only took fifteen minutes to get there.

Since she'd lost her shoes (and underwear), Walker carried her to the Silver Dildo. The whole way in his arms, she nestled her nose in the crook of his neck and breathed.

## Okefenokee Park, Campground

*"Taking pictures is savoring life intensely, every hundredth of a second."—Marc Riboud*

Later that evening, in the park's jungle-covered campground, Walker watched Callie as she slept. He smiled at the soft purrs she made in her sleep. She was such a contradiction—delicate pixie on the outside, strong as a Viking on the inside.

Stronger than him, that's for sure. Unlike her, he'd almost stroked out when he saw that alligator chasing her.

Poor thing, lost her favorite shoes and everything. That upset him too. Those shoes were her trademark. He'd taken at least a hundred pictures of her wearing them.

The park ranger thought she'd probably stumbled upon a nest. Apparently, the females attacked anything that threatened their eggs.

"If someone pissed on my children," she'd joked with the ranger, "I'd get a little aggressive too." Then she'd broken down giggling again.

Any other woman—hell, any other man—would have been hysterical in that situation, and not Callie's version of hysteria—the other kind—the screaming-for-mommy variety.

As far as he was concerned, that little spitfire deserved a medal of valor.

Since they'd been back, she hadn't left his side. And now, she was cuddled up next to him, fast asleep. He brushed away a few strands of hair stuck to her mouth, and her lips puckered as if she were kissing someone in her dreams. He couldn't resist—he gave her a gentle peck.

Her phone rang right then, and she jolted up and grabbed it. "Slow down," she said to whomever was on the line. "Start over again." She scooted off the bench. "Hold on." Covering the phone, she mouthed she'd be right back.

Outside, she perched on a stump, listening and nodding. For a split second, he turned away, and when he looked back, she was gone. He bounded down the steps. In the distance, a black dot bolted down the red dirt road like a bat out of hell.

Heart rate kicking into overdrive, he paced a path around the camper. She didn't have a flashlight, and it was darker than a cat's asshole out there.

That damn swamp was chock-full of predators. And not just animals—toothless shotgun-carrying inbreeds camped out there.

Her mental state was questionable at best. She was hurt. He didn't even have her damn phone number.

He stormed inside to get a flashlight. If he found her in one piece, he was going to strangle her.

# Chapter 15

## Lovin'

*"It serves me right for putting all my eggs in one bastard."—Dorothy Parker*

**Soundtrack:** Elbow, "Grounds for Divorce"

Callie picked a mosquito bite while her sister flipped out.

"Have you seen it yet?" Effie asked.

"What?"

"Daniel's Facebook status?"

"I defriended him. Why is he still on yours?"

"Cal—"

"What?"

"He . . . God, I don't know how to tell you this—"

"For fuck's sake. Give me your login."

Effie rattled off her user name and password, and Callie pulled up Daniel's profile. She scrolled through several benign updates until it jumped out at her—a tagged photo of him kissing Hillary.

She read the caption out loud, "'Daniel and I are happy to announce our engagement. Nuptials will take place August 15th. Hope to see you there.'"

*Her baby's due date.*

She zoomed in on the bottle of wine in front of them. Blind rage ripped through her. She'd bought it for Daniel on his birthday. It cost a bloody fortune. He refused to open it though—told her he was waiting for something worth celebrating. When he'd asked her to marry him, it stayed corked, and now he was celebrating his engagement to her best friend with her fucking bottle of wine.

They'd taken everything from her.

"Those mother-fucking, cock-sucking, assholes!" A bomb ticked inside her. She hung up on her sister and ran until she doubled over in pain and threw up.

How long were they having an affair? Months? *Years?* Obviously, he'd been fucking her friend for a long time.

A betrayal like theirs was already painful, but getting married on her baby's due date? That was a precise cut—an advanced surgical procedure. They'd not only sliced open her heart, they scheduled a date for the operation.

And while they were happily planning their wedding and drinking her wine, she was getting attacked by alligators.

The wrath and pain and humiliation boiled over, and she punched her fists in the air and let loose an animalistic roar.

Everything stilled. The cicadas stopped whirring, the frogs quit croaking, and the distant sounds of the campground ceased.

The night—heavy and black—fell over her like a funeral shroud.

*Alone.* She felt so horribly alone.

She sank to her knees and laid her cheek on the dank ground, inhaling rapid breaths into her emotionally clogged lungs.

Slowly, her chest expanded, and when it was wide open, and she was breathing normally, an odd sensation washed over her—one she hadn't felt in a long time.

Relief.

She felt relieved. That picture blasted away any remaining doubt she'd been holding onto. It was finally over. She was free. And it felt like she'd just shed a thousand pounds.

Good riddance. They deserved each other. Daniel wasn't going to treat her bitch of a friend any different. He'd end up beating her down too. Then when she was at her lowest, he'd screw someone else behind her back.

If Callie told you what happened next, you wouldn't believe her. It was like a religious experience. But she'd settle for calling it a coincidence.

Anyway, a bright light exploded in her face and took away all the darkness.

"Blue?" he turned off the flashlight.

"Walker?"

She wasn't alone. She had him.

*"Lips that taste of tears are the best for kissing."*— Dorothy Parker

**Soundtrack:** Caught A Ghost, "Like a Virgin"

Walker scolded her all the way back to the Silver Dildo. While he yelled at her, she casually slipped her hand in his. He wrapped his toasty fingers around hers and continued listing her crimes. "You didn't have a flashlight. You could have died. Christ woman, you don't even have any shoes on!"

Still holding her hand, he opened the door and shut it behind them. "If you ever do something like that again . . ." His fiery glare implied the punishment would be worse than death.

"Walker?"

"What?" he snapped.

"Will you shut up and kiss me?"

He jerked back. "Kiss you?"

"Yes, I've had a really long day, and I just want you to kiss me."

"A long day?"

She circled her arms around his waist. "Yes, and after that, I'd like you to take me to bed and ravish me."

"Ravish you?"

"Oh, all right, fuck me. I want you to fuck me."

For a good thirty-seconds, his mouth opened and closed like a fish out of water.

Her pulse skittered. What if he refused? What if he wasn't interested? Had she misread him?

At long last, a sinful sideways grin swept up one corner of his mouth. "You want me to fuck you?"

"Please."

Glasses at the end of his nose, he boosted up a brow and asked her again. "Sure about that?"

"Positive," she said, taking off his specs.

With his finger, he drew tingles along her jaw. She snuck her hand under his shirt. The smell of lemons, fabric softener, and hot skin wafted out. She gazed into his eyes and willed him to kiss her.

It worked. He pressed his mouth to hers and lightly stroked her lips with his tongue. "Ready?" he asked

She backed away. "Seriously?"

"Hell, yeah."

She sprinted to his bed, ripping off her shirt on the way. "Hurry!"

"Right behind you." He thundered after her, pausing just long enough to hurl his shoes over his shoulder.

"Shirt," she cried, "off."

His shirt flew over his head. "Pants," he shouted. "Get rid of 'em."

She squirmed out of her clothes. "Yours too! Lose them!"

He shucked them off, and The Most Beautiful Cock In The World™ sprang from its underwear cage like a mighty throbbing red beast. A choir should have been singing "Hallelujah" in the background, because glory be to God, the thing was magnificent.

She patted the bed next to her. He crawled across it like a lion and possessively dragged her into his arms. Side-by-side, nose-to-nose, gaze riveted to hers, he tucked her hair behind an ear and said, "God, I want you so bad. Sure you didn't hit your head in the swamp?" He sounded genuinely worried.

"You're not gonna change your mind or wake up hating me tomorrow, are you? This is real, right?"

The sweet vulnerability he'd just exposed? It sent her heart orbiting around the sun. That yummy man wanted her—and badly no less. Suddenly, she felt like the sexiest woman alive.

Oh, it was real all right. And she proved it by kissing every inch of his face. "I want you, Walker," she said. Grazing her lips against the sandpapery scruff of his chin, she told him again, "I want you." And once more, murmuring against his mouth, "So bad."

A savage growl rumbled from his chest. He gripped her ass in one hand and the back of her neck in the other. The feeding frenzy began. They crashed together, lips against lips, bodies banging, cock against pussy, hands all over each other—nibbling, sucking, rubbing, and grinding.

While he pinched one nipple and sucked the other, his other hand unhooked the back of her bra. *Impressive.* The man had skills. But he'd had practice. Lots of practice.

And then, as he made out with her breasts, she quietly began to freak out. Was she just another coworker conquest to him? What would happen afterwards? Would he still respect her in the morning? Did he even respect her now?

Walker raised his head and searched her face, seeking approval. At the same time, he gently pinched her nipples and sent zings of heat through her body.

Why was she upset again?

Back to worshiping her breasts he went—laving and licking. Ribbons of pleasure flowed from the tips of her nipples down through her core. She arched into him.

"Gorgeous," he said, pushing her tits together. "Sweet plums."

As he sucked, his hard-on rubbed against her leg, crying out for attention. But she couldn't reach it while he was on her boob. Wriggling free of his mouth, she scooted closer.

"Where're you going?"

"To meet my new best friend." She stroked a hand down his velvety hard shaft. A drop of pre-cum beaded at the cleft.

She smeared the silky liquid over the swollen head and continued running a hand up and down his length.

He unleashed a low man gasp. "Jesus, that feels good."

Yes, but merely touching it wasn't good enough for her. She needed to see it, taste it, *smell* it. With that goal in mind, she licked her way down his chest—made a pit stop at his nipples—and quickly got back on the road. Down, down, down she wandered, until she arrived at the destination.

She kissed her new friend hello and rubbed his dewy tip around her mouth like lipstick. Without delay, she wrapped her lips around him and engulfed him, sucking him down as far as she could. But he was simply too big. The trials and tribulations of dealing with a big dick were so . . . um, *hard*. Said no one ever.

His breathing intensified. "Fuck, that's hot. Ladies first though, baby."

She removed her lips and gave him a little shove. "Ever since I saw you in the . . ." Why remind him of the bathroom incident? She'd had enough embarrassment for the day. "Let me at him."

Like a good boy, he fell back on the pillow. "Christ, you're killing me."

Up, down, and around, she licked him.

He watched her intently, occasionally smoothing her hair behind an ear. "I love watching you suck my cock."

She hitched her gaze to his. "Mmm."

"Fuck." He yanked out of her mouth. "Your turn," he said, sounding extremely tense.

"Wait. I'm not done."

"Well, I *will* be if you don't stop. Now sit back and spread 'em." He pushed apart her legs and stared at her crotch with his brows hooked together and his lips crammed closed.

"What?"

"Is that natural?" His head tilted to the left.

She bolted up. "Is what natural?"

He stroked her patch of light peach fuzz. "Are you blonde, Bluebell? Black's not your real hair color?"

"No! Yes! Shit. Yes, I'm naturally blonde. For fuck's sake, get inside me!"

An X-rated grin curled up. "I'll be damned." He stroked her then dropped to his knees, feathering kisses on her hips, tummy, and thighs on the way down.

She whimpered. "Walker, please, put your penis inside me."

"Nun-uh, first I'm gonna eat that blonde pussy of yours." He flicked her clit with his tongue.

Heat flooded her. "Oh, all right," she grumbled, faking irritation. "I guess I can wait."

Still grinning, he slipped a finger inside her and pumped it leisurely. *Too leisurely.* She shimmied over his hand.

"Damn, woman, you're soaked." He stirred his finger inside her, making a sloshy sucking sound. After that titillating declaration, he covered her mound with his mouth and gave her clit a passionate kiss. "You taste good"—he licked it again—"real good. Like sweet cream."

Sweet cream? That was debatable. But if the man loved the taste of her vagina, then who was she to argue?

A bolt of electricity hit her center. She clamped her thighs around his head.

"Feel good?" he asked in a voice just a level above Barry White's.

She clutched the sheets and glanced up at his glossy face. "Wh-What?"

"Like when I fuck your pussy with my tongue?"

She whimpered.

"How 'bout when I fuck you with my fingers?" He sucked her clit and tapped two fingers on her g-spot.

She ground her pelvis against his mouth

Satisfied with that response, he went to town, feasting upon her like a man possessed. It wasn't long before every muscle in her body contracted. Bliss climbed to its peak and hovered on the edge. A rush of ecstasy blazed through her and she tumbled over the cliff. She cried out as painful ecstasy rolled through her body.

He lifted his head and grinned down at his handy work—i.e. her very wet vagina—and slowly worked his cock in his hand.

"Get inside me immediately!" she commanded, her voice a hoarse squeak.

"Bossy little thing, aren't you?" He caressed her drenched thighs.

"I'm begging you."

It took an excruciating amount of time for him to open the condom. Once it was finally on his incredible dick, he traipsed a finger down her wet slit. "Fuck, you're hot."

She narrowed her eyes. "Are you trying to get in my panties, mister?"

"I'd say I've already accomplished that, wouldn't you?" He slipped his finger inside her again.

"Less talk. More cock." She tugged his hand and spread-eagled on the bed, ready and willing.

He scratched his chin.

She popped up. "What are you waiting for?"

"Trying to decide which way I want you."

Forearm thrown over her eyes, she pretended to cry. "I'm in pain. Please, for fuck's sake, do me."

Mercifully, he dropped next to her, grabbed her hips and basically tossed her on top of his dick. As fast as she could, she guided him in and swirled around the tip, teasing him like he'd done to her.

He slammed his eyes shut and clenched his jaw.

"Feel good?" she asked in a seductive purr.

"It'd feel a whole lot better if you sat yourself down on my cock." His accent had thickened to molasses.

Sinking slowly, she hit bottom with a gasp. "Now that feels good."

He gripped her hips, pulled out, and slammed in. "It sure as fuck does."

She rolled her hips, stretching her pussy with his cock. Walker kneaded her tits and massaged her clit with his thumb. Lips sloping up in a sexy smirk and dimples denting his cheeks, his blue-green gaze roamed between her thighs and back to her eyes.

"God, you're incredible. Why did we wait so long to do this?"

"I have no fucking idea," he said and fucked her faster.

The gooey sound of their skin's friction filled the camper. She licked his throat then melded her mouth with his, chafing her chin against his until it burned.

They absorbed one another—breathing each other's breaths, mingling fluids, and connecting on a level she hadn't expected.

She melted around him, consuming him with passion and raw need. The tips of her nipples tightened to sore peaks as pleasure mounted. Clenching her vaginal walls, she sucked him in deeper.

He groaned in her mouth and rammed her harder. "Oh, yeah. Squeeze me tighter. I want to feel your pussy pulsing and squirting."

The dirty talk was the last spark. An astonishing orgasm blasted through her. Two more pumps and he was right there with her.

In their rapture, there was no porno moaning, or cursing, or screaming. They just held their breath and clung to each other while they came.

Chest heaving and body drenched, she lay on top of him, panting. "God," she wheezed.

"Damn," he panted. His dick twitched inside her. "I'm still coming."

"That was the worst sex I've ever had." She rubbed her nose against his sweaty neck.

His deep belly laugh bounced her head. "Fucking awful wasn't it?"

"Just terrible. How soon do you think we can have more bad sex?"

"I don't know. I'm an old man now. Maybe twenty or thirty minutes?"

She rolled off him and collapsed in a useless heap. He tied off the condom then hauled her into a tight spoon. Against her back, his damp chest rose and fell.

"I love the way you smell." He nuzzled her neck.

She faced him and laid a long kiss on his puffy lips.

He pulled back. "You . . ." He tipped her chin and kissed her again. "That . . . us . . . wow." His brows rose. "Fuckin'-A."

"Listen to you, potty mouth. Go wash your mouth out with soap."

"You're a bad influence."

"Puh-lease."

"Your pussy sure liked my dirty mouth."

"Shh"—she fanned between her legs—"You're getting her all excited again."

A warm laugh flowed out, and he tucked her back in, rubbing his feet against hers.

"Are you still wearing a sock?" She looked down at his legs.

"Huh." His sock-covered foot wiggled in the air.

She cracked up. Absolutely ridiculous, that silly sock on his carved swimmer's physique. "I'm gonna need a picture of that." She swiped the camera off his nightstand and zoomed out the lens, making sure to get his half-stiff porn cock in the frame.

He folded his arms behind his head and crossed his ankles, displaying the sock (and cock) proudly.

"Say sleaze," she said and snapped the shot.

"Stay right there, kneeling like you are." He reached for his phone. "Keep the camera to your face, with the strap between your breasts like that. Don't move." The phone's fake shutter clicked.

He grinned at the screen. "This road trip just got a helluva lot better."

# Chapter 16

## Wakin'

"Morning, beautiful." He nestled his hard-on against the crack of Callie's ass.

She twisted around, sunlight and blue mischief radiating in her eyes. He stroked her pretty face. "You are a vision, Bluebell."

"More like a nightmare. See this?" She patted the monumental rat's nest in the back of her head.

"That's some serious bedhead," he admitted.

She weaved her hands though his hair, sending tingles over his scalp. "Yours looks like you stuck your finger in a light socket."

Smiling and sighing, he caressed her body, listening to the whisper of her skin against his hand. He wandered over the curve of her breast, down the valley of her torso, around her ass, and finally between her legs, where it was slick and wet.

"What are you doing down there, mister?"

"Sticking my finger in your light socket."

Breathless, she draped her leg over his hip. "Only you could say something so ridiculous and still turn me on."

He chuckled and smeared her wetness over the rest of her pussy, making her clit nice and slippery. Over and back, he circled the ridge until it was hard and swollen.

Quietly, she panted short bursts of air. And then not so quietly, she moaned, "Oh, right there! Don't stop."

He repeated the move. "Like that?"

"Mm-hmm."

"Turn around and put your ass against me, so I can get to you easier."

She flipped on her side and shimmed back. Her nipples were so swollen and tight they looked painful. He soothed them with his tongue. As he licked her tits, he got a crazy urge to mark her. Above her nipple, in a nice secret place, he sucked his brand into her skin.

Her little whimpers turned into big moans. But she wasn't quite ready. The minute he buried himself inside her, he was going to bust a nut like a virgin, and he needed her right there with him.

He pumped his finger faster, and soon she got all quiet and tight. Legs trembling, she raised her hips and tilted her chin back.

Now she was ready.

He kissed her neck and blindly felt for the last condom. Faster than a deacon in a whorehouse, he rolled that sucker on. From behind, he dove inside her warmth. Sure enough, she came on his cock two minutes later.

Right after her, he erupted like a volcano. Honest to God, had his dick been out in the open, his cum would have shot through the roof.

"Damn," he said, still attached to her. "I wanna stay inside you all day." He held her tightly until he softened and slipped out.

They lay on their backs and held hands. She chewed her cheek and stared at the ceiling.

"Whatcha thinking about?" he asked.

"The commercial in Orlando, tomorrow."

"What about it?"

She propped herself on an elbow. "What are we going to do?"

"With the shoot?"

"No, with this." She gestured between them. "With us."

"What do you mean?"

She chewed her lip some more.

"Blue?"

"It's just . . . what now? We can't tell anyone."

"Why not? Skip doesn't care. I could call him and tell him we had mind-blowing sex, and he'd probably say, congrats, dude, and offer to buy me a drink."

Her post-coital dreamy gaze sharpened to an icy glare. She sat up and yanked the blanket around her. "Gonna go hi-five your bros now? Tell everyone you banged another office slut?"

He sat up with a jolt. "Another office slut? What the hell?"

She closed her eyes and squeezed her cheeks together with her hand.

"Blue?"

"I'm sorry. I'm—" A long, weary sigh leaked out. "I'm not worried about Skip."

"What the hell *are* you worried about?"

"Did we make a mistake, sleeping together?"

A belt tightened around his chest. "A mistake!" He vaulted out of bed and jammed his legs through his boxers.

In the background, she babbled an apology, saying something about the words not coming out right.

But he didn't care. His mind was already racing down a dark tunnel. "What happened last night, anyway? Why'd you suddenly decide to jump my bones?"

"I don't know!" She pressed her palms to her eyes.

"Dammit! Why'd you lie to me last night?"

"Will you stop!" She grabbed his hands and pulled him back to bed. "I just got out of a relationship that fucked up my whole life. I lost my fiancé, my friends, my job, my home—everything. I literally left Chicago with nothing. And I fucking hate when people say literally and don't mean it. *Literally,* I left with the clothes on my back. I wouldn't even have a job if it weren't for Skip."

He pinched a rub across his eyelids. Why did her past have to crash his party? Why did she lose everything? Did her fiancé kick her out? It didn't make any sense.

"I'm sorry," he said. For what, he had no clue. But sometimes with women, it was best to apologize and figure out why later.

She squeezed his hands. "Walker, you are the only friend I have, besides Skip. If something happens between us and the trip goes bad, I'm not only going to be bummed, I'm going to be super screwed. That's why I'm asking—did I fuck everything up by sleeping with you?"

If it were up to him, they'd be holding hands, kissing, and calling each other pet names in front of God, the RoadStream client, and everyone.

Hanging with her was the tits. And he loved having sex with her even more. Plus, she was the main reason he was getting his mojo back. But beyond that, they had something special brewing, and if she weren't so damn jaded from that other guy, she'd see it too.

Amazing the camper didn't just bust wide open with the amount of disappointment in there. Only moments ago she'd come on his cock, and now she was frowning down at her hands.

If he put himself in her shoes though—which were gone because he'd made her piss on an alligator nest—he'd probably be freaking out too. After what she'd been through, it was no wonder she was scared to get back on that relationship horse.

But he still had plenty of time to convince her they were right for each other. She'd come around soon. Real soon, he hoped. Until then, he'd be patient. Not really, but he could pretend. In the meantime, he'd act like Mr. Laid-Back and Aloof, and maybe she wouldn't feel so pressured to end things before they even began.

He caressed her cheek. "Christ, Callie. I don't want to ruin our friendship, or this trip, or anything else. Stop stressing. Let's just have fun and fuck, and not worry about things that haven't happened."

Her mouth tightened to a crimson slice. "So this is just sex, then? No strings?"

Was she relieved? Or upset? Did she even care? If they had a master's degree in figuring out the opposite sex, he'd sign up tomorrow. He gritted his teeth and ground out a smile. "If that's what you want."

"And you won't go back to hating me or get me fired if something bad happens?"

"I never hated you," he said sharply.

Once again she gnawed her lips. "Then we'll have to keep this a secret."

The conversation was starting to feel like a barbed-wire wedgie. "You still gonna keep riding my bologna pony?"

A smile peeked out from the clouds. "You're as bad as your grandma."

"Speaking of which"—he raised his chin—"you owe her forty bucks."

"Crap, you're right. Jesus, don't tell her. I'll never hear the end of it."

He pointed to his lap, and she crawled over and burrowed her head in the crook of his neck. The sweetness not only reassured him, it reignited him. He wanted her again—feverishly so. But they were out of condoms.

He pulled the sheet down around her hips and thumbed her nipple. "Think we'll fit in that shower together? I want to get you nice and dirty before we get all clean." He slapped her butt. "Then after that, I'm picking the next place. You're on probation for your little swamp idea."

"Huh?" she said.

"What?"

"I almost forgot about the gator."

"Made all the bad memories go away, didn't we?"

# Cassadaga, Florida

*"Brevity is the soul of lingerie."—Dorothy Parker*

**Soundtrack:** Portugal. The Man, "The Sun"

It was a rare summer day in southern Florida—low humidity and temperature in the eighties. The scent of crushed orange blossoms floated in the breeze. Callie lifted her face to the sky and let the sun warm her soul.

Beep!

"Did you just take a picture of me?"

Walker looked skyward and whistled. "Me? Nope."

She narrowed her eyes and smiled. "Now that we're in the Psychic Capital of the World, Mr. Rhodes, shall we find out what's in store for the rest of the trip?"

"You bet your sweet britches."

"How do you want your bullshit fed to you? Palm? Tarot? Runes? Crystal ball?"

"You decide."

"Let's split up and compare."

He picked palm reading, and she chose tarot cards. Afterwards, they'd meet back at the Chinese restaurant they'd passed on the way in.

She stepped through the tarot shop's doors into a blazing inferno of incense. She coughed and waved the smoke from her eyes. From out of the fog, a rotund woman with a fake mole materialized. She was dressed like a pirate. Or was it a gypsy?

Excited for the new story material, she purchased a Past Lives Discovery Combo Package, and the gypsy wench swept her back to a room behind a curtain with the phases of the moon.

After the woman finished her act, Callie strolled toward the restaurant. Through the window, she spied Walker in a booth, fiddling with his camera. A table of three drooling women stared longingly at him while they ate.

A mounting urge to scream take your eyes off my mancandy hit.

Walker looked up and cocked a grin. He motioned her inside with a suggestively crooked finger.

She swept open the door and released thick wafts of soy sauce and sesame oil. Other than Walker's fan club, everyone in the restaurant was Chinese—a fortuitous sign the food was authentic.

A bony man led her to the booth and told them to ask for Ho if they needed anything. She did a double take of his tag. Yes, indeed, his name really was Ho—Ho Sang, as a matter of fact.

"Over here, Bluebell." Walker pointed to the spot next to him.

She slid in the booth.

"Closer," he kept saying until she was practically in his lap. He gave her a kiss hello that felt like foreplay.

The blatant public display of affection surprised her, given he just wanted to "fuck and have fun."

Since that morning, she hadn't been able to inhale a full breath. Stupidly, she'd made an emotional investment, and he very succinctly told her to invest somewhere else.

Questioning him so soon made her seem desperate, but she couldn't stop thinking about what would happen when he inevitably screwed her over.

At least she knew where they stood. They'd be lovers on the trip. When it was over, they would be, too. She could live with that. *For now.*

"You smell like frankincense and myrrh," he said, curling his hand around the back of her neck.

"*Ugh*, I was trapped in a forest fire of incense."

He peeked down her shirt. "Still have that suck mark on your titty? Ah, there it is." On the sly, he tweaked her nipple. "Let's hurry up and eat," he said. "I want to get back to the camper and eat your PuPu Platter."

She wrinkled her nose. "Ew."

"Fold your cream cheese wonton?"

"Yuck."

"No? How about munch on your Lo Mein? Get it? Like a horse's mane but lower?"

"Please stop."

"Am I allowed to say I want to eat your pussy?" His deep voice was like auditory sex.

"That works." She bit her lips over a smile and picked up the menu. After she made her choices, she read through the beverage section and launched into an all-out laughgasm.

"What's so funny?" he asked.

"Read the beverages," she squeaked and broke down again.

He read the section out loud. "Classic Cock. Cock Zero. Diet Cock. Cherry Cock." He chuckled. "Boy, they have all the cock products."

"Wonder if they have plain cock?" she asked.

"I've got your plain cock right here."

"No, yours is more like new and improved, super-sized, hyper-caffeinated cock with a lime."

His gaze dropped to her mouth. "You thirsty, Bluebell?"

She was going to have to start bringing a change of underwear in her purse. Before she attacked her coworker, Ho came over and took their order.

He cleared his throat and ordered. "And the lady will have the large spicy hot beef, Ho, with lots of sauce."

The waiter rolled his eyes. "Seriously?"

She snorted into her napkin. After Ho left she said, "You didn't even crack a smile. You're the superhero of straight faces."

"No idea what you're talking about." His lips quirked. "So? How was your reading?"

"Oh, yes! Apparently, I'm getting married before the end of the year. And! I have a dead relative from the age of enlightenment who wants to chat."

"Is that right? And how does one get in touch with the dead?"

"Pay hundred bucks for a séance."

"Sounds about right. Mine told me my musician wife needs to know the truth before it's too late. Also, she said I'd fall in love and get dumped the same week. I asked her if that meant my wife was going to leave me. She said maybe."

She feigned shock. "You never told me about your wife."

He unfolded his napkin and placed it on his lap. "She's on tour."

"Don't tell me? Pop singer?"

"Hell, no! She plays the key-tar."

She laughed. "Hawt."

"Not as hot as the affair I'm having with a copywriter." He nibbled her ear.

"I'm having a hard time imagining you married."

"Why's that?"

She dipped her chin. "What's the longest relationship you've ever been in?"

"Two years and some change."

She almost fell out of the booth. "Really? When was that?"

"After I graduated college."

"Why'd you break up?"

"'Cause she was an unstable raging narcissist with a drug problem and an eating disorder."

"Ha! Big stamp of approval for ending that. How'd you hook up with her?"

"I was kind of a late bloomer," he said.

Young bug-eyed Walker drifted into her thoughts. She nodded fervently—a bit too fervently perhaps.

"Claudia was the first pretty girl who was into me. We fought non-stop, but I overlooked her issues because I was getting laid on a regular basis."

He peeled apart his chopsticks and rubbed them together. "I didn't really have the greatest role models. My parents were either fighting or fu—having sex. I thought that's how relationships were supposed to be. Didn't have the sense to know I was thinking with my dick."

"What did she do, your girlfriend?"

"Majored in fashion design at SCAD, but couldn't catch a break when we moved to New York, so she modeled."

Of course she modeled. A sudden burning inadequacy tossed around in her stomach. "No one after that?"

"No one long term. For years, Claudia stalked my dates. Had to shut down all my social media accounts. I'm a lot more selective now."

*Ha!* If he was selective, she was a banana. Barbie? *Please.* Though what did that say about her, now that she was also on his select service list?

Ho came by with the food. When he left, Walker asked, "What about you? You were gonna get hitched, right?"

The dumpling in her chopsticks crashed on her plate. "I . . . Yes, we were engaged."

"Why'd that guy ask you to marry him then cheat on you? You give him an ultimatum or something?"

She straightened her shoulders and shot him a look that made him sit back. "No, Walker. Believe it or not, I didn't want to get married."

"Why'd you say yes?"

Because Daniel had been an excellent liar. "Guess I was thinking with my uterus."

"Better have a chat with it. You've only got"—he looked at his wrist—"T-minus five months until you're married, Mrs. Rhodes."

"Believe me, we've already had that chat," and what a painful discussion it'd been.

Ho brought the check and a pile of fortune cookies. Walker read his. "'You will be lucky in everything.' Ha! Now that's some good fortune."

"Let me see that." She ripped it from his hands and stuffed it in her bra. "It's my fortune now."

"You've left me no choice." He slid his hand up her shirt. "I'm gonna have to fondle you now."

A hot shiver glided under his touch. "Mine sucks." She handed it to him.

"'Find a way to relax.'" He winked. "I bet I can help with that."

# Chapter 17

## Blockin'

### Studio Seven Soundstage, Orlando, Florida

*"Her mind lives tidily, apart, from cold and noise and pain, and bolts the door against her heart, out wailing in the rain."*—Dorothy Parker

**Soundtrack:** Blondie, "Rip Her To Shreds -2001- Remastered"

The day she'd been dreading had arrived. The day of the TV commercial shoot.

The instant Callie stepped through the production studio doors in Orlando, a foreboding feeling smacked her hard. A feeling that made her want to grab Walker and run.

Then she heard it—a tap, tap, tapping. Her jaw clenched as the menacing sound drew nearer.

Sure enough, Account Manager Barbie tramped toward them, wearing gut-red stilettos and a bleached smile. Without hesitation, Barbie lunged for Walker and attached herself like a tick. "Walkie! I've missed you!"

The bimbo didn't bother to greet her—didn't even glance in her general direction. Callie cleared her throat, and Barbie shot her a bitchy, *tchah*-why-are-you-still-here look.

A sudden urge to go L.A. girl gang hit—the need to scratch Barbie, bite her, pull her hair, beat her with a curling iron, stab her with an eyebrow pencil, and tell her to get the fuck off her man.

Walker hugged Barbie back and kissed her on the cheek. "Missed you too, Hot Pants."

She giggled like a stoned cheerleader.

Callie stood agog and watched the scene play out. *A hug? A kiss? Hot pants?* She crushed her fingers in a fist.

"Oh my Gawd," Barbie said with a Kardashianesque vocal fry. "I've got, like, so much to tell you." She whispered the rest of her drivel in his ear, staring right at Callie.

A few nods and smiles later, he said, "I can help with that," and confirmed it with a wink.

That line sounded mighty familiar.

The account manager pinched his chin. "I don't know what I'd do without you."

They locked elbows and pushed through the soundstage door—Barbie's obnoxious tap, tap, tap echoing behind her.

Not once did Walker look back.

Too paralyzed to move, Callie stood and stared at the doors. It felt like she'd been hit by a car and left on the side of the road.

Inside, she felt cold and hard, like she'd absorbed the concrete floor into her bones. She laughed a twisted laugh. Not because it was funny, but because he'd done exactly what she'd expected him to do. Five minutes around another woman, and he'd already thrown her to the curb.

That's what she signed up for though. No strings meant no feelings. So with a giant pair of mental gardening sheers, she sliced through every last thread.

They'd had a nice little two-night stand, and that was that. No hard feelings. Everything was fine. *Just fine and fucking dandy.*

*"If I had a shiny gun, I could have a world of fun,
speeding bullets through the brains of the folks that
cause me pains."*—Dorothy Parker

**Soundtrack:** Yeah, Yeah, Yeahs, "Heads Will Roll"

There were many, many, many negative things about Daniel, but as her boss, he'd been a stellar mentor. Since he owned the agency and had to prove he didn't just hire her because she was his girlfriend (which he did), he pushed her harder and spent more time shaping her into the perfect employee. Most importantly, he'd taught her how to fake confidence. "Pretend your words are scientific fact," he told her. "You may have the best idea in the world, but unless you can sell it, no one will buy it."

He'd trained her how to present, how to speak, how to act, what to wear, the right body language—all to sell her ideas.

Whether she'd written a coupon headline for a cheap roll of toilet paper or a million dollar celebrity-endorsed sneaker commercial, she'd applied his techniques with poise and sold her ideas with resounding success. Though most of the time her ideas sold themselves. In fact, RoadStream hadn't asked for a single revision to the campaign, which was rare since every client fancied himself as a writer.

Because she'd never met Double Dick—and since dressing well was part of the façade—on the way to the shoot, she'd even bought a few professional outfits to make a good first impression.

Wearing said impressionable outfit and sporting the aforementioned fake confidence, she waltzed up to the client as if she were the CEO of the goddamn world—even though Walker had just made her feel like the most trod upon piece of human excrement that ever existed. "Dick"—she stuck out her hand—"nice to finally meet you."

"It's Richard," he snarled and gave her limp cold-fish handshake.

"Sorry about that, *Richard*." Later, she'd kill Skip for not mentioning that little tidbit. "I'm Callie."

He flipped up his palms and shrugged. "Well, why are you standing here? We've got work to do."

A muscle ticked in her jaw as she tried to ignore his pompous-ass undertone. "Great, how can I help?"

He blinked for a minute then took out his wallet and handed her a few bills. "See if you can't find a Starbucks around here. I'm gonna pass out if I don't get a caffeine fix soon." He turned to Walker. "Want anything? It's on me."

"Coffee? You want me to get you coffee?" She gave him wrinkly-nosed smile, daring him to tell that cute joke again.

He sighed and pulled out another five. "Fine. Get one for yourself too." He faced Walker, turning his back on her. "Before we get started, I have a lot of script changes to go over with you."

She tapped Dick's shoulder. "I'll take care of your script changes."

The client turned and gave her a once-over that screamed repulsion.

Walker, who apparently spoke penis, translated for her. "Richard, Callie wrote the script, not me."

Cheeks pushed up and mouth turned down, the client stared at her with cold, creepy eyes. "She looks like a high school intern. Where's the guy who's been writing everything?"

*Someone get her some WD-40*—her jaw and right eyebrow were stuck in the shock position. Her first inclination was to show him her award-winning work for clients whose marketing budgets could pay off the federal deficit. Her second was to punch him in his dick face.

Alternatively, she stabbed him with a Murphy-Who-The-Fuck-Do-You-Think-You-Are Glare™ and said, "Guess you haven't been paying much attention to the campaign, *Dick*." She emphasized the *ick*. "I *am* the writer. The blog, the social media, your new tagline, the scripts? I wrote them all. It's also me in all the pictures." She jabbed a thumb at her chest.

"And that thirty-percent sales bump this last month?" She flashed a scary-clown smile. "You're welcome. Since you're not familiar with the work you're paying millions for, script changes go through me, not Walker, because he's an art director. Make sense? If not, I can make you a PowerPoint presentation. Gotta love a good deck." Her face hurt from smiling.

Speaking of face, Dick's turned tomato red like it was about to explode. *Uh-oh.* She must have upset the little *dick*ens. Good.

Sabrina rushed over and wedged in between them. "Hey, hey, hey, like, let's not forget, the client's always right. I'm sure the changes aren't that complicated. Walker can totally handle them. Can't you, Walkie?"

While she often joked about poisoning her Shimura coworkers, she'd never really meant it. But right then, if she had an ounce of arsenic at her disposal, she would have poured it down Barbie's throat. At the very least, she'd like to finger-flick that bitch in the nose—if only to punish her with the same nasty condescension.

The only problem was she felt a breakdown coming on.

At some point in her career, every woman has a breakdown on the job. You know, one of those moments when you involuntarily burst out crying and totally humiliate yourself? Don't deny it, everyone does it.

As for her, she'd had two breakdowns, both after working three days straight. Each time, she'd made it to the parking garage right before she'd lost her shit.

But there wasn't a parking garage at the studio. Therefore, she had to get the fuck on out of there.

"Great." She clapped her hands once. "Well, since I have a high school science project due tomorrow, I'll head back to the hotel and let you all do my job. Let me know if you need me."

"Thanks, Callie," Sabrina said, clutching Walker's arm, "but we have everything covered."

"Oops, not yet, looks like *Walkie's* got a few free limbs." She winked. "Better get on that, hot pants."

Chin in the air and still smiling violently, she shoved open the studio door, banged it on the wall, and blazed outside.

"Blue, wait!" Walker called.

Magically—it was the land of the Magic Kingdom after all—an Uber appeared and dropped someone off. She jumped in and waved goodbye to Walker with two very stiff middle fingers.

## Palm Palace Hotel Bar, Orlando, Florida

*"She runs the gamut of emotions from A to B"—Dorothy Parker*

**Soundtrack:** M.I.A, "20 Dollar"

The car dropped Callie off at the hotel the agency had booked for the night. After checking in, she sprinted straight to the bar and ordered a shot of tequila.

While the bartender poured, she closed her eyes and massaged her tight jaws. It was difficult to pinpoint exactly how she felt, but it was somewhere between livid and numb. She let out a long sigh of disappointment and dropped her forehead on the bar.

"Rough day?" someone said.

She looked up and found Eli James at the bar, staring at her with a look of bored amusement on his face. She smiled and sat next to him.

Eli was cool. Though he was another agency pretty boy, he wasn't a slut like some people she knew. In fact, she'd never seen him hanging out with anyone—guys or girls.

According to Skip, Eli was a busy man. When he wasn't working, he was DJ-ing or producing music. He didn't have time for relationships—even the twenty-four-hour kind.

Per Dick's request, Eli had created the soundtrack for the commercial. That morning, he'd flown down to present it to the client. Before he even listened to the whole track, Double Dick declared it wasn't "hip enough."

"Not hip enough for an RV commercial?" she repeated with substantial snark. "On what planet is an RV considered hip?"

"I hate that fucking word," Eli said. "People who say hip are the fucking opposite."

"Right? That tiny colostomy bag wouldn't know hip if it slapped him in his dick face."

Eli cracked a smile.

She told him her own grim Double Dick tale—carefully glossing over that part that pissed her off far more—the Walker and Barbie part.

"Another shot?" He nodded to her drink

"Only if you have one with me."

While the bartender made their drinks, she glanced around the bar. It was covered in mirrors and neon. The carpeting was a nauseating mix of brightly colored swirls. "Holy crappy décor! Whoever decorated this place in the eighties must have been on quaaludes."

"Looks like a fucking bowling alley," Eli said.

Enjoying his f-bombs thoroughly, she tapped her drink against his. After commiserating with him for a while, she felt marginally better, so she ordered another round.

They watched her first commercial on YouTube—Dr. Bob's Corn-Remover Pads—and Eli laughed so hard he cried. In return, he showed her a video of his junior high boy band, the Dream Projects, and she also cry-laughed.

Two hours, five drinks, and many giggles later, Eli invited her to check out the local club scene. But she was tipsy, tired, and needed to think. Plus, feigning indifference would require a substantial amount of energy in the morning.

On the way out, she hit the restroom, and when she came back, Walker, Barbie, Double Dick, and the rest of the production crew were sitting at a table near the front of the bar.

After a butt-load of cocktails, she was seriously lacking the finesse to deal with a band of assholios. Taking that into account, she hid in the hallway and waited for an opportunity to slip past them undetected.

So far, it looked like she'd be spending the night in the bathroom.

Barbie trotted over to Eli at the bar. Though she was all up in his grill, he took off and left. Why was she staring after him longingly? Didn't she have enough dick for the night?

Speaking of dick, Richard wogged up next to Barbie and snaked his puny arm around her waist. He whispered something apparently hilarious in her ear. She laughed boisterously, skipped back to the table, and plopped her ass down in Walker's lap.

Tequila blended burning bile in Callie's stomach. There was no way she could sneak past them. She'd just have to find her female balls, be polite, then promptly get the hell out of there.

She straightened her spine, ironed on a smile, and marched toward them. Midway to the table, Barbie wrapped her arms around Walker's neck and kissed him on the mouth.

*Fuck being polite.* Instead, she did an about-face and ran.

*"Women and elephants never forget."*—*Dorothy Parker*

**Soundtrack:** Charles Bradley, "Ain't It A Sin"

Walker was so bone-tired he could barely lift an arm to knock on Callie's door. "It's me," he whispered and knocked. No answer. He tapped again. "Blue, I know you're in there."

The door opened a crack with the chain still attached. "What do you want?" She sounded as exhausted as he felt.

"Let me in."

The door slammed in his face. He sighed and pounded on the door. "The client's two doors down. Open up before I make a scene."

The chain slid off and she flung it open, wearing the frostiest expression he'd ever seen. No doubt she was madder than a wet panther. He was too.

"Hurry up and say what you've got to say," she said, not budging from the doorway. "I'm tired."

He tossed the plastic bag he was holding on the floor, picked her up, and kicked the door shut.

"Put me down, Walker." Her voice was calm, cool, and tight.

He set her on her feet and scanned her expression. In the dim light, she looked like a shadow, but he had no trouble seeing the dark scowl on her face. More than anything right then, he wanted to make her smile.

He grabbed the bag off the floor and shook it. "Got you something." He dumped ten boxes of condoms on the bed and grinned. "These should last us for a day or two."

Boxes started flying everywhere. Several hit his crotch. Two struck his face.

Well, that idea went over like a pregnant pole-vaulter.

"I'm sorry. I'm sorry." He ducked another box. "Stop, sweetheart, I was just trying to make you laugh." Shielding his face and protecting his balls, he inched closer. "I swear, nothing happened!"

"Un-fucking-real." She darted around the room, throwing the condoms back in the bag. "Take these to Barbie's room"— she shoved the bag at his chest—"and get the hell out."

"I reckon Barbie is Sabrina?" He dropped the bag on the floor and didn't move. "I know what it looked like, but it's not what you think."

"Don't bother." She hand blocked him. "I don't need an explanation. We said no strings, and trust me, I didn't attach a thread, so just go. Now."

He reached for her, but she backed away. "Blue, Sabrina and I are just friends."

She snorted a dusty laugh. "Oh my God, is that the universal male lie? Daniel told me the same thing. 'I'm just friends with Hillary,'" she said, mimicking a dumb manly voice. "And guess what? Those two pals are getting married next month."

"Who's Hillary? Please, calm down and just listen—"

"No, you listen." She punched a finger at him. "I'm finished with men who use women and throw them out like yesterday's garbage—"

He jerked back. "That's not—you're wrong. Stop."

"Save it." Her tiny hands balled into fists. "I have no one to blame but myself. I knew what I was getting into with you. Serves me right for screwing the office manwhore to get over another one."

The venomous words shot anger through his veins. He was not, and never would be, a womanizer like his father was. He'd made that vow early in life. Callie maintained he was a player, but the truth was, she'd played him. Rebound, revenge fuck, whatever you want to call it, she'd used him. *Nun-uh,* he wasn't to blame for this situation, she was.

As far as he was concerned, he couldn't get out of that room and off that damn rollercoaster ride soon enough. "Let me remind you, sweetheart, you're the one who came on to me. And from what it sounds like, the only one doing the using and abusing around here is you."

"Get out."

"Gladly." He charged to the door. "Do me a favor? Since you can't stand me, quit the damn trip. There's not enough room for all your baggage anyway."

He slammed the door, and the instant he did, Callie started sobbing. Heart-breaking sobs. Shocking sobs. The sound drove a spike through his chest.

The woman hadn't shed a tear when an alligator attacked, yet he'd made her bawl with a few nasty words. Suddenly, he wanted to take it all back. But she wouldn't listen. From the moment they'd met, she'd already made up her mind.

Unable to withstand the sound of her misery for another second, he trudged to his room. When he turned on the light, he nearly had a conniption fit.

Flamingoes and seahorses and shit all over the goddamned room—it was a like an ugly bomb had gone off in there.

He hurled the starfish pillows across the room and tore the pink palm tree comforter off the bed. He sat on the bed and stared at the disgusting squid painting across the room.

Someone sure had a sick sense of humor. One minute he was touring the country with an incredible woman, doing the best work of his life, and the next minute, it was all over, and he was sleeping alone in a vomitus rainbow of a room, and down the hall, the incredible woman was crying her eyes out over him.

*"Woman wants monogamy; man delights in novelty. Love is woman's moon and sun; man has other forms of fun. Woman lives but in her lord; count to ten, and a man is bored. With this the gist and sum of it, what earthy good can come of it?"—Dorothy Parker*

All the emotion she'd held inside had finally popped the cork. Callie exploded and cried for two hours straight.

Once the dehydrating effects of day drinking made it impossible to manufacture any more tears, she called her sister—the most irrational person she knew—and asked for advice.

"Are you crying? Oh my God, you are. Finally!"

"For fuck's sake, you're happy I'm crying?"

"Yes! You've been so *Invasion-of-the-Body-Snatchers* unemotional about everything. I was on the verge of assembling a team of experts to pry the alien pods out of your guts. So why are you crying?" Effie snacked on something crunchy, clearly torn up about her emotional state.

"I'm such an asshole for hooking up with him," she said after relating the events.

Her sister flicked a lighter then exhaled in her ear for an infuriatingly long time. "You're not the asshole. He's back in Chicago where you left him. Stop blaming yourself. None of this is your fault."

"I must be a masochist. What's wrong with me?"

"You dated an abusive asshole."

"Daniel? He never hit me."

"He made you hate yourself, same thing. You're a textbook battered wife. You blame yourself for everything."

Was she that weak? She felt sick. "Gee, I feel much better now, Doctor Effie. Perhaps you'd like to delve into a few other things? Like my relationship with my bitchy twin sister, for example?"

Effie sighed. "Let's talk about Walker then. Take a step back and look at the facts. The man brought condoms to your room, not Barbie's. Why would he sleep with you, screw her, then come to your room and expect you to be with him? Surely, he's aware you have an above average IQ? The bimbo's to blame, Cal, not him. Did he kiss her back?"

"I don't know. I left."

"I bet he didn't. Plus, he brought you to his best friend's house and his grandmother's."

"So?"

"Would you bring a booty call home to meet your family?"

"I wouldn't bring a dog home to meet my family."

"Thanks a lot."

"Not you, fool, our parents. Besides, what was he going to do? Drop me off for a week?"

"Is he a sociopath?" Effie asked.

"No."

"Then pull your head out of your ass. The man likes you. Or he did, anyway."

Breathing suddenly became a chore.

"Are you still there?" Effie asked. "Maybe you should go talk to him."

"It's too late." There was an alarming about of sadness in her voice.

"He doesn't want me on the Silver Dildo anymore."

"The silver what? Is that what you call his dick? Never mind, don't tell me."

"What am I going to do? Skip's gonna fire me. I'm screwed."

Effie took another drag of her smoke and let it out. "Yeah, probably."

Bad idea, calling her sister. Not only was the conversation unhelpful, it was triggering an anxiety attack. "I've got to go. I don't feel good."

"Wait—"

She ended the call, turned on the lamp, and nearly threw up. How had she neglected to notice the hellish décor? "What a fucked up mess," she mumbled, and she wasn't referring to the room.

# Chapter 18

## Shamin'

"*Scratch a lover, and find a foe.*"—*Dorothy Parker*

**Soundtrack:** Handsome Boy Modeling Club, "The Truth"

*E*arly the next morning, Skip called and woke her up. Before he even said hello, he asked if she was quitting.

"Quitting?" she croaked then cringed in pain. If felt like an arrow had been shot through her temples.

"Walker said you were quitting."

He just couldn't wait to get rid of her, could he? Had to call Skip before the damn sun was up. She wobbled to the bathroom and downed a glass of water. In the mirror, her puffy face frowned back.

"I called Double Dick's boss. I've got him by the balls now. After what he did to you and Sabrina, he'll have a lawsuit on his hands if he yanks the campaign—"

"Sabrina?"

"You didn't hear? Dick handed her his room key after the shoot. She told him she was with Rhodes so he'd keep his filthy hands off her. She was worried he'd fire us if she refused."

A switch turned her anger into panic. She gripped the phone tighter. "When did Walker talk to you?"

"Several times during the shoot." Skip shut up for a long minute. "Murph?" He sounded desperately nice. "I know it's a lot to ask, but please don't quit. The tour is killing it. I've got four new business pitches out. Just hold on a little longer. If Dick tries anything else, I'll fire them. The CEO doesn't like him, so he'll probably get canned anyway."

"You're not firing *me*?"

"Um, no? Did you chop up Double D into little pieces last night or something? Doesn't matter, I still wouldn't fire you. Not that I condone murder or anything. Anyhoo, does that mean you're not gonna quit?"

He'd given her a job when he could barely afford to keep his doors open. No, she wouldn't quit, but that meant Walker would. "I'll call you back, Skip."

"You sound funny. Do you have a cold? Wait, are you quitting or what?"

She tugged on her shorts. "I don't know. I have to go."

"Yeah, you guys better boogie out of there before Penis Squirt gets an earful from his boss. Oh, and hey? Tell Rhodes I handled everything. He threatened to quit yesterday if I didn't take care of this. He was really worried about you last night."

A looming sense of loss grew in her gut.

"Sabrina, on the other hand," he chuckled. "She'd better stay the hell out of his way. Dude, Walker almost threatened to sick HR on her ass. It *was* kind of a dumb thing to do, but we all know she's not getting into Mensa anytime soon. The clients like her though, obviously—"

She hung up the phone and raced down the hall to Walker's room.

*"Take me or leave me; or, as is the usual order of things, both."—Dorothy Parker*

**Soundtrack:** Tame Impala, "Feels Like We Only Go Backwards"

Walker answered the door wearing his rumpled clothes from the night before. Without his glasses on, his bloodshot peacock glower penetrated her to the core.

"Can I come in?" she asked the floor.

He scrubbed a hand down his face and didn't move.

"Skip told me what happened . . . with Sabrina. I'm sorry if I misunderstood."

Still, he said nothing.

She drew in a ragged breath. "Okay, well, I guess I'll call Skip back and quit," and screw over the last remaining friend she had. Legs as heavy as cement, she lugged herself back to her room.

"Callie, wait."

Biting her lips so she wouldn't cry, she turned back.

He scratched his neck and huffed. "It'd be too hard to find someone else. Let's just move on and get this trip over with. We've made the roommate thing work so far . . . "

Not lover, not friend, not even a coworker—she'd been downgraded to roommate. And the trip was no longer an adventure, but a chore to complete.

Maybe she'd jumped to conclusions, but he certainly wasn't guilt-free. Straightening her previously slumped posture, she echoed the irritation in his voice. "I don't know, Walker. I don't want to crowd you with all my baggage."

"Go. Don't go. Whatever you want."

*Welp*, since he'd put it that way. She waved and walked away. "Have a good trip."

The few steps back to her room felt like the Trail of Tears. She was right back where she started—broke, homeless, and dumped. Scratch that, now she was behind the starting line— now she didn't have a job and was about to lose Skip.

Where was the brake peddle? Her life was spinning out of control.

*Now what?* Should she call Skip back? Pack? Run away? Go to Disneyland?

Someone knocked on her door, and since it could only be Walker, she didn't open it. He knocked again. "Callie?" He thumped a hand on the door. "I know you can hear me. Please don't quit. It'll be fine."

Nothing felt fine to her. "Go away."

"Open the door, please."

She sucked back the brewing tears and yanked it open. He frowned down at her like she was a cockroach. "Your decision affects a lot of people, you know."

"Hey, thanks. I wasn't aware of that." She didn't need a reminder. What she needed was a friend. And what she *wanted* was to be held.

Exhaustion, exasperation, and a medical-grade emotional hangover brought on a sudden crushing headache. Covering her eyes with a hand, she rubbed away the percolating tears.

"Callie? Don't quit. Let's just finish the trip. We don't have much longer to go."

*Wrong.* They had an incredibly long way to go.

But despite the horrid situation, an infinitesimal amount of hope remained that once they got back on the road, everything would return to normal. Whatever that was. Also, she didn't have a fucking choice.

In a voice so low a dog wouldn't hear it, she agreed to go.

"Can you be ready in twenty?"

She nodded and he left. Not once had he smiled, touched her, or called her Bluebell.

The next few weeks were going to suck hard. She'd have to motivational poster her way through it—put on a happy face, grin and bear it, walk the talk, take the 'I' out of team, dream big, be bold—and most of all, she'd have to hang in there, kitty.

# Chapter 19

## Pinin'

### Weeki Wachee, Florida

*"And if my heart be scarred and burned, the safer, I for all I learned."*—*Dorothy Parker*

**Soundtrack:** Flume, Kai, "Never Be Like You (feat. Kai)"

Overnight, Callie had traded in her normal personality—the perfect blend of sweet and sarcastic, earthy and whimsical, fiery and chill—and replaced it with a placating robot.

She flat out refused to talk about what happened. She didn't joke or talk or fight or look at him. She didn't care what they listened to, where they went, or what they ate.

Most of all, she didn't care about him.

Callie's clone kept her eyes firmly on the road and drove like she was in a hurry to get to heaven. In record time, they arrived at the lake and made their way to the mermaid show.

They sat in front of a giant aquarium and didn't say a word to each other. Red lights shined down on the water, coloring it like blood. Fiberglass clamshells opened and closed, and a rubber octopus, missing a tentacle, flapped in the current.

From the corner of his eye, he stole a glance. She sat as far away as she could. He bet if he touched her, she'd recoil.

Cheesy music blared out and an announcer introduced the show. A mermaid with a flashy orange tail floated over to the window. Bubbles floated around her head as she sucked oxygen from a tube. She smiled an underwater freaky smile and blew someone a kiss. The mermaid pointed at him, waved, and blew another.

What the hell was wrong with that chick? Didn't she see the woman sitting next to him? He glanced at his coworker. It was more than a little obvious she wanted nothing to do with him. She probably thought Callie was his sister.

Soon a whole school of fish women were blowing bubbly kisses at him. Every one of them could drown for all he cared. The tiny blue sparkle fish next to him was the only one he wanted.

Callie jumped up so fast it startled him. "I'm bored," she said, not sounding bored at all. "I'll meet you outside when this"—she waved between him and the window—"is over." And with that, she spun on her heel and stormed off.

"Dammit." He kicked the metal railing and busted his toe. "Fuck!"

Someone gasped in the audience. "Shame on you!" A few rows back, a woman threw him a crusty look and made the sign of the cross.

He doffed a pretend hat. "Have a nice day, ma'am." Then he limped his way to the exit.

In only fifteen minutes, he'd managed to maim himself, piss off Callie even more, make eyes with a mermaid, and shout an f-bomb in front of an old bible-beating lady. The way things were headed, he might as well pour gasoline all over himself and strike a match.

# Crystal Springs, Florida

*"It is more important to click with people than click the shutter."—Alfred Eisenstaedt*

**Soundtrack**: Silversun Pickups, "The Wild Kind"

Walker slinked back to the camper with a sore toe and his tail between his legs. Callie didn't seem the slightest bit upset about the mermaid show. "It's your turn to choose the soundtrack," she chirped.

Stiff as a mannequin, he sat in the passenger seat. "I don't care. Pick whatever you want." Something angry, he hoped.

Instead she chose nothing, and they drove in silence all the way to the manatee refuge, where she insisted they go paddle-boarding.

After they parked and rented the boards, Callie changed into her pink bikini.

"You're wearing that?" he said.

"Yeah, so?"

"What if it falls off?"

She dismissed him with a wave.

Along with his toe, his head began to throb. Why the hell did he make her buy that damned suit? He strapped on his waterproof camera and hurled his board in the water like a javelin.

Callie lifted a smug cheek and shook her head.

Soon they were paddling down the peaceful river on the most irritating adventure yet.

Shadows of their boards followed them under the shallow transparent waters, giving the impression they were gliding on green glass. Schools of yellow and blue fish darted past, and the damp scent of peat hung heavy in the humid air. Trees arched over the river in an emerald canopy, and egrets called to each other with old-man sneezing sounds.

It was beautiful. It was horrible.

All he could think about was pushing that scrap of pink she was wearing aside and sinking into her slick depths.

"What's wrong? Aren't you having any fun?" She lifted her sunglasses and studied him. Her eyes absorbed the aquamarine water and took his breath away.

*Hell, no.* "I'm fine." Again, he wasn't.

"Why are you scowling?"

"Didn't realize I was." He carved an oar through the water and paddled ahead.

With her out of sight, the scenery finally grabbed his attention. Just as he focused his camera on a blue heron, she coasted into view. Lying on the board with her eyes closed, she crossed a patch of sunlight and lifted her chin to embrace the warmth.

*Beep!*

She flinched and covered her face. "No, Walker, I'm not in the mood—" Mid-complaint, she crashed into the water. A moment later she emerged, huffing and puffing. "A manatee knocked me over. Did you see it? There!"

Underneath, a moss-covered boulder floated in a circle. The creature poked up its head and questioned him with peephole eyes. Silently, he spoke to it. *I'm lost, friend. What do I do? How do I fix this?*

As if the animal understood every word, it moved across the river—drowsy and sloth-like—and hit her board again.

She surfaced, sputtering and out-of-breath. "It pushed me."

A dozen more manatees sailed over. He aimed his lens and went barreling face first into the river. When he came up for air, she broke out in a riot of laughter. The sound made him sick.

A bulbous gray head raised and stared at him. Suspended in the room temperature springs, he stilled and regarded the creature. Suddenly, he felt like the biggest jackass in the world for not appreciating the moment.

Another manatee sent Callie tits over tail into the river. "Fucking assholes," she spat. "Oh, the manatees are sweet and docile. They never attack humans. Bullshit."

*Damn,* it was good to hear that smart mouth. "They're just giving you a little love nudge, is all."

She raised her oar like a spear. "They're after my blood. Where'd they go?"

"Pretty sure you'd get thrown in federal prison for that, Miss Manatee Whisperer."

"There they are!" She flipped them off. "Bye, you bunch of lard-assed bastards. No wonder you're endangered!" Tickled by her own brand of silliness, she floated on her back and giggled.

The water turned scorching hot. She wasn't even fazed by their break-up. She didn't give a damn about him. Well, screw her for using him and acting all *la-di-da* about it.

"Callie the hater," he said through clenched teeth, "hates everything and everyone, even the gentle manatees."

The joy melted off her face. That had to be water rolling down her cheeks, not tears. She was too heartless to feel anything. She scrambled on her board and took off down the river without him.

For twenty minutes, he stayed put. They needed space. Or at least he did.

An hour later, he met her back at the RV. By then, he could tell she'd built up a wall of hate. He could see it in her stony expression and wooden stance, and by the way she chucked the keys at his face.

For hours he drove, gripping the steering wheel until his shoulders hurt. Once he reached the panhandle, he parked at a trashy campsite and bolted to the beach. He swam for an hour and a half, and when he returned, she was gone, and there was a note in her place.

*Be back later. — C*

Later turned out to be one a.m. When she tiptoed back to her bunk, he was wide-awake and shaking with anger. He'd spent the last seven hours thinking something awful had happened.

Or worse, that she'd quit the trip.

# Chapter 20

## Drownin'

*"When words become unclear, I shall focus with photographs. When images become inadequate, I shall be content with silence."—Ansel Adams*

**Soundtrack**: Glass Animals, "Gooey"

alker spied on Callie through the camper window. Wearing headphones and her tiny bikini, she danced on the beach, shaking her tight butt in the sun.

Neck and dick now painfully stiff, he hightailed it to the shower and pumped gas at the self-service station. Five minutes later, he emerged, feeling no more relieved than before.

As he toweled off in the bathroom, Callie hummed and banged pots in the kitchen.

A god-awful yearning blocked the back of his throat. He dropped the towel and pressed his hands on the sink. Breakfast was their time. The time when they collaborated on ideas, talked about their day, and shared a meal. Now it was just something he had to endure.

Even though she lived with him, he missed her like crazy. He craved her witty conversation, wild laugh, and goofball humor. He wanted his Bluebell back.

In the mirror, he saw a bedraggled Walker, a man who hadn't shaved in days. It felt like he'd been eaten by a wolf and shit out over a cliff. If he didn't snap out of it soon, he wasn't going to be able to work. This trip was about finding himself, not losing his damn mind.

He opened the door, and his bikini-clad coworker handed him a plate. "You made me dick pancakes?"

She laughed. *Damn her laugh.* "Guess they do look like penises. Peni? What the heck's the plural for penis? Anyway, they're supposed to be little Floridas. See, here's the panhandle."

A smudge of flour dusted her nose. He rubbed it off with his thumb. Her dewy lips parted, and she peered up at him through lowered lashes.

Once again longing tugged him down a dark hole. "Not hungry," he grumbled and reached for the coffee.

Her natural smile turned crisp, and her glare warned him he'd better wear a protective cup from then on out. Was she back to normal? Maybe they could finally throw down, have it out, and talk about what happened.

But ever so calmly, she sat at the table with her food and started to eat.

He snatched the pancakes off the counter and shoveled in a bite.

"How are they?" she asked in a saccharine sweet voice.

"We better get moving." He threw the pancakes in the trash and barged up front. Without any warning, he started the engine and pulled out like the campground was on fire. Dishes crashed to the floor. He didn't care.

A while later, she parked herself in the passenger seat, wearing a shirt that said *oh the hu-manatee* over her son-of-a-bitching bikini bottoms. *Christ,* was she out of clothes or just intentionally torturing him?

He cranked up the air conditioning and angled the vents on his face.

"You okay?" she asked.

"Think I'm getting a fever. Mind driving?"

She placed a hand on his forehead, checking for the heat that wasn't there. Her squint called him a liar, but she took over the wheel anyway.

When they arrived in Pensacola, he burst from the camper and ran. Only an insane man would jog on black asphalt at noon in a hundred-degree heat.

He fit that bill perfectly.

On the verge of collapse, he returned to the campsite an hour later, thinking he'd burned off some of the crazy. But Callie had left another note telling him not to wait up, and he promptly went nuts again.

## Panama City, Florida

> *"In youth, it was a way I had, to do my best to please, and change with every passing lad to suit his theories. But now, I know the things I know and do the things I do, and if you do not like me so, to hell my love, with you."*—Dorothy Parker

**Soundtrack:** Rupert Holmes, "Escape (The Piña Colada Song)"

The unfortunate part about driving was all the free time she had to think. And that's exactly what she didn't want to do—think. For the last three months, she'd driven herself crazy thinking about Daniel, and now she was wasting time ruminating over Walker.

Surely someone had written a self-help book on how to live in a box with a coworker, after a brief fling that ended because another coworker fake kissed him?

Not that she actually believed it was fake, but what did it matter? It was over between them.

Living with Walker had become unbearable. He spent all his time working, painting, and as far away from her as possible. He had no interest in exploring anything. He hadn't even taken any photos for the blog.

On one hand, she didn't care. On the other, she'd do anything to be friends with him again. She believed him but didn't trust him. She wanted him but despised him.

The man made her bipolar.

In two days, he hadn't looked her in the eye once. And his conversations? One-word grunts. It wasn't like he was trying to get a rise out of her like he'd done at the beginning of the trip. No, it was more like he found her disgusting.

After Daniel, she was exceedingly familiar with that treatment. And she reacted to Walker in the same way— she steered clear, didn't engage, and tried to keep the peace.

Giving him the space he so obviously demanded, she went out every night, ate at restaurants, and watched local bands play. One day, she rented a bicycle and peddled around the beach. Another day, she went deep-sea fishing. Wherever they went, the locales kept her entertained and kept her from feeling so lonely.

The rest of the time, she focused on something other than her relationship for once—her writing. Fuck men. She had another love.

The Florida panhandle provided a wealth of inspiration too. Everything was so wonderfully tacky and weird. Retirees in matching neon green outfits, a kid with a chocolate mustache screaming at his dad, prison tattoos on a smiley grocery clerk—they all became fodder for her writing.

On the way back to the campground that afternoon, she passed a giant mechanical wizard head attached to a store. It winked and laughed and summoned her inside. What the hell did they sell in there? Magic? Maybe they had a potion to change Walker back to himself.

Turned out, they sold nothing but crapola. In one shopping trip, she'd increased the surplus of China's GNP by tenfold.

That night, she decorated the campsite with the crap from the store and tried one last time to drag Walker out of his funk. She perched the pink flamingo in the sand and draped twinkling palm tree lights around the awning.

The pornographic towels were spread out on the ground like a picnic blanket. One featured a naked man sporting a two-foot schlong, and the other displayed a naked woman with giant tits and puffy purple pubes between her legs. They were so great she sent a set to her sister, too.

She also bought Skip a half-naked David Hasselhoff towel.

Next to the towels, she placed the songbook that came with her most fabulous find—a pink ukulele.

The pitcher of drinks and ham and pineapple apps were already on the table. She gave up trying to light the shell-shaped candles in the wind. And for the final pièce de résistance, she hung a spiky blowfish over the door.

When everything was ready, she went back inside and handed one of the bags to Walker.

He blinked. "What's this?"

"Put it on and meet me outside."

He peeked inside and flicked her an annoyed look.

*That's it!* She grabbed his tit and twisted. "Put on the shirt and meet me outside." Halfway expecting him to fight, she put up her dukes and tossed him a Murphy-Don't-Test-Me Look.™

Rubbing his chest, he raised a stupid sexy brow and watched her come unglued.

Oh, he found her amusing did he? That son-of-a-chode. "Do it." She marched to the door. "Or else."

A few minutes later, he started down the steps and ran headfirst into the blowfish. "What in the fu —?" He clutched his face. "What the hell is that?"

It took everything she had not to laugh. "Oops, sorry! Guess, I didn't hang it high enough."

Still rubbing his face, he glanced around the site. "What's all this?"

"A celebration. We hit 200,000 followers today." She handed him a drink with a paper umbrella. "Cheers!"

He stared at the naked male body then gingerly sat on the towel. She didn't really think he'd do it, but he was probably afraid he'd lose a nipple.

Immediately, he took a hearty chug of his drink then spat it out, gagging and pulling at his tongue. "Ugh! What the hell did you give me?"

She tested the cocktail. A rummy lump slid down her throat. "Ack." She threw the rest on the sand. "It's supposed to be a Piña Colada, but we didn't have everything, so I made it with half-and-half and rum."

"Was the half-and-half expired? It tasted like it was curdled."

She shrugged. *Who cares? Get over it, dude.* One lumpy drink wasn't going to kill him, but *she* would if he didn't lighten up.

She clasped her hands in front of her mouth. "Yay! You're wearing the shirt."

"Yeah, thanks for making me wear a women's shirt," he said.

"It's a men's large. It's just a little snug."

"It's snug all right." He lifted his arms, exposing a foot of ripped abs. "Not to mention, there's a big dick on it. A big, pink dick, no less."

"It's peach. And that's the state of Florida."

"It says America's biggest penis awaits you."

She put her fists on her hips. "I'd thought you'd find it amusing, given your girth."

The comment made him grimace and shrink away. Yep, she disgusted him all right.

Almost defeated, but not quite, she grabbed the other pink instrument he was bound to complain about and plucked the strings.

"What's that?"

"Isn't it wonderful?"

But it wasn't the ukulele he was staring at. He reached over and tugged down her shirt. "I heart gators? Nuttier than a five-pound fruitcake," he mumbled to the wind.

"Oh, goodie, you're back to insulting me. That's better than the silent treatment."

"That wasn't an insult, it was the truth."

"Whatever." She slapped through the pages of the *Smooth Sounds of the Seventies'* songbook with unbridled aggression.

Once she found the right page, she strummed a few chords, closed her eyes, and belted out the "Piña Colada Song."

During the chorus, she stopped playing and sang á cappella. "Do you like Piña Coladas? And getting caught in the rain—" She pointed to Walker. He shook his head, so she finished the song without him.

"Where'd you learn how to sing and play like that?" he asked at the end.

"Lessons," she said. "Years and years and years of lessons. At gunpoint."

"Gunpoint?"

"Pretty much. My mother forced me to practice music six hours a day. No TV. No movies. No boyfriends. No surfing. I was only allowed to practice music. I used to hide books under my mattress, so she wouldn't take them away. This is the first time I've played anything since I left home."

"Did you want to play music?"

"God, no. But my sister was a child prodigy. At age ten, she played violin better than Perlman. Since we share the same genes, my mother assumed I just didn't practice hard enough. When I played violin like crap, she made me play piano. Then it was guitar. I was a mediocre musician at best, so she forced me to take voice lessons. My senior year of high school, she finally gave up on me."

"How'd your sister get into drugs?"

Since it was the first time he'd spoken to her in days, she answered the question. "She took Adderall and pain pills to get through the rigors of practice. Moved onto street drugs when the doctors refused to refill her prescriptions."

She remembered the exact day she'd caught Effie smoking crack. After years of putting up with her shit, Callie finally threatened to lock her up. The next morning, Effie drained her life savings and disappeared.

For two years, she'd thought Effie was dead. Then one day, Skip found her under the Manhattan Beach Pier with a bunch of junkies. Since her parents refused, he sent Effie to rehab on his dime. Another reason she loved and owed him Skip so much.

She popped her sore jaw. "Let's move on to a lighter topic, shall we?"

"What's the deal with your mother?"

He listened about as well as she made Piña Coladas. "She was a concert pianist when she met my father. A couple months later, he knocked her up with twins and ruined her life." She put finger quotes around ruined, because that's exactly what her mother said—having children "ruined her life."

"My mother heaped all her crushed dreams and resentment on my father's back. When he couldn't stand it and left, she focused her rage on stealing our childhoods."

"What happened to her?"

"She moved back to Germany. That's where she's from. Effie hates her. I pretend she doesn't exist."

He shook his head. "It's incredible the way people screw up their kids."

"Hey now—"

"If you don't want to throw away your dreams, use some damn birth control."

Why did that feel more like a jab than a general comment? "No one forced my mother to throw away her dreams."

"Kids change everything," he said. "Matt and Patty don't even have sex anymore."

"You don't want children?"

He stretched his arms overhead. "Kids are great, as long as they're not mine."

The answer disappointed her and she was at a complete loss as to why. While the waves crashed in the distance, her mood crashed ashore. The *Happy Callie Show* was coming to an end.

Walker stood and brushed the sand off his legs. "I'm gonna finish some work and call it a night."

"Already?" It wasn't even nine o'clock. "But you didn't try the appetizers."

"Not hungry."

Why did she even bother to try? She hugged her knees to her chest.

"Callie?"

She lifted her head.

"Thanks. For tonight. I wish we—"

"Yeah?"

"Never mind. Goodnight."

## Southern Alabama Coast

*"I was always sweet, at first. Oh it's so easy to be sweet to people before you love them."—Dorothy Parker.*

**Soundtrack:** Jack Garratt, "Water"

Deep in the Alabama piney woods, they spied a giant lady in the lake, four dinosaurs, and Stone Henge all at once.

Well, a fake fiberglass Stone Henge.

"But it's the same size as the real one," she said. "Faces the same direction and everything."

He leaned against a pillar and sighed. It was hotter than two foxes fucking in a forest fire, and he was overcooked, exhausted, and tired of Callie's cheer. "This is stupid," he said. "A total waste of time, money, and green space."

"I think it's rather amusing," she said. "Rich guy rolling in dough, can't figure out how to spend it, so he builds this." She spread her arms wide. "If I had money to burn, I'd use it to fight poverty or disease. After I bought a yacht and gold toe rings, of course."

Every time she said something cute, his irritability swelled. "I can't take pictures of this crap. There's no meaning here."

"How about these?"—she stabbed two middle fingers at him—"Any meaning in these?"

"Real mature. No wonder the client thought you were in high school."

Her body shook like a popcorn kernel about to explode. "Asshole," she snarled and stormed back to the camper.

"That's right! Take off again. That's what you do! When things get heated, you run."

Another bird flew in the air and not the kind with wings.

He chucked a stick at the pillar, and it bounced off and hit his head. Why did it seem like he was living out a real-life Tennessee Williams play?

Back on the RV, he mumbled an apology, but she just walked away and went up to her loft.

On the way to the next place, he kept thinking about the playwright. It gave him an idea. That afternoon, he set up camp early and took candids of Callie all day. Afterwards, he colorized them like an old movie. The pictures were stunning. She was stunning. His camera was having the love affair with her that he couldn't.

A while later, he went for a swim, and when he came back, she was gone and hadn't left a note. A storm of worry crashed down on his shoulders and blew away his semi-decent mood. All afternoon, he fretted for her safety.

At sundown, she returned—sunburned and glowing—and held up a paper sack. "I brought dinner."

Her happy-go-lucky tone made him want to stomp on baby chicks and kick puppies. "I'm not fucking hungry." That's right, he cursed, because goddammit she kept leaving.

Half an hour later, she dared to join him. On her head was a plastic beer hat with two cans on each side. She sat next to the fire, sucking beer through both straws.

"Where were you?" *Jesus*, he sounded like her dad.

"Surfing. More like floating, really. The Gulf's waves aren't quite like the Pacific's. Oh, by the way, I bought you a hat. It's on the table."

*Surfing. Beer hats. Dinner.* So easy breezy, not a care in the world. Damn her for having fun all afternoon. He stomped off, grabbed a bottle of Beam, and stomped back.

For a good twenty minutes, he drank from the bottle and kept his eyes on the flames, not saying a damn thing. A tiny belch interrupted his maudlin thoughts.

"Excuse me," she whispered.

He couldn't help but chuckle. Wearing that ridiculous hat, she was cuter than a bug's ear. "You're nuttier than a port-a-potty at a peanut festival."

She wrestled with a smile. "Truth or dare?"

Ah, what the hell. "Dare."

"I dare you to go skinny dipping with me."

Now *that* he wouldn't do. Couldn't do. Not with her. No way. He leaned back and stared up at the stars. "Not a good idea, Callie."

"Why? It's a full moon?"

Because he didn't particularly feel like being tortured by her naked body after a long day of worrying she was dead. He turned his attention back to the fire.

"Pussy," she hissed.

He snapped up his head. "What did you just call me?"

"You heard me. You can't get out of a dare."

"The only pussy around here is the one you're gonna be dunking in the ocean. Get up. Let's go."

They dashed over the dunes. The moon—nearly as bright as the sun—lit up the beach. A few feet from the tide, she peeled off her shirt and tossed it on the sand. In the breeze, her nipples puckered to hard peaks.

A creative hunger took over his sense. He wanted to paint her body with his tongue and mold her breasts in his hands like clay.

She shucked off the rest of her clothes and ran to the ocean, moonlight dancing on the globes of her ass. A wave hit her and musical laughter rang out. Then she lured him to the ocean like a siren.

He shed everything—his reluctance, his clothes, his worries—he got rid of them all, and ran to the ocean—hard dick slapping against his abs—and dove in.

Out past the break, she gave him a come-hither sign. But he stayed put. Eight feet. That's as close as he'd get. Otherwise he wouldn't be able to control himself.

But she swam to him. Her pale arms slid gracefully across the current. "Hi," she said. Drops of water dribbled down her lips. "Feels like bathwater doesn't it?"

*No,* it felt like a cold abyss to him. In fact, he was drowning.

She blasted him with salt water, burning his eyes and throat. He sucked back a mouthful of ocean, and suddenly, he really *was* drowning. Arms flailing like a madwoman, she flapped and slapped and didn't stop.

He ducked under the water and swam off. Several yards away, he hollered, "What the hell is wrong with you?"

She stabbed her arms out of the water. "I'm sick of you treating me like this!"

"Like what?" he shot back.

"It's like I don't exist. You won't talk to me. You won't work with me. You're mean. And I hate it. It's awful. I can't live like this anymore!"

What was he supposed to say? He didn't want to live like that either.

"I miss you." Her soft voice was barely audible over the crashing waves.

Three words. Only three words and she'd punched him in the heart, kicked him in the balls, and fucked him in the head all at the same time. Just a cunt-hair shy of seething, he laid it all out there. "That's awful hard to believe, considering four days ago, you claimed I was nothing more than a rebound who treats women like garbage."

Shocked, wounded, confused—she looked like a bird that had crashed against a glass window. "I never said that." "No, I believe the term you used was manwhore. Yeah, that's it."

Her lips trembled. "I'm sorry."

"Sorry about what? Being mean? Taking off every night? Treating me like you don't care? Acting like I don't exist? Dammit!" He growled at the moon. "I'm tired of this mind fuck. You want me to be nice? Then stop prancing around, shaking your ass, and asking me to go skinny-dipping. If you're gonna act like a cock-tease, don't expect me to jump for joy—"

Before he finished railing on her, she slipped under the ocean and swam away.

"Argue with me, dammit! Quit running away!" He smacked the water. "And quit swimming away, too!"

A silvery wave caught her and carried her ashore. She rose from the sea—incandescent and glimmering—and drifted over the dunes like vapor.

He didn't let out his breath until she was out of sight.

# Chapter 21

## Agein'

**Soundtrack:** Kate Nash, "Dickhead"

*B*efore Walker woke up, Callie threw herself an early morning pity party on the beach. Twenty-eight years old, with a bullshit job, no place to live, no relationship—and to top it all off, she was stuck in a moving prison with a man who hated her.

Her phone rang. "Happy birthday!" Effie cried.

"Happy birthday to you, too," she said. "It's four in the morning there. What are you doing up?" She prayed her sister wasn't high. Why else would she be up so early?

"Surfing," she said.

"Thought you hated surfing?"

"I'm filling up every single minute of the day so I don't get high."

Rather than put her mind at ease, the statement rolled a ball of worry around in her stomach. Effie was still struggling so much. Would it be like that for the rest of her life? "What are you gonna do later?"

"Nothing, really. Just gonna eat a lot of cake with my sponsor. What about you? Any special plans?"

"Nope." She watched the pink bubbly sun rise over the ocean.

"You work things out with the non-manwhore yet?"

"Still hates me. Now he thinks I'm a cock tease."

Her sister gasped with mock horror. "You made fun of his cock?"

In any other circumstance, she'd have laughed at her sister's dumb joke. But frankly, the situation wasn't funny. "I asked him to go skinny dipping last night."

"Yeah, that's pretty cock-teasy."

"It was a full moon. I wanted to live it up the last night before I turned into an old woman." Also, she'd wanted to break down the walls. Instead, she'd made them higher.

"Hey, I'm not arguing. If the Pacific weren't cold as balls, I'd do it, too."

Callie carried on with her rant. "He claims I called him a rebound, or trash, or something. I don't know. He was screaming at me, so I left." She dusted herself off and shuffled back to the Silver Dildo.

"Did you?"

"Who knows? I was so upset that night." And a little drunk, but she left out for her sister's benefit.

A car door closed in the background, and the wind howled into the phone. "Why don't you take a drama break? Go get yourself a real manwhore and have birthday sex."

She glanced around the campground—nothing but retirees as far as the eye could see. Even if she were interested in her sister's suggestion, the pickings weren't just slim—they were downright skeletal.

"Not long until we see each other," Effie said, filling in the silence. "I'm excited."

"Yep, Yosemite."

"Oh, by the way, thanks for the hideous towel."

"Hard to dry off with a two-foot dick between your legs, eh?"

"It's kind of gross. I didn't send you anything because I have no idea where you are."

*Me neither,* she thought, *I'm completely lost.* "Don't worry about it."

"Hey, I see a cute guy in a wetsuit. Gotta blaze."

She sat down and laid her head on the picnic table. Eighteen more hours till the day was over, five more weeks until the trip ended, and she could barely stand another minute of it.

"You okay?" Walker said from the camper door. Thanks to him, she was nowhere near okay. But she clamped mouth shut and didn't say a word.

"Skip emailed." He sat next to her. "Why didn't you tell me it was your birthday?"

She shot him a Murphy-Are-You-Fucking-Kidding-Me-Glare.™ "Gee, I don't know. Guess I'm too busy prancing around, shaking my ass, and teasing your cock."

He folded his hands behind his neck and closed his eyes. "I don't know whether to scratch my watch or wind my ass around you."

"I don't even know what that means."

"What am I supposed to do, Callie? I'm not any happier than you about this situation. What do you want from me?"

"Basic human kindness for starters," she said then quickly shifted her tone to apologetic. "Honestly, Walker? I don't remember saying you were a rebound. I probably said a lot of things that night. Eli and I had a lot to drink, and I was hurt and angry. I would apologize again, but I already have—several times—and it hasn't done any good."

He removed his glasses and rubbed his eyes.

"In my defense though," she said, "how did you expect me to react? I know we said no strings, but—"

"No, *you* said no strings."

"Regardless, don't you think I'd find it a tiny bit jarring to see you kissing Sabrina, not even an hour after we slept together?"

"I didn't kiss her!"

"She was all over you even before that bullshit kiss!"

"I had nothing to do with that," he shouted. "And I reamed her a new one afterwards—"

She cut him off with the slice of her hand. "No, *you* helped her throw me under the bus in front of the client."

He jumped up and waved his arms wildly. "I didn't help her do anything. You realize how many people would lose their jobs if we lost that client? Yourself included? People have families to feed. She was trying to keep him happy—"

"By kissing you? That's a pretty elaborate ruse for such a . . ." She swallowed her bitchy comment and continued. "The minute we stepped inside that studio you latched on to her and didn't give me a second glance—"

"You told me to keep our relationship a secret!"

"I said keep it a secret, not act like I have a communicable disease. Furthermore, you could have told me what happened—"

"I tried! You wouldn't listen." His voice boomed throughout the campground.

"No, you didn't try," she snapped. "After she mauled you in front of me, what you did was show up with a bag of condoms." It was an idiot move and if he didn't get that, she wanted to hammer it in.

He closed his eyes and worked his jaw for a minute before he spoke. "You assumed the worst, and there was no way I was gonna change your mind."

She blew out a deflating sigh and gave up. Why was she even arguing with him? "Fine, Walker. You were right. I was wrong. I don't even care anymore. I just want off this fucking non-recreational vehicle."

He frowned so hard it looked like he'd fractured his face. "It sucks to hear you say that."

She blinked away her tears. "You know what sucks? I thought you were my friend. Now you won't even look at me or talk to me. Guess I was just a warm hole on the road, right?"

"Just like I was your hard dick on the road?" he shot back. "Why'd you even sleep with me in the first place?"

"Why does it matter? You said no strings—"

"No, *you* said no strings."

That was the second time he'd pointed that out, but rather than ask what he meant, she filed it in the back of her mind under Confusing Topics to Analyze Later.

She slumped over and stared at the sand. "Because I cared about you. And I thought you cared about me." Not to mention, he was insanely attractive. "You made me laugh and inspired me to write. And for the first time in years, I felt happy." That she had to use the past tense to tell him those things made her indescribably sad.

"And you weren't a rebound," she added. "I was over my ex the minute I left Chicago. You meant much more to me than that. Much more."

A gust of wind whipped her hair across her face. The seagulls flying overhead dipped and changed course.

"You promised if we slept together you wouldn't hate me or ruin the trip." She sniffled and rose to her feet. "You lied."

He grabbed her hand. "Don't go, Callie. I'm sorry. This was just a big misunderstanding. I don't hate you. Not even close. Can we start over again? Let me take you someplace special for your birthday," he said. "Let me make it up to you, please."

She closed her eyes and tried to slow down the hundreds of miles of pent-up emotions whirling around in her brain. She should have been overjoyed to hear those words, but after an emotionally exhausting last few days, she felt diluted and worn out instead.

"I don't know." She dragged her heaviness up the camper steps. "I think I'm just gonna go back to bed. Maybe if I'm lucky, I'll wake up when this day is over."

# Chapter 22

## Surprisin'

### Biloxi, Mississippi

*a*bout as low down as a whale turd, that's how Walker felt after his conversation with Callie. What a bunch of tangled mistruths and assumptions. They'd wasted four days thinking the worst instead of just talking.

Time to pull his head out of his ass and repair their relationship—starting with her birthday.

After poking around on the Internet and making a few calls, he drove to Biloxi. When he arrived, he climbed the ladder and found Callie writing on her laptop.

"Ready for your birthday surprise?" he asked.

She looked up with an unfocused gaze. "Where are we?"

"At a gas station." He tossed her the bar rag. "Blindfold yourself. I have a surprise."

"Did you wash this?" She sniffed and wrinkled her nose. "It's crusty."

"Did you wash it when you made me wear it?"

"This isn't one of your spankerchiefs, is it?"

"The hell?"

"You know, your jizz rag?"

"You scare me."

Two slices of blue cut him. "Is it?"

"Hush, or I'll stuff it in your mouth. Get over here, woman." He knotted the supposed cum rag around her head.

Once he parked, he led Callie through the hotel lobby and up to the room. An old client had hooked him up with the penthouse suite. Following the bar rag removal, she blinked a few times and surveyed the room.

A chandelier in the living area dripped red crystals, and under it, a circular red velvet couch surrounded a mirrored coffee table. An entire wall was dedicated to a flat-screen TV.

In the master bedroom, a giant canopy bed rested against a wall of windows. A gas fireplace filled the opposite wall. That was a little over the top, considering the temperate weather in Biloxi.

The other two rooms in the suite were slightly smaller and didn't have windows, but were still deluxe accommodations.

Callie ventured out to the balcony. Her eyes widened. "Wow, an ocean view. Where are we?"

"Penthouse suite in the Biloxi Grand Luxor."

"You did this? For me?"

From the sound of her voice, you'd think she'd just witnessed a miracle. Like it didn't seem possible he'd done something nice. But he hadn't. He hadn't even taken her on a date. From now on, he was going to treat her right.

If she'd let him.

"Go check out the bathtub," he said.

"Holywhoreshit," she shouted from the bathroom. "An infinity pool. It's huge."

An image flashed through his mind—her in the tub, between his legs, all slick and wet. He'd have to earn that chance though, and it wouldn't come cheap.

Bouncy and eyes sparkling—she danced out of the bathroom. He'd pay the devil to see her like that every day. "Figured you'd want a real bed and bath on your birthday."

She wrung her wrists and stared at the floor. "You didn't have to do this, Walker."

He took her hands. "Let me treat you on your birthday. Will you do that for me, please? Will you just let go and enjoy yourself and not worry so much?"

The breath she exhaled sounded like it had been pent up in her chest for years.

He dug the gift certificate out of his pocket. "I booked you a spa appointment in thirty minutes. Go hog wild. Get a tune-up. Put mud on your face. Get your back walked-on. Treat yourself like a queen."

"But—"

"Hush, it's already paid for. And here"—he handed her his credit card—"buy something fancy to wear. I'm taking you out tonight."

"I'll pay for it myself."

"Callie—"

"No, you've done enough already."

He shoved the card in her pocket. "Consider it a birthday gift. And no t-shirts. Get a dress." He opened the door. "I'll meet you back here at eight."

"But what about you? Where are you going?"

"Don't worry about me." His answer seemed to disappoint her, but he had shopping to do.

*"If you wear a short enough skirt, the party will come to you."—Dorothy Parker*

Despite the ninety-minute massage, her muscles still ached. The stress from the last few weeks had taken its toll, and now she felt even worse.

In the last few hours, Walker had done a complete one-eighty—going from acting like she didn't exist to pampering her like a queen.

Her emotions had whiplash.

Then there was his generous surprise. The last time someone did something special for her birthday was never. Daniel had forgotten it the year before. The year before that, he was out of town "on business." He *did* give her a present the first year—earrings that gave her a rash.

While the sentiment was incredibly thoughtful, it was also bittersweet. In a way it was like the *Gift of the Magi*—he'd booked a penthouse suite, and she had no one to share it with.

Part of her wondered if he still wanted her, but after the things she'd said that night in Orlando, he wouldn't touch her with a ten-foot pole, let alone his nine-inch dick.

Maybe Effie was right. A little birthday nookie might be just what the doctor ordered. Fancy hotel casino in a beach town? There had to be a veritable cornucopia of men who'd be more than happy to service her. And as an added bonus, she wouldn't have to worry about the messy complications of a work road trip afterwards.

If only she enjoyed casual sex. Unfortunately, liking a person was a prerequisite for an orgasm. That's probably why she could count her relationships on one hand. Walker just happened to be the ring finger.

A birthday kiss was more in line with what she needed. That's what she'd do—troll the casino for a birthday kiss. But first she had to attract a kisser.

In addition to the massage, she had her hair and makeup done and had everything waxed. Once she was rubbed down, made-up, primped, polished, and stripped of hair, she paid a visit to the hotel's overpriced boutique.

"I need something sexy to wear tonight," she told the saleswoman when she walked in the door.

The woman gave her a grimacing once-over. "You sure do." She took off her reading glasses and left them dangling on a gold chain. "I've got just the thing. I'm Sadie. Have a seat."

The saleswoman disappeared through a door in the back and returned a minute later carrying a blue dress wrapped in plastic. "This just came in. I ordered the wrong size by mistake. Not many women will fit in a dress this small, but I bet it'd be perfect on you."

Callie snatched the hanger and dashed off to the dressing room. After she tried it on, she frowned at the woman in the mirror. The robin's-egg-blue silk dress plunged down her back and stopped a few inches above her butt. Only a thin silver ribbon held it in place. In front, the dress scooped down and barely covered her breasts.

Sadie rapped on the door. "Let's see."

Callie crept out of the dressing room, wincing as she walked.

Sadie's eyes flew open.

"I know," Callie said glumly. "I can't pull this off. Do you have something else?"

Sadie laughed. "Trust me, you're pulling it off. In fact, I bet there isn't a man in this state who wouldn't want to pull it off for you."

Turning to the mirror again, she tried to envision what Walker would think. It really was stunning. The blue made her eyes stand out, and the design made her breasts look big. Well, big*ger*. And the gathers at the waist gave the illusion (key word: *illusion*) she had hips.

"I don't know. It's pretty, but I'm not sure I'm sexy enough for this dress."

The saleswoman huffed. "Let me give you a little piece of advice. In my twenties, I had a great body, but I was so insecure I wouldn't even sleep with my first husband with the lights on. Guess what? He cheated on me left and right. Now, I'm forty-five, and I've got a hot twenty-eight-year-old boyfriend, with a great ass and a six-pack, who thinks I'm the sexiest woman in the world. Know why? Because I don't give a tinker's damn what he thinks. This body birthed two children and I'm proud of it."

Gripping her shoulders and shaking some sense into her, Sadie cried, "Don't waste that gorgeous twenty-something body on silly little girl insecurities. How you wear that dress is as important as the dress itself. Wear it proudly. Own it, girl."

She looked at the price tag. Owning it would cost a fortune. Sure it'd get her laid, but it'd be cheaper just to hire a male hooker.

*Fuck it.* It was her birthday. "You have any shoes to go with?"

*"Three be the things I shall never attain: envy, content, and sufficient champagne."—Dorothy Parker*

**Soundtrack:** Air, "Sexy Boy"

Dressed for success, Callie wore the outfit out of the store and made it back to the room with fifteen minutes to spare. Fifteen minutes to catch a buzz, gather liquid courage, and get grit in a glass.

Plain and simple, she was really fucking nervous.

Someone must have heard her cry, because a bucket of champagne was awaiting her on the table. In no time, she downed two glasses of bubbly, bypassing a buzz and skating right into bombed. Now she was relaxed.

But the tranquility lasted all of five-seconds.

Walker swaggered out of his room and caused every muscle to tense back up—including the Kegel's in her vagina.

Decked out in a tailored gunmetal-gray suit and a teal-blue tie—he looked just like Clark Kent. Just remove the glasses and presto! *Superman.*

More like *Superhotman.*

He froze and zeroed in on her boobs, lingered there for a moment, then roamed the rest of her body, blazing a trail of heat as he went. After the tour, he strode toward her and set a gift-wrapped box on the table. "Is it your birthday or mine?" he said in a late-night radio voice.

She loved the late-night radio voice.

"Damn"—he twirled a finger—"Turn around. Let me see."

Still uneasy about the slutty back, she hesitated. *Eh*, what did he care? He didn't want her. She spun around and watched his expression.

He pinched his bottom lip. "Damn." And another, "Damn." He rolled his neck a few times and paced in a circle, not smiling.

Not once had he smiled.

That wasn't quite the reaction she'd expected. But she had another friend to cheer her up. "Champagne?" She held up a flute.

"Who?" He directed his nonsensical question to her tits. You could hang a purse on her braless nipples they were so hard. But around him that was their natural state.

"Where's the rest of it?" he asked.

"I drank it."

"No, the dress. You're wearing something over it, right?" Since it was a balmy ninety-degrees outside, she hiked up an are-you-serious brow.

"You can't go out like that. You're naked. For Christ's sake, your crack's showing."

She crossed her arms. "Are you okay? What's up with the wild hand gestures? What are you, in the Italian Mafia, now? Did you change your name to Vinnie?"

He gestured wildly up at the ceiling.

Owning it, she squared her posture, raised her chin and flashed a movie-star smile. "This is what I'm wearing. And if you don't like it, you can—" She took a drink and let him fill in the blank.

That seemed to enrage him. He mumbled a bunch of southern curse words—dag nabbit, land's sake, and several versions of the Lord's name in vain—then marched across the room. "Let's go before I—"

"Before you what?"

"Never mind. Come on." He held open the door like the Queen's Guard, focusing straight ahead.

Inside the elevator, he stole a furtive glance at the same time she did. For a sizzling few seconds, Walker's eyes blasted her with heat. Had she been wearing any at the time, her panties would have melted right off.

# Chapter 23

## Gamblin'

**Soundtrack:** Chet Faker, "No Diggity"

O n their patio table overlooking the Gulf, candles flickered in hurricane lanterns. Soft music played in the background, and the ocean breeze blew off the humidity. Everything was perfect, including the woman he was with.

And to celebrate her perfection, Walker ordered a five-course meal for her birthday.

"I won't be able to get out of this dress with all this food," she said.

*Not a problem, I'll tear it off with my teeth*, he thought.

Damn that woman and her dress. He was hornier than a two-peckered billy goat. But since he was a gentleman, he cemented his gaze to her eyes—instead of her tits—and asked her about her writing.

She twirled her hair for a moment then looked out at the ocean. "I started a novel."

"Is that right? That's exciting. What's it about?"

"It's a love story."

"Can I read it?" Maybe he could help with the sex scenes.

Her fingertips traced the wine glass. "I'm not in a place where I can handle criticism yet. Maybe when I get closer to the end."

That she'd assumed he'd criticize her stuck a pin in his hope. If she didn't trust him, how would he ever win her back?

He'd just have to try harder.

The waiter arrived with the first course. Walker cracked open a crab leg and placed it on her plate. She dipped a piece of meat in butter and slid it into her mouth. A needy moan slipped out while she chewed.

"Taste good, Bluebell?"

A bright smile surfaced—the first he'd seen in days.

"What's that pretty look for?"

"You called me Bluebell."

"Sorry, force of habit."

She lowered her lashes. "No, I like when you call me that."

"Well then, Bluebell, I won't call you anything else."

Asparagus tips were the next course, and when she nibbled the tip of the phallic veggie, beads of sweat trickled down his back.

He almost poured his drink in his lap watching her suck strands of fettuccini through her wet puckered lips.

Over dessert, he captured a rogue dollop of whipped cream on her lip and licked it off his finger. She pinned a pair of hot blue gems to his mouth, and under that tissue paper dress, her nipples popped out to greet him.

Quickly excusing himself, he wobbled to the bathroom with a slight hunch and splashed cold water on his face.

Later, he took her back to the casino. Inside, orange and purple lights flashed and slots dinged and ringed. In the center, a bar ran from exit-to-exit. Callie waited for him there, and he ventured off to buy poker chips.

While he stood in line, at least a dozen men eye-raped her. He had to get her out of there. She belonged somewhere else— a gilded cage maybe—not a tawdry casino bar.

As the cashier doled out the chips, a man old enough to be her dad snaked up behind her and peeked down her back. After he got an eyeful, the Sultan of Sleaze sat next to her and heaved his fat arm around the back of her barstool.

Walker stalked over and yanked the chair out from under the guy. "Get the hell out of my seat."

The man shot up with his hands in the air and slithered away.

Callie glanced around the bar for witnesses then lowered her voice. "What's with the sudden Section Eight?"

"Section Eight?"

"Yeah, the crazy act. You could have just asked him to move."

"Forget about that guy." He grinned tightly. "Let's play some blackjack."

After a big win, which earned him an enthusiastic hug, he stupidly left her alone again at the slots. When he came back from cashing out, three frat-boys hovered over her like birds of prey.

The machine lit up, and she jumped up and cheered. One guy offered his congratulations in the form of a dirty paw on her back and a kiss on the lips. She flinched back in surprise.

He ran to her side, grabbed the little shit's shirt, and raised him off the ground. "Congratulations, you just won a five-gallon pail of whoop ass."

"Walker!"

He set him down. "Touch her again," he said warmly, "and I'll slap the taste right out of your mouth."

The little shit rubbed his neck. "Are you with this asshole?"

Still hadn't learned his lesson, had he? He cocked back his fist, but the guy's pussy friends stepped in and hauled him away.

Callie's eyebrows disappeared under her bangs. "Who are you? And what did you do with my art director?"

"He kissed you!"

"So?"

He gripped his beer like a vise. "Is that what you want? Someone else?"

"Someone else? Besides whom?"

The answer to that question should have been obvious and that it wasn't made his ears ring louder than the slot machines.

"I've spent my whole life around men who want nothing to do with me—my father, Daniel . . . you." She closed her eyes and let out a sad sigh. "It's my birthday, and I'd like to at least *pretend* there's someone out there who wants me. Who doesn't think there's something wrong with me. Is that so hard to believe?"

*That's it. No more pussy-footing around.* He set down his beer and dragged her into his arms. "I've wanted you since I met you back in that douchebag club in New York. I've never stopped wanting you. There's not a damn thing wrong with you. You're perfect. And it kills me I've made you think otherwise. I want you so bad I can't breathe. I ache for you. Honest to God, I'm in pain. I've had a headache since the last time we slept together. I've turned into an asshole. I can't sleep. I can't eat. I can't work. You don't have to pretend, Blue. I want you. All of you, and if I don't get to have you, I—"

She pressed her fingertips to his lips. "Shh, I want you, too."

He closed his eyes and slapped his palm over his heart. "Do you have any idea how happy I am to hear that?"

"Walker?"

"Hmm?"

"You can kiss me now."

He laughed and gave her a birthday kiss she wouldn't forget. Her tongue, her hands, her smell—they healed him and brought him back to life. She was his magic elixir.

Speaking of magic elixir—he'd like to taste hers.

"Upstairs!" He tossed her over his shoulder and barreled toward the exit. As soon as the elevator doors shut, he plunged a hand down the back of her dress and thrust a finger inside her wetness. She moaned and he grinned. "I've been wanting to do that all night. Torturing me, with no damn panties on."

"I've been wanting to do *this* all night." She wrapped her hand around his cock. "My God, you've been hard for hours."

He laughed. "You noticed that, huh? Jesus, I've been hurtin' for you."

The doors opened and he picked her up again and took off running down the hallway. Outside the room, he set her down, dug out the key card, and dropped it on the floor. Muttering a few curse words, he crouched to grab it, but on the way up, her legs distracted him.

"I love this dress." He slipped his head under the hem. "Jesus, Mary, and Joseph." He pushed it around her waist. "Where'd your blonde go, Bluebell?" Between her legs, it was smooth and glistening. He put his mouth on the glistening part and drew a line with his tongue up to the spot that triggered her greedy sounds.

Breathy pants came from above as he smothered his face below. Her knees buckled. Steadying her, he grabbed her ass in one hand and wrapped her leg over his shoulder.

A door slammed down the hallway. *Maybe.* He wasn't sure.

"The key," she chanted, "the key."

Mouth still attached to her pussy, he felt around on the floor.

"Hurry! They're watching."

He gave her one more lick, pulled his head out from under the dress, and wiped his face.

Down the hall, two white-haired old broads stood frozen in terror. One grabbed her throat as if she were having a stroke. The other, dressed in mink in the middle of July, said, "I'd give away my husband's brand new Beemer to have that man go down on me in the hallway."

The other replied, "I'd give away my husband."

"I'd give up my left tit," said the lady in fur. "And that's the only one I've got left."

"Maybe we can pool the three of ours and get a deal."

Callie snickered. "He's mine, bitches."

They let loose a barrage of laughs and stepped inside the elevator.

"Enjoy your evening, ladies," Walker called out.

"Ha! Enjoy yours!" they sang.

Once again he dropped the key card. "Christ on a cracker. So help me God, Blue, if you don't get that door open, I'll break it down."

Giggling hysterically, she picked it up and slid it through the lock. He sprinted to the master suite, ripping off his clothes on the way. Racing behind him, she tripped and fell on the floor. Tittering and laughing, she pointed at the chandelier. "Look how pretty. Let's do it under that."

A red light flashed in his brain and panic spread like wildfire down to the tip of his swollen cock. "How much have you had to drink, Blue?"

Eyelids at half-mast, she cocked her head and said nothing. He tallied the drinks in his head. After adding the half-empty bottle of champagne on the table, all his excitement petered away. Five drinks. Five drinks too many for a certified featherweight. Maybe she wasn't *that* drunk.

She stood and fell again, failing the sobriety test miserably.

Horse sense reared up and stomped on everything. If she woke up the next morning and regretted another night with him . . . No, he couldn't do it. Almost in tears, he yanked his tie off the lampshade.

"What's the matter?"

"I don't—" He pinched the bridge of his nose. "I can't— This isn't—" His damn tongue wouldn't let him say the words. "This isn't a good idea." His body protested so vehemently, he thought it might split open and erupt all over the white carpet.

The heat in her eyes turned to ice. "What's not a good idea?"

*Here comes the storm,* he thought. He kissed her lips, then her cheeks, then her hands. "I can't sleep with you tonight, darlin'. Not when you've had too much to drink. I'm sorry." Before he changed his mind, he ran to his room, shouting more apologies.

A shoe hit him in the back.

"Get the fuck out, you, you . . . *pussy tease.*" She sniffled and whimpered.

He banged his forehead on the door. "I know, baby, I feel like crying too. First thing in the morning, I'll climb in your bed. I promise."

Leaving her all wet and needy and wanton took serious balls. But he was a machine, a pillar, a mountain, an ox, a three-boat barge of strength.

He was a man, dammit.

And given the amount of times he jacked off that night, he was also a teenaged boy.

*"I like to have a martini, two at the very most. After three I'm under the table, after four I'm under my host."—Dorothy Parker*

Was that a fucking joke? Did he just leave her? On her birthday? The insidious insult she wanted to scream stuck to her moss-covered tongue. *Water.* She needed water.

On the way to the fridge, his gift sidetracked her. What she wanted was Walker for her birthday, not a stupid present.

She swallowed the urge to throw it in the trash and clawed off the wrapping. Fairies and unicorns danced in her heart. "Oh, Walker, you sweet, wonderful man." He'd given her a pair of pink Chucks—glittery pink Chucks.

But what he'd really given her was hope.

All she had left from her life before Daniel were those shoes she'd lost in the swamp that day. And how Daniel hated them, too. "They make you look like a kid. They're ugly. Don't let me see you wearing them again."

On the day her life crumbled, she'd dug out the sneakers from the back of the closet, put them on, and walked out the door.

The glitter Chucks fit perfectly. Of course they did—they were magic. She tapped her heels together. *I want to go to Walker's room. I want to go to Walker's room.*

*Fuck it.* She was breaking in.

Halfway there, the room started spinning. She careened towards the bathroom and called Uncle Ralph on the big white telephone.

After she emptied the five-course meal from her stomach, she staggered to bed and passed out, still wearing her new Chucks.

# Chapter 24

## Glowin'

*"His voice was as intimate as the rustle of sheets."*— *Dorothy Parker*

**Soundtrack:** Alina Baraz, Galimatias, "Make You Feel"

y the time Callie emerged from the shower the next morning, she was ravenous—absolutely starving for Walker.

Dressed in the fluffy hotel robe, she marched out, prepared to kick down his door. Lucky for the door, he was waiting for her on the couch, wearing nothing but a pair of low-slung jeans.

He pointed to his lap. "Get over here, Bluebell."

Owning it, she sauntered toward the couch, hips swaying like a super model traipsing down the runway. A foot in front of him, she tripped on the robe and fell to her knees.

He didn't laugh, but his mouth twitched like crazy.

"You didn't see that, did you?" She stood and tightened the sash.

"See what?"

"Nothing." She straddled him.

"How're you feeling?" His voice was still gravely from sleep.

"Naughty."

He removed his glasses, anchored his predatory peacock gaze to hers, then went in for a lubricating kiss. His scruff scrubbed her chin as he swirled his minty-fresh tongue around hers.

He drew back and stared at her, deep creases carving his brow. "First, we need to talk."

Her stomach twisted. Really? Rejection before breakfast? She climbed off his lap, but he hooked her with an arm and reeled her back in.

Finger under her chin, he coaxed her gaze back to his. "I can't do casual, Blue, not with you. I want strings."

Maybe she was still drunk. "Say that again?"

"I want to date you."

"Me?"

"You."

Did he even know what dating meant? "So . . . you're not going to sleep with other women?"

"And you're not gonna sleep with other men. Or look at them. Or talk to them. Or stand in the same room. Basically, I'm gonna need you to wear a burqa from now on."

She squinted a sideways glare.

Chuckling softly, he slipped the robe off her shoulders. "I'm kidding, but you're mine, okay?"

It still didn't seem kosher. "Does that mean we're boyfriend and girlfriend?"

"And lovers, and friends, and coworkers, and artists, and humans, and anything else you want to call it, as long as we're together."

As she drank in the nectar of his words, her heart sped up to hummingbird pace. "Okay," she said in childlike whisper.

"Okay what?"

"I'll be your girlfriend."

"Then I'll be your boyfriend." His worry lines lifted, his chest broadened, and his cock stiffened. It was as if she'd inflated him. "One more thing," he said.

She sighed and suppressed an eye roll. "Yes?"

"From now on, we talk. About everything. And you don't leave, or shut me out, or run away if we have a problem. I'm not your past. I'm your future—"

"Walker?"

"Yes, Blue?"

"Are you ever going to non-casually fuck me? I'm dying here, sitting on top of your boner."

"Thought you'd never ask." And with that, he gathered her in his arms and took her to bed.

Walker rested his head on Callie's breasts. The beat of her heart matched his. She was his now. And he was hers. "Know what I want?" he asked, fondling her nipple.

"What?" She ran her fingers through his hair.

"A banana split."

"Sounds healthy."

"It's got all four food groups—ice cream, fruit, nuts, chocolate fudge . . ."

Her melodious laughter reverberated through his body. "Then let's get you a banana split." She reached for the phone and ordered one from room service.

"What else are we going to do today?" she asked after the call.

"I've got big plans."

"Oh, yeah?"

"Yep, first, I want to eat my ice cream. Then I'm gonna take naked pictures of you. After that, I'm gonna have my way with you in that big bathtub."

"Then what?"

"You mean between orgasms? Think you'll get bored?"

She caressed his shoulders. "Not a chance."

"Good," he said. "Because I'm not letting you out of this room for a few days."

"But when will I wear my new shoes?"

He tickled her side until she begged him to stop. "You opened your present? I wanted to be there. So what'd you think? Like the sparkles?"

"I love them, Walker, so much."

"I thought you would. You looked like you'd severed a limb when you lost them in the swamp."

"Best present ever."

"They're just shoes, Baby Blue."

"Not to me," she said.

Later, Walker put down his sketchbook and regarded the woman he was drawing. In a ray of sunlight, still glowing from an afternoon of making love, his sexy pixie lounged against a mountain of pillows, reading a book. The ocean breeze occasionally swept in from the open balcony door and flipped the pages for her.

"Watcha reading over there, Blue?"

"Raymond Carver stories."

"Read me one." He lay beside her.

The story she read was about two couples getting drunk and talking about love. One of the characters, a cardiologist, told a story about an elderly couple in the hospital after a terrible car accident. They were in body casts and the husband's condition went downhill because he couldn't see his wife. That was love, according to the doctor, needing to see your wife just to live.

Walker completely understood that. Getting Callie back felt like he'd been cured of cancer.

"So Bluebell, what do you think love is?"

"To me, love is a verb. It's horribly cliché, but actions scream louder than words."

"My momma and daddy always said they loved each other, but they acted like they were at war."

She snuggled in his arms. "I read somewhere the Greeks have six different words for love. Platonic love, love for children and family, universal kindness, self-love . . . I can't remember the rest. And the Norwegians have a word that describes the euphoria of falling in love. Our dictionary says love expresses sexual attachment. That's so, I don't know, sad."

He ran his hand down her back. "Maybe you need your own word for love."

"Like what?"

"Hmm, we'll have to figure that out. In the meantime, I'll use love to express my sexual attachment." He scooted closer and kissed her. "For one, I love your trucker talk, especially when it comes out of those pretty lips."

"Mine! What about yours?"

"I keep my dirty words in the sheets, not on the streets."

She laughed.

"And I love your sexy laugh." He tickled her so she'd do it some more. "And I love your freckles. They're invisible until"—he kissed the tip of her nose—"you get real close. And on your back, did you know you've got four freckles in the shape of a smile?"

She hid under the sheet. He ripped it off and slipped his hand between her legs. "I love the way you melt against my hand too—all slick and silky."

And the truth was, he was falling in love with her, but if he told her that, she'd start worrying and he wasn't up for that. What he was up for was slipping between her thighs, and when he did, he made a mental note to look up that Norwegian word for euphoria.

*"Four be the things the things I'd have been better without: love, curiosity, freckles and doubt."—Dorothy Parker*

**Soundtrack:** Hundred Waters, "Show Me Love"

They turned off the lights, lit the candles, and sank into the infinity tub. She tangled her legs with Walker's, closed her eyes, and soaked her pleasantly sore body in overpriced luxury hotel bath foam.

What a glorious day! Why couldn't every day be like that? Bathing with a beautiful man after making love all day? Oh, the delicious pleasures a life with Walker would bring.

Instantly, doubt swooped in and warned her not to get attached. It was a fantasy world they were living in, where other people and jobs and monotony didn't exist. She popped open her eyes and sat up.

"You okay?" Walker stroked the bottom of her foot.

*For now.* She flashed a flimsy smile and nodded.

"Gettin' gun shy?"

"What do you mean?"

"I can tell you're over-analyzing things, getting all freaked out for nothing."

Was she that transparent?

He pinched her butt. "Stop thinking so much."

She squeaked and splashed then grew serious again. "This is all just pretend right?"

"Nope, it's real." He scooped her onto his lap and gave her a soapy kiss. "Imagine there's a bubble around us and nothing can get in." He blew foam off his hand. "Try it. Picture it's just you and me and nothing else. No second thoughts. No ex-boyfriends. No future worries."

"Just you and me," she said in a hypnotic trance-like voice, "and John Travolta . . . in a plastic bubble."

He snorted against her throat. "Can't believe you've seen that movie. My grandma has it on VHS."

"*Boy in a Plastic Bubble*? Oh, yeah, awesome film. Talk about poor taste in men. What kind of moron picks up a guy with an immune disorder, who can't even leave his vacuum-sealed room?" She snickered. "Classic corn porn."

"Corn porn?"

"Corny stoner movies. Skip made it up."

"That's a shocker."

"How about the part where she falls in love after he fondles her face with a glove? True glove!"

He chuckled. "I'm gonna make you fall in love with a glove in about thirty seconds." He plucked a condom from the side of the tub.

"I'm sure it's a collector's item," she said, tensing her vagina as she watched him roll the latex over his hard length. "You should find it and sell it. I'm sure it's worth a fortune."

"Damn right it is, Calliope Rhodes. In fact, I'm putting it in our prenup."

She was fairly certain her eyes bugged out.

"I'm kidding, nutter," he said with a foamy grin. He wrapped her leg around his waist and plunged inside. "We'll share custody."

# Chapter 25

## Buskin'

### New Orleans, Louisiana

*"Tell him I'm too busy fucking, or vice versa."*—Dorothy
Parker

**Soundtrack:** Lazy Lester, McDaniel, "I'm A Man"

They stayed in Biloxi for three days. The best three
days of his life.

Although they'd sexed it up in a penthouse hotel
that whole time, Callie told Skip a different story. According to
her, they'd been broken down in the Mississippi wilderness
and couldn't get through to the outside world. Out of the ether,
(she actually used the word ether), a bearded backwoods
hermit saved their asses.

"His name?" She flipped up her palms, asking for help.

Walker shot her a look that said you dug that hole yourself,
sweetheart.

"James, I think," she said. "Yeah, that's it, James
Patterson."

He shook his head.

"Dude, it was like *Deliverance* meets *Batman*," she said to
Skip. "Except he wore coveralls instead of Spandex. The guy
was our hero. Also he didn't butt rape Walker."

*What in the sam hill?* She was burying them up to their
necks in bullshit.

"Crazy right?" she said. "I don't know. Maybe he learned how to fix RV's in Nam. Probably why he lives in the woods— flashbacks. What's that? Um, no, he didn't charge us anything. Walker didn't get any pictures because he couldn't charge up his camera. Uh-oh, we're about to go under a tunnel. I'm losing you—" She ended the call and tossed the phone on the dash.

Over the rim of his glasses, he raised a scrutinizing brow. "Jesus, I thought you were a writer. That was the worst story I've ever heard in my life. James Patterson?"

She shrugged. "Skip doesn't read."

"Surely, he didn't believe that sorry-ass excuse for a lie?"

"Probably not, but no worries, he won't remember. There's a strong possibility he was high."

"How do you figure?"

"Because he told me he was too stoned to talk about butt rape."

"That's a pretty good indication, all right." He shook his head and chuckled.

"What?"

"Nothing, nutter. You ready to find the next butt-raping, backwoods veteran?"

"As ever." She peeled out of the parking lot.

Turned out, driving to New Orleans with her was far more terrifying than any butt-raping hermit. A tropical depression hammered the Gulf States and thick sheets of rain covered the highways. It rained so hard the animals started to pair up.

As usual, Callie waved a middle finger in the face of danger and raced the giant RV down the flooded highways. On that journey, he became a praying man. He slammed on his non-existent passenger break. "Slow down!"

Grinning evilly, she punched the accelerator to the floor.

"You lunatic! That's it. Pull over!"

"What are you gonna do, ground me?"

"Tell you what, if you let me drive, I'll give you all the oral pleasure you want," he said.

"You already do that."

"Blue, please."

"All right," she grumbled and pulled over.

Once she surrendered the wheel, he put his handwritten will to the side and drove like a normal person would in a rainstorm.

Later, she plunked down in the passenger seat. "The air conditioning's not working."

He held a hand over the vent. "It's working fine. Maybe you've got a feverrrrrr—" He swerved in the other lane, overcorrected, and almost tipped over.

Honking cars passed them with middle fingers stuck out the windows. People were willing to soak their sleeves to shoot him the bird.

"Good God all Friday, woman! Put some clothes on, before you kill us!"

"What's the matter, can't you multi-task?" she asked, wearing nothing but a wicked smile.

"Jesus."

She planted her hot gaze on his lap. "Want me to make that hard problem go away?"

"Move to the back, Blue Devil."

Somehow they made it alive to the French Quarter. He would have kissed the ground if it weren't covered in horse shit and vomit.

She plugged her nose. "What a delightful aroma."

"Eau De Sewage." He flipped open the umbrella. They huddled underneath and ran through the cascading rain, holding hands.

Hanging planters swung dangerously from wrought-iron balconies, and shutters banged loudly against the buildings. A block away, a group of colorful drunkards danced outside a bar.

"Let's get out of this," he said. "I need a shot after that death ride."

Inside, a sweaty crowd pushed them toward the bar like a riptide. After he bought a couple of draft beers, they snagged a standing table in back just as a nine-piece band crammed on stage. A husky woman with a husky voice took the microphone and announced the band. "We are the One-Night Stands." A bluesy beat started on the drums then the horns and guitars joined in.

Over the loud music, conversation was impossible, so they danced instead. He twirled his giggly girl and dipped her at the end. Then he brought out the big guns and did the robot, the sprinkler, and the running man.

"My ribcage is gonna break if you don't quit making me laugh," she sputtered.

God, he loved making her happy.

Sweat-soaked and thirsty, they headed back to the table and slugged a beer. When the next song came on, they dirty danced in the dark corner, kissing and grinding, *sweet lord.* The odds of his zipper bursting doubled.

Under her damp shirt, he molded a hand around her hot breast and rolled her nipple between his fingers. She ran her tongue up his neck and whispered in his ear, "I dare you to do me in the restroom."

The thought sliced right through the heat like a cold knife. "Oh, honey, no." He cringed. "That's just . . . no."

Her cheeks reddened, her smile flattened, and her eyes met the floor. Next thing he knew, she was no longer hugging him—she was hugging herself.

He snuck behind her and kissed her neck. She stiffened and swatted him away.

Pressure built behind his eyes. *What the hell just happened?* He grabbed her hand and pulled her outside.

The steamy rain beat the awning above. "What's going on, Blue?"

She turned away, her bottom lip trembling. "You have sex with everyone else in the bathroom."

The comment had him more confused than a baby in a topless bar. Honestly, he couldn't recall ever doing it in a public restroom. A private bathroom? Sure. But never in a bar. "'Fraid you lost me there, darlin'."

"That woman in the Boom Club bathroom! Your birthday? The tall blonde? I saw you."

"Oh, *that* woman!" He chuckled. "The Russian?"

She mocked his laugh. "So you remember now, do you?"

"I didn't have sex with her. That cracked-out mess snuck in and basically sexually assaulted me. I came this close to getting her thrown out, but a sexy foul-mouthed devil distracted me on the way."

The bar door opened and music poured out. A car splashed a loud group of bar-hoppers. They fired off curses and wobbled away, laughing and singing.

She rubbed her eyebrows. "And the blow jobs?"

"A figment of your pornographic imagination." He swept the rain off her lips with his thumb. "Blue, I'm not gonna drag you into a nasty bar and make love with you against a piss-soaked bathroom stall while a line of drunks forms outside. You deserve better."

She started to say something, stopped, and started again. "I'm sorry. I can't believe . . . I thought you'd banged two women in a matter of minutes. Why didn't you tell me the truth?"

Because at the time, he didn't give a damn what she thought. But he did now, so he kissed her until she drooped in his arms.

"Since the restroom's out of the question," she said. "How about a quickie in the Silver Dildo?"

"How about a longie instead?"

"That works."

*"He always thought the muse should be sex on legs."—*
*Lauren Beukes*

**Soundtrack:** Supertramp, "Give a Little"

A crowd gathered on the street corner to hear the tiny singer with the pink ukulele play. Even the rain stopped to listen. Walker pressed record on his camera.

Callie overturned the beer hat in front for donations then pointed to him. "See that handsome man with the camera? He dared me to get up here. Didn't believe I'd do it, so I bet him." She waved her fingers. "Enjoy cleaning the bathroom naked, Mr. Rhodes."

A few folks laughed. Then in a lush, creamy voice, she belted out the song and stunned the crowd into silence. At the chorus, others joined in, and as everyone sang, his heart did too.

During the next verse, she locked eyes with him. "'I'll give a little bit of my love to you. There's so much that we need to share . . .'"

For a second, the world stopped spinning and paused right at the moment he fell absolutely silly in love.

Someone pushed play again and the bustle and noise turned back on.

A drunk stumbled over and dropped an empty can in one of the holders.

"I'll give you a little bit of love, baby," a suit hollered then threw five bucks in the hat.

Walker shouldered the son-of-a-bitch out of the way and threw in a twenty.

Another guy tossed in a ten.

He emptied his wallet, throwing everything he had in the hat, including a business card and a condom.

The rain started again and everyone ran for shelter. Only the hammered guy remained. Then a streak of lightning shot out of the sky and the drunk stumbled for cover too.

They beamed goofy wide grins at each other while the rain poured over them. He kissed her hungrily, drinking the drops off her lips. Mouth still pressed to his, she smiled. "I made two hundred dollars, a beer can, and a condom."

"From my wallet!"

"Not all of it!" She kissed him again then hand-in-hand they strolled back to the bar.

A guy at the door stopped them. "Sorry, y'all, we're closing up. Storm's been upgraded to a hurricane. Supposed to hit in the next twenty-four hours. She's only a category one, but after Katrina, I don't take any chances."

"Guess we'd better head north then, Bluebell."

On the way to the camper, she gave a little bit of her love to a homeless person—all the money she'd earned, plus the condom and the umbrella.

# Chapter 26

## Floodin'

### Some Podunk Town, Louisiana

**Soundtrack:** The Hives, "Come On!"

$\mathcal{F}$or hours they sat in traffic, only getting as far as a hundred miles north of New Orleans. Then one of the windshield wipers blew off and they were forced to pull off on the next exit.

Torrents of rain rushed down the streets and flooded the intersections. As usual, Walker drove like an old man.

Callie twitched in her seat, dying to take over the wheel.

"We've got to park this thing somewhere." His voice was steady, calm, and completely unnerving. "See if you can find something above ground level. A parking garage or something."

She scoured the GPS and satellite maps and found a mall garage a quarter-mile away.

He slammed on the brakes and everything crashed to the floor.

She gripped the armrests. "What happened?"

"You didn't see it? Think it was a dog."

Without the wiper, all she saw was the car wash outside.

"There!" He pointed out a tiny puppy swimming across the intersection. "Dammit!" He banged his palms on the steering wheel. "I can't leave him out there to die. Be right back. Move us up the street so we don't stall out."

"Walker, no! Are you insane?"

"It'll just take a second." The door almost snapped off its hinges in the wind.

"It'll just take a second," she grumbled, plowing the Silver Dildo through the burgeoning lake. "Be right back. I'm just saving a puppy in a flood. Idiot."

When he didn't come back in the aforementioned second, she ran to the back and searched out the windows. A tree snapped in half and skidded across the road like a twig.

"No big deal, just wandering out in the dark in the middle of a hurricane." Her heart stopped and started with every crack of lightening. Hands balled in fists, she sliced her fingernails into her palms. She solved that problem by chewing off every one of them.

Still, no Walker. Fuck it. She was going out to save his ass.

Quickly stuffing herself into a rain jacket, she hurled herself into the hurricane. The darkness entombed her and the rain attacked her like BB pellets. She almost shredded her vocal cords shouting for him in the howling wind.

A black shape reached out. "Dammit, Blue! What're you doing out here?"

"You're alive!" She hugged him.

He pushed her away and pointed ahead. "Go. Now. Hurry!"

Through the rising river they slogged, dodging flying debris in their path. It took both of them to pull the camper door shut.

Walker floored the gas, but in the wind, the Silver Dildo merely inched forward. He tossed her his glasses. "Clean these off. I can't see a thing."

A stop sign hit the windshield. They both ducked. "Where the hell is the garage?" He sounded a lot less steady than before.

"It should be here. Wait. On the right! There!"

He turned and halted at the entrance. "Think we'll fit? How tall is this thing?"

She tore open the glove box and read the dimensions from the manual—exactly one foot under the clearance.

Too bad she didn't think to read the width though. They scraped through the gate with an interminable screech. She winced. "Skip's gonna shit a brick."

Up the ramp they chugged until they were five stories above ground. At the top, he jammed the camper into park. "Okay, Miss Badass Parking Queen, line us up between those cement walls."

In one sweeping motion, she accomplished the task.

Walker clapped. "Were you a valet in a previous life?"

She didn't say a word—her lungs were too busy lugging in air.

He reached into his jacket and plucked out a wet black puppy. "I gotcha, fella." The dog licked the end of Walker's nose.

"You got him?" She jumped up and hugged his neck. "Oh, Walker." Then she hauled back and punched his arm.

"Ow! What was that for?"

"You could have died out there, Captain Puppy Saver!"

He smirked. "Captain Puppy Saver?"

"It's not funny."

He lost the smirk. "Yeah, well, I'm mad at you, too. I told you to stay put."

She picked up the puppy, crawled in Walker's lap, and settled the dog in back hers. Still pissed off, she socked Walker again. The puppy barked.

"Save me from the mean lady, Leonard Nimoy," he said in a manly baby voice.

"Leonard Nimoy?"

"Look"—he held out his velvety ear—"just like Spock's."

"They look more like cow ears to me."

He clucked. "Don't listen to her, Leonard." The puppy licked his hand furiously.

After the fear of losing Walker dissipated, she cried tears of relief.

Walker wiped her cheeks and tucked her against his chest. They listened to the wind barreling through the garage like a freight train.

"Think we'll be okay here?" she asked.

"No telling." His eyes went sexual peacock. "But if we die, I'd rather go out fuckin' you."

She shot up and stripped off her shirt. "Let's go! Before we croak!"

"Right behind you." He dropped his pants.

"Condom."

"Nightstand."

"Leave those panties on," he shouted. "I'll tear them off later."

"Hurry." She was vibrating with need.

"Spread your legs nice and wide, sweetheart, I need to fuck you right now."

"Yes, sir, Mr. Potty Mouth."

They fucked like wild animals, fueled by adrenaline and the need to survive. Biting, sucking, pounding, plundering—they tore at each other with the ferocity of the storm that raged outside. Their moans trumped the thunder. And it wasn't the wind shaking the camper—they were. When they came, they both roared like lions.

On the floor, the puppy let out a pint-sized howl. Walker peered over the edge. Leonard wagged his tail and yipped again. "On a scale of one to ten, how would you rate that performance, Leonard Nimoy?" The puppy barked. "Twenty! You don't say."

Callie shook her head and smiled. "You are ridiculously adorable with that puppy."

"You mean ridiculously tough?" He tied off the condom and flopped back on the bed, panting and clutching his chest. "I feel like I just finished the Iron Man."

She lifted a sore leg. "My vagina's broken."

He propped himself up and stared at her neck. "I gave you one, two . . . Jesus, five hickies! And your hips have hand marks."

She covered her mouth. "Oh my God, it looks like a mountain lion got ahold of your back."

"You've got serious beard rash on your tits. Look how red they are."

"My face is on fire too." She pressed her fingers along her chin.

"Did we take a road trip on my ass?" he asked, "Feels like it's rug burned."

"I threw my back out."

"Sorry, baby." He brushed her cheek. "You okay?"

She whimpered. "No, can you kiss it make it better?"

"I will in a little bit. 'Fraid I can't move right now." She sniffed the air. "It smells like wet dog in here."

"All I smell is wet pussy." He grinned proudly. "And it smells fantastic."

They broke down laughing then finally collapsed in a molten heap. She stretched out on top of him. "Stay still, I want to give you an Eskimo kiss," she said.

"A what?"

"An Eskimo kiss. Like this." She rubbed her nose against his.

In return, he gave her a Walker kiss. A kiss fueled with passion, friendship, creativity, happiness, and heat. A forever kiss.

Lightning lit up the camper and a big boom followed. The trembling puppy jumped on the bed. "Get up here and snuggle, Leonard Nimoy." Walker patted the bed. "We'll all die together."

They very well could die, but at least she'd go out on top of a beautiful man.

Flat on his back with his pink belly facing up, Leonard Nimoy snored next to them.

After a while, the soft beat of Walker's heart lulled her into a drowsy dream state. On the precipice between wakefulness and sleep, he kissed her temple and squeezed her tighter. "I love you, Blue," he said and drifted off.

At least that's what she thought he'd said, but she must have been dreaming.

*"They sicken of the calm who know the storm."*—
Dorothy Parker

**Soundtrack:** Jack Garratt, "Worry"

Callie slept on top of him again. Normally, he needed lots of room and didn't like to cuddle much. But with her tiny body swathing him like a warm blanket every night, he couldn't imagine sleeping any other way. If he woke up like that for the rest of his life, he'd die a happy man.

Speaking of dying, they didn't. They'd survived the hurricane. And he wanted to celebrate . . . inside Callie.

Gently, he stretched and pinched her bubblegum-pink nipples until they tightened to hard buds.

She opened her eyes, and he slipped a hand between her legs. "Rise and shine, beautiful."

"Whatcha doing down there, handsome?"

"Making you wetter than a hurricane."

"You and your puns."

It didn't take long before she was grinding against him and reaching for his cock.

Time to suit up.

The edges of the condom stuck together and the lube was cracked and dried. But she was hungry for him and so, so ready—he just couldn't wait.

"Get on your knees, darlin'. I want it deep."

She gave him a lust-drunk smile and slowly rolled over on all fours. Strong, assertive Callie submitted to him—happily. The sight of her swollen pussy—all shiny and slick—and the heat in her gaze as she watched him take her from behind— well, he went wild. Feral. Primal. Turned into a grunting and growling cave man.

And she was his cave woman, mewling, and moaning, and meeting his thrusts.

It could have been seconds, maybe minutes, but at some point, she came hard, and at the same time, something popped and his dick drowned in liquid heat. Intense shivering pleasure spread over him and his cum pulsed out forever. Sweaty and panting, they slid down together. Brain cells started firing again and he pulled out . . . without the condom. He stuck two fingers inside her, trying to find it. Blissfully unaware of the search and rescue attempt underway, Callie contracted her muscles and moaned. Up high, he found it, and pulled it out completely shredded and dripping with cum. A beautiful cream pie streamed out with it, and he watched it flow, feeling proud he'd created such a beautiful masterpiece.

Then paralysis hit and everything turned cloudy. "Shit fire," he said. Or maybe it was son-of-a-bitch? Or uh-oh? Whatever he said, she whipped around and stared at the blown-out rubber like she'd just locked eyes with Death.

"Oh God! No! No! I'm not on the pill!"

At that very inopportune moment, it occurred to him that they hadn't discussed protection. In his mind, they'd visit their doctors once the trip was done, and until then, they'd cover up.

She jumped up and flew out the door with nothing on but panties and a t-shirt. He threw on his boxers and hurried after her, Leonard Nimoy bouncing on his heels.

At the end of the garage, he joined her. They peered over the edge and surveyed the damage. Everything sagged, weighted down with rain. Floodwater filled the roads and parking lots in every direction. Trees, cars, and debris floated like dead bodies on the lake that had formed overnight.

"This place is a disaster," he joked.

She didn't laugh.

Instead, she took off racing down the ramp, bare feet slapping on the wet concrete. From the ground floor, a banshee cried—a filthy-mouthed banshee. Her f-bombs reverberated off the walls and scared the piss out of the dog.

They dashed after her. On the bottom, he found her knee-deep in sludge, wearing abject terror on her face.

"You hurt?" It sounded like she'd been stabbed.

"We can't get out."

Ordinarily, she wasn't a drama queen, so the reaction stumped him. He waded over and took her hand. "Don't worry, sweetheart. Later, we'll go for a swim and see if we can't get phone reception. We won't be trapped for long."

"I might be pregnant." Her statement came out in a whisper-scream, like she was telling him there was a murderer loose in the building.

He chuckled. "Aren't you overreacting a bit? It's only been five minutes since my guys broke out of prison."

She buried her head in her hands. "I can't do this again. I can't."

"What can't you do, baby?"

"We're stuck. I can't get Plan B. I just lost a baby. I'm scared. I can't do this. What am I going to do? Shit. Fuck. Shit . . ."

Words kept rushing out of her mouth, but he'd only heard one thing. "Hold on. Back up. You lost a child?"

Two blue pools of tears confirmed the question. Her sobs echoed in the cave-like silence of the parking garage. All he could think to do was pick her up and carry her back.

Inside the camper, he dried her tears, made a cup of hot tea with grandma's honey, and sat her at the table. "Tell me what happened."

Several times she stopped and started. "My doctor switched my pills and I got pregnant the same month. Daniel wanted me to get an abortion, but I wouldn't do it. A week later, he proposed. Said it was his moral obligation." She snapped out an arid laugh. "The irony of that statement still blows me away."

He rubbed her back and gently guided her back to the conversation. "Then what?"

"At the end of my fourth month, the baby stopped kicking. But since I had a doctor's appointment the next day, I went ahead and taught yoga at lunch. In class, I started bleeding. I tried and tried to get ahold of Daniel, but he didn't answer.

Another yoga instructor took me to the hospital, but it was too late. The baby died before we made it. The doctor gave me a drug and it was over by the end of the night."

The Liberty Bell expression—the agony he'd captured on camera—it was on her face again. A spasm of remorse choked him. She'd suffered the loss of a child and he'd teased her about her smile.

He crushed her against him and still couldn't hold her tight enough. If he could have drained her sadness into his veins, he'd have done it. Anything. He'd have done anything to take her pain away.

"What happened next?"

"I didn't want to leave my car at the office overnight, so my friend dropped me off there. I was cramping and bleeding, so I went up to the office to go to the bathroom. I had one foot out the door then I heard a moan. I followed the sound back to Daniel's office—"

"You worked with him?"

"He owned the agency." She closed her eyes and continued. "I walked in on him fucking my best friend Hillary on his desk. Right when I opened the door, he shouted, 'I'm coming, baby.'" Another dreary laugh tumbled out of her.

He balled his hands into fists. "You never told me it was your friend." Swear to God, if he ever ran into that jerk, he was going to beat him so hard he'd cough up bones. No wonder she didn't trust anyone. No wonder she was so scared.

"They're getting married on the baby's due date."

"How'd you end up in New York?"

"That night, I called Skip. He flew me there on the next flight. I didn't even change my clothes. I just left everything and took off."

"I don't blame you." He exhaled his frustration and hugged her as hard as he could. "Why didn't you tell me all this before?"

Her lips trembled. "Because sometimes it hurts so bad, I feel like I might die."

An urgent need to reassure her arose—the need to prove he wasn't anything like her pathetic ex. "Please don't worry, sweetheart." He held her tightly and caressed her hair. "I'd never do anything like that. None of it. You hear me? The cheating, the awful way he treated you? Never."

She shook her head. "I'm ovulating, Walker."

"Sorry, my Sex Ed teacher was a Baptist minister."

"I'm at the most fertile point in my cycle. And if I take a pregnancy test now, it wouldn't be accurate. We can't even find out for two more weeks."

The lady cycle and the mysteries of womanhood weren't something his grandma had taught him. Seemed like he should have been more nervous, but he was as sedate as a Sunday afternoon.

"Let's focus on the present," he said. "For now, we'll keep making art and making love. We'll open a different box of condoms, and at the end of the trip, we'll take the test. No point in worrying about it now. Just put it out of your mind until then. Everything'll be fine. You'll see."

Boy, he hoped to hell he was right.

**Soundtrack:** MS MR, "Hurricane"

On the second day of captivity, they ventured outside. The floodwater had receded in the parking garage, and the sun was out.

Beat-up bicycles, lawn chairs, and for-sale signs sailed down the street. A mammoth tree blocked the road. Walker took pictures, and a while later, cell reception came back on.

Callie sat on the tree rubbing her sore jaw, while he relayed the events to Skip. He told him about the Silver Dildo's damage and the puppy they'd saved. He mentioned they were low on gas, and therefore, battery power, and their food and water were running out.

Multiple "dudes" and "fucks" were overheard on the other end.

Something moved in her periphery. A baby stroller glided down the street and lodged against the tree right next to her. If you looked up "ominous sign" on Wikipedia, that would be the first example.

*"Why that dog is practically a Phi Beta Kappa. She can sit up and beg, and she can give her paw—I don't say she will, but she can."—Dorothy Parker*

**Soundtrack:** Johnny Nash, "I Can See Clearly Now"

Later in the day, the heat and humidity in the garage climbed to swamp-like temperatures. Things were starting to stink. Despite their disastrous conditions, Callie's spirits soared.

She'd finally opened up, told her story, and released a gargantuan amount of guilt. Before, she'd been too ashamed to share her sordid tale. Even Effie only had the bullet-point version.

For months, she'd been mentally flogging herself. Getting pregnant was her fault, she'd driven Daniel into Hillary's arms, and most tragically, she'd convinced herself she'd killed the baby by teaching yoga.

Deep down, she knew they were irrational thoughts, but she couldn't stop blaming herself. For months, she'd suffered alone.

But the minute she'd told Walker everything, all the guilt magically disappeared. He'd helped her see it wasn't her fault.

And for the first time in her life, she had a shoulder to cry on. Literally. And you know how much she hated when people misused that word.

Still, the threat of a second pregnancy nagged the back of her mind like a mosquito bite that refused to heal. But for now, for now, she had her lover's support and that made everything all right.

For the rest of the day, she and her support system stayed busy working on the blog and their personal projects. Eventually, the heat wore them down, and they took a long nap.

When she woke up, Walker was smiling down at her, holding the bar rag blindfold.

She smiled back and his dimples deepened. "Whatcha doing, Handsome?"

"Surprising you."

He tied the rag around her eyes then led her to the parking deck. When he removed the blindfold, an explosion of warm fuzzies filled her. Outside everything was decorated with the tacky beach crap from the wizard-head store. Shell candles flickered and palm tree lights glowed. The plastic flamingo was perched next to the two pornographic beach towels. He'd placed two plates of spaghetti and meatballs on top of their beer cooler.

She clapped and laughed. Even in the worst situations, he always made her laugh. "How romantic!" She leapt into his arms and gave him a passionate thank-you kiss—because she was—so incredibly thankful—for him.

After they ate, she played tunes from the seventies' songbook, and Walker threw a ball of rolled up socks to Leonard. When the puppy came galloping back an hour later with half a torn up sock, Walker patted him on the head. "Way to go, Mr. Smarty Paws."

Leonard feverishly licked his hand.

"What are we going to do with him?" she asked.

"Reckon I'll keep him. How's that sound, Len? You want to hang out with me?" The puppy clawed his shins, attempting to scale his legs up to his lap.

"But where are you going to keep him?" Specifically, where was he going to live after the trip? And where did she fit in?

"Not sure, yet."

His indecision sank her spirits. He probably hadn't even considered a future with her. A tiny bud of panic sprouted, but she pushed aside her fears because she didn't have to worry about it. Yet.

# Chapter 27

## Movin'

### Texas, New Mexico and Arizona

**Soundtrack:** Kristy MacColl, "In These Shoes"

**Soundtrack:** America, "A Horse with No Name"

**Soundtrack:** Commodores, "Easy"

After three days, they finally broke out of the parking garage prison and made it to Houston. Miraculously, the dealership fixed the camper in two days.

During that time, they loaded up on supplies and did laundry.

For mentioning the veterinarian on the RoadStream blog, Leonard Nimoy received a free exam, shots, and a microchip.

A local pet store sponsored another post and gave him a bath, fancy organic food, way too many toys, and a bed, which he didn't need since he slept with them.

Callie also bought the puppy several smart-ass t-shirts.

As for the mobile tour—it was a resounding success. Thanks to Hot PR Chick, Skip's latest hire, mainstream media picked up their hurricane puppy story, and RoadStream sales skyrocketed as a result.

Once the camper was ready, the three of them piled in the Silver Dildo and raced through Texas. Since they were behind schedule, they drove longer hours and stopped less. And instead of writing long blog posts, they shot video clips and made a montage of their travels through the next three states—one version for the client and another for themselves.

Theirs started off with her riding a mechanical bull in a honkey-tonk bar. They lowered the speed to the same setting as a grocery store horsey ride, and Callie waved her hand overhead and rolled her pelvis in a slow sexual circle.

Later, she practiced her bull-riding skills on him.

In Austin, they swam in Barton Springs. Afterwards, he surprised his girl by hiring a mariachi band to serenade their picnic in Zilker Park. After they ate, they danced together with Leonard Nimoy sandwiched between them.

At a dude ranch somewhere in the middle of Texas, he filmed her galloping her horse off into the sunset. Over her shoulder, she shot him the sexiest look ever. Riding a horse with an erection was a mighty painful experience.

The next day, he dressed in a hat and boots and sat in front of the ranch, mimicking James Dean in the movie *Giant*. She burst into the frame and straddled him, wearing her new pink cowboy boots and nothing else. Then she rode *him* off into the sunset.

Callie had custom t-shirts made in a truck stop gift shop on the Texas state line. Hers featured a taco over each boob. Leonard Nimoy wore a tiny shirt that said *you bet your nalgas I bite*. And Walker's shirt said *mi verga es grande y peluda*. He had no clue what that meant.

Dressed in their t-shirts, the three of them posed for a family picture in front of a giant saguaro cactus shaped like a penis and balls.

Later that night, they went to a Mexican restaurant. "The waitress just translated my shirt while you were in the john," he said to Callie.

"And?"

He squinted. "My cock is big and hairy?"

"Well, it is."

In Roswell, New Mexico, they used dental floss to hang a UFO fashioned out of Leonard Nimoy's Frisbee. Midway through the scene, the puppy jumped up on the table and ran off with the spaceship in his mouth.

One day, he filmed Callie naked in bed, singing and playing "Easy Like Sunday Morning" on the ukulele, while Leonard Nimoy yelped and howled along.

He watched that clip at least three times a day.

In the mountains of New Mexico, he begged her to pose nude by a freshwater lake. Under the sun, she arched her back in a sexy pose, right as a condor-sized bird flew by and crapped on her tits.

He collapsed on the ground in a fit of laughter. In a snit, Callie flung bird shit on his face.

They left out the shower scene.

Later that night, they tried to film their moonlight swim, but Leonard knocked over the tripod, and the camera shot five minutes of him licking his balls.

On the way through Arizona, they attempted to film a music video. She made a tiny saddle out of a cardboard box and strapped it to Leonard Nimoy's back. On her ukulele, she played "A Horse with No Name," and he beat a spoon on a frying pan and sang the "la la la la" part. In the background, the horse/puppy peed on tumbleweeds and chased his tail.

They finally gave up after twenty takes because they couldn't stop cracking up.

There were many more poetic moments they shared, but most of the time, they were so absorbed in each other they forgot to capture it on film.

# Chapter 28

## Worryin'

### Flagstaff, Arizona

**Soundtrack:** Chet Faker, "Talk is Cheap"

*E*arly morning before sunrise, Walker tied the bar towel around Callie's eyes.

"We really need to invest in a better blindfold," she said, shivering in the chilly desert air. The day before, the temperature had been in the hundreds, but it'd dropped sixty-degrees during the night.

"Don't rag on the rag, lady." He brushed a swift kiss on her lips. "Stay put. I'll be right back."

It was dead quiet wherever they were. A few minutes later, he returned and steered her toward a hissing sound. "Hold still. I'm gonna pick you up."

"Don't drop me."

"What? Think I can't lift your tiny butt?"

"Considering all the times you've held me up while we fucked in the shower, I'm pretty sure you're strong enough."

A man who wasn't Walker laughed.

"Shh! Jesus, Blue." He hoisted her up and set her down next to a padded railing.

"Why didn't you tell me someone was here?" she whisper-cried.

"Didn't think you'd shout out the details of our sex life," he whisper-cried back.

Actually, if there were a megaphone handy, she'd shout it to the world. Maybe clean it up a bit first and say something like, *I'm having the best sex of my life with the most wonderful man ever.*

His finger traveled across her bottom lip. "What are you smiling about?"

"Just going over the details again."

"Before you blurt out anything else . . . Calliope, meet Jack. Say hi, Jack."

"Not a good time to use the word hijack, buddy," the guy said, detonating a full-bodied guffaw.

The ground moved and she grabbed the railing. "Where are we?"

He wrapped his warm body around hers. "A few more minutes then I'll take off the rag. I promise it'll be worth the wait."

Something clattered and the hissing grew louder. Walker's camera beeped several times then he finally untied the rag.

Above, a burst of fire filled a giant yellow orb. "A hot-air balloon!" Covering her mouth with both hands, she peeked over the basket. Below, the Grand Canyon spread out forever, its brilliant indigos and reds growing lighter by the minute.

While she watched the sun rise, a rhapsody of emotions pumped through her—skin tingling elation, heart-thumping excitement, and bubbles of tenderness that clogged her throat and filled her eyes with tears.

"You scared?" Walker asked.

She replied by cupping his face and mashing her mouth against his.

"Get a room!" The pilot chuckled.

Behind them, Hemingway's twin grinned through a white beard. He popped open a bottle of champagne and pulled out a basket of food.

But she was hungry for something different—for the beautiful man by her side.

No one spoke. And except for her heartbeat and the burner firing, there was no other sound.

She gave her lover a look that silently conveyed how much the moment meant. And he met her gaze and smiled back, quietly telling her how much her happiness meant in return. With them, words were just unnecessary noise.

*"Time doth flit; oh shit!"—Dorothy Parker*

**Soundtrack:** Robin Thicke, "Dreamworld"

They dragged their pillows and blankets outside that night and made love under the desert sky. Afterwards, she closed her eyes and caressed Walker's skin, reading his body like braille. She read sunshine and peach pie, blue silk and bubbles, pink drinks and lumpy Piña Coladas, the Rolling Stones and the One-Night Stands.

With Walker nothing felt the same. He'd turbocharged her senses. Sights, sounds, tastes, sex—he amplified everything.

Speaking of sex, with him it was downright evolutionary. She'd gone from Cro-Magnon Daniel, a mediocre lover at best, to superhuman Walker, who could dampen her panties with a dimpled grin.

One minute he was dirty and wild, and the next, he was tender and loving. That morning he'd eaten her out on the kitchen table then wiped his mouth and thanked her for breakfast.

Another time, he'd tied her up with Leonard's leash and peppered sweet feathery kisses all over her while they made love.

A few days before, he'd bent her over the bed, spanked her, and fucked her like a porn star.

Walker was pleasure personified. And it wasn't just because he was great in bed. The whole Rhodes package turned her on. His charm and warmth, his talent and intelligence, his passion and humor—everything about him rocked her world.

He made life luminous.

"Watcha thinking about, Bluebell?"

"That I can't get enough of you. I want to make Walker smoothies in the morning and wear a Walker skin suit to work."

"You scare me."

She pretended to pout.

He grabbed her bottom lip. "Just kidding, nutter. Lie next to me and look at the stars."

She stroked Leonard's satiny cow ear while she gazed at the Milky Way, splattered across the sky like white paint on black velvet. A dog barked in the distance and the puppy raised his head.

"Ah, this is so nice," she said. "I've only slept under the stars one other time—in music camp in the sixth grade."

"Bet you had pigtails," he said.

"I did!"

"I knew it. I can totally see you back then, all scrawny and scrappy. Bet you were a tomboy."

"I was! And my sister was the girly girl. She kissed the boys, and I kicked them."

"Uh-huh, figured as much."

"At that same camp, I intercepted her love note. The only love note I've ever received, and it wasn't for me." Adding a pinch of poignancy, she wiped a fake tear and sniffled.

"What'd it say?"

"Sadly, it was the most unromantic piece-of-crap ever written. It had ridiculous yes-or-no questions. Do you like ice cream, yes or no? Do you like Chopin? Remember it was a music camp. Effie hated Chopin. What else? Oh, do you like brown eyes? And so on. At the end he wrote, do you like me? And then, do you want to make out behind the boathouse?"

"Loving ice cream is definitely a prerequisite for making out behind the boathouse. So did you give it to her?"

"Of course not. Why would I do that?" That sounded slightly sadistic so she elaborated. "I checked everything no, except the make-out question, and gave it back."

"Did your sister make out with him?"

"Yes!" She blew on her knuckles and rubbed them on her bare breast. "Just call me a pre-teen matchmaker."

They chuckled together. "I've never gotten a love letter either."

"No way! I don't believe you."

"It's true. Girls ran from me when I was in junior high. Literally. And I know how much you hate that word. I asked a girl to a dance and she just took off."

"You're joking?" He wasn't *that* frightening back then. Okay, a maybe a little.

"Yep. First and last girl I ever asked to a dance."

"Aw, that's sad."

"Girls were so mean to me back then."

"Bet if they saw you now, they'd run right to your bed."

"And I'd chase 'em right back out because you're already in it."

All at once grief grabbed her by the throat. It was probably the first and last time she'd sleep under the stars with him. Every moment was a first and last on that trip. "Walker?"

"Mm-hmm?"

"What happens when this ends? When we get back to New York?"

He rose to his elbow. "What do you want to happen?"

"Nice way to evade the question."

His finger drew circles around her breasts. "I don't want it to end."

"But what about work? You're leaving."

"Let's not think about that right now."

The question that'd been plaguing her bubbled to the surface. "What if I'm pregnant?"

"I don't know," he said quietly.

"I can't get rid of a baby."

"Then I guess we'll have us a baby."

"Us?"

The space between his brows puckered. "You think I'd take off and leave you with my kid?"

"You said you didn't want children."

He sat up and rubbed the back of his neck. "Look, this is scary stuff we're talking about. You're right. I never imagined myself having kids. But I would never leave my child without a daddy."

But would he leave her? Of course he would. He wasn't the type to settle down. He'd get too bored.

No matter how hard she tried, she couldn't picture having a family with him. Not because she couldn't imagine him as a father, but because he'd made it clear he didn't want to be one.

And that caused a rift in her heart as wide as the Grand Canyon.

Callie woke up the next morning and found a folded-up note on her pillow.

*Dear Bluebell,*
*Do you like lumpy Piña Coladas? Yes or no?*
*Do you like getting caught in hurricanes? Yes or no?*
*Do you like the smooth sounds of the seventies? Yes or no?*
*Do you like champagne? Yes or no?*
*Do you like banana splits? Yes or no?*
*Do you like making love at midnight? Yes or no?*
*Do you like the Boy in the Plastic Bubble? Yes or no?*
*Do you like female pop singers? Yes or no?*
*Do you want to make out on the kitchen table later? Yes or no?*

She circled everything yes and passed the letter back to him.

"What the—? You like female pop singers?" Feigning outrage, he crumpled the paper and threw it on the ground. "I'm not making out with you."

When he wasn't looking, she smoothed out her very first love note and hid it in her suitcase.

# Chapter 25

## Strippin'

### Las Vegas, Nevada

*"What fresh hell is this?"—Dorothy Parker*

Somewhere she'd read that homicide rates went up during heat waves. On the day they shot the commercial, the plastic orange detour cones melted into puddles on the street. Anyone would plot murder in those conditions. Add a few dickheads to the extreme temperatures, and you'd be planning a first-degree killing spree like Callie was.

First on her list? The client. Shocking, right? Double Dickhead insisted the commercial be shot on the Vegas strip. Outside. Midday. In Las Vegas. In a hundred and fifteen-degree heat.

As if burning everybody alive weren't enough of a dick move, he'd also rewritten the script. We're not talking little changes here and there. He rewrote the entire thing . . . with jokes. Hilarious jokes. Hilarious, as in they were so bad they were funny.

Literally (and she never used that word incorrectly), she'd put blood, sweat, and tears into rebranding that company over the last several weeks, and Dick ruined it all by writing canned humor into the script.

She left Skip five urgent messages. "Call me ASAP. We've got Dick problems."

"The client just replaced the actors with Vegas strippers. Just thought you should know."

"Dick wrote himself into the script. Call me, motherfucker."

"If you don't call me back, I'm posting a blog article about that time in college you stole that kid's weed and got your ass handed to you by a bunch of sixth graders."

"Skip, if you ever tell anyone I had anything to do with this commercial, I'll tell Steven Segal you snuck into his party and pissed in his pool."

He never called back.

*Meanwhile, back in hell . . .*

Just like the last shoot, Barbie plastered herself to Walker. If she didn't have a life-threatening reason for her clingy behavior this time, Callie was about to give her one.

As usual, Walker didn't seem to notice the big-boobed tumor on his body. Therefore, he was third on her hit list.

Only a frozen daiquiri by the pool and four naked men fanning her face with palm fronds would have quelled her murderous wrath by that point.

She settled for a bottle of water and conversation with Eli. He'd presented another soundtrack to the client that morning, and of course, Dick thought it was awful—mostly because it was good.

"Sup?" Eli said.

She sat next to him on the curb. "Not much. Just dying of heat exhaustion."

"Yeah, whose fucking idea was it to film a commercial in the desert?"

"I'll give you a tiny guess." She pointed her water bottle at the client.

"That guy is such a tool. If he touches Sabrina again, I'm gonna beat the shit out of him."

"I'd like to beat the shit out of her." Surprising how light and airy her tone sounded, considering how serious she was.

He turned away.

She poured water over her head. "So Eli, do you have a girlfriend?"

He chuffed a laugh and sat back on his hands.

"Girlfriends then?" She emphasized the plural. "No? A strapping young man like you? I thought you'd have a different woman for every orifice."

The corner of his lip quirked.

"My sister's moving to New York. I bet she'd clean my toilet for a year if I set her up with you. She's a musician too. Looks a lot like me, but I'm cuter."

A shadow descended over them. She looked up and found Walker staring down at them with a frown on his face. He gave a curt nod to Eli. "Can I talk to you for a second, Callie?"

"I'm busy."

"Now."

Since Eli looked suspicious, she stood and followed Walker down the street. "Holyshitmas! Slow down. I don't feel like jogging in thousand-degree heat."

He glanced over his shoulder and pulled her into a cigarette butt-laden casino entrance. Before he even said hello, he gave her a toe-curling kiss. "I can't wait to get out of this hot mess." He pressed his sweaty forehead against hers. "I've got one wheel down and an axel dragging, but the end is in sight."

He took off his glasses and stared directly into her eyes. "Blue? Is Eli coming on to you?"

Ever seen that carnival game where you pound a lever with a sledgehammer and a ball shoots up and hits a bell? His question was the sledgehammer, and the bell was her head.

She shoved him with both hands. "I'm sorry. Did I hear that right? You're asking about Eli when you've got Sabrina wrapped around you like a boa constrictor?"

He stroked his hands down her arms. "Now don't go nuts on me. That's not what I'm saying—"

The director squawked on the walkie-talkie in his back pocket.

"Damn. I've got to go. Meet me in my room in one hour and I'll explain everything. Then I'll eat your pussy and maybe you'll give me a blowjob in return. Later on, let's go for a quick swim on the rooftop then fuck the rest of this day away in the air conditioning." All this was said as if he were reading a grocery list instead of a pornographic agenda

After a quick kiss and an ass pinch, he left her in the sweltering heat with a flaming vagina and a burning rage.

*"Photography deals exquisitely with appearances, but nothing is what it appears to be."—Duane Michals*

**Soundtrack:** Fantastic Negrito: "Working Poor"

Walker had spent the day shoveling out more bullshit than a tractor at a ten-day rodeo. He was over it. The heat, the client, Sabrina, her boy toy, advertising—all of it. If he didn't get between Callie's creamy thighs in the next five minutes, he was going to go apeshit.

He hoped she'd calmed down some. The way she'd looked at him earlier made a hornet look cuddly. But he'd iron things out straightaway.

He just barely stepped out of shower and got his pants on when she knocked. Dying to kiss her sweet lips, he swung open the door, "I can't wait to fuuuuuck."

Was he the unluckiest bastard in the world or what? It wasn't Callie at the door. It was Sabrina. And she was holding a champagne bucket and wearing the trashiest lingerie he'd ever seen. She didn't have on enough clothes to wad a shotgun.

A saran-wrap bustier cinched her enormous tits together and forced her nipples over the top. And her fishnet panties showcased her waxed pussy for him, God, and any other poor bastard who happened to be walking down the hall.

"What. In. Thee. Hell." He looked both ways for witnesses then dragged her in and slammed the door.

"I'm so dumb," she said with a nervous tittering laugh. "I like, locked myself out of my room, getting ice."

"You went out in the hallway in that?"

"I was in a hurry. The machine's right outside my room."

"Why'd you come here?" It didn't even matter why. His ass was grass no matter what. Full-on panic mode, he paced the room, gripping his hair.

"You're, like, only four doors down. I thought—"

"Have you lost your damn mind? You have any idea what Eli's gonna do if he sees you coming out of my room?" He didn't even want to think about what Callie was going to do.

"Call the front desk and get your naked ass out of here before all hell breaks loose. And for God's sake, wrap a towel around yourself."

If she didn't get out of there, Callie was going to string his balls up and use them for target practice.

Just then, someone knocked on the door. *Perfect. Just perfect.* Blood pressure hammering in his head, he didn't move a muscle. Maybe if he stayed quiet, she'd go away and come back after doodle brain got her door opened.

Leonard Nimoy yipped at the door. "Shut the hell up," he whisper-yelled at the dog.

Another knock.

The Queen of the Shittiest Timing in the World hollered out, "What's your room number, Walkie?"

Callie started kicking the door.

"Who is that?" Sabrina seethed. "Get rid of them. I'm naked!"

Perhaps his girlfriend hadn't heard his moronic coworker. Who was he kidding? A deaf person could have heard that loudmouth. Fists clutched, he air-strangled Sabrina's neck.

The door was now under attack. If he didn't open up, Callie was going to jam a battering ram through it.

Muttering a silent prayer to the God of Testicles, he took a deep breath and opened the door. He spread his limbs wide, trying to hide the naked woman in his room. "Hey, sweetheart."

A nice little afterthought occurred to him right then—he wasn't wearing a shirt. The scene looked bad. Real bad. We're talking breakup bad.

She ducked under his arm.

"Now Blue, before you—"

Sabrina screamed, "Oh my God, why did you let her in here?"

Callie slapped him so hard his teeth rattled then shot out the door, running down the hallway hell bent for leather. He chased after her, bobbing and weaving like NFL running back, and the only way to stop her was to tackle her like one.

They went crashing to the floor. As predicted, she tried to take out his balls. "Stop. Just— *Ow*, shit! I swear on my grandmother's life nothing happened." He got ahold of her wrists and pinned her legs with his knees. But a hand broke free and nearly twisted his nipple clean off. "Ouch! Goddammit!"

She thrashed like a wild animal.

"Stop! And just listen to me. That dumbass locked herself out. She's with Eli, not me."

Her body stilled, the rabid fury leveling off into conflicted contempt.

"Sabrina's screwing Eli, not me," he shouted. "She was getting ice and locked herself out, wearing that getup. She came to my room to call the front desk. If you won't kick my nuts off, I'll take you back, and you can ask her yourself."

Tears splashed down her quivering lips.

"Aw, Blue, don't cry." He brushed away her waterworks. "Honey, this is just a horrible, awful, terrible coincidence. You've gotta believe me."

That just made her cry harder. He climbed off her and held out a hand, but she refused to take it. "Please baby, trust me. I'd never hurt you."

She rose to her feet and dragged her feet down the hall.

Madder than a pack of wild dogs on a three legged cat, he marched to his room. Sabrina had messed things up again.

At the door, he blew out a hot breath and turned the knob. "Damnation!" he growled. "She locked us out. Boy, she's on a bullet train through stupid town. Paying attention to this?" he said to Callie. "See how easy it is to do?"

She glowered at the door as if she were willing it to go up in flames.

"Open up, Brainiac!" He banged his fist on the door.

Tits jiggling and nipples not the slightest bit hidden—Sabrina flung it open and shrieked, "Oh my Gawd, why did you bring her back here?"

The minuscule amount of patience he had left dissipated into a fine red mist. If he hadn't had to restrain Callie right then, he'd have booted his friend right out the window.

"Sabrina Driver, if you had a half a brain, you'd be dangerous. Get out of my way." He shouldered past her, dragging Callie behind him.

"I don't know which is nastier? Your outfit? Or the way you just treated my girlfriend? You mucked things up good between us last time with your brilliant idea to fend off the client, and now you've done it again."

Sabrina's mouth dropped open so wide it looked like a train tunnel. "Wait? Are you two together? I mean together, together?"

He applauded her brilliance. "Lord, you really are a super-genius. All right, Einstein, mind explaining to Callie why you're in my room dressed like that?"

She scowled and shook her head.

He turned to Callie. "Sabrina and Eli are sleeping together. Dimwit here likes to make him jealous by flirting with other men, so he dumped her. Smart man. But they hooked up again in Orlando."

"Walkie, stop," Sabrina whined. "Don't say another word!"

He ignored her and went on. "She was planning on surprising him with a bottle of champagne and her dental floss underwear, but locked herself out instead. Did I miss anything?"

She hung her head, not saying a word.

"Now I want you to tell Callie we're not sleeping together."
The account manager snorted. "What? Are you serious?"
She cracked up. "Sleep with you? Gross."

He closed his eyes and counted to ten. "Get out of here,
Sabrina."

"Gawd, you're being really mean."

"Oh, I'm sorry, please get the hell out of my room."

"*Tchah,* can I, like, borrow your bathrobe, first?"

He stomped to the bathroom, ripped it off the hook, and
threw it at her.

Finally making herself decent, she slinked to the door,
looking every bit as embarrassed as she should have. At the
last second, she spun around and begged, "Please don't say
anything. Eli doesn't want anyone to know we're . . . um, you
know."

"I don't blame him. I'd be embarrassed to admit it myself."
He slammed the door in her face.

It felt like he'd eaten a bucket of bait. "Say something, Blue."
Leonard Nimoy helped him beg by pawing her ankle. Then the
canine Benedict Arnold jumped next to her and gave him a
look that said *better your balls than mine.*

If she broke up with him, Sabrina had better get the hell
out of town. He knelt between her legs. "Darlin', please talk to
me."

She kissed his forehead. "Get up, silly, and lie next to me."

When he snuggled up tight beside her, his heart started
pumping again.

"Why didn't you tell me about her? In Florida?" she asked.

"I tried, baby."

"You've never been with her? Ever?"

"Nope, never."

"But you call her Hot Pants?"

"Sabrina and I were roommates after I broke up with
Claudia. She got me the job at Shimura. As for the Hot Pants, I

gave her that nickname after she burned her ass on the stove, having sex with one of her dates."

"All this time"—she pressed her palms to her eyes—"I thought . . ."

"Don't cry, baby. Nothing happened."

"I thought you were sleeping with her. I've been worrying about it for weeks. I'm so sorry."

He nuzzled her neck. "Easy mistake to make with her acting like a fool. Jesus, when she showed up at my door dressed like that"—he shook his head and blew out an angry sigh—"It's like the porch light's on but nobody's home. She doesn't think, she just does. Same thing in Orlando."

"But why'd you ask if I was flirting with Eli?"

"Sabrina's insecure. She thought he was coming on to you."

He paused, not entirely sure if he should admit the next part. "I guess I was a little jealous, too."

She stared at him then laughed. "Have you looked in the mirror lately? Do you have any idea how amazing you are? Inside and out? Not to mention, you have The-Most-Beautiful-Cock-In-The-World.™"

"TM?" He grinned. "Did you trademark my cock?"

"Of course. It deserves its own brand and maybe an athletic cup sponsorship. But I'm not finished. What about the others? Liberty? Avery? What's-her-face? The receptionist?"

"You're the only one I've been with at the agency."

She raised her brows and shook her head.

"You look as confused as a cow on Astroturf."

"I don't get it. Women throw themselves at you. And you're so . . . player-ish with them. This whole time I thought you were—"

"A manwhore. I know."

"But why? Why didn't you set me straight? Same with the club that night? Why didn't you tell me the truth?"

"You wouldn't have believed me."

"That's ridiculous. Not saying anything is as bad as lying. Don't do it again."

"I promise. Boy Scout's honor." He flashed the sign.

"Nice try. That's the Vulcan greeting."

"Whatever. I promise it won't happen again."

She reached for the phone and dialed room service. "Do you have banana splits? Great. And extra whipped cream please. We'll be indisposed for about forty-five minutes. Could you bring it up then? Thank you."

She didn't look confused anymore. Now she looked like a jungle cat hunting for prey—eyes shining bright, cheeks flushed, lips all wet.

"Indisposed? What are you up to, naughty girl?"

She straddled him and unbuttoned his pants. "Pretending you're a manwhore."

"In only forty-five minutes?" He helped her take off his clothes.

"That's for the blow job." She stroked him nice and slow. "The banana split's for after."

He laid back and sighed. "I've been waiting my whole life to hear a woman use the words blow job and banana split in the same sentence."

She smiled around his cock.

"Jesus, I'm not gonna last five minutes."

"Hmm?" She pulled him out of her mouth. "You want me to call them back?"

"Hell, no, get those lips back on me. I'll use the other forty on you."

# Chapter 30

## Fallin'

### Yosemite National Park, California

**Soundtrack:** alt-J, "Pusher"

*a*s Effie's arrival drew closer, Callie's jaw pain worsened. What if her sister had lied about being clean? After all, that's what she did—lie and get high.

All night she stayed up, fretting her sister would show up wasted and embarrass her in front of Walker.

That would be a minor offense compared to the other things she'd done. For instance, she'd stolen Callie's ID and drained her hard-earned savings. The same day, she'd also hocked her surfboard, her bike, her guitar, and her jewelry. All told, she made off with about sixty grand worth of Callie's shit.

To this day, she still resented Effie for not selling her precious violin that was worth a small fortune.

Effie had bled her emotional and financial resources so dry she'd had no choice but to sever contact. And cutting off her twin felt like cutting out part of her heart.

Though she talked to her almost every day, it'd been almost two years since she'd last seen her sister. Which made it all the more troubling when she couldn't bring herself to greet her.

Rather than question her bizarre behavior, Walker offered to welcome her sister. When Effie arrived, he held open the car door and helped her out. In slow motion, she shook out her long blond hair as if she were in a shampoo commercial and delivered him a dazzling smile.

Her body was no longer emaciated, and her skin had a healthy glow. She didn't seem strung out or raggedy. On the contrary, from her chill demeanor and carriage, one might have mistaken her for a yogi, rather than a former drug addict.

For the first time in years, Effie looked . . . *healthy.*

Callie let out her breath and darted out the door. They crashed into each other's arms and laughed through their tears.

Effie pulled back to examine her. "What the—? What happened to your hair?"

Walker gawked at the twins. "Mercy, it's creepy how much you two look alike." His eyes darted from sister to sister. "Blue, is that what your natural hair's like?"

"Hers was longer," Effie said. "Down to the middle of her back. Give me the name of the hairdresser who did that to you. I'm gonna kick their ass."

She glared at her sister. "I needed a change." The day after she'd moved to New York, she'd made an appointment with Skip's hairdresser Colt, a man who wore more makeup than her, and asked for a whole new look. He begged her not to cut it—got down on his knees even—but three hours later, she'd stepped out of the salon with a chin-length black bob and a new tougher identity.

"I like your hair," Walker said, smoothing his hand over her head. "The color makes your eyes stand out."

As if she'd suddenly been cured of blindness, Effie's eyes went wide. "Whoa," she said to Walker. "You are beautiful. Callie mentioned you were hot, but . . . wow."

He stuffed his hands in his pockets and gave her a shy aw-shucks smile.

Her sister rolled up to him, wrapped her arms around his waist, and laid a cheek upon his chest. "Oh, he's so tall and tight and dreamy." She sniffed. "And you smell fantastic. What is that, lemons?"

Not hesitating for a second, Walker gave her a big bear hug back. It felt like Callie had just seen a tearjerker movie with a happy ending.

Effie had never really learned appropriate social skills. She never had the chance. From the time she was four, she practiced violin fourteen hours a day.

Also, she probably had a touch of undiagnosed Asperger's. Except hers was reversed. Instead of shrinking away from touch like others on the autism spectrum, she threw herself at people.

Personal space wasn't a concept Effie really understood. She routinely hugged UPS men, strangers on the street, and convenience store employees, to name a few of the victims.

Likewise, Effie didn't have a mental filter. If you thought Callie was bad, Effie was a thousand times worse.

Most reacted as though she were insane. But Walker just squished her in a hug without a second thought.

Leonard Nimoy trotted over to say hello. She picked him up and kissed him on the mouth. "Wook at you, you wittle cutie!"

"Uh, Eff, he just spent the last fifteen minutes licking his ball sack."

"Couldn't be any worse than smoking. Speaking of which . . . you mind?" She dug out her cigarettes, lit one up, then blew smoke on everyone as she surveyed the mountain peaks. "Kinda looks like we're in a Bob Ross painting," she said.

Walker laughed. "You mean because it's so pretty it looks like we're in a cheesy oil painting?"

"Do I detect a fellow Bob Ross fan?" she asked.

"You betcha. Favorite after school show on PBS."

"His voice is so soothing," Effie said. "Not to mention, the man said mind-boggling things. His quotes are like Zen Koens." She scrolled through her phone. "'We tell people sometimes, we're like drug dealers—we come into town and get everybody absolutely addicted to painting.'"

Walker chuckled. "We don't make mistakes. We just have happy accidents."

"Wow, I'm thoroughly impressed with your Bob Ross knowledge. The man was brilliant."

"I dressed up as him for Halloween in college."

She laughed. "That's awesome."

Callie loved Halloween. Maybe they'd dress up together next year. A subtle pang in her chest reminded her not to think that far ahead.

"Here's another one," Effie said. "'There's nothing wrong with having a tree as a friend. Trees cover up a multitude of sins.'"

"'How do you make a round circle with a square knife?'" he chimed in.

All three chortled then let out aftermath-of-a-good-laugh sighs.

"Sooo . . ." Effie said. "What have you kids been up to today?"

They exchanged secret smiles. They'd spent the afternoon in bed.

"I see, so you've been hiking a lot?"

That made Walker laugh.

Effie took another hit and regarded him for a moment. "Did Callie tell you I was a crackhead, Walker?"

"I thought you were a violinist?"

She blinked then burst out laughing.

He covered his eyes. "That's nuts. Y'all even have the same laugh."

Effie smiled. "I love him, Cal."

"I love him, too."

Except the wind rushing through the pines, everything went dead silent. Because the words had so effortlessly tumbled from her mouth, it took her a minute to figure out why two pairs of blue eyes were staring at her.

*Fuuuuuck.* Did she just tell her brand spanking new boyfriend of six-ish weeks that she loved him? Any minute now and he'd run screaming for the hills.

Effie cleared her throat. "So what can I do to help? Want me to build a fire? I'm amazing at lighting shit up."

She could just kiss her sister right then.

"Nope, y'all kick back and relax. I'm fixin' to make dinner."

"Even the way you talk is sexy. Let me know if you ever want to have a threesome with twins." She said this as if they routinely had sex with men together.

Walker glanced at Callie for help.

"She's kidding," she said, squinting at Effie.

"Phew." He flung pretend sweat off his brow and made a beeline for the camper. "I'll let you two catch up."

"Nice to meet you, Walker. Enjoy the new masturbation material."

"Yep. Will do."

*"Be still with yourself until the object of your attention affirms your presence."—Minor White*

**Soundtrack:** Jake Shimabukuro and Charles Yang, "While My Guitar Gently Weeps" (YouTube)

Walker left the sisters alone and went for a long hike. While he wandered, he whistled, feeling like a bird flying over a mountaintop, his heart soaring with joy over Callie's accidental declaration of love.

Since then, as crazy as it sounded, he couldn't think of anything he'd rather do than father her child.

As if the universe sensed what was on his mind, the trail opened up into a bluebell-filled valley.

In no time, he gathered a bouquet and rushed back to camp. The sisters were huddled together at the picnic table. He kissed Callie on the neck and gave her the flowers. "Wild bluebells, for my wild Bluebell."

"They're gorgeous." She threw her arms around him and thanked him with a kiss that made goosebumps rise on his skin.

"Yo," Effie said. "I'm still here."

"Better get used to it. I can't keep my hands off your sister."

Later that night, Callie went inside to prepare dessert. The second she was out of earshot, Effie drilled him. "What are your intentions with my sister, young man?"

He chuckled. "Uh, yes, ma'am. I'd like your permission to court your daughter."

Her expression sobered. "I'm serious, Walker. She's really fragile."

"Sure we're talking about the same person? The woman inside who's tougher than a one-eared alley cat?"

"She puts on a good act."

He scratched the scruff on his cheek. "You think she's not being real with me?"

"I think she's terrified you're going to hurt her."

"Did she tell you that?"

"No, but I know her."

He stood and dropped another log on the fire. Sparks flew up and snapped. Callie's twin stared at him, waiting for an answer.

"I'm in love with her, Effie."

"I know. I gather you haven't told her yet?"

No, he hadn't, because she'd flip out and start predicting the end. "See, your sister's kinda like holding a grape seed"— he pinched together his thumb and forefinger—"if you squeeze too tight, she'll shoot out of your hand. She scares easily, and if I pressure her, she'll think someone else is trying to run her life. I know it sounds dumb, but she has to say it first. And I'm not talking about what happened this afternoon. She needs to say it when means it."

Effie bounced over and hugged him. "Too bad you don't have a twin. I want one of you for myself."

"Hey now, I'm taken."

"Your girlfriend in there? The one who's probably eating all the chocolate? She's my heart and soul, not to mention, she saved my life. I haven't been worthy of her love for a long time, but I'm trying to make up for that. So if you hurt her, I'll kill you." Based on the cold blue lasers cutting through him, she wasn't kidding around.

"The last thing I'd ever do is hurt her. And sweetheart, you're worthy of everyone's love, not just your sister's."

Her mouth opened then quickly lowered back to pensive position. Though the sisters had virtually the same eyes, Effie's looked haunted—even more so than Callie's at the beginning of the trip. God knows what she must have experienced as an addict.

She hid her quivering lips under her teeth. "Thank you, Walker."

"For what?" He stood and patted her shoulder. "I'm gonna go see what your sister's up to."

"Is that code for making out?"

He winked. "You're a pretty smart lady."

"Hurry up. I'm hungry for dessert. Sweets are how us former addicts get off, you know."

After they ate piles of s'mores, the sisters put on a show—Effie on the violin and Callie on ukulele. They played "While My Guitar Gently Weeps." At one point he had to get up and stoke the fire so they wouldn't see *him* gently weeping.

When everyone went to bed, he tried like crazy to be quiet, but when Callie's pussy tightened and pulsed around him, he roared out, "Fuck, you feel good."

"I hear you, assholes!" Effie yelled. She climbed down the ladder and stomped to the door. "I'm going out for a cigarette. Let me know when you're done."

"Better take a sleeping bag," he said. "You might be out there all night."

*"Only photograph what you love"*—*Tim Walker*

**Soundtrack:** Time For Three & Jake Shimabukuro, "Happy Day"

*The golden hour.* The last hour of sunlight when everything has a warm glow. The time of day when most photographers get a hard-on. That's when he took the pictures.

Clouds puffed in the sky like pink cotton candy. And the waterfall behind billowed down the canyon like melted butterscotch.

Both dressed in white, the sisters looked like fairytale princesses against the mystical backdrop.

He captured hundreds of images of the bewitching twins. Together, apart—it didn't matter—the camera loved them.

He loved them.

They were Yin and Yang—different, but the same. While both had the same arctic eyes, Callie's were lighter and more hopeful, and Effie's seemed darker and wizened.

Their hair—short black feathers versus golden blond ropes—added more disparity.

Even their postures were distinct—Callie's pin-straight and edgy and Effie's slouchy and almost broken.

He captured the nuances of their relationship as well. Their expressions as they spoke their secret twin language, their laughs, their embedded desolation after a terrible childhood—he caught it all.

One shot after the other, drums beat in his chest. Every time he released the shutter, he thought, *this is it! This is the one.*

For weeks Callie had been pushing him to tell a story with his photography. "Give people more than a pretty picture. Make them wonder."

Now he knew what she meant.

Later that night, he couldn't sleep. He was too drunk with excitement. He'd been waiting for that moment his entire life. That moment when he'd congratulate himself on a job well done. That moment when he could honestly say, *goddamn, I'm good.*

That glorious day, on that magical mountaintop, with the incredible woman he loved, he'd reached it. The pinnacle. The goddamn-I'm-good moment. And he'd never felt so high in his life. No joke. From then on out, he had a non-stop buzz.

*"Last night, while I lay thinking here, some Whatifs crawled inside my ear, and pranced and partied all night long, and sang their same old Whatif song."—Shel Silverstein*

After a long hike, Callie and her sister sat on the banks of Mirror Lake and talked. At the beginning of her career, she'd written an ad for an air freshener called Mountain Breeze. It smelled like a truck-stop urinal cake and not at all like the damp pine needle scent surrounding them.

This was the thought she had right before her sister blurted out, "Pregnant?"

She darted her gaze toward the Mormon family picnic on the opposite bank. "Lower your voice."

Effie's eyes bulged. "When will you find out?"

"In five days."

"What are you going to do if you are?"

She tried to skip a stone across the water, but it sank on the first try. Her sister's question was the same one she'd been asking herself. "Guess I'll be a single mom."

Her back straightened. "Single? Why? What about Walker?"

"He doesn't want kids. And I'm not going to force him to parent a kid he doesn't want."

Effie didn't need a second explanation—their parents, the Daniel situation—she understood completely. "What if you're not?" she asked. "Then what?"

"I don't know. He's quitting the agency and leaving New York."

Dragging her hands from her eyes to her mouth, Effie wiped away her confusion and uncovered frustration. "And what about you?" she asked, placing angry pauses between each word. "Where do you end up?"

The ache in her chest inflated. "Nowhere. That's the point."

"So that's it? You're telling me in five days, it's over?"

Since she didn't know the answer, she picked up another rock and chucked it into the lake.

"Do you want to go back?" Effie asked.

"I don't have a choice. You're coming to live with me."

"Forget about me—"

"Other than you and Skip, I don't have any reason to stay there."

"Why don't you quit, too?"

"Right. And then what would I do? Where would I go? How would I live? And on what money?" She didn't bother to hide her scorn. If her sister hadn't stolen her savings, she'd at least have the cushion of time to make a decision.

Effie stared at the ground. "I'm sorry about the money," she said, reading her mind. "I promise I'll you back someday."

The tragic level of remorse in her voice heaped a pile of guilt on Callie's already overburdened shoulders. She puffed a resigned sigh. "Money wouldn't solve everything. Remember the last time I gave up everything for a guy? If I did that again, I'd be like a female Bill Murray, repeating the same stupid mistakes over and over again like that movie *Ground Hog Day.*"

The muscles around Effie's mouth tensed as if she were desperately holding back a frown. "What about the book?"

Her sister was grasping at straws. Unfortunately, she'd already grasped all of them, used them twice, and recycled them again. "I'm not finished with it. And there's no guarantee it'll get published when it's done."

"Maybe your weird friend from college could help. The uber-jaded, rich chick? What's-her-name? The publisher?"

"Oh yeah, Barbara! Wow, I forgot about her. How do you know her?"

"I hung out with her and Skip a couple times after I got out of rehab."

"Skip knows her?"

She shrugged.

Barbara. Good old Babs. Callie *should* look her up. They majored in creative writing together. Now she was some sort of bigwig at one of the major publishing houses.

Effie lit a cigarette.

"Seriously?" She coughed and waved her hand. "Are you going to smoke that out here? And stink up the fresh air?"

"What can I say? I'm an addict."

"Nice way to take responsibility for your actions."

Smoke circled around her head as she slowly blew it out. "I'm doing the best I can right now, Callie."

She took her sister's cigarette-free hand and squeezed it. "I'm sorry. I know how hard it's been. And I'm extremely proud of you. Really. It's remarkable how far you've come. You're so incredibly talented. I guess I'm just dying for you and the rest of the world to figure that out."

Effie sniffled. "Thanks. I needed to hear that." She stared out at the lake for a minute then said, "Everything will be okay, Cal. Love will prevail and all that shit. You are in love with him, right?"

"I don't really know what love is." The truth was she did love him and spiritually so, but if she admitted it out loud, it'd be real, and when it was over, which it would be in five days, the pain would be so intense she'd never recover.

Effie studied her with a suspicious glint. "What do you mean you don't know what love is? Even *I* know what love is and I've never had a boyfriend. It's all the beauty in the world. All the stories, the music, the art . . ." Softer she added, "Love gives me a reason to live."

How did her formerly homeless junkie sister have a better outlook on love than she did?

"Besides, Walker's different. He's nothing like Daniel."

"You've only spent forty-eight hours with him."

"I only need thirty-seconds to figure out if someone's a creep. Daniel never said anything nice to you. That jackass probably criticized the way you slept."

"He did."

Effie scoffed. "Walker, on the other hand, worships you, warts and all. Even with your dreadful haircut. Are you going to keep it like that?"

"How do you know?"

"Because you look about five years older—"

"Not my hair, ass. I'm talking about Walker. How do you know? What if this is all just a fantasy? What if we can't make it outside of our RV cocoon?"

"But what if you can? Or what if you're pregnant? Or what if you're not? What if a tornado blows you away? Or what if your vagina burns up in a freak accident aboard the Silver Bullet? You can't think that way. You just have to go for it."

The sun peeked out of a rolling cloud. As the warmth flooded her, she imagined a blue-eyed boy with glasses, sitting atop Walker's shoulders. Another cloud passed and the sun disappeared.

"Dildo," Callie said

"Huh?"

"Silver Dildo. Not silver bullet. Silver Dildo."

Effie tossed her hair over a shoulder. "I don't know what yours looks like, but my dildo doesn't look like a metal bus."

"I don't know," she said, not delving any further into the debate. "But in five days, the magic dies."

Neither could refute that fact, so they reached for each other's hand and held on tightly all the way back to the Silver Dildo/Bullet.

# Chapter 31

## Lightin'

### Northern Oregon Coast

fter Effie left, Walker and Callie ambled north through California, paused for a night in Napa Valley, then continued up the Oregon coast.

The RoadStream campaign had close to a million fans by that point. America loved the fake couple (who weren't fake anymore) and adored their goofy puppy.

Leonard Nimoy even had his own Facebook page, which Callie made the mistake of checking that afternoon. She read the comments out loud.

> *Are Callie and Walker getting married at the end of the tour?*
> *Are Walker's photos for sale?*
> *I'd like to take a ride with Callie.*
> *1 Corinthians 6:18-20. Praize Jesus.*
> *i kill that UGly bitch. WAlker is to HOt for dat ho.*

"I need a bodyguard," she said, slightly on edge.

"I'm watching your body right now," he mused.

"Funny, but at the same time, not funny."

"I thought you'd be more upset about the marriage one," he said.

No, that hadn't upset her at all. Not at all.

"Aw, come on, Blue. You know trolls don't have lives. When they're not vomiting hate, they're probably watching reality TV in their moms' basement, eating orange food and feeling miserable."

"Orange food?"

"You know, cheese curls, mac and cheese, orange soda . . . whatever. Email Liberty and have her remove that crap. Especially the one about riding you."

Callie tossed him a flagrantly incredulous smirk. Aside from his vision problems, if aliens landed on Earth and needed a sample of the perfect male specimen, Walker would be the man to nab. That he was even remotely jealous struck her as absolutely ridiculous.

He zigzagged his gaze from the road to her. "Why are you looking at me like that?"

"Like what?"

"Like you're gonna rip off your clothes or masturbate in front of me and make me wreck."

"Excellent idea, but unfortunately, we just passed the exit. Pull over and let me drive."

"Get the blindfold, you sexy peacock, you."

"Sexy Peacock, huh?" He climbed over the console, stuck his hand down her panties, and gave her a tingly kiss. "How 'bout you tell me where we're going?"

Though his sexual syrup voice was turned up to eleven and his fingers felt fantastic, she had a mission to complete. "You're distracting me," she said, grabbing his hand. "Get the blindfold!"

"*You're* distracting *me*. Keep kissing me like that and I'm gonna bend you over the table again."

The mere mention of that morning's shenanigans set off an oven timer in her body—*ding!*—she was ready to go. Though she was sufficiently pre-heated, she still had a plan to carry out. "Get the rag!"

A second later, he came back with the bar towel. "Smells like pine cleaner."

"I used it to clean the counters." She tied it around his head.

It was hard to tell with the blindfold on, but she was pretty sure he rolled his eyes.

Despite Walker's screams, she flipped a bitch in the middle of the highway and turned into the Lighted Inn. The owners converted the lighthouse and keeper's residence into a bed-and-breakfast.

After she checked in, she led a blind hottie and a bouncy puppy up the ancient winding staircase to the tower.

"Hoo-boy." He exaggerated winded breaths. "Is this your surprise? A stair climber workout?"

"You'll see," she sang.

Once they reached the top, he squeezed her breasts. "What are these? Is this the surprise?"

She tore off the blindfold. "Mwahaha! I'm locking you in the tower tonight." The glass-encased room made it seem as if they were standing in a snow globe—without the snow. of course.

His eyes moved to the clouds rippling like bed sheets above, then to the Pacific crashing violently against the cliffs below.

A puffy circular bed filled the room. He knee-walked over it and peered out the window. "Where'd you find this dump?"

She knelt next to him. "Shitty view."

"Awful." A dubious let's-play-Spin-the-Bottle grin swept up one side. "Ever had sex in a lighthouse, Bluebell?"

She flapped a hand. "Hundreds of times."

"Better show me the ropes then."

*"Love is like quicksilver in the hand. Leave the fingers open and it stays. Clutch it and it darts away."—*
*Dorothy Parker*

**Soundtrack:** Duffy, "Syrup & Honey"

The next morning, they strolled on the beach with Leonard then parked him out back with the owner's mutts.

Part of the charm of a bed-and-breakfast was, of course, the breakfast, and at the Lighted Inn, it was a seven-course five-star meal prepared by an award-winning chef. The host led them to a long communal table in the dining room where Callie sat while Walker snapped a few shots of the lighthouse from the bay window.

Already seated at the table was a couple that looked like Viagra models. The man, white-haired and embossed with permanent laugh lines, nodded a hello. His companion, a dead ringer for Debbie Harry, greeted her with a foreign accent she couldn't quite place.

Callie introduced herself.

"Walt Trainor," the man said with a honeyed southern accent. "And this is my girlfriend, Veronica Henrikson."

Walker froze mid-stride. "Did you say Walt Trainor? Thee Walt Trainor? The photographer?"

"Not sure if I should admit it, but yes, that's me."

She snapped her gaze back to Walt. *Holyshitdicks!* Walker's childhood dream dad was sitting at their table.

"You are familiar with Walter's work?" Veronica asked.

An awkward silence set in as star-struck Walker fish-mouthed and struggled to speak.

"Actually, Walt," she said, helping him out. "You're Walker's idol."

He nodded and found his voice. "Yes, sir. Your work inspired me to go into photography."

"Call me Walt, kid. Sir makes me feel old as dirt." He stood and shook Walker's hand then gestured to the seat next to him.

"Kinda of embarrassed about this," Walker said, "but in sixth grade, I mowed about a thousand lawns so I could buy one of your prints. *The Gift.* That's the one I bought."

"What an egregious waste of your hard-earned dollars," Walt said.

Veronica waved a hand. "Oh Walter, please don't pretend you're humble. We all know what a big head you have." She turned to Walker. "It always pleases me to meet his admirers." She squinted at her boyfriend. "I thought they were extinct."

Walt squinted a smile back. "I told you they were still out there."

"How'd you end up here?" Callie asked.

"Ronnie's good friend lives in Portland. She recommended this place." He took a sip of a coffee. "Where y'all from?"

Walker puffed out his chest. "Same as you, sir, er—Walt. Born and bred in Savannah."

"Son-of-a-gun. From my hometown and everything. Small world."

Small indeed. Ending up at the same remote B&B as Walker's fake dad? What were the chances? Heck, she'd even have to break out her favorite word: serendipitous. Know how many times she'd used that word to describe something? Exactly zero. But that encounter was seriously fucking serendipitous.

The hostess came over and Walt ordered a bottle of champagne. After he filled everyone's glass, he held up a flute. "To new friends . . ."

With the looming risk of pregnancy squarely on her mind, Callie only took a sip. Everyone else, however, plowed through the first bottle in minutes.

After the second bottle, Walker morphed back into his laid-back self and told the tale of their road trip so far. In return, Walt and Veronica shared stories about Sweden. By the end of breakfast, fake father and son were BFFs.

"So how did you and Veronica meet?" she asked.

A sentimental sparkle flashed in Walt's eyes. "Africa. Thirty-years ago. I was on assignment for *National*

*Geographic* and Ronnie replaced my assistant, who contracted malaria. Hasn't left my side since." He reached across the table for her hand. "Ronnie's a photojournalist. Award-winning. But don't tell her I told you that. Her ego's big enough as it is."

"Ha!" His girlfriend shook her head and muttered, "Helt otroligt," which Callie assumed was the Swedish translation for asshole.

"So you're not married?" she asked.

"Believe you me, I've tried to put a ring on her finger. But she won't let me. See, I'm an old fashioned guy, and Ronnie, well, she's Scandinavian."

"I already love you deeply, Walter. I don't need a piece of paper and a ring to prove it."

"The least you could do is tattoo my name on your inner-thigh."

She shook her head. "Hur kunde jag falla för denna galna mannen?"

The photographer turned to them. "In case y'all were wondering, she said she'd tattoo herself first thing in the morning."

Veronica rolled her eyes. "Yes, that is exactly what I said."

Long-term (seemingly) happy relationships always fascinated Callie. By the time thirty years rolled around, most marriages went the way of the dodo bird. That couples like them still existed, much less remained deliriously in love after decades together, filled her with giddy hope.

Then again they probably didn't have kids. "No children?" she asked, eager to find out.

Veronica's gaze dropped to her plate. Walt was still smiling, but his eyes weren't. "No," he answered. "No children."

Most people wouldn't notice, but Callie instantly recognized the loss written on their faces. Had they lost a child too?

"How long have you two been together?" Veronica asked.

They'd only been together eight weeks. If they subtracted the days when they weren't actually couple, their history didn't amount to much. Certainly not thirty years.

"We got together on the road," Walker said, smiling at her.

"Ah, newbies." Walt raised his glass. "Fresh lust."

Veronica threw him a look that said *don't go there*.

He gave her a slight nod and cleared his throat. "I see you've got a fancy camera, kid. Know how to use it?"

"Not like you, that's for sure."

"Let's see what you got."

He handed over the camera. "I'd be grateful for any tips that'll help me quit my day job."

"I'm sure they're amazing since I inspired them." Walt winked. The South was awash with winkers.

Walt scrolled through the photos, revealing no clues as to what he thought.

Under the table, she wrung her wrists, fighting the urge to look over his shoulder. Walker hadn't shown her a single shot of his personal work since the dreaded Liberty Bell photo. But she'd seen the rest of his work and knew whatever Walt was looking at had to be amazing.

The photographer passed the camera to his girlfriend without a word. His non-reaction couldn't have been a good sign. Walker's face fell, and deep in her belly, she felt his disappointment.

Veronica, however, viewed his work with wide eyes and multiple "wows." She passed back the camera and wiggled her brows at her boyfriend.

"Yep. That's what I thought too," Walt said, somehow reading her mind. "Time to quit your day job, kid."

"Hilarious," Walker said dryly. "Go on, I can take it. Tell me what you really think."

"Serious as a stroke, kiddo. That Yosemite stuff? Never seen anything like it." He dug a card out of his pants and passed it over. "You at all familiar with our little gallery in Savannah?"

Walker nodded, looking a bit pale suddenly.

"Twice a year, we sponsor a show featuring new photographers and artists."

"Walt's notoriety brings in wealthy investors and national media," Veronica chimed in. "Most do quite well after a showing. I believe our last artist made seven figures."

Walker shook his head and downed his drink.

"So, my boy, what are you doing six weeks from now?" Walt asked. "Want to show your stuff in our gallery?"

He choked. "I must be drunk. For a minute there, it sounded like Walt Trainor just asked me to show at his gallery."

"Can you make it?" Veronica asked, looking and sounding dead serious.

"Sweet mother of God." He clutched his chest and wiped a fake tear from his eye. "I hope no one minds if I cry like a little girl."

She reached under the table and squeezed his thigh. Seeing him light up like he'd just seen Santa, had to be one of the most beautiful moments she'd ever witnessed. The last few weeks, he'd been so dedicated and happy with his work. And it had finally paid off—he'd made it.

While she was absolutely thrilled for him, sorrow settled at the base of her throat. Walt's golden ticket had just stamped a final expiration date on their relationship. Now Walker had a good reason to quit his job, leave New York, and pursue his passion full-time.

Which meant their time together was coming to an end.

*"When people look at my pictures I want them to feel the way they do when they want to read a line of a poem twice."—Robert Frank*

**Soundtrack:** Sleeping At Last, "I'm Gonna Be (500 Miles)"

*Yee-haw!* Lightning had just struck his merry-go-round. Walt Trainor wanted him to show in his gallery! Running into him couldn't have been a coincidence—it had to be destiny. Actually, it was Callie. Thanks to her sweet surprise and photogenic face, his dream had come true. He could quit his job, and if Callie ended up pregnant, he could support her while she wrote books and stayed home with the baby. They could live a passionate life together, doing what they loved. Nothing sweeter than that.

She'd given him a gift. And he needed to show her his deepest appreciation. "Come on, woman." He tossed her over a shoulder. "You're slower than molasses on a cold day."

She thumped his back. "Put me down! You'll kill us on those stairs."

A hundred stairs were nothing. He had a brand new life force. In the room, he yanked down her shorts.

"Walker!"

"Sorry, baby. I need you." He knelt down and buried his face between her thighs.

"Walker!"

"Blue!" He stuck a finger inside her and tapped it behind her clit. Her slick heat coated his hand.

"Holyshiiiiyesss," she hissed.

"Yes, what?"

"Yes. Continue. Go. Don't stop."

"Fuck baby, you taste so sweet. Get up on my face, so you don't fall."

Across his body, she laid in a sixty-nine. Tendrils of pleasure caressed his body. It felt so good—her writhing on top of him, sucking his cock at the same time. But he wanted to make love, pour himself inside her, make babies, merge their souls. He wanted to open the windows and shout, *I love you, Blue.*

And she loved him too. She didn't have to say it. He felt it. But she was still scared—still his little grape seed.

Afterwards, they clung to each other, not talking, just feeling. She quivered against him. He tilted up her chin. Tears trickled down her cheeks. "Why are you crying, baby?"

"I'm just so . . . happy for you."

The thing was she didn't look happy. But he read faces about as well as he read minds. And since the show guaranteed their future together, she had to be telling the truth.

"Hand me the camera," she said, sniffling.

He passed it over.

"I want to capture this moment for posterity—the day you became a famous photographer!" She focused the lens. "Smile, handsome."

And boy did he. He smiled with every muscle in his body and every ounce of his soul.

# Chapter 32

## Rainin'

### Seattle, Washington

*"Love is for unlucky folk, Love is but a curse. Once there was a heart I broke. And that, I think is worse."—* Dorothy Parker

**Soundtrack:** Above & Beyond, "Love Is Not Enough"

*T*hey dropped off the Silver Dildo at the dealership, ending their trip with no more pomp and circumstance than as if they'd dropped their laundry off at the dry cleaners.

"Goodbye, Silver Dildo, I love you." She blew the camper a kiss and turned to Walker. "Are you crying?"

"Hell, no." He took off his glasses and wiped his eyes. "Okay, maybe a little. That damn camper changed my life."

He was the one who changed her life, not the camper.

The tightness came back. The same tightness in her chest she'd had when she started the trip. The next day, they'd fly back to New York and everything would be over.

Of course it rained all day. A cold, piercing rain. An end-of-summer rain. An end-of-sunshine-and-warmth rain.

They headed straight to the hotel, took off their clothes, and got under the covers.

"Should we watch TV?" he asked glumly.

"I guess." They hadn't watched TV in two months and turning it on felt like turning off her happiness.

He flipped through channels.

"Stop right there. Go back," she said. "Let's watch this—*An Officer and a Gentleman*."

His brow arched. "Is this a chick flick?"

"There's tons of male-grade violence. It's Richard Alpha Male Gere in his alpha male costume, getting all alpha male-y."

"Alpha male costume?"

"His military outfit," she clarified.

Groaning, he tossed her the remote. They nestled against each other—Walker using her as a pillow and Leonard using her pillow as his bed.

At the end of the movie, she let out a happily-ever-after sigh. "I love how he rescues Debra Winger from her shitty factory job. Will you do that for me? Rescue me from my shitty advertising job?"

"Only if you do the same for me. Think you can carry me like that?"

"I'll get a wheelchair and roll you out."

"Or I could just walk."

"The theme song is the tits, too."

He sang a mock version in a deep gravely voice.

She swooned and fluttered her lashes. "My hero."

"Can you play that on the ukulele?"

"Only if you sing a duet with me."

"Done."

At that, she tossed back the covers and headed for the bathroom. He serenaded her on the way. "Blah, blah, blah where we belong."

She closed the door and squeezed her eyes shut. There it was—the pregnancy test—lying unopened on the counter. Officially, her period was late.

Bile rose in the back of her throat as she peed on the stick. When she got up to flush, she stared down at the toilet in shock.

She'd gotten her period.

Holding her breath, she stripped off her clothes and climbed in the shower. Then she let go and sobbed.

No more storybook fantasies of being married to Walker. She wasn't having his blue-eyed baby with vision problems. Now he'd leave the agency, leave New York, and leave her.

Walker pushed back the shower curtain, holding the pregnancy test. "I can't understand this thing. What does the line mean? Are you pregnant?"

"I peed on that."

He dropped it like it was hot. "Well?" he asked.

"I just got my period."

He pumped his clasped hands over his head as if he'd just won an Olympic medal for not knocking her up. "Whew, thank Christ in heaven." He was absolutely beaming.

Only if a puppeteer pulled the strings to her mouth would she be able to smile back. "You're free."

His brows gathered. "What do you mean I'm free?"

"Nothing to tie you down now." Agony barbed her tone with sarcasm.

"Blue—"

She turned off the water and buried her face in a towel.

"Hey—" He sat on the toilet. "I don't understand. Are you upset you're not pregnant?"

*Yes. No. Maybe?* She just wanted to be with him. God, she was pathetic—like a woman from another era—wanting to be pregnant so she could stay with the man she loved.

He cupped her chin. "Just because I don't want kids right now, doesn't mean I don't want them later. That's what this is about right? You're afraid I don't want kids?"

True, a man who didn't want kids wasn't the man for her. But that wasn't everything.

"I love you, Blue. I know it's probably too soon to say it, but I don't care. I love you."

She stared at a rusty spot on the bathtub drain. "Love," she echoed. That didn't change a thing. No matter which way she spun it the result was the same. If she held him back, he'd resent her. Then at the very least, he'd cheat on her like Daniel had. Or worse, he'd end up like her mother—a cruel, empty shell.

The throbbing ache of guilt had hovered over her like a rain cloud her whole life. She didn't want to live like that anymore. Not with Walker. She loved him too much to be the source of his misery and too much to have him be the source of hers.

"I'm sorry, Walker, but love's not enough."

He jerked back like she'd shot him.

"Love isn't going to make this work. You're leaving. What do you want me to do? Have a long distance relationship with you? That won't work and you know it."

Sad peacock eyes pierced her. "Come with me."

She covered her face, blocking the view of her misery. "I gave up everything for the last man who told me he loved me. And look where that got me. Love is a word, not a solution."

"I'm not asking you to give up your life—"

"Let's say I go with you. What am I gonna do? Follow you around like Leonard while you take pictures? What happens if I chase you and we don't work out? Am I gonna be shit out of luck and have to start all over again?"

"You don't have to chase me. You could write. You could freelance. I don't have to quit right now. I can stay in New York."

"No, I won't let you. I won't let you give up your dreams for me. I'm not going to be the person you resent for the rest of your life."

He continued his plea. "I'm not gonna resent you. Stop, Callie. Please don't do this. Please don't throw us away. You're predicting the end before it's even happened."

But it had happened. They'd driven for months only to reach a dead end. "We had a nice fling, Walker, but outside the RV fantasyland, we simply don't work. Our relationship doesn't translate to real life."

Anguish contorted his face. She could almost taste the blood from the wound she'd inflicted. Breaking his heart, so he wouldn't break hers. How sickeningly ironic.

"You ever gonna get tired of running away from your problems?"

"I'm not running. Don't you get it? I'm staying. I need my own path, Walker, not yours."

Anger barged in and hardened his expression to stone. Using his forearm as a bat, he swept all the hotel toiletries off the sink, sending them crashing to the floor.

He stormed out, and minutes later, fled the room with his suitcases and Leonard Nimoy in tow.

She couldn't move. Or breathe. Her lungs had turned to blocks of ice. Shivering painfully, she sat frozen on the edge of the bathtub, chilled blood slugging through her veins.

He didn't even say goodbye. Or put up a fight. He just walked out and slammed the door.

It was as if he'd slammed the book shut at the end of their story. As if everything had been make-believe. As if the fairytale had ended.

Unhappily ever after.

**Soundtrack:** James Blake, "Retrograde"

Walker got the call right after Callie dumped him. He was in the hotel lobby trying to book another room for the night. A faceless voice on the other end robotically fed him the information.

"Mr. Rhodes, your grandmother collapsed yesterday. We'd like your permission to move her to a hospice."

The statement wrapped around his neck and squeezed his pounding pulse into his ears. "What do you mean collapsed? Where is she? Who the hell are you?" He paced the lobby, yanking Leonard with him.

"Dr. Sen. I've been caring for your grandmother at Savannah General. Her chart listed you as the power of attorney."

"Are you telling me she's dying?"

"Sorry, I assumed you knew."

"What on earth's wrong with you? You tell me my Grandmother's dying like it's an item on your to-do list. How about showing some goddamned compassion?"

A woman at the counter sidestepped away from him. He lowered his voice. "Why did she collapse?"

"As you know, she's had cancer for quite some time. It spread rapidly over the last month."

"It came back? When?"

The doctor cleared his throat. "She discovered a nodule under her armpit six months ago. With her advanced age, she opted out of treatment."

"What do you mean she 'opted out?' Why the hell would she do that?"

"She stated she'd already been through chemo before and didn't want to die bald and full of poison."

Oh, Josephine, you crazy old bat.

Deboned, useless, and utterly destroyed—he crouched on the floor while pain pecked his heart like a black crow.

"Sir? The hospice?"

He stood. "I'm in Seattle. I'll catch a flight out as soon as I can. Think you can do your damn job and keep her alive until I get there?"

"Sir, I know you're upset— "

"Upset? Buddy, I'm about two hundred levels above upset." He hung up the phone, handed Leonard's leash to the concierge, and weaved toward the restroom.

The mirror was the first to go—he shattered it with his fist. Next, he kicked the shit out of the trashcan. Then he ripped the paper towel dispenser off the wall and threw it against the toilet.

After his meltdown, he went back out and booked a ticket home.

# Chapter 33

## Dyin'

**Soundtrack:** Télépopmusik, "Breathe"

*D*awn crept through the window and brought delirium with it. The ache lodged inside her like an unwanted visitor—probably staying for good this time. She hadn't eaten nor slept since Walker had left the night before. Her body shook, her throat throbbed, and her mouth tasted like blood.

In her backpack, she dug for a cure—a pill, a salve, a bandage that might fix her pulverized heart. She dumped out the last two months of her life on the floor—the blue dress, the X-rated towels, the stuffed beer can, her love note. On the bottom of her bag, Walker looked up at her.

She pulled out his junior high picture and examined the nerdy little boy who'd grown into the handsome man she loved. All the sudden, despair punched her in the chest and stole her breath.

Everything went black. Forever, she hovered in nothingness, spinning and fighting. Somehow air slipped through the darkness and the lights turned back on.

A storm of dust motes swirled above her in a sunbeam. "Walker! Come see how pretty this filth is!"

Reality crashed through the door. No need to point out beautiful photo ops. No more late-night whispered conversations. No more silly anecdotes.

He was gone.

All the weird thoughts and quirks and faults—all the things he loved—she'd have to lock them back inside her head.

She sat up. How did everything in her room get so beige? Without Walker the world had turned back to bleak.

The day grew lighter, and as it did, her mind cleared. What if somehow they could make it work? What if they could live happily ever after? "'What if I fall?'" she recited to herself. "'Oh but, darling, what if you fly?'"

Don't be such a pussy, Murphy!

Their flight wasn't until ten. She still had time.

She ran down to the lobby. The attendant was fast asleep with his cheek propped on a fist. She cleared her throat and woke him up with a start. "Remember me?" She waved her fingers.

The guy squinted.

"I checked in yesterday with a man and black puppy? Walker Rhodes?"

He rubbed his eyes and rose to his feet. "The tall guy with glasses?"

She nodded frantically. "Do you have his room number?"

"He checked out last night. Went to the airport." He reached under the counter and handed her a phone. "The driver dropped this off. Guess he left it in the van."

"Call me a shuttle." She snatched the phone and ran upstairs to pack. Their seats were next to each other on the flight home. That gave her six hours to fix everything.

But he wasn't at the airport. According to the airline, he'd canceled his flight.

Without his phone, she had no other way to contact him. And the chances of him buying a new one in the next twenty-four hours were nil. Other than checking in with work, his grandma, and Matt, he'd made zero calls on the thing. They hadn't even exchanged numbers. Why bother? They'd been inseparable.

She emailed him. Three times. Nothing.

But he'd come to the office on Monday and resign in person. He'd say goodbye to his friends and she'd do the same. Then they'd leave on their next adventure together.

Two days. She just had to get through two days.

Then she'd tell Walker she loved him and get her happy ending.

She would.

## Savannah, Georgia

*"I dwelt alone, in a world of moan, and my soul was a stagnant tide"—Edgar Allen Poe*

**Soundtrack:** Black Atlass, "Paris"

A super-sized portion of sorrow had been served to Walker in the last twenty-four hours. And you know what? It tasted like a shit.

It was the worst day of his life.

As if Callie dumping him weren't God-awful enough, he'd flown six hours in a middle seat, between two dudes as tall as him, while Leonard cried and whined under the seat.

Then he'd lost his phone and couldn't check in on his grandmother.

After that, he'd driven four more hours from Atlanta to Savannah and rushed into the hospice to find a comatose skeleton in Josephine's place.

The whole way there, he'd worried about her dying there. He kept thinking she'd want to be at home. But evidently, she'd picked out the place months before.

He could almost hear her laughter ringing through the hallway as she toured the building and joked with the nurses. "This place ain't bad . . . for a cemetery."

And that's how it smelled, like death. Sterile death. It was nothing more than a mortuary disguised as a nice hotel. Though she'd never see it, she even had an ocean view.

He thought it would be like a hospital. But the only clue it was a medical facility was the morphine drip that slowly sucked her into delirium.

Only twice she'd woken up. Once, mumbling something that sounded like, "Don't forget the special brownies in the ice box." He had a pretty good idea what "special" meant.

The other time, she'd carried on a conversation with Ted Turner.

He begged the nurse to turn off the drugs so she'd know he was there. But his grandma was in horrible pain, the nurse told him, and would suffer greatly without the medication.

Even the non-stop morphine drip couldn't have calmed the rage he felt after hearing that. While he was out gallivanting around the country with a woman who'd called him "a nice fling," his grandmother—the woman who'd saved him from foster care and raised him—had been suffering in pain.

It was suffocating, dammit, the dry desolation he felt.

In only a few hours, her health declined rapidly. Again, he begged the nurse for help.

The woman shuffled over to him, her large, polyester-clad thighs swishing as she walked. "She was probably just waiting for you to get here before she let the good Lord take her home." She placed her hand on his shoulder. "I'll pray to Him and ask for an easy passage."

He scoffed. "While you're at it, ask the *good* Lord why he gave her cancer in the first place."

The nurse just smiled and patted his shoulder.

Josephine moaned. He took her hand—just wrinkled wax paper over bones. The last twenty-fours hit like a tidal wave and he broke down and wept.

"Aw, Sugar Bear."

He lifted his gaze and found Josephine awake.

"Don't be sad." Her words came out a gasp at a time. "It's my time. I've had a great life."

"Why didn't you tell me, Grandma? I would have been here for you."

On her once-vibrant, now gaunt face, a strained smile curled up. "Can't fall in love on a deathbed, can ya? That's what you did right? On your trip? Fell in love?"

"Yes, you meddlesome old woman. I fell in love." For both their sakes, he left out the part where Callie also broke his damn heart.

His grandmother smiled, closed her eyes, and said her last words. "You owe me forty dollars."

# Chapter 34

## Writin'

### Manhattan, New York

*"Writing is the best antidepressant."—Fierce Dolan*

**Soundtrack:** Miss Li, "I Can't Get You Off My Mind"

The minute Callie landed in New York, she booked an appointment with Colt, the hairdresser who'd chopped off her hair before. It took him three hours to bleach out the black and return her to blonde.

Then she donated her t-shirts and went shopping. "I'm back," she said to the dressing room mirror.

Now all she had to do was get Walker back.

Monday came and went and he never showed. But no one else did either. Skip had taken everyone to the Catskills on a fucking bonding retreat.

By that point, the amount of emails she'd sent Walker had gone several levels beyond crazy stalker bitch.

Dozens of people called his phone. Betty, Jane, Rosemary—who were these women with old-school names? Why were they suddenly calling him? Did they know about the break-up? Why hadn't he replaced his phone yet? None of it made sense.

That day, she didn't eat or sleep.

On Tuesday, when he didn't make it, she developed a sharp pain under her ribs. But surely, he'd make it in the next day.

He didn't.

Desk-by-desk, she asked everyone, and not a soul had heard from him.

The panic attacks came back with a vengeance on Thursday. Several times she'd almost gone to the emergency room. She booked an appointment with a doctor for the following week. By then though, she'd be well on her way to Savannah.

When Walker didn't return Friday, she charged up his phone. Given the forty-seven calls he'd missed—including one from Sabrina an hour before—he hadn't replaced it yet.

She rushed to the account manager's desk with his phone in hand.

"Oh my Gawd," Sabrina cried. "I, like, didn't even recognize you. Is that your natural hair color?"

"Did you just call Walker?"

"Yeah, hey, where do I send flowers for his grandmother's funeral? I know it was yesterday. Is that tacky? Sending flowers after it?" She tossed her hair. "Why aren't you there?"

Callie dropped the phone and sank to her knees, feeling like she'd been buried alive.

Sabrina picked it up. "Are you okay? Do you have asthma? My sister has that. She has to carry around a geeky inhaler."

"Call an ambulance," she rasped. "I'm having a panic attack."

Nonplussed, Sabrina yanked a paper sack out of her drawer. "Here, breathe into this."

The trick worked. She stopped hyperventilating.

"Scary, huh?" Sabrina said. "I get those a lot." Lowering her voice, she added, "Advertising causes them." She peeked around the cubicle. "I don't think anyone saw. Let's go to the ladies' room."

Callie gripped the sink in the bathroom while vomit swirled in her stomach. "She died?" Maybe she'd heard it wrong the first time.

Sabrina nodded. "Of cancer." Her head tilted to the side. "You guys are still together, right?"

In the mirror, a pale ghost stared back at the account manager and whispered, "I don't know."

"He's not coming back, you know? He quit."

The walls closed in on her. She wrenched open the door and ran down the hall. Frantic stiletto taps chased her. She took the stairs.

All day she wandered around Manhattan like a zombie. Never had she felt so lost. By the time darkness fell, she looked around and realized she really was lost. Literally. And she could give a shit less if she'd used the word correctly.

She didn't have her purse, but she still had Walker's phone, so she used it to call Skip. Forty minutes later, a limo rolled up.

Her friend lounged in back, wearing all back and a pair of mirrored stoner shades. "Hey, Blondie! How in the hell did you end up in the Bronx? Dude, how you been? Haven't had time to jack off lately, thanks to you. We won five new clients. You believe that?" He paused and waited for the normal social pleasantries to follow—*the greats, fines, not muches,* and *how are yous*—the polite conversational lies that stuck in her throat.

"Dude, you look like shit." He removed his shades. "Have you been crying?"

She stared out the window at a middle-eastern peddler selling knock-off designer purses to a smiling tourist with a fanny pack cinched around her huge waist. *That woman is about seventy-bajallion times happier than me,* Callie thought.

He tugged her chin. "Look at me. Ah, shit. You fucked Rhodes, didn't you?" He pushed a button and slid down the partition. "Hey, Allen? Change of plans. Can you take us back to my place?" The driver nodded and the glass slid back up.

"Why didn't you warn me? Now I don't have a creative director, and the client wants to rig a fake wedding." He flopped back on the seat and huffed. "Let's hope Hot PR Chick can fix this debacle." He poured brown liquor into a glass and handed it over. "Sad about his grandma." Another beat of silence passed. "Murph?"

She turned.

"You're looking worse than when I picked you up from LaGuardia. Should I feel guilty? I thought Rhodes was one of the good guys?"

She smiled weakly. "Skip Shimura you're the kindest man I've ever met. Don't worry though, your secret's safe with me. That trip changed my life. Walker was the best thing that ever happened to me." A sob escaped and let out the rest of her misery with it. "I think I lost him, Shimmy. I got scared. What should I do? I don't know how to get ahold of him."

"Sorry, Murph. We shut down his email when he quit last weekend. He's still in Savannah I think. Least that's where he arranged to have his stuff sent. Honestly though, I doubt he's in the frame of mind to deal with relationship shit right now. Give it some time. He's dealing with a lot of negativity."

And she'd made it more negative. But how long should she wait? And when should she get in touch with him? And how? And what should she say when she finally did? These questions she kept to herself because Skip wasn't exactly a relationship expert.

He dude-slapped her back and attempted a smile.

She braced herself.

"Come on, Murph. Snap out of it. What's that old saying? You can't be happy with someone if you're not happy alone."

See? His advice sucked ass. "That's a steaming load of crap. Who the hell's happy being alone?"

"What about this one? If you love someone, set them free. If they don't come back, they've probably found a better piece of poontang."

That earned him an I-Can't-Even-Believe-You-Said-That-Shit-Murphy™ glare. The reminder was redundant. She was already painfully aware most women would sell their organs for a chance to date Walker.

The limo pulled in front of his building. "Nothing you can do about it now," he said with all the tenderness of a rock. "Stay at my place tonight. We'll eat ice cream, watch chick flicks, and chat about your man probs."

"Are you serious?"

"Fuck no. But we can eat sushi and sit in the hot tub. I've got some killer weed and bunch of great corn porn. Ever seen *Boy in a Plastic Bubble?*"

*Walker My Love,*

*I trudge through my days with a heavy heart. I'm not even sure I'm alive. For weeks, I've been trying to get in touch with you. If this letter doesn't work, I'm hiring a skywriter to fly across country.*

*I wish I could have been there to comfort you after the loss of your grandmother. I also wish I had had a chance to thank her for raising such a wonderful man. Josephine was an original, that's for sure. And evidently, she was clairvoyant, too. In only an hour, she'd figured out I was in love with you.*

*And she was right. I am in love with you. Allow me to translate—in your southern language of bad similes—just exactly how much I love you.*

*Mr. Rhodes, my love for you is bigger than a penthouse bathtub and brighter than the Milky Way in the desert sky. It's hotter than dirty dancing in a dive bar and more powerful than a hurricane. Around you, I feel higher than a hot-air balloon in the Grand Canyon and drunker than a tequila-soaked nudist swinger. And with you, my love, I'm happier than a giant water gun fight on the Fourth of July. And without you, I'm lost in a shoe-sucking alligator-ridden swamp.*

*You are my sun, my moon, my inspiration, and my color.*

*There's a Hindu word for the love I'm feeling—viraag (not to be confused with Viagra)—the crushing emotional pain of being separated from someone you love. I'm viraag without you.*

*I didn't mean anything I said in Seattle. I was scared. My worst fear though is I've lost you forever.*

*I miss you desperately. If you miss me too, hurry up and come get me.*

*Love, Bluebell*

# Chapter 35

## Willin'

### Tybee Island, Georgia

*"I've never been a millionaire, but I know I'd be just
darling at it."—Dorothy Parker*

*M*ort Howard, Josephine Rhodes's attorney and
close family friend, did things a little different
from most lawyers. Reading wills was somber
work, so instead of dressing up in stiff suits and ties, he
donned Hawaiian shirts, long shorts, and flip-flops.

And when it came time to read Josephine's will, he took
Walker to his favorite watering hole on Tybee Island. He sat
him at a wobbly plastic table on a deck overlooking the
crowded beach, ordered a round of drinks and a basket of hush
puppies then got down to business.

"Sorry about your grandma, son," Mort said. "Helluva lady.
Not a boring bone in her body. And a damn fine herb
gardener, too." He winked.

Walker huffed a joyless laugh. "You too, huh? Had to stop
using her phone because I kept getting requests all hours of
the day."

Mort clucked his tongue. "Sharp as a tack, that woman, a
regular weed-dealing Robin Hood. Not sure you if know this,
but she marked up her goods for wealthy people and gave the

rest to cancer victims. Called it her non-profit pot." He held up a hand. "Well, that's not entirely true, she earned a profit."

"I didn't even know she was dealing." A gull landed on the railing and snatched an old french fry. He threw a hush puppy at it and hit Mort's shoulder by mistake. "Sorry, man."

His attorney brushed off the crumbs. "You pissed Jo didn't tell you she was sick?"

Beyond the sandcastles, the waves, and the sailboats, Walker stared at spot out in the ocean, far, far, far away from where he was sitting.

"That's gotta hurt, I know," Mort said. "Tried to talk her out of it, but she didn't want to ruin your trip."

He rubbed his chest. On and off for weeks, he'd felt like he was on the verge of having a heart attack. "Let's get this shit over with, Mort."

The lawyer tossed back his drink then yanked a folder out of his beat-to-shit backpack. He leafed through the first few pages and began. "I, Josephine Rhodes, being of sound mind"—he chuckled—"at least she was when she wrote this will." He continued the reading. "Yada, yada, yada . . . will to my grandson the following . . ." He listed the Cadillac, the house, all of her assets, her investments, and a gargantuan sum of money.

Walker leaned in and cupped his ear. "Say that last part again?"

An ill-timed hearty laugh burst out of Mort. "Thought that might pique your interest. Josephine left you a nice chunk of change."

"Jesus Christ, where'd she get that kind of money? Investments? What the hell? That can't be hers. Jo was so tight she squeaked when she walked."

"Eh, she was a damn good investor, made a fortune from her"—he coughed—"post-retirement income. Also, your grandpa was loaded. He set up a trust for you and your mama before he died. She made a fortune off that interest alone. Plus, there was your mama's life insurance and your daddy's child support payments—"

"Child support! Since when? That man never sent me a dime."

Mort winced. "Sent a check every month from the time he left your momma. And also paid for your college tuition—"

He slammed his fist on the table, sending the silverware clattering to the floor. A flock of old hens stopped clucking and stared. He didn't care.

"I paid for my own goddamn education. And I busted my ass working from the time I was ten. That old hag! For Christ's sake, Mort, I taped my broken glasses together and wore them for two years because she told me we didn't have a pot to piss in."

"Never said your grandmother was sane, just a good investor. Bottom line, Walker my boy, you're a wealthy man now." He handed the will over. "Doesn't replace your grandma though, does it?"

Had she been alive, he would have strangled the woman.

A chill passed over him. He didn't mean that. If she'd been alive, he'd have taken care of her instead of letting her die alone.

"Know what she asked me to do?" Mort said. "Dress up like that old Ed McMahon fella in eighties' Publisher's Clearing House TV commercials and deliver a giant check to your door. You're lucky I have a little dignity."

"Crazy old bat."

"Hey, son? Do me a favor? Now that you're rich? Buy yourself a phone. Any idea how hard it was to track you down?"

He didn't need a damn phone. The only two people he wanted to talk to were gone.

# Chapter 36

## Showin'

### Trainor Gallery, Savannah, Georgia

*"There is no place for grief in a house which serves the Muse."*—Sappho

**Soundtrack:** Velvet Underground, "Pale Blue Eyes"

The photographers sat at the bar in the back of the gallery and drank the "good scotch" in celebration of Walker's successful show. When most of the liquor was gone, Walt asked, "How come your girlfriend's not here?"

Walker one-eyed the bottle and filled his glass again.

"She still in the picture?" Walt pressed.

"Nah."

"Her idea or yours?"

"Hers."

"She know she's your muse?"

"No idea what you mean."

Walt gave him a pointed look and swept a hand around the gallery. All fifty of his framed photographs featured Callie.

The Liberty Bell photo was the first to go and the shots of the twins sold right after that. A dull ache developed in his gut as a line formed at the cashier, and one-by-one, his memories of Callie were sold off.

There was only one left—his favorite—the one of her in the penthouse. At the last minute, he raised the price astronomically so it wouldn't sell. He just couldn't let it go.

By the end of the night, it felt like she'd died right along with his grandmother.

"You getting any work done since she left?"

For six weeks, he hadn't done a damn thing except sit on his grandmother's porch and drink.

"Wanna talk about it?"

He threw Walt a warning look over his glasses.

"You act like I just asked you how many boxes of maxi pads you want from the store." He held up his hands in surrender. "Fine, she's your muse, not mine. Mine's at home waiting for me in a nice warm bed."

Walker swirled the ice in his tumbler. "I told her I loved her and she said it wasn't enough. Said we were just a fling."

Walt tugged his ear. "Come again?"

"That's what she said."

"Kiddo, as a photographer, I'm somewhat of an expert on reading subtext. What she told you? That's a hundred-percent crap. Callie was gaga for you. Tell Dr. Walt the whole story. Maybe there's something you're leaving out."

Recapping his heartbreaking saga sounded about as much fun as a poke in the eye. But he hadn't talked to anyone since she'd left, and if anything, he just wanted to get it off his chest. So he went ahead and recounted the highs and lows of the trip and everything that led up to the breakup.

"That's it?" Walt asked. "You just walked out the door? Didn't argue with her? You just up and left?"

Since the question was rhetorical, he poured himself another scotch.

"Hell, kid, you should have stayed there and fought it out. You gotta fight for the woman you love." He punctuated his statement with a karate chop on the bar.

"Didn't really feel like sticking around after that."

"Bully for you. Coulda had you some grade-A make-up sex."

Walker hunched over his drink. "Why don't you just take me out back and shoot me, man?"

The photographer chuckled. "I know how you feel. One time Veronica and I broke up . . ."

The man was out of his ever-loving mind if he thought it was the right time for a cute breakup-get-back-together story. "Walt—"

"Let me finish. I swear there's a moral to the story." Walt reached for the remote and turned down the music. "So the day Ronnie showed up with those cheekbones of hers . . ." His glazed gray eyes went heavenward. "That woman, she made me crazy. And not in a good way. Had to use reverse psychology just to get shoots done—tell her not to do something, so she'd do the opposite. A thorn in my saddle, that damn Swede."

After a hearty swig off the bottle, Walt continued torturing him. "All my stuff you see in the museums? The best work of my life? That's 'cause Ronny pushed me so hard—right over the edge most days. Lord, I love that woman." His voice cracked on the last word.

He ambled behind the bar and pulled out a bag of peanuts. "When we finally got together? Talk about sparks! Ka-boom!" His hands made an exploding bomb gesture. "I think we changed the weather pattern that night!"

"Man, I don't want to hear about your sex life—"

Walt cut him off. "Didn't want kids before. After her though, I wanted a whole gaggle of 'em. I kept picturing a bunch of little Veronicas running around. We sure had fun trying to make babies until it didn't work. Fertility treatments started—jacking off in a cup and all that. Finally gave up after four years of bad news."

"That sucks, man. You woulda been a great dad."

A deep frown took over Walt's slaphappy grin. "Know what she did after that? Up and left me! Wrote me a damn sticky note that said I needed a whole woman, not someone barren."

"A sticky note?"

"I know, right? I'm still pissed about that. The love of my life leaves me and she can't at least find some damned notebook paper?" He popped a few peanuts in his mouth and washed them down with a slug of scotch.

"She just up and vanished. I went crazy trying to find her." He tore at his hair for effect. "Worst time of my life. Finally hired a private investigator and found out she'd gone to Alaska. Frigging Alaska. Want some water? These things are saltier than a deer lick."

He shook his head.

Walt filled two glasses anyway and put one in front of him. "So I fly up to Alaska on this plane put together with toothpicks and duct tape. I frigging snowshoe to the lodge she's staying at. Know what she does when I got there? Tells me she didn't want to see me. You believe that?"

Walker grabbed a handful of nuts.

"She put up a helluva fight too when I wouldn't leave. Told me she hated me." He put his elbows on the bar. "Know what? I didn't believe her for one goddamned second." Walt's peanut-encrusted spit flew everywhere as he blabbed on.

"Three days it took me! Three days in the North goddamned Pole to convince that stubborn Swede I could live without children, but I sure as hell couldn't live without her."

The drunken photographer stared at him like he expected a grand chain reaction of clarity to suddenly hit.

He shrugged. "Cute story, Walt, but I don't get how this relates to me and Callie?"

"That bullshit Callie fed you? Same thing. Bet you money she thought she was doing you a favor by breaking up with you. Bet you cold hard cash."

No way, was he buying that gift-wrapped explanation.

"I'm serious," his hammered friend said, "I'll bet you a frigging grand. Head up to New York. If she blows you off, you'll be a thousand dollars richer. No skin off your back."

If she blew him off again, it'd be more like ripping the skin of his balls. "I'm afraid that ship has sailed, Walt."

"Well, then if the wind will not serve, take to the oars!" Folks in Venezuela had probably heard him shout that.

Walker sat back in his chair, shaking his head at his shit-faced idol.

"Plan on making a career out of photography, do you?" Walt asked.

He shot him a look that said duh, obviously.

"Then you gotta fight for the muse!" He karate chopped the bar twice. "Go get her. Bring out the big guns if you have to. Gotta snowshoe to the North Pole? Hire circus performers? Put on makeup and dress in drag? So be it." The last karate chop sent nuts flying everywhere.

Walt paused for a drink then yelled, "And none of this pussy-texting or emailing either. Get your ass up to New York and do it face-to-face. Show her you'll pull out all the stops. That you won't go down without a fight. Focus on one thing, my man"—he karate-chopped the bar with each syllable—"Make. Up. Sex."

Walker snorted. "You're a weird son-of-a-bitch, you know that?"

"A weird son-of-a-bitch with a hot woman who's been with me for thirty years. Trust me. I know what I'm talking about. Call me when you get her back and I'll take you both out to dinner and pay for it with my winnings."

# Chapter 37

## Tryin'

### Savannah, Georgia

*"The sun's gone dim, and the moon's gone black. For I loved him, and he didn't love me back."*—Dorothy Parker

hen Callie didn't hear from Walker after she sent the letter, she flew to Georgia to surprise him at his show.

On his grandmother's porch/furnace, she awaited him. She didn't read or look at her phone. She didn't move. She just sat in the rocking chair—rigor mortis stiff—staring down the street, waiting for Walker to come home.

After one hour, her hope atrophied. By the third, it vanished completely.

He wasn't there. He wasn't anywhere.

No longer able to put off her primary needs for water, food, and a bathroom, she dragged herself down the steps and headed for the rental car.

"You one of Josephine's herbal clients?" Across the street, an elderly man limped down from his shady porch, wearing pinstriped shorts and tasseled brown loafers with no socks. He gave her a suspicious once-over with rheumy, glaring eyes, and took a step closer. "She passed on." He jabbed his cane down the street. "Go on, git."

"I'm here for her grandson."

He raised an insolent chin. "Walker?"

"Yes! You know him? Is he here?"

"Was here." He wiped his neck with a waded up bandana.

"When will he be back?"

"Not anytime soon."

She lugged scalding air into her lungs, licked her parched lips, and gave him a wax-museum smile. "Any idea where he went?"

"You here for the show? If so, you missed the opening. It was last week."

"I thought it was this week!"

"Nope."

"He's gone?" Her vision started to pixilate.

"Left the day before yesterday. His art's still at the gallery though. Will be for the next month."

"He left?" She still couldn't believe it.

"Yes, ma'am. Asked me to keep an eye on things and call the cops if I saw anything strange."

His squint suggested he was about two-seconds away from calling the cops on her. Add to that his get-off-my-lawn attitude, his intentionally vague responses, his shiny, bald head, and his stupid fucking shoes—plus a pinch of her dehydrated delirium and bursting bladder—and you'd get what she had: a staggering urge to bludgeon him to death with his own cane.

"When will he be back?"

"Didn't say. Told me he was going on a road trip."

A road trip. The world spun around her. She collapsed on the sidewalk and put her head between her knees.

An exasperated huff came from the man. "Come on. Let's go inside. In case you plan on trying anything, I'm a card-carrying member of the NRA."

It was dark when she jerked awake on the couch. Pipe smoked hovered around a lamp and a pair of varicose-veined legs stared at her. "You're the woman in his photos," said the man attached to the legs. "Didn't recognize you at first. Your hair's different."

She jammed fists into her eyes. "I'm sorry. I don't—"

"In Walker's photographs? You're the one in all the pictures." He stood and held out a hand. "Pierce Stanley. I apologize for not inviting you in earlier. Didn't realize it was you. There are sandwiches and sweet tea in the kitchen. You got a place to stay tonight?"

Getting Walker back was the only plan she'd made. "I . . . no. Not yet."

"Sleep here then. I've got an extra bedroom."

"No, I'll find a—"

"Nonsense. Josephine told me about you. She was like a sister to me. Stay here. I'm too old to try any funny business." He limped to the kitchen. "When you finish eating, I'll show you how to get to the gallery."

As it turned out, Mr. Stanley had known Walker since he was a baby and had a limitless supply of childhood stories. How little she knew about her lover. Or ex-lover, since he'd obviously moved on.

She'd read somewhere it took half the time you were with someone to get over them after breaking up. It'd been exactly six weeks and they'd only been together two months. Their brief love affair wasn't long enough. He didn't miss her. He had no reason to—they didn't have a history.

"Miss Callie?" Pierce said. "Better get going. The gallery closes in an hour."

**Soundtrack:** Banks, "Waiting Game"

At the gallery, a college girl with too many facial piercings, ping-ponged her gaze from the walls back to Callie. "That's you, right? In the pictures? Your hair is different, but that's you, right?"

She glanced at the walls and found herself staring back. Silence crowded the space as she made her way around the room and relived her memories—now spotlighted, framed, and enlarged.

By the time she reached the last one, a profound sense of loss swallowed her spirit, and in its place, emptiness grew like a massive black hole. Deep wracking sobs poured out, soaking her shirt and pooling on the floor.

"Are you okay?" hook-face asked.

Obviously fucking not. She circled the room ten more times and eventually managed to squeak out a question. "Do the red dots below mean they're sold?"

The girl pulled her lip ring and nodded.

Every piece had sold except one—her favorite.

In the Biloxi penthouse, she lounged in bed with a book on her lap, looking blissfully happy. Her naked breast peaked out from the tangled white sheet, and one leg dangled off the bed. On the nightstand, a half-eaten banana split melted in a dish, and on the floor, her glitter Chucks reflected the light. Sunlight streamed in from the balcony and illuminated her outstretched hand as it summoned the artist to bed. It was titled: Forelsket.

"Do you know what this means?" she asked the girl.

"It's Norwegian." She read from an index card. "It's the euphoric feeling of first falling in love."

Callie crumpled to the floor and bled tears. "I don't care. I want it." She needed it. "That's his most expensive piece."

She slid her credit card across the floor without bothering to ask for the price.

# Chapter 38

## Livin'

### New York City, New York

*"I hate writing, I love having written."—Dorothy Parker*

Callie lugged what remained of her heart back to New York, determined to get on with her life. It was time to deal with the consequences of her stupidity and figure out how to live alone.

During the day, she buried herself in work and scoured Manhattan for apartments. For weeks, she'd been living in perpetual hotel limbo—absolutely certain Walker would come back.

At night, when she couldn't sleep, she worked on her book. A week later, she finished the first draft.

Dying for someone to read it, she looked up her old college friend Barbara and met her for dinner at a posh restaurant on the Lower East Side.

When her friend walked through the door, everyone in the restaurant dropped their forks and stared at the Amazonian queen. Flaming red hair and wild green eyes, she stood six-feet tall with a haughty demeanor that made her seem like royalty. That is, until she opened her mouth.

"What the fuck is up, whore?" Barbara said with a thick Long Island accent.

"Not much, slut," she replied.

They ordered a bottle of wine and discussed the last five years. Normally, conversations between women revolved around men, but for once, the topic never came up. She'd almost forgotten what it was like to focus on herself.

Hanging out with Babs also made her realize how much she missed female friendships. Or rather, *intelligent* female friendships.

Conversation with Hillary had been akin to reading Cosmo. In other words, unless the topic included men, sex, fashion, makeup, celebrity gossip, or the next fad in diets, they didn't discuss it.

During a pause in her refreshing conversation with Barbara, she gathered her courage and pushed the manuscript across the table.

"What's this?" Babs picked it up with a perfectly manicured hand.

"My book."

"Oh, I get it now." She flopped the manuscript back on the table. "You're not interested in a friendship. You wrote the great American novel and want me to publish it. Do you have any idea how many manuscripts I get every day? I don't have time to read shit like this. Get an agent." She slapped her credit card on the table, sending a strong signal the conversation was over.

Though her friend was richer than God, Callie replaced the card with her own and tried not to think about the enormous debt piling up after buying Walker's photograph. "I got this."

"Don't bother. I'll just expense it." She took out her phone and scrolled through her texts.

"Hey, Babs? I didn't expect you to publish my book. I just wanted your opinion. No one else has read it, and you're the only person I know in New York, other than Skip, and he doesn't read."

Her attention snapped back. "Skip? Skip Shimura? He's here?"

"He took over his dad's agency. I work for him now"

All the sudden she didn't look so eager to leave. "No shit? You have his number? No, wait"—she dug out a business card—"give him my card."

"Maybe all of us can go out some time?"

"Really? That'd be great." From the way her eyes lit up, you'd think she'd just been given an ounce of gold bullion. "Are you busy Friday night?"

"I'm pretty much free for the rest of my life, but I'll see if Skip has plans."

Babs slid her gaze over to the manuscript then let out a resigned sigh. "Okay, I'll read the first few pages tonight. If I think it has promise, I'll hook you up with an agent. But I'm warning you, I will tell you if it's a fucking piece-of-shit."

*"I'd like to have money. And I'd like to be a good writer. These two can come together, and I hope they will, but if that's too adorable, I'd rather have money."—Dorothy Parker*

On the way back from signing a lease on an apartment, Callie strolled through Central Park. Orange and gold leaves rained down from the trees, and the air was as crisp as an apple.

Her phone vibrated. It was Barbara. "Where the fuck are you?" she shouted.

"Central Park."

"Text me the closest cross streets. I'll send a car."

"What? Why?"

"I read your book last night. The whole motherfucking thing."

"And? Is it a piece-of-shit?"

"It's fantastic, hooker. I'm going to publish it. It needs editing though. Why didn't you spell-check those last pages?"

Her legs locked up and she almost dropped the phone. "What? Are you serious?"

"You didn't give this to anyone else, right?"

"Uh-no."

"Good. I've got legal working on a contract."

She sank into a pile of leaves. She'd done it. She'd finally realized her passion. And Walker was the only person she wanted to tell. Only he would have cared as much.

"Text me the cross streets, ho-bag. Oh, and by the way, did you come up with a title yet? Your manuscript doesn't have one." She paused. "Whore?"

"Road-Tripped," she said. "That's the title."

# Chapter 39

## Savin'

### Madison Avenue, New York City

**Soundtrack:** Joe Cocker, Jennifer Warnes, "Up Where We Belong."

**Soundtrack:** The Jackson 5, "I want you back"

*a* week later, Walker's photograph arrived at the office. It took all day to build up enough courage to brave a look. When she finally did, it felt like a semi-truck had crashed through her chest.

While she was in the throes of a deep depressive episode, some asshole starting playing the theme song from *An Officer and a Gentleman*. She almost threw up on her desk.

Ready to commit an act of violence to get it turned off, she shot out of her seat and ran straight into . . . "Walker?"

He set an old eighties' boom box on her desk and shut off the music. "Hi, Blue."

She closed her eyes, took a deep breath, and opened them again. "Are you really here?"

A cautious smile played at the corners of his mouth. "I'm here to rescue you from your shitty advertising job."

"Wh-What?"

He swooped down, picked her up, then stumbled. "Whoops, sorry, Gere made it look easy."

The whole agency stood and applauded. Avery whistled, Sabrina cheered, Eli nodded, and Skip dude-slapped Walker's back.

"Thanks y'all," he said and swept her out of the entrance. "I owe ya big-time."

By the elevators, he set her down. "Like your blonde hair. Makes you look soft and sweet." He whispered in her ear, "But we both know that's a lie." They stared at each other for a moment then he said, "God, I'm so happy to see you."

On the verge of fainting like a fictional eighteenth-century heroine, she locked her trembling arms around him and squeezed him as hard as she could. "I'm afraid if I let you go, you'll disappear."

"I'm not going anywhere."

With her attached like a human suckerfish, he shuffled onto an elevator full of people. He yanked the Screw It bar towel from his pocket. "Gotta blindfold you, darlin'."

As he tied it on, she inhaled his lemony-Walker scent and burst into a sobbing, shoulder-shaking mess. "Walker?"

"Yes, Blue?"

"How many people are still on here?"

"About ten."

"Great." She continued the ugly crying.

On the ground floor, he led her outside and untied the rag. Palm on cheeks, she released a Murphy-Gaspy-Wheezy-Tear-Soaked-Laugh.™

Double parked in front of the building—where the whole trip began—sat the Silver Dildo gleaming in the sun

"Is that—?"

"Yep."

"But how?"

He tugged her up the camper steps and a larger version of Leonard Nimoy greeted her at the door with a bark and a furiously wagging tail. "There she is, Len. Got our girl back."

Someone outside screamed, "Fuck you! Move that fucking heap of—"

Walker slammed the door and sat her in the passenger seat. He knelt between her thighs and gave her a kiss that made her feel like she was made out of helium.

"Got your love letter," he said smiling cheek-to-cheek. "My very first one. I tried to hurry up and come get you, but I had to buy the Dildo back from the dealership in Seattle and drive it all the way here."

"Where are you taking me?"

"On a big adventure. Then I'm bringing you home to Savannah."

Her heart screamed let's go, but her head screamed slow down. "What? No! I can't."

His smile shriveled.

"I mean, yes. Yes!"

He collapsed on the floor, clutching his chest. "Jesus jumped-up Christ, woman! You scared the hell out of me."

"What I mean is I can't just leave. Your picture—it's upstairs. My sister's moving here. I signed a lease. I bought clothes. My book—"

The dimples came out full force. "Effie told me. I'm so proud of you. I knew you could do it. And I can't wait to read it." He kissed her again. "Your sister's moving into my loft next week. Forget about the clothes. I'll buy you new ones. Skip's taking care of everything else. As for the photo, it'll be waiting at the house. You're getting your money back, by the way. What were you thinking, spending that kind of money?"

Formulating an intelligible response wasn't an option at that point, so she stared at him instead.

He dug a key from his pocket and dangled it. "I bought our storefront in Savannah. Remember our dream place? My grandma left me some money—"

"Oh, Walker, I'm so sorry."

"Shh, let me finish." He patted his leg. "Come on, Leonard. Bring the surprise, boy."

Leonard perked up his ears, fetched something from the back, then plopped down and started chewing on it.

Walker swiped the box from the puppy. "You have no idea how long it took to train him to do that."

She hiccuped a giggle.

"I was gonna wait until after we got to Intercourse"—he winked at the innuendo—"but I'm too excited." His Adam's apple bobbed as he took her hands. "I love you, Blue. I love your humor and your strength, your passion, and your creativity. I love your nutty personality. I love living with you and going on adventures. I love your potty mouth and your smooth sounds of the seventies' ukulele songs."

The blubbering laugh she choked out sounded a bit like she was dying.

"You okay?"

She nodded and he continued. "I love everything about you, dammit. And I need you. And you need me. And I don't want to spend another second without you."

He opened the box and revealed a platinum engagement ring with a blue diamond setting. "Baby, Bluebell, I want to spend the rest of my life with you. I want to travel the world then make babies and raise them in my grandmother's house. I want to make you the real Mrs. Calliope Rhodes. Will you marry me, Callie?"

A sugary sensation swept over her. Imagine bathing under the sun on a tropical island and there's not a cloud in the sky. Then picture yourself sharing a banana split with the man you love while you float on a raft together across a warm cerulean sea off the island's white sandy beach. That's exactly how she felt—warm and floaty and filled with love.

"Fuck yes, I'll marry you!"

He slipped the ring on her finger, and all at once, every horn on Madison Avenue honked. The engagement kiss included lots of heavy petting and moaning.

"Mmm, if we weren't about to start a riot, I'd make long sweet love to you right here on this floor."

She gazed into his happy peacock eyes. "I forelsket you."

"Is that how you pronounce it? I've been saying four el skillet."

"I like how you say it better."

"Let's hurry up and get out of this damn city so I can ravish you." He sat in the driver's seat and started the engine.

"Yes, please, hurry up and ravish me." Leonard jumped in her lap and she buckled her seatbelt.

"What's the soundtrack, Mrs. Rhodes?"

She flipped through the stations and found the perfect song.

He gave her the most dashing dimpled smile ever, reached for her hand, and together they rode the Silver Dildo off into the sunset.

# Epilogue

## Five years later. Their backyard. Savannah, Georgia

**Soundtrack:** Talking Heads, "Once In A Lifetime-Remastered"

*O*ut in the garden that night, they drank champagne in celebration of Callie's third book release and Walker's successful show at Bluebell's Gallery, Creative Coffee House & Yoga Studio.

Strings of palm tree lights twinkled in the oak tree and a pink flamingo perched on one leg below it.

A four-year-old fairy with big blue eyes, gossamer wings, and a muddy yellow dress pranced over and sat in Walker's lap. He smoothed her tangled, blonde hair and pointed to his cheek. "Give Daddy some sugar."

Josephine put her arms around his neck and gave him a chocolate ice cream-coated kiss. "Daddy, Parker won't let me up in the tree house. He said boys only. Will you put him in time-out?"

"Did you remind your brother you're the one who painted all the stars on the sides?"

"Hey, poop face," tiny Josephine yelled. "Daddy says you're in time-out."

He shook his head. "Child, you have a mouth like your mother's."

Josephine's twin brother Parker—a replica of his father from his glasses to his lanky frame—zoomed over with Leonard Nimoy on his heels and almost knocked Callie off her chair with a hug.

Walker pretended to be stern. "Did you tell your sister she couldn't play in the tree house?"

"She keeps telling me what to do. She's not the boss of me," he said.

Veronica laughed. Walt and Veronica, Parker and Josephine's adoptive grandparents, spent winters in Georgia to be with the kids. "Parker, sweetie, come sit in your grandmother's lap. I want to tell you a secret. Women are always the boss."

Walt coughed "bullshit" into his fist.

Callie and Walker sent each other a secret smile.

He winked and handed their child to Walt. "Jo, go visit your grandpa. Mama and I need to take care of something." Her husband took her hand and led her toward the house.

Veronica yelled behind them, "Make sure you lock the door! Don't want any fairies interrupting your *something*."

"Come on, woman!" He slapped her butt. "You're slower than pond water."

"Ouch," she said with a seductive brow wiggle.

"There's more where that came from. Now get upstairs!" They sprinted to the bedroom and locked the door.

He slid his lips against hers. "Have I ever told you how much I love you?"

"A few times."

"Have I ever told you how much I love that sexy sundress?" He untied the strings at the top.

"It's all I can stand to wear in the heat."

"You feeling hot now?" He slipped a hand under her dress. "You naughty girl, you're not wearing any panties."

She undid his pants. "Easier access."

"Keep them off for good, then."

"In two days, we're spending a month with the kids aboard the Silver Dildo. Therefore, talk dirty to me."

He gave her long blonde ponytail a tug. "How hard do you want me to fuck that sweet pussy?"

"Keep talking."

Quite a few more naughty words were spoken during a lightning fast foreplay session.

"Hurry, I need another orgasm." She bent over the dresser. "We've been gone too long. They'll be here any second."

He punched inside her. "That fast enough?"

She moaned in response.

Soon, the dresser was pounding against the wall.

"Daddy?" The doorknob rattled. "What're you doing in there?"

"Helping your momma move some furniture, baby girl." He rammed Callie harder and made her moan again.

"Is it heavy? Is momma hurt?"

"No, baby. Go on downstairs. We'll be out in a bit."

The child disappeared and let them finish with a bang. *Literally.* And you know she never used the term incorrectly.

"I'm feeling pretty four el skillet, Mrs. Rhodes," he said, buttoning his pants. "How 'bout you?"

"I always feel four el skillet with you, Mr. Rhodes. Always."

# Acknowledgments

I gave up a lot of time-wasting activities to write this book: TV, Facebook, exercising, showering, my personal life, taking care of my son... Not that my son can read dirty romance novels yet, but I'd like to personally recognize him for being one patient little boy. For six months he kept saying, "When are you going to finish the book, mom?"

It's done, cutie. Thank you for letting me be creative.

Speaking of moms, I wouldn't have been able to do it without mine. She entertained her grandson on the weekends, so I could lose myself in my dreamy couple's relationship. I doubt she'll ever read this book because it has dirty words and sexy scenes, but in case she does, thanks, Mom!

In addition, I'd like to thank my beta readers, Kate, Lucy, Susan, Rebecca, Laurie, and Beth. None of them had ever read a romance novel until I shoved this down their throats.

Another special thanks to my structural editor, LS King.

And a great big kiss to Murphy Rae at Indie Solutions. Not only did she design a fabulous cover, she dealt with my newbie author pain-in-the-assishness while she was nine months pregnant.

By the way, the poet who wrote the *What if I fall* poem is named is Erin Hanson, check out her fabulous work.

# About the Author

Nicole Archer's lengthy career as an advertising copywriter not only polished her writing skills—it provided a lifetime of book material. Many months her book purchases are as high as her mortgage. As a single, full-time working mom of a beautiful, brilliant, and horrifically energetic son, she has little time to do much else besides work, write, read, drink wine, and breathe. In real life, she lives in Dallas, Texas, but she'd rather live in Switzerland.

Check out nicolearcher.com for questions, images that inspired the book, the soundtrack, deleted scenes, upcoming work, her random musings, or if you just want to email her and go out and get tacos and margaritas.

If you sign up for the newsletter, you'll be the first fans offered promotional pricing. FYI, she hates spam—the email and the canned meat.

Follow her on Facebook at user name /nicolearcherauthor and on Twitter @nicolearcheraut.

# Review Me

Hey, Fabulous Reader! Raise your hand if you liked this book? Or better yet, rescue me from my shitty advertising job and leave a stellar review everywhere. Positive reviews are critical to the survival of new indie authors, and I'd be ever so grateful if took the time to write one.

Please review me on Amazon, Goodreads, or wherever you purchased your book.

Love,
Nicole

# Coming Soon! Ad Agency Book 2

## Head-Tripped

Effie Murphy moved to New York to start a new life as the violinist she was meant to be. Broke, beat-down, and lonely, she's on the verge of giving up. When her twin sister learns this, she sends her former ad agency coworkers to the rescue.

Finn Clark, the leader and DJ of the hottest electronica band in the world, lives with Eli, a graphic designer at the agency. When Finn meets Effie, they end up spending three incredible days together. The problem is Finn's leaving. Worried he'll lose Effie while he's gone, he takes a huge risk and invites her to play violin on his European tour.

Finn and the band members of Urban—a rag-tag bunch of misfits—welcome her on the tour with open arms, and for the first time in her life, Effie feels like she's part of a real family. But when details of Finn's past surface, she fears she'll lose him and her new family, if he finds out about hers.

**Sign up on nicolearcher.com for updates.**

21125794R00194

Printed in Great Britain
by Amazon